Hi Richard -
It was nice
enjoy the bo

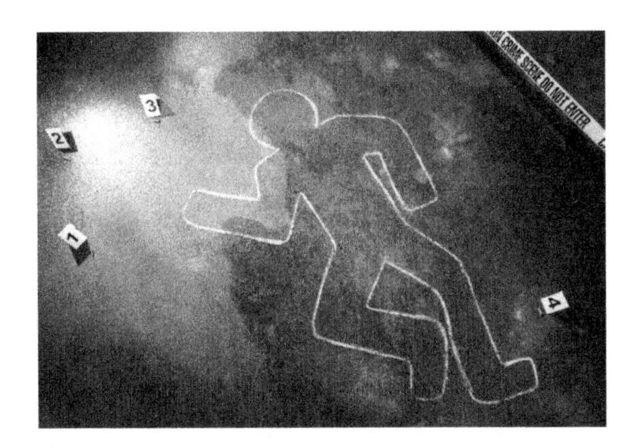

When DNA is Wrong

When DNA is Wrong

This book is fiction. The factual scenario mentioned in this book is a real one, though. Sometimes, our law enforce community is plagued with the same problems mentioned in this novel. All of the characters, names, and events contained herein are also fiction. If you see an event, person, or activity that is similar to that in the novel, it is purely coincidence.

For more information, please contact me.

Authoring by Jeff Beckett
(517) 626-0098
Jeffbeckett@jeffbeckett.com
www.jeffbeckett.com
Printed in the United States of America.

Acknowledgements

I always put my acknowledgements in the front of my books. Without the great and inspiring people in my life, the book wouldn't exist. So, why stick them in the back?

God – I've said from day one that I'm not going to be an author unless I can glorify God, through his Son, Jesus Christ. This is what it's all about. In recent years, I survived a traumatic brain injury and I very strongly believe I would be dead without his blessings. I'm a Christian author – the type that you can tell is a Christian. My writing greatly reflects his awesome glory.

My family – They are the best part of my life and have done a great job to support and foster me. I have no doubt in my mind that I couldn't do this without them. Thank you, my dearly beloved. May God bless you through his Son, Jesus Christ.

Samantha Markham – Okay guys, here's the hard truth. This lady did quite a bit of editing and writing for this novel. She is, what they call, a 'ghostwriter.' She's not just pesky ghost with me though. Even though I paid her fairly, she deserves credit for all of her work. Thank you, Sam.

I hope you enjoy the reading and find it exhilarating. My other novel is Lord Falkin's Majestic Treasure – the Eye, if you're into fantasy reading. If not, I've got many more books to come.

In Christ,

Jeff

Chapter One

Meredith Maloney didn't appreciate being woken at four o'clock on a Sunday morning. It was part of the job sometimes, of course, but she didn't have to like it. Nor did she feel any compulsion to hide her thorough dislike of it. Stewing in the passenger seat of her partner's Dodge Challenger, she chewed on a slice of cold pizza she'd snatched from her kitchen counter on her hurried way out.

"Do you mind keeping that sauce off the upholstery," the man beside her huffed. With one eyebrow arched, he flicked his focus between the road ahead and the woman who was carelessly close to ruining the interior of his beloved vehicle.

Casting him a sidelong glance, Meredith swallowed the mouthful she'd been munching. "You know, Cox, maybe you ought to see someone about this clean fetish you've got going on." She eyed her partner slowly, taking in the suit he'd dressed himself in despite the day and the ungodly hour of it. His dark hair, which was almost black except for a little early graying around the temples, was neatly combed and gelled. How did he get smartened up so fast? And why would anyone bother even if they could?

Her own long, auburn hair hadn't seen a brush that morning. She'd scooped it quickly back into a ponytail and she wasn't bothered about the knotted strands that had caused uneven lumps. She'd hauled on a pair of jeans and a sweater, and had just managed to clean her teeth and splash some water on her face. But that was as much beautifying to herself as she was prepared to do at that time of day.

"It's not a fetish," Jenson Cox muttered, ignoring the sharp green eyes that he could feel trained on the side of his face. "This car was expensive, I've had it less than a month, and I don't want you making a mess of it."

"It's not just about your car. It's just everything. You're a neat freak, Cox." With a light scoff, she continued. "You must be great fun in the sack. Don't want to go making a mess of those sheets, huh?"

"Better than sheets that haven't been cleaned for weeks," he shot back.

"How would you know how often I change my sheets?"

"How would you know what I'm like in bed?"

She took a sharp intake of breath, readying to hurl something at him in reply. But her exhausted and frayed brain had to admit the man had a point. Although she'd spent enough time around him to make a pretty well-educated guess, she had no hard evidence. Not that she *wanted* evidence. Cox was, she had to admit, one of those classically good-looking guys. His dark eyes and impressive physique occasionally caused a fluttering of excitement in her.

But he was far too uptight; did too much thinking. Maloney liked to keep her romantic relationships simple. When certain urges overwhelmed her, she gave into that primitive drive without much thought.

She wasn't sure if Cox even had a primitive drive. During the year they'd been working together, she had seen several younger officers and rookies flutter their eyelashes at her outwardly attractive partner. Some had even been so bold as to ask him out, but he always turned them down. She assumed, at first, that he had a wife or girlfriend, maybe even a boyfriend, but in the months that followed he'd never once mentioned a relationship.

"How 'bout we focus on our job?" Jenson said, thumbs tapping restlessly at the steering wheel.

When he was first assigned to work with Maloney, he didn't think he'd be able to last a month - she was moody, combative and sarcastic at every turn. Almost everything about her rubbed him the wrong way. Somehow, though, he had found ways to work around it and, usually, he managed to give it as good as he got. And, although he'd admit it was somewhat childish, his own exasperation was reduced by the certain knowledge that he chafed on her nerves just as much as she chafed on his.

Slouching back in her seat a little, Meredith tossed the last piece of pizza crust into her mouth, before mumbling around it. "Fine by me."

A subtle smile pulling at the corners of his mouth, Jenson counted that as another battle he'd won. The grin hurriedly faded, though, as he tossed his attention to her. Noticing the way her greasy fingers were closing in on his leather seats, he leaned forward and popped the glove compartment open. Easily finding a pack of wet wipes, he flicked them onto her lap before putting both hands back on the wheel.

"Seriously," she sighed, ignoring the wipes and rubbing her hands over the denim covering her thighs. "Seek help."

Biting on the inside of his cheek, Jenson ignored her. He knew from experience that was the best way to deal with her. Sometimes, it was the only way to deal with her. Besides, they should both have more important things on their minds than petty bickering. As infuriating as Maloney was, Cox knew, when it came down to it, she was a professional. And, although he wouldn't ever tell her, she was a damn good detective.

Sighing, Meredith picked the wipes off her lap and tossed them onto the dashboard. She noticed as she did that she'd left oily finger marks on the shiny packet. That was bound to irate Cox, but he wouldn't notice it for some time.

The Challenger slowed and stopped in front of three patrol cars with their emergency blue lights still flashing. Crime scene tape had already been stretched across the home's driveway, and a couple of uniforms shuffled aimlessly back and forth in front of the flimsy barrier. A handful of early-rising nosey neighbors were huddled in a loose circle across the street. One middle-aged man pointed to the house. Even without the benefit of hearing him, Meredith could tell he was assuming an air of authority when, in reality, he knew Jack. There was always one.

For the sake of a quiet life, she pulled the sleeve of her sweater over her still slightly greasy hand as she popped open the car door and stepped out into the dark, slightly damp morning air. Striding a few paces along the sidewalk with a sudden burst of energy, she didn't wait for Cox. She knew he'd only be a step behind her.

As she approached the cordon, one of the uniformed officers lifted the yellow crime scene tape with a deferential nod. Maloney said nothing as she ducked under and headed to the open front door. Behind her, Jenson said, "Thanks," as he bent to pass through the tape.

It was a standard suburban, three-bedroom house in what was usually a quiet part of the city. It wasn't crime free, no part of Chicago was. But it was not an area used to seeing clusters of CSI and homicide detectives.

A cop at the entryway stood back as they approached. "Mornin' Maloney," he said with a tip of his head. "Cox," he added.

"What have we got?" Meredith asked, not really looking at the tall, slender officer whose radio crackled with a muffled voice at the other end. Instead, she eyed the walls of the hallway. The clean, neat wallpaper was interrupted by two pictures; one a print of Niagara Falls with a rainbow hovering in the mist, the other a photograph of a man and woman. The picture was taken on a beach somewhere, and the pair had bronzed skin and broad smiles.

Her gaze drifting down to the hardwood floor, she spotted smears of rusty colored blood; partial footprints that had already been numbered and logged by the CSIs.

"Deceased is Alec Renaudin," the cop replied. "His girlfriend had been away for the weekend. When he didn't show at the airport to pick her up, she assumed he'd forgotten, and so took a cab. When she got home, she found him in the living room with his head smashed in."

"Where is she now?" Cox wondered, one hand slipped casually into his neatly pressed pants while he gave the uniformed officer his full attention.

"Upstairs. She's in a pretty bad shape. Paramedics had to sedate her."

Crouching, Maloney studied the blurred prints. The tread that made them looked like sneakers or running shoes and they were fairly large, she guessed about a ten. "Did we manage to get a statement from her before they drugged her up?" she asked, still examining the floor.

"She was too hysterical to say much of anything."

"Okay," she sighed, pushing herself back to her feet. "Let's take a look at the victim first."

Silently, the officer led the pair of detectives down the hall to the living room. He stayed just outside, and gestured to open the door. Maloney stepped inside first, avoiding more bloody footprints that had been left on a beige carpet. Unlike the entryway, this room was not clean or neat.

A glass coffee table in the middle of the room had been turned over and a large crack zigzagged through the middle of it. There must have been at least two drinking glasses on it, because there were two small brown stains where liquid had been spilled. One of the drapes hanging in front of sliding doors that led out into the backyard had been ripped from its hooks. Two of the walls were daubed with blood splatter. And there were smudges and streaks of crimson all over the carpet.

"Definite signs of a struggle," Cox pointed out needlessly.

Beside the upturned and cracked coffee table, a body laid lifelessly. One arm covered his face, as though he'd been trying feebly to protect himself. The part of his head that could be seen was visibly concave, and his salt and pepper hair was stuck in clumps. His white shirt was soaked with blood, and a large pool of the stuff had spilled out in an almost perfect circle around his head. Maloney thought it looked like some kind of halo; a twisted version of the kind of thing you'd see in stained glass images in church.

"Has the ME taken a look?" she asked, flicking her face over her shoulder toward the cop who still lingered at the threshold.

"Yeah, she's ready to take him downtown when you've got what you need."

"And CSIs are done?" Cox added.

"Yep."

"Somebody need me?"

Recognizing the voice, Maloney turned. Dean Anderson stood in the doorway. One thumb hooked in the belt loop of his black jeans, he grinned. Noticing Cox, he gave him an acknowledging nod. Cox returned the gesture, but did not manage to offer the cocky forensic investigator a smile.

"You've been working in here?" Meredith asked.

"Uh-huh," he replied, stepping forward. "Nobody told me you were on the case." His smile turned crooked as he continued to look at her. "It's been a long time."

It had been weeks since they talked, but she didn't see the need to get excited. He was, after all, not what she was looking for in a romantic or personal relationship. At times, he was just too arrogant or weird.

Best way to deal with it was to not deal with it at all. "So, what have you got so far?" she wondered, turning her own eyes to the man lying in a pool of his own blood.

"Probably nothing you can't work out for yourself," he replied casually as he took a step closer to the victim. He pointed to the dent in the man's skull. "Blunt force trauma."

"Weapon?" Cox chipped in.

"Nothing in this room."

"But what are we looking for?" Maloney asked. "Thin, metal object maybe?"

"Tire iron," Anderson continued, picking up her thread. "Something like that." Getting up, he glanced at the walls. "The struggle probably didn't last long. The first blow to his head might have caught him off guard, 'cause he wasn't able to defend himself very well."

Humming in agreement, Maloney looked at the spilled drink. "Things started off civil enough, though."

"We've got some prints and trace off the glasses," Anderson informed her. "Hopefully, we'll have a DNA match. That'll make your job a lot easier."

"Almost takes the fun out of it," she replied flatly. "Have we got a TOD?"

"Difficult to be exact," Dean replied, one hand sliding through his dusty blond hair. "Doc's putting it sometime between ten and eleven at night."

"And he was found at?" Maloney asked, directing the question at the uniformed cop behind her.

"Little after 3 a.m., Ma'am."

"The question is, are we dealing with pre-meditated murder," Cox sighed. "If Renaudin's attacker brought a weapon with him, that suggests he came here with a plan."

Pursing her lips in thought, Meredith strolled the width of the room. "Do we know if he'd made any enemies recently?"

"You'd have to ask his girlfriend," Dean replied with a shrug.

"Is she in any condition to talk?" When she received nothing but another shrug, she turned away from the men and walked back out into the hall. She only paused briefly before mounting the staircase.

The master bedroom was easy to find, because there was an officer posted outside the door. She gave Maloney a tip of her head.

"Is she awake?" the detective asked.

"I just went in there with a glass of water," the young woman replied. "She was awake then."

"Lucid?"

Blue eyes squinting and brow creasing, the youthful cop moved her head indecisively. "Not sure whether she'll be much use to you."

Knowing she was about to take something of a shot in the dark, but having nothing to lose, Maloney stepped to the door and lightly tapped her knuckles against it. "What's her name?" she asked quietly of the uniformed woman.

"Sandra Hager."

"Ms. Hager," Meredith called through the closed door. "May I come in?" Without waiting for a reply, she pushed on the handle. The hinges gave a slight creak as she slowly and quietly wandered into the room. "Ms. Hager? I'm Detective Maloney, I wonder if I could ask you a few questions."

The woman laid on the bed on her side with her knees pulled up close to her chest. She wasn't asleep. Her hazel eyes were wide open, but they were fixed on some spot seen only by her. Some of her dyed blonde hair had fallen over her face, and must have been tickling, but she wasn't annoyed by it. In fact, she didn't even notice.

"Ms. Hager?" Meredith persisted. "I know this is a difficult time. And I apologize for having to do this now. We want to do everything we can to find the person who attacked Alec, and to do that I'm going to need your help."

The woman blinked, and then her blurry eyes realized someone stood beside the bed. They seemed unwilling to cooperate as she urged them up to the detective's face, though, and she had to blink again before they'd obey her instructions.

"Ms. Hager?" Meredith spoke quietly and took a step closer. When she was level with the blonde woman's face, she crouched. "Can I call you Sandra?"

Opening her mouth to speak, Sandra found that the sounds she wanted to make came out distorted and strange. She couldn't seem to make a word, at least not one she recognized. But the vague sound was close enough to a 'yes' for Maloney.

"I know you've been through this all before, but can you tell me what happened when you got home?"

"I…I…" Stuttering, Sandra Hager swallowed and took a couple of hasty breaths. "I just walked in and he was…"

"You didn't touch anything?"

The woman shook her head as best she could while it was still resting on the pillow.

"Did you touch Alec?"

Again, the dazed and confused woman, with a strand of blonde hair obscuring her eyes, shook her head.

"Was he expecting a visitor last night that you knew of?"

"Uh…no…" Her throat raw, the words were feeble.

"And do you mind if I ask where you've been this weekend?"

"Vegas," she mumbled, completely bereft of emotion. "A friend's bachelorette party. Alec didn't want me to go."

"Why?"

"I dunno...He...We haven't been together very long. I guess he thought I might cheat on him or something."

Maloney nodded, and tried not to place any accusation in her next question. "And the two of you argued about that?"

"No," she replied swiftly. "No, we hadn't ever argued. Alec wasn't that kind of man. He was soft-spoken, he was...He was good to me." As she spoke, her hazel eyes filled with tears and in the process of trying to sweep them away she finally moved the hair off her forehead.

"Okay," Maloney soothed. "So would you say Alec was the kind of man who got along with everybody?"

"Most people."

"Was there anyone in particular who might have had a grudge against him? Colleagues? Ex-friends?"

Squeezing her eyes shut, Sandra bit her lower lip. "No," she said before sniffing back fresh tears. "No one he told me about. But we didn't talk much about his work. We didn't talk much about anything really. It wasn't that kind of relationship."

Not bothering to ask Ms. Hager to elaborate, Maloney focused on a different tack. "Did you speak to Alec after you left for Vegas?"

Struggling to swallow with a dry throat, she shook her head. "He drove me to the airport Thursday afternoon, and I didn't hear from him again. I did try to call him Saturday evening before I got on the plane to come home...There was no answer."

"Was it unusual for him to not pick up?"

"Sometimes he'd leave his cell lying around. He hated it when people were glued to those things."

"Alright," Maloney breathed, the backs of her legs beginning to go numb. "I think that's everything I need for now. I'd like to talk to you again when you're feeling up to it, though."

Closing her eyes, Sandra nodded, her head still not willing or able to lift itself from the bed.

Stifling a groan as pins and needles tingled down her calves, Meredith pulled herself back to her full height. The conversation hadn't exactly been illuminating. But she was as sure as she could be that Hager had nothing to do with her boyfriend's death. For one thing, she had nothing to gain. And for another, those shoe prints downstairs were far too big for the diminutive woman curled up in the fetal position. And then, of course, there was the ferociousness of the attack. Tire iron or not, Alec Renaudin's head had taken a battering from someone with strength and what seemed to be a serious anger management issue.

Of course, if the DNA had a match in the system, the whole case could be done and dusted by lunchtime. Maloney hoped so, because that would mean she'd be able to spend the rest of the day where she should have been right at that very moment…in bed.

Chapter Two

Maloney stifled a yawn, but that didn't stop the purposeful motion of her feet. Nor did the draining of her coffee, or placing the freshly emptied Starbucks' cup on the sill of the large lab window as she passed it. Reaching the door, she shook off the remaining fatigue and braced herself for the chill that would meet her on the other side. Not bothering to knock, she strode into the pathologist's lab. As always, the room was spotlessly tidy, with its sanitized white walls and strip florescent lights. Three empty and dazzling clean tables glinted under the glare of the bright bulbs. At a fourth, Maloney found the doctor hovering over the naked, pale body of Alec Renaudin.

A pair of protective glasses over her own thin-framed spectacles, Laura Farrow bent close to the dead man's head. Studying the marks left by the weapon that had cracked open his skull, she lifted one carefully shaped eyebrow.

"What have you got for us?" Maloney asked, sliding her hands into the shallow pockets of her jeans.

"Come look at this," Farrow replied with a cock of her blonde head.

Shuffling closer to the stainless steel examination table, she leaned in to get a view of what the doctor was staring at. Squinting, she gazed at the large freshly cleaned wound; without the tsunami of blood that had flowed from it, flecks of white bone could be seen jutting out.

"What am I looking at?"

With one latex glove-covered finger Farrow pointed to the marks that were preoccupying her on the man's forehead.

Maloney shifted closer still. She spotted what the doctor was gesturing to, but she couldn't decide what it was she was looking at. The indentations seemed precise, the shapes defined, and yet, at the same time, difficult to discern.

"Is that a horse shoe shape?" she wondered, pointing to one of the tiny marks.

"I think it's a 'U'," the doctor replied, righting herself and lifting the protective glasses from her eyes. Pushing them back on her head, she adjusted the frames of her spectacles.

"A 'U'?"

With a soft hum, Farrow nodded her pleasantly plump face. "The one before that looks like a backwards, upper case 'D', and the one after seems to be an 'N' in reverse?"

Still staring hard at the man's brow, Maloney shut one eye and scrutinized the indentations until she saw what the ME had been seeing. "Yeah," she murmured quietly. "Yeah. So, something was written on whatever hit him?"

Blue eyes wandering back to the print that had been indelibly left, Farrow slipped out of her gloves with a snap of rubbery latex. "Definitely."

"Dun-" Maloney whispered to herself, turning to face the woman next to her. "Any ideas what caused it?"

"Well, as you may already have gathered, he was struck repeatedly with something metal and pretty weighty. There were traces of oil in his hair, too."

"Oil?"

"Motor oil."

Maloney glanced down at Renaudin's body before meeting Farrow's eyes again.

"So, a tool of some kind?"

"Sounds about right to me."

"Tire iron," Maloney added thoughtfully.

"Could be."

"No, it is," she replied, feeling suddenly less tired as a familiar pulse of adrenalin started to move through her. There was nothing quite like getting a hot lead to perk the young woman up. "Dun is Dunlop," she explained rapidly.

A subtle smile forming on Farrow's face, she tossed her gloves into a small trash pale beneath the table. "That's why you're a detective making the big bucks."

To that quip, Maloney scoffed. "Big bucks," she muttered beneath her breath. "Yeah, right." Sweeping a few unruly locks of hair behind her ear, she changed the subject. "Is there anything else you can tell me?"

"I'd say the attack was emotionally motivated, there was a lot of rage here. It probably only lasted about five minutes, but your perp kept hitting him for a short while after he was dead. He or she really meant this. You're looking for someone right-handed. But that's nothing much you couldn't have already figured out at the scene, right?" the doctor replied with her trademark mix of professionalism and empathy for the poor unfortunate who had ended up on her slab. "Sorry."

Maloney shrugged it off. "That's okay." As far as she was concerned, they probably knew all they needed to. She'd certainly solved cases with much less to go on.

A knock at the door turned the attention of both women.

Politely opening the door fractionally, Cox leaned just the upper half of his body across the threshold.

"Morning, Jenson," Dr. Farrow said, her cheeks flushing slightly.

It was no secret to Maloney that the doctor had something of a crush on Detective Cox. It was just a silly crush, though, because the ME had been happily married for close to a decade and had two young children she adored. He didn't seem to notice, though. If he did, he hid his reaction to it phenomenally well.

"Hey," he said with an amiable smile.

"We know what weapon we're looking for," Maloney told him eagerly, and with a grin that was ever so slightly smug. She expected him to ask her what it was, and she looked forward to being able to tell him what she'd figured out.

However, the question she was hoping for didn't come. His face didn't even flicker. Instead, Cox was more concerned with what he had been planning to say.

"We've got more than that; the DNA recovered from one of those glasses at the scene is in our database."

Maloney felt a faint pang of disappointment. Not only had that stolen her thunder over the tire iron, but it may have rendered the whole issue moot anyhow.

"Who've we got?" she asked, reminding herself that the only thing that really mattered was that they'd caught whoever killed Mr. Renaudin.

"I've got an address," he replied, grinning with even more smugness than she'd been flashing at him. "Come on, I'll explain on the way." With a jerk of his head out into the hallway, he moved back and let the door swing shut.

Maloney rolled her eyes as she followed, hating it when he treated her like a dumb donkey. Laboriously hauling her feet to the door, she tossed a, "Thanks for your help," over her shoulder.

"Don't mention it," Farrow called across the space between them, her voice echoing on the tiled floor and walls. "Good luck catching your man!"

"Yeah, thanks." Closing the door gently behind her, Maloney was pretty sure she didn't need any luck.

***

It was a little after midday, and the slither of sunlight that sliced into the room through a gap between the drapes was making him feel sick. His alarm first beeped at seven o'clock, because he'd forgotten to turn it off before he went to bed. It had subsequently received an irritated slap of the 'snooze' button six times over the course of the following hour and a half, by which point it surrendered itself to complete silence.

And the room was almost silent, except for the occasional soft snores emanating from the dark head that had just buried itself under the covers to hide from the nauseous sun.

He didn't know what time he'd finally crawled into bed last night. It was late. Very late. Or early, depending on how one looked at it. But he wouldn't be able to be any less vague than that. And when his head did meet the pillow, he was out like the dead.

He wasn't particularly feeling among the land of the living now, either. In fact, he might have gone so far as to say he felt worse for the leaden sleep.

But, the good news was he could stay exactly where he was all day long. And that's exactly what he intended to do.

Someone else, though, had different plans.

The banging was almost deafening loud. But, for several seconds, he couldn't work out where it was coming from. Were the damn neighbors remodeling again?

Grumbling, and squeezing his eyes shut as though that might keep some of the sound out as well, he tried to remember whether the Miltenbergers had mentioned anything about DIY. Truthfully, he never really paid that much attention to that motor mouth Ron; the man was far too in love with his own voice.

The knocking came again, and was even louder this time.

"What the-?" he muttered, tapering off as he realized the noise, which was prompting shooting pains in his skull, was coming from his own home. From downstairs.

"Ugh." The comment tossed toward the ceiling, he threw off the sheets and heaved his unwilling body off of the mattress.

Dressed in only an A-shirt and boxers, he couldn't be bothered to put anything else on. The heel of his right hand rubbing at his half-open eye, he wandered downstairs with a sulkiness that was reminiscent of his young son. He was too tired and too lacking in self-awareness to recognize it, though.

As he got to the bottom step, the pounding at the door resumed.

"Alright, alright!" he hollered. "I'm coming!"

Ready to hurl an irritated insult, and maybe even a fist, at whoever was impatiently thumping. The man twisted the lock and opened the door while his free hand rubbed through his sleep-tussled dark hair.

"What do you...?" His question was cut off as one of the two people on the other side of the door held out an ID card and a Chicago PD badge.

She gave him a slight smile that was wholly insincere, as was the apology she uttered next. "Gabriel Summers? We're sorry to wake you, sir. I'm Detective Maloney, and this is Detective Cox."

While the woman spoke, the man beside her pulled his ID from his inside pocket and flashed an identical badge.

"We need to speak with you," she continued. "Is it alright if we come in?" Not waiting for a reply, she stepped across the threshold, pushing his stunned silent form aside with a brush of her shoulder.

"Wh-What?" As though a bucket of ice water had been tossed over him, Gabriel was suddenly very alert. Brown eyes wide, but hand still restlessly moving through his hair, he twisted his face over his shoulder to watch the movement of the woman who'd invited herself in.

She was eyeing the walls casually, while she slipped her hands into her pockets.

"Mr. Summers," the male detective said as he wandered into the house too, "would you mind telling us where you were last night and into the early hours of this morning?"

"I-I-" Shaking his confused head, Gabriel glanced between the two cops. It had been a long time since he'd had any trouble with the law, and he was out of practice. The cool, 'couldn't give a hoot' routine he used to employ wouldn't come to him as easily as it used to.

Squinting, he closed the door behind Detective Cox and took a deep breath as he tried to remember exactly what he'd done the night before. Some of it, and that included all the bits post-Vodka were blurry.

"I went to a bar, but I left early-About ten."

"And then?" Maloney asked, pausing in her examination of the hallway to look at Gabriel.

"I came home," he replied, brow creasing with lines that aged him.

"Did you go out again?"

Those furrows growing ever deeper, he shook his head. "No."

"Anybody here with you, sir?"

"Uh-No. No, I was alone."

"So, no one can confirm where you were?" Cox asked.

Fist tightening at his side, Gabriel tossed his knuckles to the door with a hard punch. "I just said no, didn't I?"

Eyebrows creeping upward, Cox glanced at his partner before addressing his thoughts to the man in front of him again. "Just relax, Mr. Summers. We're just trying to establish some facts."

Too irritable to relax, and feeling even more pissed under the patronizing glare of those azure blue eyes, which looked unusual on a man with such dark hair, Gabriel felt perspiration prick his temples.

"What facts? And why?" he demanded.

There came no direct answer to either of his questions, but Maloney did speak in reply.

"Do you know a man named Alec Renaudin?"

He should have been used to the tough way cops conduct their questioning. That's the sort of thing one never entirely forgets. Yet, the familiarity of it had faded a little over the years, and he was subsequently feeling pushed onto the back foot. And that's exactly what the stuck-up woman with the badge wanted to do to him, wasn't it? He knew her type. She thought she was smarter than him. She thought she could talk him in circles, until she'd got him confessing to something. No, that wasn't going to happen.

"How about you tell me what's going on, or you get out of my house?" he shouted, trying to open the door again, but finding his fatigued and hungover fingers struggling with the lock.

"Sir, this will all go much smoother if you just cooperate with us," Cox insisted, stepping unthreateningly forward and urging Gabriel away from the door.

"What do you want from me?"

"For starters, we want to know whether you're acquainted with Alec Renaudin," Maloney replied firmly.

Her partner tossed her a glare. He knew she wasn't helping to calm the situation. Of course, she was no fool, she knew it too. But she was missing her bed, and she was far too irritable to mess around.

"Do you know him, Mr. Summers?" Cox said, playing the 'good cop' in the hopes of easing the mounting tension, which he could imagine turning ugly.

Prodding at the inside of his cheek with the tip of a furry tongue, Gabriel stared at Maloney. He hated her, he knew that much already. Turning to Cox, he slowly eyed him. He didn't exactly care for this dude, either. He was a pig, after all, and all pigs were jerks. But he was better than the woman looking down her condescending nose at him.

"No," he muttered. "I've never heard of him."

"You sure about that?" Maloney chirped close to gleefully.

Gabriel almost bit back, but quickly screwed his angry hands by his sides. She was trying to bait him. She wanted to get a reaction so she could haul in him on some trumped up charge. He had to stay cool.

"I don't know any Renaudin," he eventually said, but it was impossible to keep the contempt for her from his voice.

Not taking quite as much pleasure in this game of cat and mouse as his partner, Cox slipped a hand into his jacket and pulled out a photograph. Offering it to Gabriel, he asked, "Do you recognize this guy?" He was willing to give the man the benefit of the doubt, maybe Renaudin was a nameless fella he'd met in the bar, who offered him back for a drink.

Growing more annoyed at this waste of his time; time that could be spent in bed, he gave the picture only a cursory glance. "Don't know him."

"Well..." Maloney breathed, still smiling as she took her hands from her pockets, leaned against the wall and folded her arms across her abdomen. "See, Mr. Summers, this is where things start to get a little weird, because your DNA was found at Mr. Renaudin's house. Would you care to explain that?"

Scoffing Gabriel shook his head incredulously. "There must be some mistake. I'm telling you, I've never seen that guy before and I've definitely never been in his house."

"No mistake, sir," she insisted, a tilt of her head flicking some of the hair that had fallen from her sloppy ponytail off her shoulder. "Your DNA was collected from that house, and matches the DNA we have on record for you."

"Someone messed up, because I wasn't there."

"No, Mr. Summers," Cox quietly said, picking up the trail from where his colleague left off. "There can't have been any error. It was checked three times, and was a 100% match with you."

"You need to start being straight with us, sir," Maloney jumped in. "Because, this morning, Mr. Renaudin was found dead."

Fists squeezing and relaxing as quickly as the pounding of his heart, Gabriel shifted anxiously on his bare feet. "What the...What are you trying to say?"

"I'm not saying anything," she replied, with a quirk of one shoulder. "I'm asking you to tell us how you know Mr. Renaudin and what you were doing at his home sometime last night."

Gabriel instinctively found himself looking back at the door. Cox, however, had slickly moved and was now blocking his escape route. He was sweating visibly, much of that was a result of the alcohol last night, but he could not deny that some of it was definitely fear.

"Let me ask you another question, Mr. Summers," Maloney breathed, still enjoying herself. It wasn't quite worth getting up so early for, but it was close. "What size shoe do you take?"

"None of your business."

"Sir," Cox muttered, beginning to lose his patience, "we are conducting a murder investigation. And, right now, you're obstructing it. Do you understand? Now, we can talk here or we can drag you down to the station and you can answer our question there. Clear?"

"Really makes no difference to us," Maloney added.

Chewing at his lower lip until he tasted the faint metallic tang of blood, Gabriel weighed his options. He was pretty sure he would be heading to the police station anyway. "Ten," he spat out.

"And do you own a Dunlop tire iron?"

Eyes squinting as his entire face scrunched, Gabriel tossed his hands to the ceiling. "I don't know what make it is..." he growled. "Maybe."

"Where would that tire iron be, Mr. Summers?"

"In the trunk of the car. Where else would it be?"

Hand moving smoothly behind him, Cox opened the door. Even though he'd never touched the temperamental lock before, he managed it with much more ease than Gabriel's trembling hands.

"Would you mind letting me take a look, sir?"

Their questions no longer seeming like questions at all, Gabriel saw no choice but to accept. He pointed to the Ford Focus' keys in their usual place; in the basket on the small table next to the door.

Cox nodded his gratitude, swept them up into his palm and wandered outside. Maloney remained behind, keeping a close eye on Gabriel and one hand ready to reach for her gun. She didn't trust this guy. He obviously had a temper, and if he gave her any reason whatsoever, she wouldn't hesitate to take him down.

"Where's the family, Mr. Summers?" she asked, as though she were an overly-nosey, but a friendly visitor.

The last thing Gabriel wanted to do was engage in chit-chat with this woman, but he knew well enough that it wasn't chit-chat.

"I don't see what it's got to do with you," he started gruffly. "But my wife and kids are in Pennsylvania, spending the weekend with her parents."

"You didn't go with them?"

"Obviously not."

"How come?"

Now the self-satisfied cow really had stepped outside the bounds of her so-called investigation. He felt himself lurch as though to take a step toward her, but his feet didn't even move before a breeze behind him brought the other cop back into the house.

Cox twirled the keys around his index finger as he glanced at Maloney. "Nothing in there," he said. "No tire iron."

Something passed between the two detectives. A look that was all, but it meant something to them. Something that made Gabriel edgy.

"Well...It...My wife must have taken it for her car. Maybe she lost hers or something?"

"Really, Mr. Summers?" Maloney responded, using her shoulder to push herself away from the wall. "We can talk more about that down at the station."

"What the heck are you talking about?"

"Gabriel Summers," Cox said, reaching behind him and taking hold of the cuffs in his belt, "I am arresting you on suspicion of the murder of Alec Renaudin."

"Oh, for crying out loud," Gabriel muttered.

"You have the right to remain silent," Cox continued, stepping forward. "Anything you do say, can and will be used against you in a court of law."

"I don't know anything about this." Hands suddenly pushing forward, Gabriel tried foolishly to shove the detective away from him.

Cox's sober, and much more agile reflexes leapt into action. Taking hold of Gabriel's wrist, he soon had his arm pulled up behind his back while he forced him face-first against the wall.

"You have the right to an attorney," Cox said, slapping the cuffs on. "If you cannot afford an attorney, one will be provided for you."

"I'm telling you, I don't know who this guy is!"

Rolling her eyes, Maloney wandered forward giving her partner a pat of congratulations on the back as she passed him. The day wasn't over by a long stretch, but, hopefully, the worst of it was behind them. And, with any luck at all, the whole case would be wrapped up quickly and cleanly.

Chapter Three

Gabriel shifted, causing the overalls he wore to rustle. His own clothes had been taken off of him, and bagged for forensic testing during the humiliating processing routine. Some of that routine had been modernized since the last time he was a participant of it, but much of it was close enough to feel like habit. But, of course, that didn't make any of it easier to stomach. In fact, it may have made it worse.

His fingers laced but fidgeting restlessly as his wrists rested on the edge of the melamine-topped table, he stared directly ahead of him. The walls of the small room were a solid gray not broken by windows, the only light was from a bulb directly overhead that flickered. It was only slight, but it was enough to be annoying. And he was certain it would give him a headache if they left him sitting there long enough. Maybe that's what they wanted to do.

The hangover probably wasn't helping. In some ways, it was giving the whole thing a surreal quality. Had any of it really happened? Perhaps it was just a bad dream. However, the pounding of his pulse behind his eyeballs reminded him that this was no nightmare. This was very real; it was definitely happening.

Releasing a pent-up breath, he tried to relax. Otherwise, he knew, he'd play right into their hands. They'd left him here to stew; to get all wound up so he'd say something unguarded in the heat of the moment. He wasn't going to let those cheap tricks work, he wasn't going to let them win.

Closing his eyes, he counted the slow seconds as he let air pass in and out of his lungs. It was something Jennifer did when she'd taken up yoga during her pregnancy with Nate. Gabriel had no idea if it worked or if it was like those stupid anger management techniques, and he'd even derided Jen for it at the time. However, he was willing to try anything.

He was right, though, it didn't work. Giving up almost as soon as he'd begun, he slammed the heel of his hand against the table. The clunk caused the metal legs to creak, but the bolts holding them to the floor prevented them from moving.

As that sound continued to echo around the otherwise empty room, the door that was the same shade of gray and so indistinguishable from the walls, opened.

Detective Cox walked in first and, as he did, he glanced up at the camera, which was protected by a dome of dark plastic. Maloney followed, reading from a manila file as though it were the daily news she was casually taking in.

Hand holding the loose end of his tie close to his abdomen as he sat, Cox settled into one of the seats that was also securely attached to the solid floor.

"You sure you don't want an attorney?" he asked.

The question, in different guises, had been asked three times. Gabriel's answer remained the same.

"I don't need an attorney; I haven't done anything wrong."

Slapping the file down, Maloney announced herself and her partner for the benefit of the tape. "I don't think," she added, sitting down and resting both elbows on the desk, "you quite understand the severity of your situation, Mr. Summers." With a small smile, she pointed to the document beneath hands that loosely dangled at the wrists. "We can place you at the scene of a murder. And not only can't account for being there last night, but you also deny having been there at all."

"That's because I haven't ever been there," Gabriel snapped.

"Do you know how DNA works?" she responded tartly. "It doesn't lie, Mr. Summers, but people do."

"I've told you, you've made a mistake."

Cox sighed softly and lifted his gaze to the grid pattern of the dropped ceiling. "And we've told you repeatedly that there couldn't have been any contamination of that sample."

Hands screwed into familiar fists, Gabriel swallowed the impulse to slug the guy in his clean-shaven jaw. "Then someone is trying to set me up," he ground out through snarling teeth.

Scoffing lightly, Maloney let her elbows slide off the shiny desk as she leaned back. "Do you think that's likely, sir?"

"You're the cops, it's your job to find out."

"It's our job," she returned smartly, "to find the person responsible for Alec Renaudin's death. "And, I'd say, we've got him."

"Why? Why would I murder a man I've never met, huh?"

As Cox slammed his hand on the desk, Maloney jumped and twisted her face toward her usually mild-mannered partner.

"You were at the house," he insisted angrily. "You were there, and you met him. Stop messing around with us, Gabriel."

Frowning, Maloney slipped her hand beneath the table and grabbed hold of Cox's thigh in an effort to gain his attention. It worked, and her partner's annoyed eyes were suddenly turned on her. He seemed to ask silently 'what?' with his creased brow. Equally silently, her pointed look told him to stop being an ass. She wasn't sure what had gotten into Cox since they made the arrest, but it was very obvious to her that the 'bad cop' approach wasn't going to work with Summers.

That little hissy fit back at the house was proof that they were dealing with a big kid. And, as far as she was concerned, the only way to deal with a big kid was to give them something that would make them reach adulthood in a hurry.

"Mr. Summers," she offered in a mild voice, which was an effort for her. "You've got quite the record." Releasing Cox's leg, she peeled open the manila file and read a few of the choice hits from it. "First arrest was for assaulting your math teacher when you were seventeen. Your next brush with the law was battery at the age of eighteen. Attempted assault with a deadly weapon when you were twenty."

"You know what we call that, Gabriel?" Cox muttered rhetorically. "Form."

Struggling not to be baited, Gabriel slowly stretched his fingers and stared down at the flexing of his knuckles.

"You're quite a violent man, Mr. Summers," Maloney added.

"I got into some scrapes when I was a kid," he replied, hands still clenching the hair on the crown of his head. "I went through a rough patch and I made some mistakes. What? I've got to pay for that forever?"

Titling her head while she began to read again from the document before her, Maloney sighed quietly. "Mistakes? You can say that again. A couple of years later, you were involved in a bar fight," she said, casting her partner a sidelong glance in the hopes of stalling any further comment he'd been planning to toss into the mix. "You put a guy in the hospital. And, I'd say, you would have been looking at jail time on that occasion if it hadn't been for your victim..."

"He wasn't a victim," Gabriel interjects. "He was a-" With a humorless scoff, he stopped himself and shook his head. He'd been about to do it again; he'd been letting them rile him.

"Your victim," Maloney continued as though the man in front of her had never opened his mouth, "had been seen at some point that night with a knife. And, of course, you had a lenient judge, who bought the possibility of self-defense and sentenced you to mandatory anger management classes. How'd they work out for you, Mr. Summers?" Smiling slightly, she lifted her eyes to him.

"I stayed out of trouble since then," he replied stiffly. "So, what do you think?"

One palm smoothing over the tabletop, Cox settled back in his chair. Upper body remaining stiff despite the relaxed position, his focus moved to Maloney, who was uncharacteristically silent in the face of their collar's sarcasm. With her fingers still toying idly with the papers in her file, she simply stared at Gabriel, waiting for him to say something else.

"I think you've either been lucky or you've kept your nose clean," Cox said, his deep voice easily filling the room. "Either way, something changed last night."

Sucking his lower lip between his teeth, Gabriel bit down hard as he raked both hands through his disheveled hair. "Nothing changed, because I didn't do anything," he eventually breathed. "Why won't you listen to me?"

"We'll listen to you when you start being straight with us."

Still quiet, Maloney turned her attention back to her file and rifled through a few sheets until she found a glossy black and white photograph, which had been blown up. The image was distorted for being enlarged, but it was clearly a security camera's still.

Calmly turning the photo around, she pushed it toward Gabriel with just her forefinger.

"We checked out your whereabouts last night, and confirmed you were at a bar called Crossing Downtown." With that same un-manicured finger, she pointed at the grainy picture and a man sitting at a bar.

The guy in the photograph was staring up at one of the many huge TVs in the place, and he was watching a basketball match on it while mournfully nursing his beer.

Barely glancing down, Gabriel shrugged. "I told you that's where I was."

"Yeah, but, see, here's the problem." As Maloney spoke, her pointer slid along the picture, sweeping across the bar four stools along from where Gabriel sat, until she reached another man. "This is Alec Renaudin."

Tongue prodding at the inside of his cheek, Gabriel snorted. "I am telling you, I don't know the guy. I don't know why you're trying to pin this on me. But I..."

Cox's palm lifted sharply off the table before slamming back down on it. "Watch it! And I suggest you listen to me very carefully, Summers," he yelled. "We have got you drinking with the victim, and we can place you at his house. You are in a heap of trouble like you've never been in before, understand? And the longer you continue to lie about being at Renaudin's home, the worse this is all going to look to a jury. Because, you better believe, this one is going to trial."

Her partner's sudden protective streak caught Maloney off guard and, for a moment, she was unsure whether to feel grateful or patronized. A mixture of the two warring in her, she tried to clear her head of the whole issue and get back to the matter at hand.

Defiant, Gabriel threw himself back in the chair and folded his arms across his chest. "I don't know the guy, and I wasn't there."

"So, how do you account for your DNA on a glass found in his living room?" Maloney asked, genuine curiosity creasing her brow. She wondered how the man in front of her could possibly hope to get away with this? Even if the murder was committed in the heat of temper, which looked highly likely, he'd had time to think about his story. He could have claimed to have left Alec alive and well. Instead, he foolishly chose to deny being there at all. That made him, arguably, the most stupid criminal she'd ever come across.

"I'm not saying anything more."

Thoughtfully running her tongue across her lower lip, Maloney looked to the man seated beside her.

"Are you sure you've got nothing else to say?" Cox demanded, preempting what the answer would be and already getting to his feet.

Gabriel said nothing as he stared at the man with raw contempt.

In amused disbelief, Maloney shook her head. "I strongly suggest you rethink the attorney thing, Mr. Summers," she said quietly as she got to her feet. "You are going to need a phenomenally good one."

***

A phenomenally good attorney was out of Gabriel's price range. Instead, he had to make do with the public defender assigned to him. The guy also had four other cases on his docket, something he reminded Gabriel of almost constantly. And he, like the cops, was unwilling to believe that Gabriel was oblivious as to how his DNA wound up in that house.

Scott Gattis was running on caffeine, a jelly donut and just three hours sleep when he met with Gabriel Summers for the fourth time. It had been three months since the file had been slapped on his desk, and, from the moment it did, he didn't know how the heck he was going to defend this guy.

Meeting him in person hadn't helped. Summers was uncooperative, and acted like the whole world had it in for him. In his fifteen-year career, Gattis had met plenty of people with a chip on their shoulder, but no one had been so self-defeating and stubborn. And this morning's discovery was the last straw.

Massaging the nape of his neck, Gattis paced the width of the small room. His fingers trembled of their own volition, and he realized he shouldn't have had that second espresso. Knocking the toes of Derbys he hadn't had time to polish against the already grubby-marked wall, he turned and placed his hazel eyes on the silent man seated at the table.

Dressed in a gray round-necked sweater and a pair of what looked very much like lounge pants, the man frowned. But that wasn't unusual. In fact, it was a permanent feature of his face, those deep lines that were going to be wrinkles if he kept doing it for much longer.

"Do you realize what kind of sentence you could be looking at here?" Gattis demanded as he reached the chair opposite Gabriel's and leaned his hands on the back of it. He had a slightly Southern accent, which he'd clearly made efforts to shed. A little of it lingered though, and was even more noticeable when he was pissed off about something.

Lifting his face slowly, Gabriel met the man's eyes, but refused to answer his question. "Have you spoken to my wife?"

"Not since the last time I was here." Pushing his wire-rimmed glasses up his nose, Gattis exhaled. "Can we focus?"

"I don't know what any of you people want from me. I have told you everything I can."

"Oh, really?" Sweeping a hand over prematurely-thinning hair that he kept shaved close to his scalp, the lawyer cocked his head. "Well, you certainly didn't tell me about your trial for assault thirteen years ago."

Refusing to be chastised like a child, Gabriel rolled his eyes. "Figured you already knew. Isn't it your job to research the facts?"

"I do not have time to spend hours sifting through your background. If you want me to help you, then you have to start helping me. Now what else have you been keeping to yourself, huh?"

Indignant, Gabriel sniffed as he rubbed the heel of his hand against one darkened eye. He struggled to remember the last time he slept properly. The bed was so damn hard, and his head refused to leave him in peace for five minutes anyway. The oblivion of unconsciousness, something he desperately craved, refused to come.

"Gabriel, are you listening to me? If you withhold information that could be pertinent in your trial, I can't defend you properly. And if you want to continue playing these games, you can find someone else to defend you, because I've had my fill of them."

"I'm not the one playing games. I have told you the truth about that night."

"No, you haven't. Because you haven't told me why you were at Renaudin's house, what happened while you were there, and what time it was when you left."

Leaping out of his chair, Gabriel pounded the side of his fist on the table. "Why won't anyone listen to me? I wasn't there. I've never been there in my life!"

Despite the cop guarding the door, Gattis was concerned about the volatile nature of the man in front of him, and not just for his own sake. If Gabriel went postal on his counsel, what slim chance there was of a favorable verdict would be blown completely out the window.

Trying to calm himself, and hoping that would simultaneously diffuse the leaden atmosphere in that claustrophobic room, the attorney took a couple of deep breaths before even attempting to speak again. And when he did open his mouth to talk, it was with a voice a touch lower than before.

"The evidence puts you there, Gabriel. It's conclusive, and we have to find a way to explain it if we're ever going to convince a jury that you're not guilty of murder."

"Wh..." Blinking, he took the older man in slowly. "What do you mean, 'convince a jury'? I am not guilty of murder."

Gattis wanted to believe all his clients were innocent, but he wasn't some newly-qualified naïf. He knew how the world worked. He knew how the justice system worked. Everyone deserves a trial, even when their guilt is patently obvious. And it was his job to try and secure a 'not guilty' regardless of his feelings toward the person he represented and the crime they were accused of committing. There were times, though, when his feelings refused to stay politely on the sidelines where they belonged. Like one of those over-enthusiastic football dads, his feelings sometimes screamed at him as if they'd like to take his place and play the game themselves given half a chance. He had to be careful about that; had to keep thing in check.

"You don't believe me, do you?" Gabriel asked, squinting slightly and putting crow's feet at the corners of his eyes to match the lines on his forehead.

"What I believe is not the issue here," he responded with a professional detachment that answered the question as surely and clearly as if he'd yelled, 'no'. "I have a job to do, and in order to do it, I need your cooperation."

Scuffing the floor with beaten up sneakers, Gabriel clenched his teeth and felt the tiny muscle in his jaw contract.

"What I need you to do is start being honest with me, because the DA is pushing this trial through as quickly as he can. I am doing everything in my power to stall things, so that when we wind up in court we have a case to present. But we can't drag this thing out indefinitely. And, at the moment, I have precisely diddly and squat to present."

"I don't want to be represented by someone who doesn't believe me," Gabriel muttered.

Chuckling at his client as though the thirty-something was just an adolescent having a stroppy tantrum, Gattis picked up his papers from the desk.

"What I suggest you do is think long and hard about what it is you want, Mr. Summers," he said, tapping the edge of his file on the table to neaten the pages before whipping it under his arm. "If what you want is to see your kids grow up, then you need my help. So when you decide that you're ready to take this conversation seriously, we'll talk again."

As he headed for the door, Gattis wasn't sure whether he'd rather wash his hands of the whole case. In that instant, he did. But part of him already knew that was just fatigue and bad temper talking. Once he'd had a chance to calm down, his sense of responsibility would kick back in. Gabriel Summers needed legal counsel. Truthfully, he needed all the help he could get.

Chapter Four

Jennifer Summers wiped at the weary, frustrated, irate tears that left their sticky and weaving tracks down her cheeks. Those tears had come and gone over the last eighteen months. Bouts of them had become less frequent in recent weeks, but they were no less draining and she was no more able to stop them than she had been the day she returned home to find her husband had been arrested. A torrent of emotions, too many to count and some she couldn't even lend a name to, had rushed through her during the hours, days, weeks, and months since that moment. There were times she'd felt sure she was losing her mind.

How could everything in her life have gone so badly wrong? It didn't seem real to her. She was sure it had to be some horrible dream that she was about to wake up from. And yet, somehow, in the midst of that storm, life went on as normal. She went on as normal. She had to, there was no choice in the matter. Occasionally, she might lock herself in the bathroom and sob. Sometimes, one of the older kids had found her quietly weeping while she prepared their dinner. But she did carry on. She fed them, bathed them, read them bedtime stories, ferried them to school - she did all of the things that were expected of her, because she had no choice.

And because she had to carry on for their sake, she carried on doing the normal things for herself - she ate and she slept, although most nights she needed half a bottle of wine or a couple of Xanax to get there. On occasion, she'd drunk a little more wine and even combined it with the pills. It was only in the mornings, she realized how selfish she'd been to risk leaving her children without either of their parents.

So, guilt was added to the swell of emotions she thought she might be about to drown in. But there was some relief in being able to shift the blame. She was trapped in a situation not of her making nor of her choosing; none of it was her doing. Being a single mother had never been part of the plan, and she was facing that future anyway. And that realization, which hammered away at her brain like a persistent downpour of winter rain, provoked anger in her. An anger at herself. An anger at the injustice of life. An anger at the world. Mostly, though, an anger that was directed squarely at him.

Leaning against the kitchen counter, she exhaled a slow and shaky breath as silent tears blurred her vision of the room. She sniffed, but it did nothing to dry the dampness in her eyes. Squeezing them shut as the phone began to ring, she willed the noise to stop. That sound grated on her already tattered nerves.

Less than a week after Gabriel's arrest, she'd gotten an unlisted number. But it hadn't helped. The calls kept coming; reporters wanting to get the inside scoop from the 'murderer's wife', other people calling just to hurl abuse at her. Five times over the last eighteen months she'd changed the number. And, mercifully, the stream of incessant calls had begun to die down. They were much less frequent now than in that first month, when the phone barely stopped ringing and she had to resort to unplugging it for hours and sometimes days at a time.

Poor Nate and Amy barely remembered a time when they were allowed to answer the phone. They both knew now never to touch it. That was just one of many things about their lives that was abnormal. And, in the grand scheme of things, she knew that was one of the more minor issues. However, those minor things mounted up in Jennifer's mind, and caused her to worry constantly about their well-being and their future happiness. Would this mess them both up for the rest of their lives? How could it possibly not?

As the phone continued to ring, Jennifer released a taut groan through gritted teeth and swiped the thing off the counter. “Hello?” she snapped, hauling the phone to her ear.

“Uh-” The male voice on the other end of the line hesitated. “Sorry, Jen, is it a bad time?”

“Pete?” she asked, her fingers rubbing at her lined forehead. She was certain the last year and a half had aged her thirty times over.

“Yeah,” he replied. “I’m sorry to bother you. I just wanted to check that you and the kids are okay.”

Sniffing again, she smiled sadly to herself - those were the only smiles she’d been able to manage in so long that she’d almost forgotten what it felt like to smile properly. “That’s kind of you,” she murmured, her voice cracking.

Pete worked at the same insurance company as Gabriel, the two had been on friendly terms. In fact, Pete had even had dinner with the family on a couple of occasions in happier days. Unlike the rest of the well-wishing, can-we-do-anything-to-help calls, Pete’s hadn’t stopped after the initial drama had passed. He was a good man.

And sometimes, as she’d been lying alone in her bed, staring at the ceiling in search of a sleep she knew she wouldn’t find, she’d think about what her life would have been like if she’d married someone like Pete instead. She felt no pleasure in those thoughts. She knew it was a betrayal of her marriage, and the man she’d loved so deeply she’d sworn to spend the rest of her life with him. But those two o’clock in the morning musings wouldn’t listen to reason and would not be silenced by accusations of inappropriateness.

“Have those vultures been hounding you again?” he asked, his voice stiffening slightly.

"I got a couple of calls yesterday," she replied. "But it's fine." That was a lie, and she had a feeling he must know it. However, he didn't call her out on it, and she didn't try to take it back. They both let it hang their, obvious but untouched.

Eventually, he broke the silence by changing the subject. "How'd the visit go?"

"Oh, it was-" How could someone explain what it had been like, what it was like every single time? The heartache. The feeling of uselessness. The anger. The desperate longing to believe her husband, but the doubts that niggled at her and refused to be ignored.

"It was the same," she sighed.

"You know, Jen," he offered with a quiet exhale of his own, "everything's gonna be alright. I know it all looks bad right now, but it'll be okay. I mean- He's innocent, right? So when the trial comes around-" He allowed his words to drift untethered, suspecting that she'd rather talk about something else. Anything else.

He never knew quite what to say, and hated that he stumbled over what he wanted to tell her. He wanted to make it better, to comfort her somehow. Yet, it was impossible. Nothing could make the situation any easier for her. It was one of the most awful things that could have happened, and no amount of pep talking would magically take the previous eighteen months away.

"I'm sorry," he mumbled. "I didn't mean to- I just-"

"I know," she whispered. "I know you mean well."

An ever so slightly awkward silence drifted between them, seeming to make the very air in Jennifer's kitchen thick.

"Well-" Pete muttered, his finger audibly tapping on the back of his phone. "I really just called to make sure you're okay."

"Thanks," she replied. "I really appreciate it."

"And you let me know if there's anything I can do," he added sincerely. "You just call me anytime. Day or night."

Grateful, Jennifer found her lips tugging into that melancholy smile of hers again. She wasn't sure whether it was his kindness that was filling her lower lids with tears again, or if it was the stark reminder of how unkind the rest of the world had been. Either way, as she blinked another heavy droplet swerved a curved path down her cheek until it met her upper lip and she licked it away.

"Thank you," she managed to say, although the words were hoarse and she couldn't be sure he'd hear them.

He did. "You're welcome. Bye, Jen."

She cleared her throat and swallowed before saying, "Bye," in return, but he'd already gone. The line was quiet. The back of her free hand wiping at her face, she turned and replaced the phone. Letting her eyes slip closed, she leaned on the counter for support as she emptied the contents of her lungs and felt her entire body tremble.

"Mom?"

Clenching her eyes a little tighter, she willed herself not to respond with the curtness that pulled at every overwrought nerve in her body. She hadn't always been able to quash that, there had been times she'd snapped at all three of her children, even the baby. And that was another sandbag of guilt to weigh her down.

"Yes, sweetheart?" she said, pulling herself together. With a quick sniff, she turned to flash Nate a smile and show him her 'mommy face'.

Little Nate was not so small anymore. He was just a few months from his eighth birthday, and he was several inches taller than the last time his father saw him. He'd abandoned George long ago, Gabe would have been pleased about that, but, of course, the father hadn't been around to witness his son's coming of age.

Jennifer silently wondered how many other milestones in the boy's life would be missed by his dad.

"Mom, are you okay?" he asked, taking a shuffled step forward. When he reached the breakfast nook, he climbed up onto a stool, something Gabe didn't even know he could now manage on his own. Resting his elbow on the counter, he let his chin fall into the palm of his hand as his dark hair flopped into his eyes.

His difficult seeing her reminding Jennifer of something else that needed to be done, she leaned forward and swept his bangs back from his forehead, and made a mental note as she did to take him to get a haircut.

"Mom?"

He hardly ever called her 'Mommy' anymore, and that caused a twinge in her heart. He wouldn't be her little boy much longer. Time was passing so quickly, and yet it was also dragging so slowly. How was that possible?

"I'm fine," she eventually said, answering his question. "Where's your sister?"

"Watching TV with grandma."

"Why don't you go back in there?" she urged with a gentle tilt of her head. "I'll get started on dinner."

Not moving, the boy still sat with his face resting on his palm. As he spoke, his jaw was constricted, but it didn't seem to bother him that he couldn't open his mouth properly. "Mom, how long before Dad comes home?"

Resting her forearms on the counter between them, Jennifer lost the ability to maintain her 'mommy face'. It was a question both of the older kids had asked often. Like most things, it had become less frequent. They had both adjusted. And, most of the time, she was convinced that they were handling things better than she was. Well, of course, they would be. They were too young to understand. At least, they had been too young to understand. Nate was beginning to reach an age where he might overhear something that he understood. Jennifer dreaded the day she might have to tell him the full story. She pleaded with God that Gabriel would be home long before that day, and she'd never be forced to have the conversation that would no doubt break her son's heart.

"Truthfully, I don't know, honey," she answered, having decided a long time ago that she wouldn't tell any of her children a deliberate lie. She might be tempted to bend the truth slightly in order to spare their feelings, but she would not do anything to destroy their trust in her. Trust, she knew, was a precious thing. And far too fragile to risk breaking.

His young brow frowning, Nate glanced down at the counter then back at his mother. "Some guys at school... They were saying stuff."

Feeling her pulse rate quicken, Jennifer trembled. "You know," she started, trying to offer him a confidence and calm she didn't feel. "People will say stuff, Nate. It's best to ignore them, right?"

As if she hadn't even spoken, he continued. "They said Dad did something bad. They said he hurt someone."

Holding her breath, Jennifer waited for him to finish the story with something worse. But nothing else came.

"Dad-" she slowly began, carefully weighing how to phrase what she wanted to say. "Dad has been accused of doing something. You know what that means, right?"

He nodded his small head, but didn't lift it off his hand as he did.

"It doesn't mean he did it," she added, feeling the need to elaborate even though he clearly understood. "It means someone thinks he did something. And soon, they're going to realize he didn't do anything wrong. Then he'll be back home with us. Okay?" Smiling, she swept her hand through that over-long hair again.

His young but serious face bobbed up and down in another nod, but the chewing of his lip suggested he wasn't entirely satisfied. "But how long's that gonna be?"

"I don't..."

"Nate."

Both mother and son turned to the door to find Nate's grandma walking into the room. Pulling her knitted cardigan around herself, she folded her arms beneath her bosom as she approached the pair with solemn features and thin lips.

"Nate, go back in the living room with your sister."

"But, I..."

"Don't argue with me, Nate."

She'd always had a way. Something in that tone, which meant there was no negotiation to be had. Jennifer had only once caught herself using it, and immediately swore never to do so again. She didn't want to turn into her mother. Of course, her mother reminded her that she'd turned out okay, and there was, therefore, nothing wrong with her approach to parenting. That was a point that couldn't be argued with, but Jennifer still wanted to bring her children up her own way.

Sure enough, though, Nate obediently slid off the stool and made his way back into the other room.

"There was no need to talk to him like that," Jennifer muttered, pushing herself off the counter and moving toward the refrigerator.

"He's too young to know about these things."

"I wasn't going to tell him everything," she insisted, opening the door and grabbing some vegetables out of the salad crisper. "But he keeps asking, and I can't side-step the issue forever, Mom."

Still holding her arms tightly around her slender frame, the older woman shakes her dyed blonde head. "You think a seven-year-old can possibly understand any of this?" Scoffing, she added, "You want him to know his father is a murderer?"

"Gabriel is not a murderer," she replied through gritted teeth and in hushed tones. Slamming the refrigerator door shut, she dumped the ingredients for dinner down and pressed cool hands to burning hot cheeks. "He is not a murderer," she repeated even more quietly.

"I warned you when you married him. You're really naïve enough to think men like that change?"

"Alright," she breathed, arms flopping listlessly by her sides. "Alright, I knew he had a problem with his temper. I knew he could be violent. But this is not- He's not capable of this."

"How do you know that?"

"He's the father of my children," she returned, trying to keep her voice down so the kids wouldn't overhear. "You're suggesting that Nate, Amy and Jamie's dad could do something so awful?"

Blinking her gray eyes, Jennifer's mother simply regarded her daughter for a while. "I know you keep clinging to that," she said, stepping forward and unraveling her arms from her body. "I know you have to, because the alternative is too terrible to contemplate."

Jennifer opened her mouth to contradict the woman who puts an arm around her. But as she was pulled into a hug, she lost the fight to speak, to argue, and to hold back the tears.

Running a hand over her daughter's trembling back, the blonde-haired woman hushed her just as she used to when she was a little girl. "It's alright," she murmured. "It's going to be alright. You've got me. You've still got your family."

"Gabriel's my family," she replied, the words muffled by emotion and the woolen shoulder her face was pressed against. "I can't turn my back on him."

She breathed slowly before answering. She had been trying to get the girl to see sense for months now. She could not ignore what was right in front of her eyes.

"And what if he's guilty?" she asked, trying to pose the question calmly.

"He isn't." Lifting her face, Jennifer stepped back and shook her head defiantly. "He isn't. He can't be."

Not fighting to pull her back into her embrace, she folded her arms again. "Then why can't he explain his DNA being there? Has he even tried to tell you how that happened?"

It was a conversation they'd had before. Many times. And Jennifer's answer was always the same. "I don't know. Something must be wrong."

"He's lying to you that's what's wrong," her mother snapped. "Whatever happened that night, he was there, and he's lying about that."

Silent tears hurriedly spilling onto her cheeks, Jennifer shook her head. It was all she could do. She didn't know exactly what it was she was saying 'no' to; the possibility that Gabriel had an even darker side than she could ever have imagined; the fact that she could have married a man capable of beating someone to death; that her marriage was in pieces and, regardless of what happened, might never be repaired.

Maybe she was saying, 'no' to all of it. To everything. The whole mess that she did not want to be part of. In that moment, she would have sold her soul for all of it to disappear. Because she could not completely block out her mother's words. She wanted to. But they were always there in her subconscious. They had been there all along; they'd been questions she'd asked herself dozens, no hundreds of times.

"Jenny," her mother crooned gently. "You can't keep playing the devoted wife to a man who lied to you; to a man who's a monster."

She wanted to shout back, 'He's not a monster.' However, those words wouldn't come. And she realized for the first time, it was because she no longer believed they were true. She didn't know Gabriel anymore. Everytime he'd thrown a punch at the wall; everytime he'd smashed something in anger; everytime he'd scared her, when he'd given her a flicker of doubt in the certainty that he'd never put his hands on her- it all came flashing in front of her eyes like a movie on a cinema screen.

Perhaps the man she married wasn't the one she thought he was. That was an agonizingly painful proposition, but it was one she could no longer ignore. Why wouldn't he tell anyone what he was doing there that night? Why wouldn't he at least tell her? Surely, there was only one reason he'd lie about it. There could only be one, and it made her want to vomit.

"It's going to be alright," her mom said, but it was a platitude she could well have done without. Nothing was alright. Nothing could ever be right again.

Chapter Five

Maloney leaned back in her desk chair, causing it to squeak. Screwing her face up, she wondered why the department budget couldn't stretch to half decent office furniture. She supposed it wasn't the most important thing on the city's agenda, and they might have had a point about that, but she at least deserved somewhere comfortable to sit while she sifted through all the paperwork, didn't she?

It had been a long week. And the worst of it was a case that she couldn't crack: A homeless man had been shot and killed in the early hours of Saturday morning. There were no relatives concerned about the guy, no obvious motive for the killing, no witnesses, and no real clues. Nobody else seemed to care a great deal-except Cox, maybe. But he had that kind of obsessional personality. For everyone else, though, it was *just* a homeless guy; he wouldn't be missed, so his death didn't appear to matter. It mattered to Maloney, and not just because she hated to leave a case unsolved. It mattered because the guy was a human being, and he deserved justice just like everyone else.

Lifting her feet to the edge of the desk, she sighed and tipped her face to the ceiling. She hated that feeling; that sense that someone needed her help and she wasn't able to give it. Sighing, she blinked at the spitballs someone else had left on the cream ceiling above her head.

"For heaven's sake," she murmured. "I'm working with a bunch of kids."

"What?"

Head falling down and snapping to her right, Maloney watched as Cox sauntered alongside her desk, then planted his butt on the edge of it. When she remained silent, he asked his question again.

"What are you muttering to yourself about?"

"Just the-" she half said, tossing her eyes to the ceiling to indicate the rest of what she simply could not be bothered to say.

His gaze followed hers and his mouth scrunched in disgust. He refused to linger long on it, though, and soon put his focus back on her. "What are you still doing here? Thought you were finished an hour or more ago."

Shrugging sullenly, Maloney dragged her feet from the desk and sat upright again. Twisting the swiveling chair, and prompting it to clunk and grind as it moved, she faced him. "What are you, my keeper now?"

Arching one of his jet black eyebrows, he folded his arms across his abdomen and sighed. "Is this always how it's going to be?"

"What do you mean?"

"This," he said, gesturing with his head at the space between the two of them.

She pursed her lips in reply and lifted her palms toward the unpleasant ceiling. "I don't know what you're talking about."

"The ornery sarcasm."

"Probably," Maloney replied unapologetically, as she looked at her computer keyboard, although there was nothing of any interest to be found there. "Sorry, Cox. If you wanted some Starsky and Hutch-style partners bonding thing, you're out of luck. In case you hadn't already noticed, that's really not my thing."

"I had noticed," he assured her, crossing one ankle over the other. "You know, it's a shame, though, because I can just see you in one of those chunky-knit sweaters."

Maloney didn't want to laugh, she was feeling too dejected, and she definitely didn't want to encourage his wisecracks. But she couldn't help herself. Stifling the snicker, though, she quickly tossed back, "For your information, I would have been Hutch."

"Yeah, maybe," he replied with a subtle nod and a smile tugging at the corners of his own mouth.

She peered up at him. Their eyes met briefly, and for a second she allowed herself to think he wasn't such a bad guy after all. In fact, she realized that, in their odd kind of way, they complemented each other. They made a pretty good team. And she'd never tell him, but she held a respect for him that she did not have toward any of her other colleagues. For a second, she wondered if that meant they could work well together in other aspects of life. However, she quickly dismissed that thought with a shake of her head. Her and Cox? That was a crazy proposition. Laughable really. And dangerous, too. She forcefully warned herself not to get sentimental, knowing it was a luxury she couldn't afford. That way lay vulnerability, and if there was one thing Maloney refused to be it was vulnerable.

"Anyway," he sighed, breaking the silence that had begun easily enough but had turned awkward the longer it hovered between the pair. "I was just coming to tell you that my buddy in the DA's office told me that Gabriel Summers' trial is coming up next month."

"Oh," Maloney replied, nodding. The preliminary hearing had been months ago, and although she'd never forgotten about Summers, she had allowed him to fade into the shadows of her memory. "Well, that must be a relief for

Renaudin's girlfriend. She's been waiting a long time for the system to work." She knew that the slow-moving wheels of justice were there for a reason; to ensure a fair trial, and reduce the miscarriages of justice that might occur if cases were fast-tracked. Nevertheless, there were plenty of times she wished those wheels could move a little quicker than they do.

"Hmm." Chewing the inside of his cheek, he glanced at the gray carpet by his feet before adding, "They're still trying to negotiate a plea, apparently."

"And he's not biting?"

"Uh-uh," he responded simply.

"Why?" she huffed, lounging back in her seat and swiveling the chair idly from side to side with tiny movements of her feet.

The creaks and clicks of the chair filling the space between them, Cox frowned at her like a father irritated by a noisy toy. Maloney, however, did not pick up on the subtle expression. Or, if she did, she chose to ignore it.

"I mean-" she added, gaze drifting up toward the spit-balled ceiling again. "It just doesn't make any sense. He has to know he's never going to get away with it. What game is he playing?"

"I don't know," he replied with a light lift of one shoulder. "I guess he must think he can get a 'not guilty' verdict."

"With his DNA at the scene, and him denying he's ever been there?" she retorted swiftly.

"Hey, I'm not the one trying to claim my innocence with blood all over my hands," he returned smoothly. "You'll need to ask Mr. Summers whether he was dropped on his head as a child."

Exhaling loudly, Maloney turned to the window and watched the fat, cumbersome snowdrops swerving awkwardly in the wind on their way to the ground. Not turning away from the winter scene, she asked, "Do you ever think about that tire iron?"

"The one we couldn't find?"

"Yeah," she replied, her face still turned to the window. "It was the one piece of the puzzle that was missing."

Pushing himself off her desk, Cox ran his hands down his thighs, straightening the neatly pressed crease in his pants. "Yeah, well, sometimes you don't need every piece of the puzzle to know it's a picture of Munch's The Scream."

Quirking her head over her shoulder, Maloney frowned at him. "You had a very strange childhood."

***

Gabriel sat with an elbow propped on the table and a fist gripping some of his own hair in a way that looked painful. If it caused him any discomfort, though, it did not show on his face, nor did he stop. His other hand laid on the table, his palm flush to the surface. Bruises shaded his knuckles, and spots of scabbing blood dotted each of the five fingers.

He was missing his daughter's birthday. Funny thing was, Gabriel had never enjoyed his children's birthdays when he was at home for them. They'd been stressful, noisy occasions; often spattered with tantrums. He'd had precious little opportunity to have a drink, because Jen had always been on him to 'do something' with the kids. And doing something with the kids was never any fun, they were still too young; Nate couldn't even play catch properly, Amy only wanted to have freaking tea parties, and the baby could barely hold his head up.

Of course, things would be very different at home now. And he'd missed precious moments of his kids' lives that he couldn't get back. That particular day was an obvious one, a birthday, but every single day since his arrest moments had been stolen from him.

"Gabriel?"

The voice nudged him unwillingly from his thoughts and he lifted his face to show the bloodied cut under his right eye and yellowing bruise on his left cheek.

"Gabriel, are you listening to a word I'm saying?"

"I'm listening," he gruffly replied, that hand still tugging viciously through his thick, dark hair. "I'm listening. Alright?"

Pulling at his tie, Gattis loosened the microfiber knot before popping open the button of his collar. Then, as he let go of a sigh that was borne of several months' struggle, he rubbed both hands at his cheeks. A slight rasp of stubble accompanied his weary breath, creating an overture of frustration.

"You're not listening to me. And you haven't been listening to me for the last year and a half."

"You're not the one who's lost the last year and a half of your life," Gabriel shot back.

"I've got news for you, working on this case is eighteen months I dearly wish I could get back," he muttered in reply, shaking his head. "Do you honestly think this," he paused long enough to gesture an overworked hand at Gabriel's face, "is going to help anything?"

Flipping his eyes upward, Gabriel wondered if the guy sitting across from him had ever spent a day in the real world, with the kind of men he was now spending twenty-four hours a day with.

"The guy started on me," he insisted, sounding to Gattis a lot like an overgrown adolescent. The attorney kept that opinion to himself, though. He had no great desire to have his head removed from his shoulders.

"You don't just ignore things like that," Gabriel continued. "Not in here. Not if you don't want everyone to think you're a wimp."

Noticing a smudge on his lenses, Gattis slipped his glasses from his face. "I don't pretend that you're in an easy position," he said, picking up the end of his tie and wiping at the greasy mark. "I don't pretend that anything about this is easy." Eyebrows scrunching, he lifts the glasses toward the light on the ceiling and realizes it's not a greasy mark at all but a scratch. "Damn it," he mutters to himself before putting them back in place. Making a mental note to get his spare pair out of his desk drawer at the office, he resumed his focus on the matter at hand. Leaning forward, he placed his forearms on the edge of the table between them and laced his fingers gently.

"You're a smart man, Gabriel, you have to know how this is going to look to a judge. You must know that the prosecution can use you fighting with other inmates and being belligerent with the guards to establish a pattern of violent behavior." Internally he added, 'Which you have.' It seemed counter-productive to mention it aloud.

"I have already been stitched up by the system," Gabriel snapped. Wild, bloodshot and sleep-deprived eyes staring hard at his counsel. "You think things can get any worse?"

"Hmm." Gattis tilted his face. "You think it can't, huh? How about this? The DA is going to be pushing for the harshest sentence, meaning you could be looking at spending the rest of your life in jail."

Gabriel heard the words perfectly well, but there was no external reaction to them. In truth, there was little internal reaction, either. It wasn't a possibility that hadn't occurred to him. He knew exactly what he could be facing. He was now numb to the prospect; it was like a cast iron weight in his stomach, but he'd become used to the sensation. And, for much of the time, while the dark clouds of depression and despondency hung over him, he wondered if it really mattered much. Would it matter to Jennifer or the kids?

Jen had been visiting less often, she'd made excuses about being busy. He noticed the change in the expression in her eyes, though. The words, "We will get through this, honey," which she'd spoken so passionately in the weeks just following his arrest were nowhere to be found anymore. And now, whenever he told her that he'd done nothing wrong, she avoided his eyes.

She'd lost hope. And, if that was the case, then nothing damn well mattered anymore.

"Gabriel," Gattis said again, feeling like an algebra teacher trying to get through to a student who simply did not want to learn. "We have to be real here."

With a half-smile that flashed a snarl of white teeth, Gabriel snickered in return. "It doesn't get any more real than this." They were never going to be pals. This guy was no different from the rest of them, he would be just as content to see him rot in hell as those that arrested him.

Finally letting go of his hair, which had grown too long and was now covering some of his ears and managed to meet his collar at the back, Gabriel let his gray hoodie-covered arm flop down hard on the tabletop.

"You think this is some sort of game?" he added.

"No," Gattis replied, somberly shaking his head. "But I sometimes wonder if you see it that way. I wonder if you appreciate the consequences of your actions. And I don't know whether you ever met Alec Renaudin or not, but I do know that you've been fighting with inmates with little or no concern for how that might bias a jury against you."

"I told you, you can't walk away..."

"I know what you told me," the attorney interjects, losing all patience. "But I am telling you, I have got to somehow mount a defense for you. And that job is hard enough as things stand without you helping the prosecution!"

Gattis almost cursed. As a young man, despite his mother's protests, he'd used swear words with zeal. After she'd passed away, though, it started to feel as though she could hear him everywhere. Suddenly, whenever he swore, it felt like it was in her presence. The wrongness of that shook him out of the habit altogether. That is until Gabriel Summers came along and stretched every last vestige of his composure to breaking point.

"Look," he added, forcing a calmness into his voice, although he did not feel it. And the restless motion of his fingers as they slipped between one another suggested it, too. "I have to be straight with you, I don't like the chances of us getting a 'not guilty' out of a jury. It was going to be almost impossible before, but now..."

"So, I was supposed to just let myself get pummeled?"

"Well, it might actually have made you more sympathetic to the twelve people who are going to hold the rest of your life in their hands," Gattis pointed out with uncharacteristic churlishness. "But what's done is done, and the only thing we can do now is be pragmatic."

Gabriel still stewed in resentment at the implication that he should have done nothing to defend himself. Did this smart-suited jerk have any idea what it was like in a place like this? He wouldn't last five minutes. They'd eat him alive. And Gabriel couldn't find it in himself to much care about which brand of pragmatism the man was about to come out with.

"The DA is still offering a plea bargain," he said, his lips thinning in anticipation.

"Uh-uh," Gabriel blurted, shaking his head vehemently. "We've been over this a hundred times, I'm not pleading guilty to something I haven't done."

"I need you to take this offer seriously, Gabriel," he replied, dismissing his client's words entirely. "If you accept it, you'll be looking at twenty-five to thirty. If you turn it down, the worst case scenario is life without parole."

"Worst case scenario?" Gabe scoffed.

Lifting one hand to his face, Gattis pushed his glasses further up his nose. "With your history and your less-than-illustrious conduct while you've been bound over for trial, I'd say it's a very real possibility, yes."

"No," the dark-haired disheveled man insisted. "No, that's not going to happen."

"The violence of that murder was..."

Slamming his hand down, Gabe yelled, "I didn't do it!"

Closing his eyes and leaning back in the chair, Gattis moved his head from side to side in bewilderment and disbelief.

"Why won't anyone listen to me?" Gabriel demanded. "Why won't anyone believe that I didn't touch that guy?"

"Listen..." Eyes opening again with a sigh, the attorney placed his hands between his thighs and shrugged. "It doesn't matter what I believe anymore. Maybe it never did matter. All that matters is what I can get a jury to believe. Now, I could try to convince them that you were intoxicated, that there was some self-defense involved, although that would be tough one to swing given the state of that poor guy's head. Nevertheless, I could give them a handful of mitigating circumstances that might make this go better for you. None of which are going to fly unless you admit to being there. Do you understand that?"

Gabriel felt his upper teeth with his tongue. Then, slowly, he began to nod. "I understand," he muttered. "I understand that everything about this a pile of steaming poop, and that you're no better than the rest of them."

"Alright," Gattis said, pushing his chair back and getting up. "Alright, Gabriel, this is getting us no place." Sweeping his jacket off the chair, he slipped into it, not bothering to push his tie back into its usual place. "You need to think long and hard about this plea thing, because it is the last chance we're going to get."

Hating his use of the word 'we' as though they were somehow in it together, Gabriel snorted in response. They weren't in it together at all; he was alone. Completely alone. The only family he had, his wife, had begun to turn her back on him. And whatever the future held, once the trial was over, he'd have to face it without the assistance of the useless counsellor standing in front of him.

"You know what?" he said as Gattis made a move for the door.

Twisting his head over his shoulder, the attorney wore an expression of vague hope. "Yeah?"

"You can tell the DA to get lost."

Clenching his jaw as he glanced at his shoes, Gattis swallowed. By the time he lifted his face again, he was nodding. "If that's what you want," he sighed in defeat. "I might use slightly different vernacular if it's all the same to you, though." Placing his hand on the door, he turned to leave again. But stopped himself. "Take the night to think about it, Gabriel. Really think about. And call me if you change your mind, okay?"

With a huff of unamused, tired laughter, Gabriel shook his head. Would the man ever give up? He knew one thing with absolute certainty, though: Nothing would ever persuade him to plead guilty.

Chapter Six

The room was so much smaller than Jennifer Summers had imagined a court room to be. It didn't look grand or prepossessing, like they always did on TV. The judge's desk was elevated, and it had Old Glory hanging from a flagpole behind her chair. But it didn't seem that much different from a school room or a college lecture hall.

It was mundane in many ways, with its cheap pine-veneered desktops and faux leather seats. The air-conditioning was poor, either not pumping enough cool air into the room or making it feel like a refrigerator. And of the twenty or so seats in the public gallery, which was really just a sectioned off part of the floor space, only five of those had been filled for all of the fourteen days of the trial. She, her mother, and brother accounted for more than half of those. There was a woman of about the same age as her, who was constantly tearful. Jennifer assumed she was a loved one of the victim. That poor crying woman was supported by a man who looked a lot like her, so she guessed he must have been a member of her family.

On this, the final day, though, the gallery was crammed; the other fifteen or more chairs were filled with journalists, some of whom had flitted in and out during the previous days, but none of whom saw the entire trial as interesting enough to follow it from beginning to end.

She'd expected the trial to be longer. She'd expected there to be passionate speeches, and dramatic shouts of 'objection!' There had been none of those things. It was simple for the most part. And it was sickening the rest of the time. There had been four expert witnesses, who discussed Alec Renaudin's injuries. They'd talked in detail about which ones were caused as he'd tried to defend himself, which had been inflicted after death, which ones might have killed him. That endless dissection of the gory details was accompanied by equally gory images displayed on a large TV screen that was turned mostly to the jury. But Jennifer, and everyone else in the room, could still see it well enough. And it turned her stomach.

As the rolling dry heaves shook her, she'd looked at the man sitting on trial. She tried to imagine him capable of such a thing, and came close to actually vomiting when she realized it wasn't all that difficult. What made it worse was that he still flatly refused to explain what he was doing at that house on the night of the murder. The prosecution pressed him on that over and over again. The defense attorney, Gattis, ignored it altogether, knowing that, if Gabriel wouldn't tell the truth, there was nothing that could be said or done to make the presence of his DNA look any better.

Throughout the two weeks, Gabriel had been mostly quiet. His face an emotionless mask, it was difficult for anyone, even his wife, to tell what was going on in his head. To a complete outsider, like those reporters, it must have looked as though he didn't care. Jennifer couldn't believe that was true. She wouldn't accept that he wasn't thinking about his children, about her, about everything he stood to lose if things went against him.

Gabriel had glanced over his shoulder once, the very first time he was led into the room, to look at his wife. He'd tried to meet her eyes, to make some connection that would mean nothing to anyone else, but everything to the two of them. Like those looks they used to share during the first few years of their relationship; before the kids had come along and life had become a humdrum, sexless list of chores and stress.

But as he'd found her eyes, she blinked and turned her gaze toward the floor by her feet.

The last vestige of decaying hope died right then and there. In its place rushed in all the anger, bitterness and resentment he knew how to handle. And he could handle a lot. Unlike the hope that had been struggling to grow in the barren conditions of his soul, those negative emotions flourished.

He knew that he probably looked impassive as he sat listening to the case being made against him, and the feeble attempts of his defense counsel to refute them. And the truth was, he was impassive. Impassive to his own fate anyway. The deck had always been stacked in someone else's favor. He had been gypped in every hand he'd ever been dealt. The only question was, why had he begun to let himself think that things could change? Why had meeting Jennifer seemed like the turning point, when it was actually just another bend in a road that led to hell?

The trial happened in the background. He heard it well enough, he saw the images, and he followed the lines of questioning. And if he'd wanted to, he could have tuned into it more clearly or commit some of it to memory. But he didn't want to do either of those things. And so, while it all played out, like a television that stays on all the time even when no one is watching it, he let his thoughts wander. He wanted them to turn to happier things: the night he'd met Jennifer, the first time they made love, that summer afternoon he'd proposed. Yet, every time he tried to steer his brain that way, it dragged his conscious thoughts back to the reality that all those things were gone. Long gone. And maybe they were never real anyway. Because maybe he'd never been real.

The man he was with her was different from the man he'd been before. He wanted to be different for her. He'd wanted to give her the world, because she was beautiful, sexy, smart, kind, loving, and so the world was exactly what she deserved. In those early years, she'd looked at him as though he was some kind of superhero; the best man she knew. And he so desperately wanted to be what she saw. He would have died for her back then. But had he really just been kidding himself? Had she been kidding herself, too? Had anything ever changed? Or was he always the same screw-up, with a quick-temper and even quicker fists?

Eventually, her blinkered view of him widened. And she started to see what everyone else had seen; what her parents had warned her about. She'd stuck by him, though, he had to give her credit for that much. She'd been sure that he could change. And she'd been certain that he'd never harm her. She still trusted him, even though the illusion of perfection and of the superhero had been shattered. But once it had been, once she woke up and realized that he wasn't the best man she knew, Gabriel no longer had anything to strive toward.

And now, when she couldn't even look him in the eyes, he knew that trust had gone as well. The faith that he could be a better man was all dried up. When he looked at her now, he didn't know who he wanted to be, because there was no standard to measure himself by anymore. He was nothing to her. And so, he was nothing to himself.

And as the judge returned from her chambers and asked the jury if it had reached its verdict, there was no pounding of his heart as he'd expected there would be. There was no dry mouth. There was no trembling in the backs of his knees when he was told to stand. He was nothing. What happened to him didn't matter.

Jennifer chewed her lower lip as the foreman of the jury got to his feet. He was a reluctant spokesperson and looked a little nervous, but he was doing a valiant job of hiding it. Lifting a balled hand to his mouth, he cleared his throat before answering the judge's question.

"We have, Your Honor."

The woman beside Jennifer slipped her hand over her daughter's. She glanced down at the fingers smoothing over the back of her clenched fist and found her vision blurred with tears. Flipping her hand over, she gripped her mother tightly; so tightly she suspected she might be hurting her. But she couldn't lessen the grasp.

"And how do you find the defendant, Gabriel Summers, in the count of murder in the first degree?" the judge asked, as she picked her reading glasses off the bench and slipped them onto the end of her nose.

So ordinary, Jennifer had time to note. The woman who was about to announce her husband's fate looked like a librarian.

The foreman shifted his weight from one foot to the other and looked at the card in front of him, despite the fact he must have already known whether he was about to provide a one or two-word reply.

"Guilty," he stated.

One word. One word that was spoken, heard and faded in the blink of an eye. But it seemed to echo on and on in Jennifer's head.

Gabriel stared straight ahead of him, showing no more emotion that he had through the whole ordeal. But then, something snapped. Slamming both palms down on the table in front of him, he jumped to his feet.

"No!"

Beside him, Gattis rushed to stand and placed a calming arm on Gabriel's back. However, Gabriel simply shrugged him off.

The judge tapped her gavel before yelling, "Mr. Summers, I suggest you sit down!"

"No!" Gabriel shouted again, spinning to face his wife. "No. Jen, please, baby! You've got to believe me."

"Bailiff," the judge ordered, a flick of her head at the man saying everything else that needed to be said.

"Jen, for God's sake, you can't think I-" Angry tears began to prick Gabriel's eyes, he wouldn't let that sign of weakness stain his cheeks, though. Sniffing them back, he stiffened. "Jennifer, listen to me!"

The hand that held her mother's was growing ever tighter. She did listen. And she watched him, with a pain in her heart that couldn't have been more profound if someone had stabbed her in the chest. She watched the anguish play out on her husband's face; a strange mixture of pain and rage. A counter-intuitive fluctuation between begging and commanding, as he both pleaded with her and insisted that she believe him all at the same time.

She was so mesmerized by the wealth of emotion she could see in a face that had up until that moment shown none, she didn't notice the six feet and five inches of broad-shouldered bailiff that strode up behind Gabriel. As the big, bulky black man wrapped an arm around her husband's chest, she saw Gabriel fruitlessly try to shake the guy off. However, unlike Gattis, the bailiff wouldn't be swiped aside like a pesky insect.

"Don't make this harder on yourself, Mr. Summers," the bailiff said, tugging the smaller man back.

Refusing to give up the struggle, even though it was quite clearly one he would not win, Gabriel continued to shout to his wife. "I didn't do anything, Jen! You have to believe that."

As she blinked, heavy silent tears streamed down her face; tears that she'd wanted to shed for the last two weeks. Tears she'd wanted to weep as freely as that other woman, the one who'd also lost someone she loved. But she hadn't been able to. They wouldn't come, and they'd stayed bottled up inside her like a poison slowly eating her from the inside out. She didn't feel a whole lot better for their flowing.

Flailing his legs as he was half-carried and half-dragged from the courtroom, Gabriel never stopped yelling. And his pleas lingered for Jennifer long after he'd left the room and his voice could no longer be heard.

"It's alright," her mom whispered, leaning closer to her and letting her forehead rest on her daughter's temple. "It's alright."

On the other side of her, her older brother, Michael, wrapped a strong arm around her shoulders. "Don't listen to him," he urged. "He's not your problem now, okay? You've just got to be strong for the kids."

She sniffed and turned to him. His blue eyes, which had driven the girls crazy since he'd hit puberty, stared solidly and sincerely back at her. She shook her head, unable to acknowledge the idea that Gabriel was no longer her problem. He was a part of her. His problems were her problems-weren't they?

His hand rubbing circles between her shoulder blades, he refused to let the matter sit. "I mean it, Jenny. You have got to start thinking about yourself. The kids need you. You're everything to them now. You can't let him drag you into this trap he's trying to pull on you."

His mother agreed about everything he was saying. "He's right," she crooned softly. "The children need you, and you need us. Come back to Pennsylvania, Jennifer."

"But-But, Gabe-" she mumbled through tears that refused to stop.

"Never mind about Gabe," Michael insisted. "He's done this to himself. You need to stop worrying about him, because, Lord knows, he ain't been worrying about you. Maybe he never did, Jenny."

"Come back home," her mom repeated. "Let us help you with the kids, and support you. You can get your life back together, and try to leave all this behind."

Jennifer shook her head, but she couldn't manage to find the words to argue. And deep down, she knew that was because she didn't want to argue. She wanted what her family was offering; someone to take care of her for a change. She needed help. Because for almost two years, she'd been floundering, just keeping her head above water financially and keeping a tentative hold on her sanity. And she already knew, although her head tried vehemently to deny it, that her heart had given up on Gabriel.

***

Katherine Roser picked up the freshly boiled kettle and poured the steaming water into a mug that already contained a teabag. It was chamomile. She'd never really cared for it. But a friend at work said that it was good for insomnia, and, as she didn't like the thought of taking pills, she thought she'd give it a try. In her mid-fifties, she was also starting to get hints of arthritis, and she was reliably informed chamomile was good for that, too.

Getting old, she had already decided, was no fun. There were some benefits, though. The older she got, the less inclined she became to making mistakes. And, heaven knew, she'd made some huge ones. Age and experience definitely had advantages over youth and girlish dreams. She just wished she could have the youth all over again, carrying the experience she currently had. Things would have been very different.

Sighing as she waited for the tea to steep, she glanced around the small apartment. It wasn't much for an entire lifetime. An empty, one-bedroom apartment. No husband, no real career. She loved what she did. It gave her a sense of peace to know that she was helping people, and truly making a difference in the lives of others. But it wasn't a career. It wasn't ever going to make her rich.

"Beware of covetousness," she whispered to herself. "A man's life consisteth not in the abundance of the things which he possesseth."

It was true. She knew that. She knew it all too well. She just wished that life didn't have to be the way it was; that, in the winter months, she didn't have to make a call between turning the heat up or being able to afford to eat. But she did enjoy her work in the community, helping young mothers, visiting lonely elderly folks, and trying to get some of the homeless off the streets. It was important work. It was God's work. And of that fact, she was very proud.

Finally lifting the teabag from the cup, she pressed it against the side with the back of a spoon, then popped it into the trash. Rubbing her fingers across a lower back that was tender from a poor night's sleep on an uncomfortable mattress, she picked up the mug in the other hand and turned in search of Luna, her three-year-old Siamese mix, who had been found as a stray. Katherine had taken the poor thing on, and fed her up, while her owner was waiting to be found. A year later, the owner either hadn't been found or hadn't really lost her in the first place. So, Katherine and Luna had remained together. It was apt in a way, the middle-aged woman thought. Two strays with only each other for companionship.

With a soft meow, Luna's blue eyes and soft gray fur appeared from the back of the couch.

"Hey, girl," Katherine said, smiling as she left the open kitchen and took the couple of steps it took to reach the living room.

The television had been on since she came in, she liked the noise of voices, because it made her feel less alone. She hadn't really been paying attention to what was on, though. And as she found the local newscaster on her screen, she reached for the remote on the coffee table as she blew tentatively on her still scalding hot tea. She'd never liked the news. It was always bad. It was always sensationalist; making sinful acts seem like the route to fame.

Before she could change the channel, though, the pictures on the screen alters and her finger simply hovered over the button. Blinking, she tilted her head and squinted with bad eyes as the words from the broadcast chilled the air around her.

"Gabriel Summers was convicted this afternoon of the brutal murder of Alec Renaudin two years ago. Judge Noll said in court today that the savageness of the attack meant Summers will be looking at thirty to life. Sentencing is expected early next week."

The man on the screen was first shown in a mug shot, his face grim, hair messy, dark rings under his eyes. Still, though, there was something about him that was eerily familiar. When the image changed to a relaxed shot, obviously taken in happy days, she lost her grip on the cup in her hand. It fell to the floor quickly and shattered on impact, sending Luna racing back for the safety of the couch. The piping hot tea splashed up, catching both Katherine's feet and legs.

"Ouch!" she hissed, leaping back as the liquid burned through her socks and the linen pants she was wearing.

Even the pain couldn't prompt her to take her gaze from the television screen, though. She knew those deep brown eyes so well. How could she ever forget them? She once thought that they contained the entire world. Finding it difficult to swallow, she noticed the shape of his face, the line of his jaw, they were also exactly the same. He looked exactly the way his father had looked when she first met him. There could be no mistake. The man in that picture; the man who had just been convicted of killing someone, was her son.

"Oh, Lord," she murmured, looking to the ceiling and beseeching Him for advice.

Another voice in her head was the only one she heard in response, though. It was her own voice, and it was telling her that she knew. She knew all along that it would come back to haunt her. That the past wasn't done with. It could never be buried. And that that sin hadn't been forgiven. Perhaps it never could be. She was sure of one thing. She couldn't ever forgive herself, even if The Almighty could.

Chapter Seven

Gabriel Summers stalked the width of the small space, from the white metal desk and chair that were bolted to the wall, the floor, and each other to the cubby, which was designed to hold clean clothes and what few hygiene products he was permitted. The space between the two was ridiculously small – only two and a half paces, and they weren't even full strides. He prowled that tiny space repeatedly, though. Not seeming to tire of the fact he could never get far. And it was something he'd spent a lot of time doing over the precious eight weeks, two days, and seven hours.

Once he'd stayed up for thirty-eight hours straight, and done nothing but pace.

Eventually, of course, that period of raw energy had burned itself out. Neither mind nor body could sustain it, despite his desire to. At that point, he'd collapsed on the low bed with its foam mattress, which was so thin it was still just like lying on the solid steel frame beneath. Most nights, he wondered if it would be more comfortable on the floor. Not that comfort rated high on his list of concerns. But it was just another way that he was being treated like a dog.

Pausing in his restless traipsing, he ran his hands through his hair, gripping the thick dark strands. Then, bending forwards, he released a howl of frustration. The sound bounced off the white-tiled walls, reminding him that no one was listening. No one cared. It was as if the walls themselves were mocking him.

Spinning on his heels, he studied the rest of his cell: the steel can in the corner and the tiny sink next to it. Everything was so claustrophobic. Only a small amount of natural light crept in through the grated re-enforced window that was too high to see out of. Everything about the room reminded him he was trapped. And every second he spent in that room, he felt himself dying. There was no life there. There was no existence. It was only waiting. Waiting, counting the days, and slowly dying. Death wouldn't even do him the favor of coming quickly.

Still fisting his hair, he scuffed his way to the bed and sat with an exhaled, "Ugh!" Slumping forward, he dug his elbows into his thighs and rubbed his palms over the stubble on his cheeks. Trying to remember the last time he'd felt alive, he screwed his eyes tight shut.

His mind, which had been constantly whirring for what felt like an eternity, scoured every thought and feeling he'd had over the last few weeks. A small thing that, would have been enough. That was all he could hope for now, after all. He dwelt on a couple of times, when he'd been lying on bed, and felt an unexpected, but familiar twitching that caused a rush of blood to his groin. There had been nothing to account for the sensation, it was spontaneous and, more importantly, unwelcome. It was just a natural process of his body, like breathing; it wasn't something that needed to be encouraged. His brain hadn't prompted it, and his thoughts didn't follow the instinct either. He felt no urge to do anything about the subtle ache that came with his erection – it couldn't even be called arousal. But that sensation was as close to a reminder of the fact he was living as he got.

Occasionally, thoughts of his wife and his children had entered his head. But he'd been quick to push them aside. It was too painful to think of them, and, in those moments, he was glad of his state of anesthesia. Numb was both good and bad. It was both his friend and his enemy. It was both necessary and unwanted.

Leaping up, Gabe pounded the side of his fist against his orange-clothed thigh before resuming his endless and pointless pacing. As he reached the metal cubby, he kicked it, but it was far too sturdy to make a dent. And the pain it caused his foot wasn't enough to make him really feel. He spun and crossed to the other wall. When he reached the desk, which was empty – always empty. He threw a punch at the white tiled wall. The crack that followed was that of bone rather than of tile.

"Crap," he groaned, hauling his hand back reflexively and cradling it in the other hand. Cuts on his knuckles already oozed blood that seeped through the gaps in his fingers and dripped slowly to the floor.

"Oh well," he whispered, trying to move his damaged hand and realizing that he couldn't. The pain shot up his arm, tingling nerves all the way to his shoulder. It hurt like crazy, but he was glad of it. It was at least a feeling. And pain, physical tangible pain, was just about the only thing he was willing to feel.

As the door rattled and the clunk of a lock turned, he lifted his face. Privacy was a luxury he didn't have. They'd just walk in whenever they wanted. They didn't even bother to check if he was on the can.

"Summers?" The voice was one Gabe recognized. Jake Kirkley was one of the newer guards at the correctional center. He was just twenty-five, and had only been working at the jail for eighteen months, so he still had that naïve notion that he was doing something for the betterment of society; that he could make a difference in the lives of the men he was charged with watching over.

He was, as far as Gabe was concerned, a goody two-shoes. A boy scout. One of the world's bleeding hearts. And, by that stage, Jake was beginning to get on Gabriel's nerves.

The young guy, with one of those baby faces that made him look even younger than he was, but which was belied by a muscular frame, stepped inside the room. "Thought I heard something. Are you-" He came to a slow halt as he saw Gabriel bent forward at the waist and still babying his injured hand.

"What happened?" Jake asked, the question coming with a mixture of weariness and concern; like a father who just knows his kid is always going to keep getting into these scrapes.

Gabriel didn't appreciate the tone. He wouldn't have appreciated it from anyone, but he especially didn't appreciate it from a guy who, at a decade younger than him, was really still no more than a kid.

"Nothing," he said, snarling as he backed to the bed and sat down again. He left a small but persistent trail of blood in his wake, which did nothing to reassure the young guard.

Taking a step forward, Jake placed one hand on the hip of his black pants while his hand swept through his sandy blonde hair. The motion of his arm stretched the light gray passant on his shirt into a loop. Then his light blue eyes fell to the floor, and he followed the drips of crimson further into the room.

"You need to go to the infirmary?" As he asked the question, he let his hand flop to his side, or as close to it as he could get with the thick and well-equipped belt he wore.

Gabriel shook his head but didn't lift his face as he replied, "No." Attempting to flex his fingers, he discovered that not one of them seemed to move much if at all. There was a good chance something was broken. But he still didn't want to see the doctor. It'd heal just as well on its own. And he certainly didn't want anything for the pain.

"Gabriel-" Jake sighed and toyed with the black wristband on his right hand, which bore four letters in white,

'WWJD'. "I know it's tough, but you've got to accept it in order to adjust."

"Why don't you get lost?"

The younger man slowly felt the edges of his teeth with his tongue before attempting to respond. "You're going to be here a while, man. Fighting it, fighting yourself and what you've done, isn't going to do you any favors."

Eyes still down, Gabriel refused to even acknowledge him. Instead, he watched the droplets of blood that seeped from him – a sign that he was alive. And yet, he was definitely dead.

"I was thinking-" Jake continued, his youthful naïveté combined with his desire to help making it impossible for him to read the very loud and clear signals Gabriel was sending him. Or perhaps he could read them, and was simply determined to ignore them. Something told Gabriel it was the latter, and it made the man all the more infuriating.

Ceasing the fiddling of his wristband, he flicked his eyes toward the door before continuing. "The new chaplain started this week, and I figured you might want to talk with him."

"Why would I want to talk to him?" With a scathing frown, Gabriel lifted his head. At the doorway stood a stranger. A man who looked anything but a chaplain. For one thing, he wasn't middle-aged and pot-bellied. He was an athletic-looking, thirty-something. He wore faded Levis, with a tan leather belt, and a blue plaid shirt with sleeves rolled up to his elbows. One thumb was tucked in a belt loop, and he leaned casually against the doorway. The only sign of his calling was the well-worn black leather bible he held in his free hand. He smiled warmly, his dazzling teeth seeming all the brighter for his cool ochre skin tone.

"Gabriel," he said, his smooth baritone voice filling the room with ease and rumbling gently over the tiled walls. "I'm Matthew Beaman. Pleasure to meet you."

The man sitting on the bed was instantly annoyed by the pleasantries. In his view, they didn't match the surroundings. And they were utterly worthless to him. He was happier with the walls that ignored him, because at least they were honest. They didn't pretend to give a hoot about him.

"Look, Pastor Beaman, I..."

"Just Matthew is fine," he interrupted. "Or Matt if you prefer."

Eyes narrowing, Gabriel studied the man with suspicion. "What do you want from me?"

A subtle, deep chuckle rumbled up from him as he shook his head. "I don't want anything from you, Gabriel. I was hoping that I could help you."

"Really?" he scoffed.

Matthew glanced at Jake and something passed between them that suggested the hostile reception was not altogether unexpected. The younger man shrugged slightly before taking another step forward in an attempt to get a closer look at Gabriel's hand. However, it was snatched back from his sight before he had a chance.

"I just want to make sure you don't need that looked at," he grumbled, gesturing to the hand that Gabriel was protecting like a bear with an injured paw.

Matthew, meanwhile, took a step forward, but still lingered just inside the threshold, as though he was at least somewhat respectful of Gabriel's space and the fact he hadn't been invited into it.

"Jake tells me that you're holding onto a lot of anger," he pointed out calmly, tucking his bible under his arm and folding his hands loosely in front of him. He then nodded at the injury as proof of his statement.

Although, of course, there didn't need to be proof. In the two months since his conviction, Gabriel had been in half a dozen fights. One of which had resulted in the broken jaw of a fellow inmate. He'd almost clocked a guard, too. He was told that he'd been lucky that his fist didn't make contact. However, he didn't share that view. After all, what were they going to do that would be worse to him than what had already happened? Punishment beyond what he was currently serving was superfluous.

The lectures he'd received from the warden didn't make a dent. And that was no surprise to anyone. Jake had obviously filled Matthew in on these things. Gabriel knew that, under different circumstances, he would have been angered about being the subject of discussion, as though he were some kind of intriguing experiment. Right then and there, though, he couldn't give a hoot what they'd talked about.

"Your frustration is understandable, Gabriel," Matthew continued, undaunted by the lack of response or even eye contact he was receiving. "You're carrying a large burden, and you're trying to carry it alone."

"Are you a pastor or a therapist?" Gabriel retorted.

With a soft half smile, Matthew shrugged. "The two aren't mutually exclusively. In fact, they're not at all dissimilar. My job is to offer you my ears should you need them, my advice if you ask for it and, most importantly, to guide you to a much worthier set of ears and a more knowledgeable source of advice."

Gabriel rolled his eyes. "I haven't been to church since I was a kid. If God is up there, he's done jack to help me so far. And I don't want his help now."

"Well, He wants to help you, Gabriel, whether you're aware of it or not."

"Oh, yeah? Then why did he let this happen?"

Inhaling slowly, Matthew considered his next words carefully before opening his mouth again to speak. "Why did he let what happen?"

"Why didn't he stop me from winding up here?" Gabe spat, grabbing a towel that had turned gray with hundreds, maybe thousands, of washes. He wrapped it carefully around his hand, flinching from Jake's help as the young guard leaned forward to offer it.

"You know why you're here, Gabriel," Matthew responded, placing no emotion or accusation into the assertion. "You hurt someone, and that needs to be dealt with."

"I didn't hurt that man!"

"Guilt is a terrible thing to hold in your heart," the pastor continued. "But there's nothing He can't forgive, as long as you recognize the sin and repent for it."

Gabriel could see that this conversation was going to get him nowhere. Still clinging to the towel, he got up and strode the three paces toward the door. He expected Matthew to step back, or at least blink. But he didn't move. He was a fairly solid guy, but he was smaller than Gabriel; a couple of inches shorter and slim rather than broad shouldered. Yet, there was no fear in his dark brown eyes as the man he believed to be a violent thug approached him.

Standing just a few inches in front of the man holding the bible, Gabriel studied him. He could swing a punch at his jaw and land him on his butt, there was no doubt in his mind about that. And part of him wanted to. The part of him that didn't care anymore whether the whole world thought he was a hotheaded jerk and a murderer. After all, he was one. He'd been branded now. And that was a mark that could never be sponged away. So, what the heck?

However, as his left hand fell away from his tender right one, and balled in a fist at his side, he found it would do no more than that.

"I don't feel any guilt, because I didn't do anything wrong," he said, teeth clenched.

Jake took a step toward the pair, and placed a hand on Gabriel's shoulder. It was a warning as much as it was an attempt to calm him.

But Matthew stayed motionless, his breathing even and his posture relaxed. "We all feel guilt, Gabriel. It's part of the human condition. It isn't possible to exist without wronging others, whether in thought or in deed. And it is our innate relationship to God that tells us these things are wrong; that makes us feel guilt. All have sinned, and come short of the glory of God," he added, quoting Romans 3:23. "But his capacity to forgive us, and to love us, is limitless. All we need do is ask for it."

Despite himself, Gabe listened to the man. The words, smooth and clear, entered his mind whether he wanted them there or not. Unaware of it, the hand at his side slackened its tight grip on itself. However, he shunned that brief moment of comfort as quickly as he'd inadvertently let it in.

Shaking his head, he grasped hold of the towel again, squeezing down on his knuckles to stop the bleeding.

Jake felt the subtle sag of Gabriel's shoulder. Surprised by the reaction, he glanced at Matthew and found himself grinning. He had known all along that he would be able to crack into the man's hard outer casing eventually. But he'd never imagined it would be that simple. However, God moved in mysterious ways, he told himself. And perhaps, he moved in quick ways sometimes, too.

Matthew wasn't smiling. His face was relaxed, but unlike the enthusiastic young guard, he could tell that there was far more work to be done. The expression on Gabriel's face suggested he was fighting something. And although he would help the man before him in every way he could, ultimately, the battle was his alone. Matthew would beat the path for him, but Gabriel had to walk it. And the new chaplain wasn't yet convinced that this prisoner was willing to put one foot in front of the other.

"Do you want me to leave?" he asked, already knowing the answer to that question, but giving Gabriel the opportunity to voice his feelings.

The grinning lips of Jake fell open. With a shake of his head, he silently expressed his surprise. He felt sure Matthew was getting somewhere, why would he give up when they'd just started to see some progress?

"Yes," Gabriel sighed. "I want you to leave, and I don't want you to come back. I didn't ask for your help, and I don't want it, alright? So you can take your bible and your God, and you can shove it. God doesn't care about me. So I sure don't care about Him." Turning away from the chaplain, he stalked back to the bed, sat down and stared at the floor.

"Matt," Jake muttered, "you..."

"It's not my intention to interfere," Matthew said, talking to Gabriel rather than his over keen, young friend. "I just wanted an opportunity to introduce myself and let you know that my door is always open."

Gabriel scoffed. "No door in this place is always open."

"True." The chaplain gave a rueful smile that Gabriel never saw as he ran a hand over his buzz cut black hair. "But you know what I mean," he added with more seriousness in his dark voice. "If you ever need to talk about anything, you know where to find me. And when you're ready to let some light into your life, God's there, too."

Shaking his head, Gabriel kept his eyes on the floor. "Just leave, please."

Matthew politely stepped back. Jake hovered closer to the door for a moment, mouth ajar as though he was ready to argue the point. But with a quiet nod from the older man, he relented.

It was only once they were on the other side of the door, and the cell was shut and locked firmly behind them that he said what he'd wanted to say several seconds earlier.

"You were getting through to him, I don't..."

"Jake, Jake, Jake," he murmured with a smile as he put his arm around the younger man's shoulders. "You can't force these things."

"But, he was listening."

"Well," Matthew replied, hedging with a slight tilt of his head while the two men strolled along the narrow prison corridor. "I had his attention for a few seconds. But that's not enough. God will keep talking to him, and, when Gabriel is ready, he'll accept Him into his heart."

Not so certain, Jake shook his head as he stepped out from under the older man's arm. "Summers is stubborn; I really think we've got to keep pushing. And I think you could..."

"It won't do any good," Matthew insisted. "It's got to come from him. And it will. Just trust that God will reach him, Jake."

Exhaling, the zealous prison guard's shoulders slumped a little. "If you say so," he eventually muttered.

On the other side of that cell door, Gabriel was watching the thin fabric of the overused towel go red in patches. His fingers still wouldn't move when he tried to force them to. And the pain was growing worse as his adrenaline faded. Chewing on the inside of his cheek, he silently cursed God for everything that had happened to him.

Chapter Eight

Katherine had always believed there was a certain smell to old churches. It didn't matter which city she was in, and she was fairly sure it wouldn't matter what country in the world either. There would always be *that* smell. Old incense that had woven its way into the walls, and pews, and every porous surface. The scent of burning wicks, even when none of the candles were lit. The warm odor of wood. But there was something more to it, she was sure. It smelt like home. More like home than any other place had ever, and could ever, smell. She wasn't sure she had a right to that sensation of comfort and safety, though.

The centuries' old place was quiet and deserted. Her footsteps echoed in the high-ceilinged, cavernous space. She strolled slowly along the nave. Then pausing a few steps from the chancel, she looked up at the depiction of Jesus smiling as he held a small child on his knee. Katherine felt the corners of her mouth lift in response to the image. But it didn't linger. Her thoughts soon shifted to the sacrifice that man had made.

She wondered if there was any moment at which he knew fear. She was convinced he must have done. He may be God's son, but he was also one of us. He felt all the emotions we feel. He knew what it was to love, he knew what it was to fear, he knew what is was to be betrayed. Yet, somehow, he found peace. He knew he was here for a bigger purpose. He would not only save all of us, but serve as a constant reminder of what we should be striving for. And so, he had faced death calmly.

As she swiped at the silent tear that had drifted onto her cheek, Katherine knew she would never be able to face her own fate as gracefully as he did. She also knew she had failed to live up to his example. She had been so much weaker than him. She had made mistakes, she had been cowardly, she had been sinful, she had allowed her body to be degraded and used.

Worse still, she'd even let lust get the better of her inside the very walls of a church not unlike this one. That very first time it had happened in the vestry. Of course, He would have known about it no matter where it had happened, but to do it right under His nose-. She disgusted herself.

But he'd said it was alright, hadn't he? He'd told her love was nothing to be ashamed of. And he'd convinced her that he *did* love her. All that did, though, was give the woman another stick to beat herself with. She'd bought it. She'd been stupid, and naïve, and believed things that so obviously weren't true. She'd been so ridiculously desperate for it to be true, that she'd let herself believe a lie. And, with that piece of youthful stupidity, he'd betrayed her. But part of her wondered if she deserved that betrayal, because she, in turn, had betrayed God and she'd betrayed Jesus. And, in her heart, she knew that none of this would be happening if she hadn't.

Katherine recognized herself as unworthy of that man with the child on his lap, who had died for her. She knew she wasn't worthy of his father, either. And, despite her best efforts to put her life on a better path, she knew that she would always remain unworthy. Tainted. Some stains could never truly be washed out.

The tears flowing freely, but still soundless, she staggered to her left and clung to the wooden pew for support. "What have I done?" she whispered. Sniffing and wiping the back of her hand across sticky, damp cheeks she slumped to her knees. Eyes tightly clenched, she laced her hands in front of her.

"Please," she begged quietly. "Please-I didn't mean-." Faltering over tears that came too hard and fast, she dropped her face to the hands she was squeezing together before her. She made continued efforts to speak, but the words were really no more than dolorous sounds, their meaning entirely drowned out by her sobbing.

The sudden presence of a hand on her shoulder startled her. Flinching, she glanced back, shrugging the weight of fingers from herself instinctively.

"I'm sorry," the man said.

Blinking, she tried to clear the tears that blurred her vision. With a sniff, she unlaced her hands and turned toward him. He wore a concerned smile that reached his pale blue eyes. Olive skin suggested he might have some Mediterranean ancestry. He wasn't overly tall, but he was considerably larger than her five-feet-three-inch frame. His thick head of light brown hair was graying a little around the temples, and he had a slight bulge of excess weight at his abdomen, but, despite all this, she guessed he was only in his early forties.

"I didn't mean to frighten you," he added, straightening as he withdrew the hand that had touched her. "I just wondered...Is there anything I can do for you?"

Grasping hold of the seat next to her, Katherine pulled herself to her feet and rubbed the heel of her hand across wet cheekbones. "I'm-I'm okay," she mumbled. It was an obvious lie to both of them.

"I'm Glenn," he said, hands sliding into the pockets of his dark pants. "I'm the new minister here. I-uh-I think I saw you on Sunday, right?"

"Yes," she replied, not looking at him as she slumped into the pew. She remembered his service. He talked about the importance of relying on a spouse as a partner in every aspect of life. His words were beautiful and heartfelt, and they'd made her feel even more wretched for the life and family she might have had if only her decisions had been different.

He smiled softly as he took a few steps and sat on the other side of her. "I came here from a small congregation in Derby, Kansas," he said. "This big city thing is taking some getting used to."

She had noticed the subtle accent. Nodding, she was grateful that he wasn't pushing her to talk about what was bothering her. Katherine did sense, however, that he wasn't mentioning his move from Kansas for his own benefit.

"I don't know whether there'll be as much chance to get to know my parishioners here," he continued, eyes leaving her face and moving to the image of Jesus hanging on the wall ahead of them both. "I hope so," he added quietly. "I'd like to think that big city or small town, we're all children of God and we should love each other as unconditionally as we love those who are family by blood."

Realizing she was wringing her hands, Katherine ceased their restless motion by clamping them between her knees. "Do you think-" she began slowly, "God loves us all unconditionally as his children?"

His smile growing wider, Glenn twisted his face to the woman on his left.

"Yes," he said emphatically. "There's no question, He does."

"No matter what we've done? No matter how awful?"

Features drifting into a sober expression, he twisted in his seat and allowed his arm to drape on the back of the pew that stretched behind Katherine. Inhaling slowly, he weighed his thoughts as he skipped sympathetic eyes over the distraught woman.

"I think so," he eventually said. "After all, if a child of yours came to you and confessed that they'd done something terrible, but that they were sorry for it, could it ever diminish your love for that child?"

"I don't..." She stopped herself suddenly and shook her head. "I don't have any children," she murmured.

"A parent's love is an immense force," he replied. "It's forbearance and unconditional nature are personified."

That was another of those things that Katherine wanted to be true. She couldn't quite let herself believe this one, though. Unconditional hadn't been the brand of love her parents had practiced. And if they had known about-Well, things were bad enough with what they did know. They weren't prepared to overlook mistakes. They could not abide weakness.

"Some things are too much," she said, her eyes focused intently on the hands she still held between her legs. "Too much even for a parent's love."

"Perhaps." Nodding, Glenn paused before adding, "But God isn't just an ordinary parent. Humble yourselves, therefore, under the mighty hand of God so that he may exalt you in due time: Casting all your anxieties on him; because he cares for you."

Lifting her face to Christ, Katherine drew in a breath that caused her entire form to tremble. She didn't need him to quote chapter and verse to her. She already knew the text inside and out. She knew that there was evidence of God's capacity for love throughout. However, she also knew that He was capable of anger and He would mercilessly punish when He deemed necessary. And she could not shake the sense that she was being punished now. But guilt just stabbed deeper into her heart, because she was not the only one being punished. And while she deserved it, those others were innocent.

Glenn watched the consternation on the woman's face for several seconds. He tried to interpret the troubled furrow of her brow and the nervous chewing of her lower lip. But he could not imagine what was tormenting her, and he wasn't sure if she wished to unburden herself.

"If you came to be alone with God, I will-" He started to get up as he spoke, but Katherine grasped his arm.

"I need help," she whispered, the words clawing at her throat on their way up. "I need-I don't know what to do."

Slowly re-seating himself, the minister placed his hand on Katherine's shoulder. And, this time, she did not jerk away from him.

"We are all lost sometimes," he admitted softly. "There's no shame in admitting that. Or in asking for help."

"But there is shame in admitting what I've done," she insisted. "I know He already knows, and I have begged hundreds, maybe even thousands of times, for His forgiveness. But I- Some things can never be forgiven, can they?"

"I don't believe God has it in him to not forgive if we truly ask for it."

Katherine shook her head vigorously. "No, I have asked. And He hasn't forgiven me."

"How can you be sure of that?"

"Because..." Her rapid answer cut off as she silently considered how much she wanted to reveal. The man was warm-hearted, she didn't doubt that. But there was still so much shame in her story, it bred like a cancer in her abdomen. Every passing year, the tumor became bigger, heavier. The burden was becoming too much to bear.

"Because the consequences of my actions are still being felt, more than thirty years on."
A hand still on his parishioner's shoulder, Glenn nodded his understanding. He didn't want to contradict her outright, and knew that wasn't the way to reach her. He did not agree with her perception of The Lord, though.

"And something terrible has happened recently because of the-the choices I made."

"I don't think we can take that as evidence of God holding a grudge," he replied softly with a subtle smile.

"Then what would you call it?"

"We can't understand His reasons. There are many things we're not yet privy to," he added, looking into her eyes with full sincerity in the words he spoke. "Perhaps it will make sense one day. Perhaps it'll never make sense. All we can do; all we *have* to do, is trust Him."

Deep down, Katherine already knew that. And she wanted to trust him. She so badly wanted to believe that everything would work out for the best. And, for years, she wondered if they had. It hadn't eased her guilt any, but she had at least hoped that things had been better than they would have been if she'd chosen differently. Now, though, a man had died. And what if that were all her fault?

"Maybe-" Glenn began softly, leaning closer to the woman as he squeezed her shoulder lightly. "It isn't Him you feel you need forgiveness from. Are there others you need to make amends with?"

Eyes blurring again, she gave a shift of her head that passed for a nod but wasn't an obvious one. "But I don't know how to apologize to him," she muttered. "He's-He's in prison."

"You can't visit?"

Struggling to swallow with a scratchy, dry throat, she blinked. "I called the jail, and they told me that I have to be on an 'approved list'."

"Ah," Glenn responded. He wasn't well-versed in the penal system, but he was aware that prisoners had a list of pre-agreed visitors. "Yes, of course. And this man refuses to permit you to visit him?"

She chuckled, but there was very little actual humor in the sound. And what little amusement there was in it was directed solidly and derisively at herself. "He doesn't even know who I am," she whispered once the self-scathing laughter had abated.

Glenn still wasn't sure if he understood the picture, but he was starting to comprehend the source of the woman's deep distress. She felt she had wronged someone who considered her a stranger, someone who may never allow her to apologize for whatever it was that had happened – something she clearly felt great remorse over. It was clear to him that she would never forgive herself or accept God's forgiveness until she had earned this man's forgiveness, too.

"Perhaps you could write him," he suggested quietly. "Sometimes we're able to say much more in a letter than we ever can when we are face-to-face with someone."

She had considered the possibility. But what she had to say was... Well, it wasn't the kind of thing that could be blurted out in a letter. She needed to look into his eyes, she needed to make him understand, she needed to ensure that he knew how very sorry she was. None of those things could be done in a note.

"I...I can't...I need to see him."

"Well," the man beside her breathed, "perhaps you could explain that need to him. You could ask him for the opportunity to speak directly. And, if he refuses, with your permission, I could perhaps write on your behalf. I don't claim that I'll be able to perform miracles," he added with a chuckle. "But there's a chance that we might be able to get through to him together, isn't there?"

Lifting her face to the minister, she met his eyes. She could tell that he was serious, that he genuinely wanted to help. So few people did these days, unless there was something in it for them. But he did. She had no idea whether his plan would work. Nevertheless, she was willing to give it a shot. After all, what did she have to lose?

"Thank you," she said as a final stray tear glanced off her cheek.

Dismissing the gratitude with a disarming shrug, he smiled. "That's what I'm here for," he insisted. "That's what we're *all* here for; to help each other."

Chapter Nine

She'd always hated packing. Always hated moving. She and Gabriel had already done it twice during their marriage; from their first apartment to a small house when Nate was born, then from that home to the one she now stood in after Amy came along. Jenny knew that everybody hates packing, and that moving is never anything other than stressful. But this time it was all so much worse. She wasn't just sorting through memories that were bittersweet while she looked forward to an exciting future. There was no exciting future this time. And there was no sweetness to any of the memories she was stowing away. They were all just bitter.

At least the house was quiet now, though. The kids had been driving her crazy. Nate, bless him, had been trying to help, but he'd already broken a vase and the frame that held his parents' wedding picture. There was something fitting in that, she supposed. Certainly symbolic anyway. Amy had been whining the whole time, because she wanted to go to the park. And little Jamie, who was a not-so-little almost four-year-old now, had spent the past hour yanking on his mom's jeans and craving her attention. Eventually, when it all got too much, Jenny's mother took all three kids out for pizza.

In normal circumstances, Jenny wouldn't have wanted them stuffing their faces with junk. But, on that day, she couldn't have cared what they were eating or how much of it they were managing to wolf down, as long as it allowed her to finish this darn job.

"What about these photo albums?" Pushing a hand through his sandy blond hair, Pete strolled in from the living room with a cardboard box held under his other arm.

She offered him a small smile of gratitude. He'd been so good to her since...Well, since the beginning of all this crap really. He'd been even more of a rock since the conviction. He'd suggested she stick around; that it would be good for the kids to be around familiar things. She'd considered it, and even seen his point. She had to admit, she was worried about dragging the children, especially Nate, away from their friends. But she couldn't stand being so alone. She needed the support of her family, and she needed to live in a place where people didn't nudge each other every time she walked by.

"Umm," she replied, wondering if she really wanted to keep the pictures. She couldn't imagine ever wanting to look at those images of her stupid, happy face when she was first married, a new mom, and totally naïve about where it would all end. She paused, nibbling her lip as she contemplated telling him to just throw them in the dumpster she's rented. She'd thrown out a lot of stuff – at least all the stuff she could afford to buy new. She wanted to start fresh.

Although, there could never be any fresh start. Some slates could simply never be cleaned.

"U-haul," she eventually said, deciding the memories, although painful, were ones she couldn't quite let go of.

He nodded, but didn't move. "You know, Jen, you need to stop beating yourself up over this."

Shaking her head, Jennifer leaned the small of her back against the kitchen counter and folded her arms across her abdomen. She wasn't exactly sure how he knew she was beating herself up over it, she certainly hadn't told him that she had been. But he was a perceptive man. One of the world's nice guys.

"It's-" she began, having no clue what she wanted to say. "It's all just so hard."

"But it's not your fault."

"No," she agreed softly. "But I'm the one who has to try to explain it all. I'm the one who has to pick up the broken piece and try to hold them all together."

Stepping forward, he slid the box he'd been carrying onto the counter. "You've got people around you who want to help," he said. "You don't have to do this all on your own."

"I know." Sighing, Jennifer tossed her eyes to the ceiling. "I know that my parents and my brother want to help, and that's why I'm moving. I need that support, Pete. But-"

"But what?"

Eyes still trawling the ceiling, she rubbed idly at the back of one of her wrists. "But I'm still the one who's got to somehow answer the kids' questions about why their dad isn't coming home. And Nate's old enough now that-Well, he wants to understand why mommy and daddy aren't going to be together anymore. And- What do I tell him, huh?"

Leaning a fraction to his right, Pete rested his hip on the counter and sighed. "I don't know." Having no children of his own, he had no frame of reference. He tried to think of something helpful to offer. But there was nothing, and he suspected that no one could give her a beautifully packaged answer that would make the world a better place again.

"Do you-" he continued hesitating. "Do you want me to try to talk to him? Maybe..."

"He'll listen better to a man?" she interrupted with a defensive jut of her chin.

"No, that's not what I meant," he responded calmly. Pushing himself away from the counter, he took another step closer and met her eyes. "He's at that age where he needs a good male role model, right? And I-I want to help is all I'm saying, Jen. And if you can think of any way that I can, all you have to do is ask. You know that, don't you?"

Her irritation melting rapidly, she exhaled. "Yeah, I know." Offering him a shaky smile, she unfurled her arms and placed a grateful hand on his chest. "You're a good man, Pete. And a good friend."

Attempting to smile in reply, he only managed a lopsided one. "I hate seeing you like this," he murmured. "You deserve-better." Lifting his right hand, he brushed the hair away from her cheek with the backs of his fingers.

Jenny's eyes slipped closed and she found her face unconsciously leaning into his touch. His hand was so warm. His skin was a little dry and rough from all the dust it had been exposed to over the course of the day, but it felt wonderful. How long had it been since someone had touched her like that; shown her any *real* affection? God, it was almost too long to remember. As her eyelids flickered open again, she found herself staring at his blue gaze, which was intent on her face.

"I worry about you," he said. "I just-I wish there was something I could do to make it all go away."

Without being aware of it, her focus shifted to his slightly parted lips. As his face grew closer to hers, she had time to register what was about to happen, and that it wasn't exactly right. A tiny voice in her head told her that she was still married. That it was wrong to let this happen. But a much louder voice insisted that she wasn't the one who had done something wrong. She was being punished for something that had absolutely nothing to do with her. And if she now had the opportunity to feel good for the first time in more than a year, a misguided notion of loyalty wasn't going to stop her.

Pete's mouth merged softly with hers, his arm smoothing around her back and pulling her gently until her body met his. His kiss was gentle; wary even, as though he might be worried that she'd push him away. But she had no intention of pushing him away. Lifting her hands to his shoulders, she urged him closer and whimpered softly as she parted her lips from him.

There was only a flicker of doubt in Pete's mind. Yes, Gabe had been a buddy and a work colleague. But that man didn't deserve a friend's fidelity. He didn't deserve his family. And he definitely didn't deserve this woman. She was so much stronger than Gabe ever gave her credit for. She was beautiful, and loving, and she'd married a man who was never worthy of her.

As his palm cupped Jenny's cheek, Pete let the tip of his tongue stroke her lower lip. She tasted a little bit like vanilla, and he wondered where that had come from. But the thought didn't have time to linger for very long. As she slid her tongue into his mouth, all thoughts left him. His grip on her tightened as he realized he was nowhere near close enough to her warm, soft body.

Jennifer felt herself weaken as he pulled her firmly to him and she felt his breath on her cheek. Her legs trembled slightly and she started to believe she was relying solely on him to keep her on her feet. It had been a long time; far too long since she'd felt what she was experiencing in those moments: Wanted. Desired. Sexy. Like a woman, rather than just a mom.

Even before the arrest, Gabe hadn't touched her like this, as though he'd die if he didn't have her for years. Sex between the two of them had become practically non-existent. And the infrequent times they had made love, it wasn't really making love. It was perfunctory and over within ten minutes.

"Jenny," Pete murmured, his lips leaving hers long enough for him to draw breath as he turned her and pushed her gently back until she was pressed up against the refrigerator door.

"Oh, God," she gasped.

His hands smoothed up her torso and molded her breasts through the ratty old T-shirt she was wearing. When he kissed her again, there was none of the slow hesitancy of the first time. It was fiery, passionate, and intense. He needed her, and he was determined to show her how much.

Her own fingers found their way under the polo shirt he wore and she ran them over the hot skin of his abdomen. As she felt him twitch in response, she chuckled against his lips. Ticklish, she thought, while she pressed herself into his generous palms.

"Jen," he whispered. "I..."

Covering his mouth with hers, she silenced whatever it was he was about to say. She didn't want to hear it. She didn't want to think. She just wanted to feel. She wanted to feel good, because that was something she hadn't felt in a very, very long time.

Not needing any further encouragement, Pete let one hand slip down and smoothed across the waistband of her jeans. He felt and heard her moan softly as he popped open the silver button.

Inhaling, Jenny waited for the sensation of his hand on that part of her that suddenly felt very restless. But as she filled her lungs, the scent of him filled her instead. There was a subtle mint from his shower gel, and a soft clean smell from a laundry detergent that still clung to his clothes. But underneath both of those was a musky smell. An afternoon of lifting and hauling had left him sweaty, and that salty, masculine scent was him. As individual as his fingerprint.

Without willing it to, her brain sharply reminded her that the smell was unfamiliar. For more than a decade, the only man she'd been this close to was Gabe – the man she'd promised to love and be faithful to for the rest of her life. He'd betrayed her. Yet, she'd still made a promise. And even if she hadn't, was she really ready to have another man touch her, to see her body, which was so different now from the last time she dated?

Placing her hands on Pete's chest, she pulled back panting for breath. "Stop."

His hands left her, but he didn't move. "Jen, it's okay."

"No, it's not. I-I can't. We can't, Pete." Baser instincts were still warring with that notion as she pushed her hands through her loose hair and tried to calm her rampant breathing.

"I'm sorry," he sighed, pulling back far enough to yank his glasses from his face. Tossing them on the counter behind him, he pinched the bridge of his nose as he continued to talk. "I'm sorry. I shouldn't have pushed so fast. We can slow down. It's not a problem."

"It's not just that-" Shaking her head, she realized she had to move away from him before temptation caused her to toss all other concerns aside. "I-I can't-"

He let her pace toward the other end of the room, but he wasn't prepared to let the conversation end there. He'd waited too long to tell her how he felt; he wasn't going to lose the opportunity to say it now.

"Jenny, please listen. I've...Well, I've had feelings for you a long time and I..." As he watched her face drift into an expression of shock, he changed tack. "Look, I don't want anything from you. I don't expect my saying that to suddenly make everything alright, and I'm not saying I can fix all the things that have turned out so crappy in your life." Pausing for breath, he ran his fingers through his hair again and wondered what it would have felt like to have her doing it; gripping it maybe in the heat of passion. Quickly shaking the thought, he let the hand drop to his side.

"All I've ever wanted was to try to help you, and the kids," he eventually sighed. "And, I think, if you let me, I could do that."

"Pete..." she mumbled.

"We can take things slow," he insisted, pre-empting what she might say. But he was off the mark.

"It's not that." Shuffling in the empty space that used to be home to the small kitchen table, she glanced out the window. What Pete was offering was seductive; a chance to try again; a man who would treat her well, because there was no doubt in her mind that he would treat her well; stability and love for her and for her children. And yet, there was something that stopped her. She couldn't put her finger on what it was. She wondered if it was because Pete had been a friend of Gabe's, and so there would always be that horrible reminder. It was a plausible reason, and she tried to cling to it. But she couldn't quite manage to. She knew it was something else. Something just out of her grip to understand and impossible to explain. But she felt it. The wrongness of it, even though she had every intention of divorcing her husband.

"You're a wonderful man, Pete. And I...I think I could have very easily..." With a quirk of her head she gestured to the fridge. "Just now. But I...I just can't..."

"All I'm asking is that you give it some thought, that you give us some thought. Maybe in time, you'll..."

"I don't have time, Pete," she replied. "I need to bring some normality to my kids' lives."

"And I can help you with that if you stay."

His eyes were sincere. He wasn't just throwing crap her way because he thought it was the only way he'd now get the sex he'd so narrowly missed out on. Jennifer knew the difference between a man who meant what he was saying and one who didn't – some lessons Gabe taught her very well. But she couldn't. Part of her hated herself for the fact she wasn't willing to accept what this decent, considerate, caring man was offering. Had Gabriel truly made her believe that she didn't deserve good things in her life? Whatever the cause, she couldn't.

"I need to go, Pete. I need to be in Pennsylvania. The kids need to be near a proper family, and I need a fresh start."

"Jen..."

She didn't want to let him finish. "I think you should go now, Pete."

The motion of his chest a little heavier than usual, he stared at her and tried to think of some way to change her mind. Running his tongue along his lower lip, he tasted her again and shook his head.

"Alright," he eventually sighed. "If that's what you want, I'll go. But if you change your mind..." Not bothering to finish the sentence, because it's end was so abundantly clear, he picked up his glasses. Leaving the room, he didn't look at her.

She didn't look at him, either. She couldn't.

Chapter Ten

Lying on his back, he stared at the off-white ceiling. Shallow breaths undulated his chest and that, coupled with the odd blink of his eyelids, was the only movement to suggest he was still alive. Although he would have scoffed at the definition of 'alive'. Heart beating. Oxygen filtering in and out through his lungs. Was that it all took to be alive?

The letter he'd just read laid on the mattress by his unmoving hand. He had no idea who the woman was or what she wanted with him. Just a lonely, middle-aged do-gooder with too much time on her hands, he assumed. Either that, or a relative of Renaudin, who wanted to vent her anger or forgive him, so she could move on. Whichever the answer, he would have laughed at the whole thing if he could have found the energy to raise anything – even a smile.

It was ridiculous really, he thought, he had never had such a prolonged period of inactivity. And the result was that he had never been more lethargic. But it wasn't really exhaustion that had him feeling so dog tired all the time. Not physical exhaustion anyway. It was his stupid brain that was keeping him tired all the time. It was the thoughts that bombarded him. It was the voice, in the dark shadows of his mind that told him life wasn't worth the effort it took to draw breath. Sleep. That was all he wanted to do, because sleep was oblivion. And, boy, how he longed for a deeper one; one that came with a boatload of booze; or, better yet, one there was never any waking up from.

But, here he was, with the guards regularly checking the contents of his cell for anything he could use to harm himself, and making sure he couldn't seek out that oblivion on his own. And so, somehow, he had to find the will to do the things he didn't want to do. All of the things that took more strength than they ever should. Every single thing took an inordinate amount of effort; even simple well-practiced things, like urinating. Reading that stupid letter had sapped him of the scrap of energy he'd had.

When the tap came at the door, he couldn't even find the strength to groan. And he wanted to groan, because he knew who it would be. He'd started to knock a few weeks ago, which was just a ploy, Gabriel assumed, to get him on his bible-bashing bandwagon. He'd curtly told him not to bother; after all, no one else did. Nevertheless, Jake had stubbornly persisted with the politeness.

He didn't bother to wait for a reply, though, knowing, after the better part of two months, that he was unlikely to get one. Scuffing his feet slightly, he wandered into the room and found Gabriel exactly where he expected to. Exactly where he always was.

"Hey, Gabe. How's it going today?"

He hated that he'd taken to calling him that. Like the knocking, though, he'd lost the will to complain about it. He couldn't even manage to twist his head. Still staring at the ceiling, nothing in his face would even indicate that he acknowledged the young man's presence.

"It's your yard time," Jake added, smiling and placing a brightness into his voice. "It's a beautiful day out there."

Gabriel didn't move. Didn't speak. Didn't even blink. He hadn't been interested in going outside for over a month. It just seemed to taunt him. The sun he could only feel on his face for thirty minutes. The fresh air that tasted of freedom, but was a lie. He didn't want to be in touching distance of all the things he was missing. That and, of course, he just couldn't be bothered to move.

"Come on, Gabe. The exercise is good for you." Taking another step toward the bed, Jake held his hands loosely stretched in front of him, one hand wrapped around the other wrist as he rocked on his heels and continued to smile. "The fresh air," he added. "And the sunlight. Hey, man, you need that vitamin D." Chuckling, he tried to coax something, he knew for a fact it wouldn't be a smile, from the prisoner before him.

Gabriel blinked. It was not much of a sign, but Jake figured he might be starting to get through to him.

"You can't stay here like this for the rest of your sentence, Gabe," he urged, lowering his voice and softening his tone. Although, with his irrepressible youthful enthusiasm, it still sounded far too chirpy for Gabriel's liking. In fact, as far as Gave was concerned, Jake was like a puppy; too eager to be liked, too happy to be anything other than ignorant.

Part of him well aware that anything he said to the younger man would only encourage him, he couldn't help the mumbled, "Just leave me alone."

Jake filled his lungs slowly and released the air through his lips. He tried to remember what Matthew had told him about giving Gabriel time and space, and letting him come to one or both of them when he was good and ready. But patience had never really been one of Jake's virtues. He knew he could help. And he wanted to. It seemed stupid to stand by and watch this man needlessly suffer. For a few seconds, though, he schooled the instinct to open his mouth again. He urged himself to think carefully as his fingers toyed with his WWJD? wristband.

"Gabe, I know-" Stopping himself abruptly, he planted his hands on his hips and shook his head as he pondered the direct or indirect approach. He knew which Matthew would take, but then Matthew's soft sell approach wasn't working either, was it?

"Look, I know your wife filed for divorce," he said slowly, part of him knowing as the words slipped out that they may not be the best idea he'd ever had. But at least they'd stir something in him. They'd pull some life out of the very lifeless-looking man on the bed. Sure enough, Gabriel's head twisted sharply to the young guard.

"Isn't anything in this place private?" he demanded. "My personal life is like some soap opera to you guys?" Anger gripping him, he bolted up and swung his legs off the side of the bed, knocking the letter as he moved. That one sheet fluttered to the floor unnoticed by its recipient.

Jake saw it, though. "I'm sorry," he mumbled. "You know what's like in here, word gets around. And-I-It's just that-Well, it's crappy, I get it. You're upset and you have every right to be, but these things happen." Stepping forward, he swept up the letter and apologetically offered it to Gabriel. "You've got to find a way to go on," he added. "Maybe these things happen for a reason."

Refusing to take the piece of paper, Gabe looked up into the younger man's eyes. "You haven't got a clue," he stated gruffly. "Go on for what? Huh? What is there to keep going for? What reason could there be for any of this? I've lost my whole life!"

Swallowing, Jake couldn't answer and his gaze drifted to the letter in his hand. Gabriel saw the direction of Jake's focus, but he couldn't have cared less. Let him read it, he thought.

"Go ahead," he urged, shifting one shoulder as he swiveled, lifted his legs again, and flopped back onto the mattress with limp limbs. "It's already been read by one of you jerks anyway, right?"

All the mail was opened and checked before being passed on. It had to be. Jake wasn't going to deny that letters were also read, and that some of the men and women tasked with that particular job enjoyed it more than they should. Especially when girlfriends or wives wrote detailed and graphic love letters to their incarcerated men. Jake didn't share their salacious interest. And he didn't relish the thought of reading about the details of Gabriel's divorce, either.

"It's between you and your wife, Gabe. I don't want to..."

"It's not from Jenny," Gabriel muttered in reply. His focus had returned to that spot on the ceiling, where he looked at everything and nothing. "It's some woman who's been writing me for the last three weeks. Go ahead," he repeated. "Knock yourself out."

Jake rolled a shoulder discomforted by the fact that Gabriel was suddenly sharing something of himself, and not sure this was the 'something' he wanted him to share. However, he wondered if this might finally be an opening; a way to get closer to the man who was so determined to shut the whole world out.

"Some woman you know?"

"No," Gabriel replied, eyes not moving and lips only barely shifting enough to allow words to pass through them. "I don't know who she is."

Jake's brow creased as he wavered between a curiosity to read the letter and his sense that it was wrong to do so. "Why would someone you don't know write you?" he asked.

Gabriel, however, was done. The conversation was over. He had said all he was willing to say. With a short sniff, he flicked one hand in a 'how the heck would I know?' gesture. Jake cocked one eyebrow as he glanced between the man on the bed and the paper between his finger and thumb. Slowly, he lifted the sheet and focused on it.

Dear Mr. Summers,

I understand why you've ignored my last three letters. You don't know me, and you have no reason to be interested in what I have to say to you. But there are things I need to discuss with you that I cannot write. We are connected in a way that you don't, and can't, appreciate yet. And there are things that I need to apologize for. Please let me try to explain. That is all I am asking for. Let me try to help you if I can. I need to do that for you, Gabriel. I need to make up for the mistakes I've made. We all need forgiveness Gabriel, and you must now understand that more than anyone. And perhaps, together, we can find it. Please know, that I only want what is best for you. And if you refuse to see me, I'll accept your decision. But I am begging you to give me a chance. One visit is all I am asking. And if you never want to see me again after that, I promise I will not contact you again.

Please, just think about it.

Katherine Roser

The creases in Jake's brow had only deepened over the course of reading. And as he lifted his eyes back to Gabriel, he couldn't understand why he wasn't as intrigued. He should be even more intrigued. This was *his* life the letter was talking about after all.

"Aren't you the least bit curious?" he asked.

Gabe grunted something that might have been "Why?" but it was impossible to be absolutely sure. Jake scanned the letter a second time and released a steady breath.

"Are you sure you don't know her from somewhere?" he probed. "Someone you've forgotten maybe?" He already knew the questions were pointless, the woman had said Gabriel would have no idea who she was. Yet, they must have known each other at some point in time. Otherwise, how could she have done anything that needed apologizing for?

Not bothering to lift it from the hard pillow, Gabe shook his head. Jake moved his own in bewilderment in return.

"Gabe," he sighed. "I really think you ought to give this woman a chance."

"Why?" The sound of the sullen question was very much like a child. But Gabriel didn't care that that's what he sounded like. "I don't owe her anything."

Running the tip of his tongue along the inside of his lower lip, Jake folded the letter neatly and laid it on the bed beside Gabriel's left hand.

"No," he agreed softly, stepping back and looping his thumb in his belt. "You're right, you don't owe her anything. You don't owe anyone anything, Gabe. Not even yourself. But you think this is the way to spend your life? You think even if you try, you can really shut everyone out? You can't, Gabriel, because the world doesn't work that way. We're all dependent on each other whether we like it or not. You need to interact with other human beings."

"Why?" Gabriel retorted, his head moving, but nothing else. "You think it'll help me to know that there are people out there who have a life that's lost to me now?"

"Nothing is lost to you as long as you don't shut your heart up and pretend that nothing and no one matters." Jake knew exactly what Matthew would have said to him if he'd been there. He would say that this wasn't the right way. That he had to go in calmer and let Gabe make a move in his own sweet time. Problem was, it didn't look like Gabe would ever make a move. And Jake feared that, if something didn't change soon, if Gabriel didn't find some sense of purpose, he wouldn't be able to find the will to keep breathing much longer. He had all the hallmarks of suicidal ideation. Jake knew the signs. He recognized the complete lack of value Gabe had for his own life. The death wish that kept him cooped up and motionless on his bed; not getting any exercise and barely eating anything.

"What do you want from me?" Gabriel yelled, still lying flat on his back with only his face twisted towards the younger man. "You thought God can save me? Now what do you think, this woman can save me?"

Jake didn't know whether it was better or worse to see some fire in the man who was once so full of rage that he broke his own hand on the wall. Better, he supposed. At least anger was something. It was an emotion. The depressive state he'd been in was nothingness; an apathy to everything. And that was infinitely worse than anger. Anger had energy. It had feeling. It was *something*. And so perversely, as those incensed eyes stared at him, Jake began to smile slightly.

"This is not about saving you, Gabe," he said, his own tone quieter. "This isn't about saving anyone. But this woman knows something; something that concerns you. And it's insane that you don't want to know what that might be."

Rolling his dark eyes, Gabriel's face slipped back to the ceiling. "What difference will it make?"

"I don't know," Jake admitted. "But you don't know, either. And you won't know unless you agree to see this woman. What you've got to ask yourself is this, what have you got to lose? What would it all amount to, huh? A waste of time? Well, let's face it, you've got plenty of it to waste, right?"

Gabriel didn't reply. Still and silent, he continued to stare upward. But Jake felt certain there was something different in his eyes now. He couldn't define exactly what had changed in them, but there was hesitancy where there had once been solid determination not to budge, not to listen, not to be moved. Things were no longer as concrete as they were as little as thirty seconds ago.

"Maybe you'll regret seeing her," Jake added with a shrug that he knew would only be seen out of the corner of Gabriel's eye. "But you might regret not seeing her, too. And I've always thought it was better to regret doing something than regret not doing it."

Lips pressing inward, Gabriel's teeth dug into the inside of them gently. There had been a time, when he was Jake's age, when he'd lived a life full of regrets. But the heaviest ones had been those missed opportunities. Those jobs he hadn't had the guts to go for. The master's he'd thought about doing, and then decided against. He'd almost missed out on asking Jen out, too. And, although part of him scoffed at the great loss that would have been, even in his dejected state, he realized the very existence of his kids depended on the few seconds it took him to smile at the woman who would become his wife and say, 'do you want to go out sometime?' What if he hadn't done that?

He was positive whatever this Roser woman wanted couldn't affect anything in his life so profoundly as that. But, Jake was right, he didn't know what impact it would have until he found out who she was and what she wanted.

"So...?" Jake breathed, smiling some more. "What do you say?"

"I don't..." Gabriel began, before cutting himself off with a deep exhalation that emptied his lungs entirely and left them aching.

"I could get the ball rolling." Not waiting for a reply, Jake forged on. "I can get her on your approved visitor list. Just say the word, Gabe. Come on..." he added, chuckling. "You know curiosity is going to get the better of you sometime."

"It's not curiosity," Gabriel insisted, suddenly flipping onto his side and putting his back to the guard.

Smile falling and shoulders slumping, Jake knew he'd blown it. He'd pushed too hard. Matthew was right...

"But alright," Gabe added gruffly. "Get her added to the list. I'll see her."

A grin stretching his face until it hurt, Jake tried to hide the sense of victory from his voice when he replied, "Sure thing. I'll get the paperwork moving."

Chapter Eleven

Katherine shifted on the metal chair, which had been cold when she sat, but had quickly warmed with the temperature of her body and, after only a few minutes, had become almost unbearably hot. Her breath was quick and shallow, and it had been ever since she set foot in the building. She'd even hesitated on the elevator ride up to the second floor. Was she doing the right thing? She had been so sure she was; that she was doing the *only* thing she could do. Yet still, the doubts plagued her. What did they say about sleeping dogs? Perhaps the past was in the past for a reason and should remain there.

Her hands had been trembling as she filled out the requisite visitor form and read the rules on what she was allowed to wear and not allowed to take into the communal visiting room. As she sat waiting, though, those same hands had become very still. They were also icy cold and she wasn't sure if she'd be able to move them if she wanted to.

In truth, it wasn't just fear that had left her numb. It was shock. Despite the strength of her pleas, and her strong desire that they be heard, a part of her had been sure he'd remain unaffected. She'd been sure there would be no chance to ask his forgiveness; to try to explain how and why things turned out as they did. And all the words she thought had been so carefully rehearsed for more than three decades left her.

The door buzzed and opened. In he walked. Except 'walked', she decided, wasn't the right word. He shuffled, like a man whose feet weighed a ton. She couldn't decide whether that was reluctance or a lack of energy on his part. Eventually, she guessed it might be both.

Gabriel dragged himself forward, squinting curiously at the woman while he tried to remain disinterested. All week, when he'd found himself anticipating this day, he'd told himself he hadn't agreed to any of this to satisfy his own interest. He'd done it to stop the irritating letters, and the even more annoying coaxing of Jake: the smiling man, who escorted him into the room as though he'd achieved something miraculous.

Trying to ignore him, Gabriel's dark gaze fell on the woman. She couldn't have been much more than fifty, but she wore the concerned wrinkles of a much older woman. Her brunette hair was graying around the temples and was swept away from her face and clipped at the back of her head. As he drew closer still, he could tell she was finding it difficult to breathe. He wondered if she was scared of him. He was, after all, a convicted killer. Perhaps, he'd been right, when he guessed she was a relative of the murdered man – someone who wanted to find closure or offer some fatuous gift of salvation. Either way, she was wasting her time. He didn't want salvation, and she wouldn't be able to find any closure. Not from him.

What Gabriel could not have envisaged were the thoughts that actually drifted through her head as he gradually neared her. She was noticing small things. The glint in his eye, which was dull, but unmistakable. The slight dent in his left cheek that would become a larger one if he smiled. Did he ever smile, she wondered? He must have...before. She prayed he had. She prayed that he'd known happiness. He looked so incredibly familiar. And yet, he was a stranger. Regret clawed at her heart. But she couldn't quite identify what it was she regretted most. Perhaps it was everything. It felt as though something was fighting to be first, though.

His shuffled steps slowed as Gabriel neared the edge of the bolted table, which stood like a barrier between him and the older woman. Silently, he peered at her. Moistening his lips, he waited for her to speak first. She didn't. Staring up at his tall frame, she felt even smaller than usual. And although she knew she had to say something; that the whole reason she came was to say something, nothing would emerge from her nervous lips.

"Take a seat," Jake suggested. Only it wasn't quite a suggestion, Gabriel knew that. It was an order. He *had* to sit down. But the grinning Jake had managed to make it sound graceful. If Gabe had been able to block out his surroundings, he'd think he'd popped around to a friend's for dinner.

With a subtle scoff at the idea, the prisoner finally lowered himself into the seat. As he did, Katherine's heart began to pound so violently that it seemed set to rip itself right out of her chest. Her right leg jiggled with nerves and, try as she might, she couldn't stop the motion. She was glad that it was at least under the table and not visible to anyone else. But it was irritating her.

Settling back into the seat, Gabriel maintained his silence. He stared at her, waiting and indifferent, as though she had put him out by asking to see him.

"Th-thank you," she eventually murmured. "For agreeing to meet me," she added by way of explanation. She knew it wasn't really necessary, but she found that once the words started, they were difficult to stop again. "It was kind of you. I know-I know you probably don't want to talk to a complete stranger, and I-" Forcing herself to pause, she took a deep breath that trembled its way into her lungs and caused her to visibly shiver.

Gabriel studied the woman opposite him while trying to retain the dispassion in his features and his eyes. He couldn't decide how he felt toward her. Compassion? Concern? He'd thought those emotions were dead. And he didn't want to feel them. But there they were. Slight. Maybe just embers of the real thing. But he did feel them. And that knowledge made him just as uncomfortable as she was. Unlike her, he masked his with stillness and silence.

"How are you?" she suddenly blurted. "I mean-Are you-? Well-How are you?"

He lifted one shoulder before placing his cuffed hands in his lap.

She exhaled slowly and nibbled on her lower lip. She'd been imagining this afternoon for a month, ever since the visiting order came through. She had tried to anticipate how she would feel sitting near him, seeing him no more than a couple of feet away. She couldn't have bargained on the reality of it. How surreal and confused it felt. How wrong. How right. How full of joy. How full of sadness. How much she'd lost. How much she had to gain.

"Maybe I shouldn't be here," she mumbled, eyes falling away from his face as she gently shook her head. "I don't want to do the wrong thing." Katherine no longer knew what the 'right thing' was. So many times in her life, she'd gotten it wrong. And this could be another one of those huge mistakes that she'd spend the rest of her days regretting. She didn't want to upset him. He had a right to know the truth. But at what price would the truth have to come after all those years?

"I'm sorry, Gabriel," she whispered, pushing herself off the chair.

"Wait," he replied, the word coming before he had the chance to second-guess it.

His deep voice even sounding like one she knew well; the one she still heard in her sleep sometimes. She numbly resumed her seat. Swallowing stiffly, she met his deep eyes, trying to scour them for something she couldn't name. She wasn't even sure if she knew what it would look like if she found it.

"I want to know how you know me," he said.

"Well-" she breathed. "I-I don't really. I saw you on the news the day when you were convicted."

His brows drew closer together as he scowled. "So, you're just some do-gooding liberal, who wants to offer me comfort or a chance to unburden myself?"

There was so much irony in that question. If the circumstances had been any less tragic, Katherine might have laughed at both the idea of her as a do-gooder and the notion that she was there to let *him* unburden himself.

"No," she whispered. "No, I didn't lie when I said that we are connected. But I don't know you, either. Not really."

Gabriel sighed as he shook his head. "Look, I know everybody here thinks my time has no value, so it can't be wasted. But..."

"I'm not here to waste your time," she quickly interjected. "I promise, that's not what I'm here for. This is just- What I have to tell you is hard. And I don't know where to start, and you're so- Well, you're not making it any easier."

Chuckling, he tilted his head to one side. "You want me to make this easier for you?"

She hadn't expected him to, but she also hadn't expected him to make it so much harder. Mentioning that wasn't going to help anything, though.

"I just-" she flicked her eyes to the ceiling briefly before continuing. "I thought you agreed to put me on your visitor list because you wanted to see me. But I'm getting the impression you really don't want me here."

"I agreed to shut you and him up," he pointed out with a taut shift of his head backward.

Katherine's gaze shifted over his shoulder to the young guard who was wandering along the rear wall. He was keeping his eye on all of the visitors, just like the four other guards in the room, but she recognized him as the one who had brought Gabriel into the room. She looked him over, and thought how young he seemed to be in that kind of job. She noticed the compassionate look in his blue eyes; a sincere expression. She didn't know what he had done to help persuade Gabriel, but she wished she could thank him for it.

"Why don't you just tell me whatever it is you want to tell me?"

At the sound of his voice, she dragged her attention back to his face. Hesitantly, she nodded. However, it wasn't as simple as that. This wasn't something a person could just blurt out. But where to begin?

"Can I ask you something first?" she wondered quietly, almost too quietly to be heard.

"You can try," he scoffed. "Can't promise I'll answer."

"Do you have a family, Mr. Summers?" She couldn't account for why she'd called him that. Perhaps she thought the respect would move him more effectively, or maybe it was that she wanted to distance herself slightly. First names was too intimate for two people who'd only met three minutes earlier. Although, technically, they had met before. It was fleeting, but they had known each other. And as that thought crossed her mind, an involuntary smile twitched at the corners of her mouth. It wasn't an entirely happy expression. She could feel the sadness it prompted, and the way it tugged at her heart.

Gabriel had been contemplating ignoring the question or telling her to mind her own business. But as her soft pink lips twitched in a moment of pain and wistfulness, he faltered.

"Yeah," he eventually mumbled. "Yeah, I have a family. I did have a family anyway."

"Children?" she asked, tears threatening and a lump in her throat not letting anything more than that one strangled word through.

Squeezing his fists, he again felt the rush of desire to refuse to reply. It left him just as suddenly, though. Ebbing away like a calm ocean being pulled back to an amber sunset on the horizon. And then it was his own mouth's turn to shift in a strange mixture of joy and discomfort.

"Yeah," he said, the edge in his voice suddenly softening. "Yeah, I have three."

"You miss them?" She phrased it as a question, even lifting her tone at the end. But they both knew it wasn't a question.

Gabriel bit his cheek until he tasted blood. He didn't want to speak; didn't want to expose the wounds that scarred his heart to anyone let alone a complete stranger.

"You always want the best for your kids," she continued, saving him the need to fill what was becoming an awkward silence. "You want them to be happier than you were, don't you?"

Thinking of all the overtime he'd put in, trying to make sure those little ones were well taken care of, Gabriel nodded. "You have children?" he then wondered, realizing that somehow he'd let her steer him way off topic.

She leaned back slowly and eyed all of the people around them. Women in the twenties and thirties, visiting boyfriends or husbands. A couple of them were holding very young children: one just a baby in arms, the other sitting quietly on his momma's lap. This was no place for them to be. No place for a family.

"Have they ever visited you here?" she asked.

"You didn't answer my question."

Her gaze leaving the scruffy-haired little toddler who looked innocently between his parents, with no possible way to understand where he was or why he only saw his daddy for an hour at a time, Katherine hauled her focus back to the man in front of her.

"It's complicated," she finally replied.

Thoughts of his own kids vanishing, he left gnawing on the inside of his mouth. "What does that mean? Either you have children or you don't."

"I don't," she replied, satisfied that it was the truth. "But I did." Unshed tears turned her eyes glassy and her vision blurred.

Gabriel wasn't sure what she meant. Had her kid died? Was she the mother of this Renaudin guy? If she was, she must have had him young.

"Look, I don't know how you think we're connected..." he began to say, but she quickly cut him off.

"I'll explain. I'll explain everything." It was now or never, she determined. What she was about to say must be said. There was no way around that fact. She had no idea how the news would be received. And she dreaded making everything worse. But she was forced to ask herself whether there was a worse. Surely, Gabriel's life had sunk as low as it could go.

"I just-" she continued to murmur. "I need for you to understand, so I think I'm going to have to start at the beginning."

"I'm not really one for long stories."

She was silent a second while she pondered on giving him the shorter version. But she couldn't imagine only giving him the bare, emotionless facts. He needed to know everything, so that he could have the whole picture. Otherwise he'd fill in those blanks on his own, and the conclusions he'd draw were bound to be bad.

"Please," she whispered. "Let me tell you how I came to- How I played a part in where you are now."

With those words, Gabriel's interest was captured, bound and held. "You what?" he demanded.

"It's not like that," she insisted, shaking her head. "I never meant- I only wanted what was best."

"Just tell me what you're talking about."

"Gabriel," she said, as she lost the fight against those escaping tears. "I'm your mother."

Chapter Twelve

Thirty Five Years Earlier

The back door slammed shut, the bang echoing across the dark, damp lawn. With tears slipping down her cheeks, the woman, who was really still just a girl, ran across the slick grass, her feet almost slipping out from under her in her haste.

She heard the door crash open again and his shout. "You get back here, Katherine!"

Determined not to do anything he said - ever again - she kept walking. She didn't even glance over her shoulder.

"If you don't get your butt over here now, don't you bother coming back! Do you hear me?!"

She wanted to tell him that was fine by her. She had no intention of going back and she wasn't prepared to be treated like a child anymore. She was nineteen; old enough not to get the third degree for being out after midnight. And old enough to date whomever she wanted to date. What made it all the more infuriating was his insistence that Karl wasn't good enough had nothing to do with integrity and character.

"I mean it, Katherine!" he hollered.

She knew he did. And she meant it, too. She'd meant what she'd said during their blazing fight inside: she was tired of him controlling her every move; telling her what to major in; telling her that she should date, and eventually marry, some guy from his work, who'd he'd decided was perfect; telling her not to smoke or drink. Okay, she was still technically too young to be drinking, but, for God's sake, everyone else was doing it. Why did he have to make such a big deal out of everything?

It wouldn't have been so bad, she thought, if she'd at least had Mom on her side. But her mother was too busy criticizing her clothes, and her hair, and her makeup, and reminding her she looked like a tramp and that no good man would ever want her.

It was all too much. She wanted out. She *had* to get out.

Her vision blurred with tears shed and unshed, she pushed upon the gate and was relieved that no sound of running feet or shouts followed her. Rushing out into the muggy night, she headed to the one place her feet naturally led her.

But when she got there, he didn't greet her as she expected. In fact, he didn't even invite her in. Keeping her on the porch step, he stepped outside and closed the door behind him. His eyes moved over her, and lines appeared on his brow as he studied the tear-streaked face in front of him.

"Karl," she said, sniffing. "I- I just had a huge fight with my dad."

"Again?" he replied, some of the tension leaving his forehead.

"It was really bad this time." Sure he didn't understand, she continued, "He's kicked me out. I need somewhere to stay until I figure out what I'm going to do."

Glancing back at the closed front door, as if he were afraid it might not have been shut after all, he sighed softly. "Katie, you can't stay here. My parents would go nuts."

"But-" she mumbled. "But-"

"Besides," he added softly. "I've been thinking that- Well, maybe we ought to call it quits, you know?"

Stunned and silent, she blinked at him and a stray tear wove its way down her cheek.

"I don't want to be the reason you and your dad fall out," he explained. "And- And I just don't see us working out, do you?"

She *had* seen them working out. She'd seen them getting married. She'd seen herself bearing his children. She'd seen them being a family, and then growing old together. She'd seen all that. She'd wanted all that, and she'd assumed he wanted those things, too.

"It was fun," he said. "I like you a lot. But- I mean, come on. It's just- We both need to be real about this."

Despite his solid stream of words, which came with a tone that implied good sense, Katherine still didn't understand what he was telling her. She understood the sentences; understood their meaning, but she couldn't comprehend where they'd come from. Had there been clues that this was coming? Had she just been burying her head in the sand and ignoring the fact that their relationship wouldn't work long term?

Her quivering lips parted, but as she drew a breath to speak, the motion of the door opening stalled her. A rush of air struck her face as a young woman stepped out onto the porch. Lithe, shapely, beautiful and dark-skinned, she grinned broadly at Karl.

"That couch is getting kind of lonely without you," she said before noticing the other woman. "Oh, hi- I-" As she scanned the pale features of the girl in front of her, she tilted her head in concern. "I'm sorry, am I interrupting something?"

"No," Karl quickly muttered, curling an arm around her waist and steering her back to the open doorway. "No. I'll just be a sec, okay?" He kept an eye on Katherine as he made none too subtle efforts to keep the two women apart. Once he'd closed the door again, he turned fully to her. "It's- I can explain."

"Don't bother," she spat, spinning on her heel and striding down the steps. The anger heating her cheeks dried up the remaining tears. She wasn't sure if she wanted him to chase after her or not. At least it would show he cared. Although, she was no longer sure she could believe he ever did. He obviously didn't care about her as much as she cared about him.

She kept walking with absolutely no idea where she was headed. And when she got to the bus stop at the end of the street, it suddenly occurred to her that she had nowhere to go. There was no way she could step foot in her parents' house again. Even if she'd been prepared to swallow her pride, she wasn't prepared to continue living under the thumb of her manipulative father. There were no other relatives she could stay with, because they all lived hundreds of miles away. She only had a couple of friends, but she didn't feel close enough to either of them to ask if she could bunk on their couch even for a few days.

What the hell was she going to do?

And as spots of rain began to pelt down from the inky sky, she felt sure the whole world hated her. "Damn it," she muttered, glancing upward as the stream of water grew steadier and harder.

She had a little money. But not much. It would have to do, though. And it would at least get her a bed for the night; she'd worry about longer term plans in the morning. However, the nearest motel was ten miles away. And she wasn't even sure if the stinking bus that came this route went anywhere near there.

Rain striking down on her, she tried to figure out some sort of plan, while her clothes soaked and started to cling to her skin like plastic wrap. A slosh of slowing tires pulled her focus up and she watched as the gray sedan idled by the curb alongside her.

"Hey, sweetheart," said the man winding his window down until the rain splattered his shoulder and face. Katherine had never seen him, or his slightly scruffy beard and engine oil smeared hands, before.

Chewing nervously on her bottom lip, she willed him to move on, even though it seemed very obvious he wouldn't. Her standing like a mute wasn't going to change the situation, yet she didn't want to encourage him by speaking, either.

"You okay?" he asked. When all she did was nod, he added, "You look like a drowned rat. Why don't you jump in? I'll give you a ride."

Something about the way his green eyes raked over her made her sure that would be a very bad idea.

"I'm fine. Thanks. I'm- I'm waiting for someone," she lied.

"Well, you can get in and I'll wait with you," he suggested, his gaze still pouring over her as though he thought he had a right to.

"No," she replied, trying to force a polite smile. "Thanks. But, I'm okay."

"Sweetheart, you're going to catch your death of pneumonia," he argued, chuckling. "I won't bite."

Her attention shifting from him, she glanced up and down the quiet street, hoping there might be someone who could come to her rescue. However, there was no one.

"Really," she eventually murmured, returning her focus to the man. "It's kind of you, but I'm okay."

Scoffing, his eyes moved over her body again. But there was something different in the look now, something contemptuous. "Whatever, sweetheart," he said, his hand moving swiftly to the window and winding it back up. Foot slamming on the gas, his car lurched away from the curb, sending a miniature tsunami Katherine's way.

The lower half her jeans were saturated with grimy water, but she was certain that, if that was the worst she'd received from him, she was lucky. Watching his taillights disappear into the distance, she couldn't bring herself to breathe a sigh of relief. After all, what if he came back?

"Crap," she whispered beneath her breath, more desperate than ever to come up with some kind of solid plan. One thing she did know was that standing motionless was getting her nowhere and probably leaving her more vulnerable. So, she began to walk. The headwind driving the rain into her face, she forged on almost blind, until she heard the soft purr of another engine and the swish of wiper blades.

Stopping, she twisted her anxious eyes toward the sound.

"Hello," a friendly, deep voice said. His window open halfway, she could see him clearly. He had smooth tanned skin, raven hair that was just long enough to have a slight curl, deep dark eyes, and a grin which put a dimple in his cheek. He was handsome and kind of boyish, although she guessed he must have been at least thirty.

"Uh- Hi," she replied.

"It's not really the night to be out for a stroll," he joked. "Can I offer you a ride?"

Hesitating, Katherine reminded herself that just because this guy looked pleasant enough didn't mean he was pleasant. She'd seen Psycho.

"I'm just on my way to the church," he added. "But I can take you wherever you need to go."

"The church?" Katherine echoed. "At this time of night?"

He cocked his head self-deprecatingly. "I forgot a sermon I was working on, so I've got to go back and get it."

She was about to repeat the word 'sermon' before realizing she might start to sound like an idiot. "So, you're a- a minister?" she wondered.

"Yeah," he said, his smile broadening. "Nicholas Harrington." Reaching out the window, he extended his hand to her. "Nice to meet you."

Relaxing, she reached for his palm and shook his hand. "Katherine Roser," she replied, offering him a shy, rain-bedraggled smile.

"Well, for goodness' sake, jump in, Katherine," he urged, with a light chuckle and a tilt of his head. "You going to get soaked to the skin."

She didn't bother to tell him that she already was. Instead, she dashed around the rear of the car and gratefully jumped into the passenger seat. He smiled kindly before putting the car in gear and driving away.

They chattered aimlessly about the downpour and the likelihood of more of the same before the summer was out during the ten-minute journey to the church. And once they arrived, she strolled inside and into his small office. Waiting by the door while he fetched the papers he'd come for, she watched a few drops of rain drip from his hair and weave a path down his neck. Moistening her lips, she couldn't account for the strong desire she had to lick those droplets of water from his skin. It was wrong. She knew that. He was a man of God, a married man at that; she'd seen the wedding ring while he was driving. He was pure and righteous, and no doubt devoted to his wife. If he knew the kind of thoughts running through her head, he'd think she was wicked. Nevertheless, they wouldn't stop.

"So-" he sighed, lifting his face and the paper he'd been searching for. "Where can I take you now, Katherine?"

"Oh-" she murmured, realizing she hadn't give it much thought. "I- Um- Well, a motel, I guess."

His jet black eyebrows lifting in mild surprise, he perched himself on the edge of his desk. "Not home?" And when he received nothing more than a brief shake of her head, he added, "Can I ask why?"

"It's a long story," she muttered, eyes dropping to the floor.

"Well-" he replied, smiling. "I like long stories. And I'm a good listener."

"I'm sure you want to get home, Mr. Harrington." Katherine replied quietly.

"Please, it's Nick. You make me feel like my grandfather." Laughing, he urged her nearer with a jerk of his head. "And my wife's at her book club tonight." He shrugged as he set the sheet of paper back on the desk and gestured to the vacant chair near him. "I'm in no hurry to be anywhere."

She wasn't sure she wanted to discuss it - any of it. But there was something so warm about him. The atmosphere that surrounded him was so easy and welcoming. And so, as she obediently moved to the seat he offered, her mouth opened and the night's events tumbled out much more candidly than she imagined they ever could.

He was telling the truth. He was a good listener. Listening was all he did. His eyes fixed on hers, he didn't stop her and reprimand her for being ungrateful for all her parents had done. He didn't frown at her when she admitted part of the reason she'd dated Karl in the first place was to irk her father. And he didn't roll his eyes at her foolishness over the reality of Karl's feelings for her. Patiently, he let her talk. Compassionately, he nodded occasionally. Concern seemed to mar his brow. He cared. Of that much she was certain. He cared more than anybody had in a long time. And that made the urge to lick his neck, to kiss his lips and to feel his arms around her, even stronger.

"I see," he eventually breathed once she'd finished the story at the moment his car had pulled up alongside her disheveled body. "And- You have nowhere to go?"

"Not really," she replied.

"Well-" A half smile tugging at his lips and placing that dimple in his cheek, which was even more handsome to Katherine now she could see it properly, he got to his feet. "You could stay at my house for as long as you need."

"I- I couldn't," she gabbled. "I don't want to be an imposition."

Gaze moving softly over her face, he shook his head. "It wouldn't be an imposition, Katherine." Taking a step closer, he peered down at her with amiable warmth in his deep eyes. "I do have to tell you, though, Katherine," he added quietly. "I agree with your father on one point. You should stay away from those boys who only want one thing from you. Your body is a sacred thing, it belongs to God, and you..."

"No," she blurted, suddenly aware of what he was inferring. "No, I didn't- Karl and I-" Blushing furiously, she tried to find words that rose awkwardly in her throat and rested even more uncomfortably on her tongue. "I'm- I'm- I'm a virgin." In truth, she was fairly sure that was one of the reasons Karl had lost interest. He'd made no secret of the fact that being denied anything more than second base was beginning to annoy him.

Nick's eyes brightened and his grin dazzled her. "Good," he said, one hand reaching for her face. The backs of his fingers grazed her cheek gently and a shiver moved through her, which she hoped he didn't see or feel. He meant it as a paternal gesture, she was sure. The fact she felt more, and wanted more, was amoral.

"Good girl," he whispered. "That's a gift you should only give to a man worthy of it." His gaze was so intently focused on her that she found it difficult to swallow. But then, suddenly he broke eye contact. Withdrawing his hand, he leaped to his feet.

"Right," he said, his smile seeping into her pores. "Let's go then, shall we?"

"Um-"

"I won't take no for an answer. It's not an imposition. We have a spare bedroom," he added. "And I make a mean spaghetti and meatballs." Before she had a chance to argue, he was leading her back to the car.

Later that night, as Katherine lay in the soft but unfamiliar bed, she listened to the sounds coming through the thin walls from the next bedroom. Soft gasps, heavy breathing, deep groans, and sensual whispers. Closing her eyes, she found herself sinfully wishing that she was the one making those gentle moans of pleasure while he sought ecstasy from her body.

A couple of weeks passed, and neither Nick nor his wife, Susan, seemed in a rush to heave Katherine back out onto the street. Being around him, though, was getting harder. He had no qualms about sitting close on the couch, his thigh pressed against hers. He would touch her often: a brush of her hand, a stroke of her knee, a rub of her back. It was all friendly, she told herself. The feelings those touches stirred were only in her head and nothing to do with his intention. Yet, every night, she dreamed of his hands. His lips. And the swell at his groin, which her eyes often drifted to no matter how many times she willed them not to.

On a sunny Sunday, long after the service, Susan had already left to drive a couple of the more elderly members of the congregation home. Nick and Katherine tidied away, and then moved into his office.

"I'm glad you've welcomed God into your life these last two weeks," Nick said, gracing her with his trademark grin. She didn't bother to tell him that a large part of the reason she had was to impress him; to make him proud of her; to please him. And, apparently, it was working.

A hint of a blush heating her face, she sat down and shrugged. "I'd never really given religion much thought until I met you."

"Hmm," he replied, leaning against the desk just in front of her. "You know, Kate, I think there's more that you'd like me to open your eyes to." He'd taken to calling her Kate just a couple of days after meeting her. She liked it in a way that she knew was girlish, but was completely powerless to prevent.

"Wh- What do you mean?"

"I've seen the way you look at me, I know what goes through your mind. Those guilty little thoughts you have." He spoke low, and his smile remained, giving her the impression he wasn't angry with her. But if he wasn't upset, what was this about? Confused and not daring to reply, she simply stared at him with her mouth slightly ajar.

"Do you ever touch yourself while you think of me, Kate?"

Her blush raging hot, she gaped at his entirely unashamed eyes. "I- I-"

"It's alright," he insisted, chuckling. "We all have those thoughts. We're all prey to those feelings."

Still unwilling or perhaps just unable to answer his question, she squirmed in her seat. As his hand went to her knee, she stilled and the heat in her cheeks spread throughout the rest of her body.

"You want me to make you a woman, don't you, Kate?" he whispered. The question not sounding altogether like a question, it was as though he really had been able to see into her thoughts.

"Your- Your wife," she managed to force out. "It's-" She shook her head, trying to reconcile the look in his hungry eyes with the spotless pillar of moral virtue she'd seen preaching to his congregation just an hour before. Every single person in that church had looked upon him the same way she had: beyond reproach. Now, it seemed, there was something else lurking in him. A tenebrous side, which both thrilled and frightened her in equal measure.

"I would leave her for you."

For a second, doubt gripped her. Would he? Would he really be willing to throw away his marriage, and the whiter than white image he had, and his position in the community - for her? But perhaps he would. Perhaps he loved her more than he'd ever loved Susan. Perhaps he felt the same way about her as she felt about him and would be prepared to turn his back on the rest of the world if it meant they could be together.

"Nick," she whispered.

His fingers swept higher, grasping her thigh in a way that could not be mistaken for friendly or paternal.

"Tell me you want me," he said. "Tell me you want me to touch you. Tell me you want me inside you."

The warmth in her body all seemed to settle between her legs and she parted her thighs for his roaming hand. “I- I want you,” she gasped.

That first time, on his desk, it had hurt. He’d warned her it would. But it was a pain she was glad to feel for him. And as she heard him hiss, and pant, and grunt, and finally roar with pleasure, her own discomfort was forgotten. She had done that to him. Her body had given him all that joy, more she was sure than she’d ever heard from his marital bed.

After that, his need for her was unmasked. Whenever they were alone together, he would take her as though he thought he might die if he didn’t. She loved him. She hungered for him. She couldn’t get enough of his affection, and his lust fueled hers in ways she could never have imagined.

And then, almost exactly three months after the Sunday afternoon she gave him her innocence, she discovered she was pregnant.

Chapter Thirteen

Gabriel ceased to hear the lull of conversations swirling around him. He simply stared at the woman while her hurried flow of words came to a tearful, juddering stop. He knew the implication of what she had said and the facts that lay within all those words unspoken. But he wasn't able to register it all. He waited. Waited for her to spell it out in plain English. However, as tears filled Katherine's eyes and wedged a lump in her throat, she became incapable of saying anything at all.

"You're-" Gabe started sluggishly, as if his mouth could only move in slow motion. "You're my mother?"

Katherine forced down a swallow as she nodded. "I-I'm so sorry Gabriel," she murmured. "I was young and- And when I told him I was pregnant, I thought he'd take care of me, take care of all of us. But he told me there was no way he'd leave his wife. No way he'd risk the shame of having a child with a girl who was still only a teenager. He told me I had to go away so no one would know, and then I'd have to give you up for adoption."

Her babbling stopped only long enough for her to draw breath. "I was scared, and I knew I couldn't look after you on my own- I wanted what was best for you. I wanted you to have a family and all the things I couldn't give you." She ran out of steam again, and stared into eyes she wished desperately would believe her.

Gabriel's glare, meanwhile, remained rigid and impassive. He didn't know whether he believed her or not, and the truth of what she'd told him wasn't his only, or even his first, concern anyway. Feeling the lava of anger rising in him, he breathed fast and shallow while every muscle in his body tightened.

"Just like that?" he said, his jaw tense. "It was as easy as that?"

"No." Katherine shook her head, some of her hair falling from its loose clip and slipping over her face. "It wasn't easy. Of course, it wasn't. I didn't want- I didn't want any of it to happen."

"Maybe you should have thought about that before you opened your legs."

She leaned back, as though he had physically struck her. Numb head still shifting pleadingly from one side to the other, she continued to contain a stream of tears that wanted to wash down her cheeks.

"And why this?" Gabriel demanded, wary of keeping his voice low, not just because he didn't want anyone else to hear the conversation, but because he didn't want to be unceremoniously escorted back to his cell for causing a disruption. "Why did you come here now, huh? I meant nothing to you then. So why do I suddenly mean something now?"

Katherine, sniffed as her knuckles brushed at her damp cheeks. "I wanted you Gabriel," she said, her voice trembling. "And I've thought about you every single day since you were born. I loved you. And I thought I was doing the right thing, the only thing I could do." Her breath catching in her raw throat, she paused long enough to gather herself. "I won't pretend I didn't do anything wrong, Gabriel. I know I did. And I've prayed for God's forgiveness with all of my heart."

Gabe's eyes drifted towards the gray ceiling and he exhaled a scornful huff.

"I have," she insisted, assuming his derision was disbelief rather than disillusion with the entire concept. "All I wanted was for you to be happy. I wanted you to have a loving, supportive family. And I assumed, all these years, that you'd had those things. I knew the Summers must have been able to offer you much more than I ever could have done. But then- when I saw on the news- I- Well, I began to wonder, if I'd done things differently, whether-"

"Right?" Gabe spat, his dark eyes made even darker by the weight of his resentment and rage. "So, you're some slut who tossed her child aside and now you want me to say, 'Oh, it's okay, don't worry about it,' and make you feel better about that?"

"I made a mistake when I was still just a kid myself, Gabriel," she replied. "I'm no angel, and perhaps I don't deserve God's grace, but I've repented for what I've done." Before speaking again, she leaned gently forward and held his angry focus with a calmness she was sure wasn't all of her own making. "I think it's time you repented, too."

"What is it with you people?" He only just managed to catch himself in time to stop from shouting. But his voice was still too loud, and it drew the attention of the guards.

It was Jake who raised a hand to his colleagues, assuring them he'd deal with it as he approached the pair. "Everything okay over here?" he muttered, keeping one thumb looped in his belt as he glanced between Gabriel and his visitor.

"Fine," Gabe snapped, not looking up at the young guard.

"Am I going to need to take you back early?" Jake replied, sounding to Gabriel as if he were talking to a pre-k child.

"No," Katherine quickly interjected, reaching for Jake and grasping him gently by the sleeve of his black uniform shirt. "No, please. I need- I need this time."

Jake quirked his head sympathetically. "Okay, but you're going to have to keep it down over here. You hear me, Gabe?" he added, twisting his face to the prisoner.

Gabriel toyed with the notion of telling the smug guard that he would happily go back to his cell now; that he *wanted* to go back. But the truth was that buried deep under all his anger toward the woman sitting across from here, were a mound of questions that only she could answer. And, for a split second, when he looked into her eyes, he saw a flesh of Amy. This woman was a part of him. A part of his children. That thought brought with it a conflicted sensation the like of which he had never known. He hated the fact she was an indelible feature in his family and had been even when she'd been invisible all those years earlier. He hated her for abandoning him and leading him to believe he wasn't wanted. Yet, there was some comfort in that glint of familiarity in her features. And perhaps he hated her for that, too.

"It's fine," he eventually mumbled, his attention finally lifting toward Jake. "I'm calm. I'm cool."

Jake wasn't entirely convinced, he'd known Gabriel long enough to have more than a passing knowledge of his moods and the expressions he wore. Gabriel was far from 'cool' or 'calm', that much was obvious. But Gabe had also become something of a 'project' with him, and he was without doubt the most stubborn he'd come across so far. Something about this small-framed woman made him think she might hold the key to breaking down some of that tough exterior. One thing he was certain of was that it was worth a shot, because Lord knew there were no other bright ideas waiting in the wings.

"Alright," he said, nodding a little stiffly. "If you need me at all, just give me a wink," he added, smiling as he spoke to Katherine.

She attempted to offer him a grin in return. The only one she could summon was meager, but it was abundant with genuine gratitude. She was silent as she watched the young man walk away, but she internally spoke a brief prayer for his safety and happiness. He deserved those things, she was sure.

As Gabriel continued to look at his biological mother, picking out features she shared with either himself or one of his kids, he began to laugh. It was shallow, not reaching deep in his belly like a real laugh should. Instead, it was a laugh filled with bitterness and disillusionment.

"What?" Katherine asked quietly, salty tear-tracks tightening the skin around her mouth and making it slightly difficult to move it properly.

"It's ironic," Gabe muttered. "Life is ironic. You haven't wanted anything to do with me for the last thirty-six years..."

"I did..."

He refused to let her interrupt. "And now, you're the only family I've got that actually wants something to do with me. My wife's divorcing me and won't even speak to me. She's as good as taken my babies from me. All I've got- Is the woman who abandoned me when I was a day old. How's that for irony, Mom?" He emphasized the last word, managing to make it sound both sarcastic and insulting.

Katherine weighed her response carefully, stalling the instinct to simply get up and walk away from the man who so clearly didn't want help from her or anyone else. But, of course, she knew well enough that we don't always know what we need. She certainly didn't always know, and what she thought she did know had led her so terribly astray.

Eventually, she began to nod. "I suppose it is ironic," she said, unshed tears still distorting her voice. "But don't make the mistake of thinking you weren't wanted Gabriel. The pregnancy obviously wasn't planned, it was stupid of me not to think about the consequences of my affair with that man, and it was naïve of me to expect him to react differently. But if it had been my choice, if there had been any other way, I would have kept you."

Gabriel wasn't sure whether to believe that or not. But there was one thing he could be certain of. "He didn't want me, though, did he? My father."

She hesitated, knowing the truth would make things worse, but also recognizing his right to the truth – even if it was unpleasant. "He- He was confused and scared."

"Selfish, you mean," Gabriel insisted. "He was selfish and he was a jerk. Because he must have realized you'd get pregnant. He must have known..." Cutting himself off before his voice grew any louder, he raked his teeth harshly over his upper lip. "Who is he? Where is he?" Those questions were asked calmly and with an edge of resolve that made Katherine shift in her seat.

"I-"

Setting eyes that were impossible to read on his mother's face, Gabriel said, "I want to be able to speak to him."

"You can't," she whispered. "I'm sorry. He- He died two years ago."

The first word that flirted with Gabriel's tongue was 'good'. He was glad he was dead, and hoped he was rotting in hell. On the other hand, though, it meant he would never be able to look the guy square in the eye and tell him he was a lousy excuse for a human being. He'd never be able to slug him in the jaw. He'd never be able to take a hammer to his skull- Shaking that thought off, Gabriel gradually straightened in his chair.

"I'm sorry," she repeated. "I know- I know you deserve more than that, but I-"

"It's fine," he muttered. "I don't suppose he and I would have had much to talk about anyway." With something that fell between a sneer and a smile, he shrugged.

"Gabriel." His mother, who was still struggling to conceive of herself as the mother of this man – a man who had taken the life of another. "I came here, because I wanted to apologize. I wanted you to know the truth about me, and about why I gave you up. But I also- I wanted to help you. I'm so desperately sorry if your decisions were affected by the path I set you on. I- I-"

"You're here to assuage your own damn guilt?" It wasn't much of a question. He knew the answer or, at least, strongly suspected he did. What surprised him, though, was her reply.

"Yes," she admitted candidly. "Yes, that's part of it. But I know what it's like to do something terrible. Something you don't think anyone will ever forgive. I know what it's like to carry that shame around with you, and know that to everyone else you're just a horrible, defective human being."

"Look..."

This time, she did not let him interrupt her. What she had to say was too important to be bull-dozed over. "You're not a horrible person, Gabriel. And neither was I. People sometimes do horrible things, but it doesn't mean they're evil. Do you understand what I'm saying? Circumstances can make perfectly ordinary people do a thing that disgusts them and haunts them for the rest of their lives."

The subtle flicker of his eyes over her shoulder leaves no doubt in her mind that he's not really listening, but she forges on regardless. "But there is a way we can all seek redemption. There is one person who understands that there is no evil in my heart or yours- You have to turn to Him, Gabriel. He'll guide you."

Slumping back, he attempted to cross his feet and realized he couldn't stretch his legs out far enough, because there was a metal division that ran from the middle of the table to the floor. Sighing, he adjusted his feet again, but could not manage to find a spot that was entirely comfortable.

"Look," he said, "if it sets your bible-pushing mind at rest, you've nothing to feel guilty about. You didn't do anything that resulted in that man's death. You couldn't have done, because I didn't kill him."

"Gabriel..."

"I didn't..."

As Katherine moistened her lower lip, she tasted the salt from all the tears she'd shed. She wondered, in a fanciful instant, whether she could taste all of the tears she'd ever shed from the moment she'd discovered she was pregnant until the present day. It seemed that way.

"All the more reason for you to turn to a power greater than yourself," she eventually said. Katherine wanted to believe that her son was innocent, she would have given almost anything to know that her child, the tiny boy she'd held for a few days before he was whipped away from her arms and her life, had not committed something so irrevocably awful. Perhaps, she acknowledged, that was why she could believe him. She wanted it to be true. But then, she had wanted the things his father had said to be true, too. And they most certainly were not. Nevertheless, she wasn't going to force a confession from the man in front of her. And it was right- "No force on Earth has been able to help you. So where is the harm in looking elsewhere?"

Gabriel shook his head in amusement, but he didn't have a pithy comeback for that simple question. What was the harm? If Jake and Matthew and this woman were wrong, what would he lose? He admitted, it would be nothing. It was only silently that he could admit that much, though.

"I know how angry you must feel," she continued. "Not just for this, but for every time life's treated you unkindly. But we're not alone, Gabriel. "He understands our pain, and He wants to help us if we only look to Him."

"He helped you, did He?" he grumbled sardonically.

Her reply came without hesitation or artifice. "Yes." With a quick nod, she added, "I won't pretend that my life has been easy and that I don't still carry a heavy burden of regrets, because I do. But without Him, I don't think I would still be here. I wouldn't have been able to carry this load without knowing He is taking some of the weight from my shoulders."

"Time's up, folks!" A cheery voice came from the back of the room, and Gabriel recognized it as Jake's.

"Can I see you again?" Katherine asked.

Gabriel had already been about to stand when the question came his way. He paused and then shot her a query of his own. "Why? What more is there to say?"

"I don't know. There are lots of things we could talk about. Anything. Everything. You could tell me about your children." She was careful not to call them her grandchildren, because she knew she had no right to make any claims on them. Although, deep in her heart, she felt every bit their grandmother.

When Gabriel winced, however, she knew that mentioning them at all had been a mistake. "Or not," she added quickly. "We don't have to talk about anything you don't want to. If there are more questions you want answered, though, I'll tell you everything I can. And... Well, you said yourself that I'm all you've got now."

"So?"

"So, you don't really want to cut me out of your life... do you?" She was prepared for his response to be 'yes'. In many ways, she was surprised he'd even let her spend as much time with him as he had.

Clicking his tongue, Gabriel glanced up as Jake approached the table and asked him to stand with a quick flick of his head.

"I'll... um... I'll think about it," he said quietly, as he got to his feet.

"Okay," she replied, offering him a broad smile. "Thank you. And, uh, is it alright if I write you again?" She had to lift her voice slightly, because he was already being led from the room.

However, before he was escorted through the door, he tossed his face over his shoulder and said, "If you want."

It was hardly an enthusiastic endorsement, but for Katherine Roser it was so much more than she'd dared hope for. Her eyes rising to the ceiling, she mouthed a 'thank you' to the heavens.

Chapter Fourteen

Days turned to weeks and weeks turned to months. Steady and reliable. Sometimes Gabriel was certain the march of time was the only steady, reliable thing in his life. But it wasn't quite the only thing.

There was Katherine. He had no intention of calling her 'mom', and she didn't seem to expect it. However, she'd been writing him at least twice a week since her visit. And, although, he'd never admit it out loud, he'd grown to look forward to those often-long letters. Some of them answered questions he'd had for years. Gradually, she revealed more about those months she was pregnant and hadn't known where to turn. His sympathy for her slowly mounted, he began to understand her choice to have him adopted. He wasn't sure if he could ever entirely forgive her, though. And he was more than a little irritated by her refusal to discuss the man at the heart of the whole issue.

At times, it still seemed as though she were protecting him. Protecting his memory.

I might have been young, Gabriel. But I was old enough to know better. He wasn't some terrible monster. He was human, like me. Like you. He was imperfect, and he had desires he couldn't or didn't want to control. But, so did I.

Gabe read those sentences dozens, maybe even hundreds, of times and tried to find the same forgiveness she held for the man she'd sinned with. But it wasn't that simple. If it had just been the affair, and the hypocrisy of it, perhaps he could have found it in his heart to recognize the weakness. After all, he knew he had plenty of his own weaknesses. His father, however, wasn't just a poor excuse for a preacher. He'd made a baby with this young woman, and his choice not to face the responsibilities filled Gabe with rage that flooded his entire body and spilled over as he threw his fist at the wall.

Katherine's letters weren't all packed with explanations and pleas for forgiveness and understanding, though. Many of them were mundane. She told Gabriel about her cat. She told him about the charity work she was doing, even going into great detail about a young man, Brody, who had been homeless since he was twelve.

On some level Gabe knew that, just a few short weeks before, he wouldn't have been slightly interested in these letters or the humdrum accounts of life they contained. But he enjoyed them. He anticipated them and he drank them in gratefully. They were a connection to the outside world. And they were a connection to someone in his own family, someone who cared about him.

That was something else in his life that was steady and reliable – the lack of contact with his wife and children. Katherine had encouraged him to write to Jenny, she said it would do him good and possibly open the lines of communication. It had all sounded like pseudo marriage counseling baloney to him. He resisted her pestering for the better part of two months, reminding her that Jen had already made it as plain as day she didn't want anything to do with him.

Katherine was just as dogged about that as she had been about arranging the visit, though. And, eventually, as much to shut her up as to satisfy his own curiosity about what a letter home would achieve, he wrote. It was only brief. He didn't know what to say, and couldn't find the words for what he did want to tell his wife. The days slipped by and there was no response. He was angry. Bitter. And despondent about the prospect of never knowing what his kids were up to, their grades at school... and even further into their futures, what universities they went to and whether they got married.

And yet, the reliable lack of response from Jenny did have one upside. Gabriel could at least tell Katherine he'd tried, and that it had been a big, fat waste of time and effort.

Some nights, Gabriel had found himself staring at his cell's ceiling, pretending he were somewhere else and fantasizing about his wife. As he felt his body responding to those thoughts, he remembered all the times over the course of their marriage he'd let stupid things come between them. He'd let petty arguments prevent them being as close as they should have been. He'd let work dictate his life to the point he was tired and stressed, and he'd taken it out on her and the kids. When his mind refused to focus on anything other than her in the middle of those lonely nights, he was bombarded by all the missed opportunities. The times he could have jumped in the shower with her. The evenings they should have packed the kids off to one of Jen's friends, so they could spend the night alone and uninterrupted.

When those thoughts swirled in his head at two o'clock in the morning, he wondered if he deserved to be where he was. Maybe he deserved to have lost her.

But there was one final constant and reliable aspect of his existence. Jake. Every day, without fail, the young, spiky-haired man would drop by Gabriel's cell. At first, those visits were explained by some pretext or other. The feeble excuses soon stopped, though, and he started to admit he was just 'checking in'.

And that checking in sometimes occurred several times a day. Like the letters from his mother, Gabriel had conflicted emotions toward the daily pestering of perpetually cheerful Jake. He resented it in many ways. Some days he couldn't fight back the urge to tell the younger man to get lost. Although, there was a part of him, that same part Katherine was touching, which was softening. Perhaps it was because there was just too much anger and hurt and pain to hang on to. It was a load that was psychically impossible to carry for any length of time. Whatever the reason, it was beginning to slip away. And the knowledge that people cared about him was like a life preserver to a drowning man. The problem was, there were times, as it floated toward him, he wasn't sure if he wanted to be saved.

Jake, though, saw the change. Even when Gabriel was pissed with him, there wasn't that same edge to his voice and his eyes. Even when he was too depressed to lift his head off the pillow, there was some sign of life in his features. Things were changing. It was gradual, but it was happening. And Jake was determined to keep that momentum moving in the right direction. Even if it meant making a complete pain in the ass of himself.

"How's it going?" Jake said one morning.

Gabriel lifted his face from the letter he'd been writing, and turned to the cheerful whistling of the man propping his shoulder against the doorframe of his cell.

"How do you think it's going?" he muttered, with a shake of his head.

The prison guard knew Gabe was irritable, but the hostility had mellowed. There was even a hint of humor to some of his complaints now. He'd actually become vaguely approachable. Not to all of the guards, of course. And to hardly any of his fellow inmates. Jake's persistence had paid off, though, because Gabriel did at least talk to him now.

"I was speaking with Matthew..."

"Not this again," Gabe huffed, cutting the younger man off.

"I just think, it might be..."

"You think too much," Gabe interrupted again. "About things that are really none of your business."

A soft smile played at Jake's lips as he swayed gently, his shoulder still leaning against the wall. "Your welfare is my business, Gabe."

"Oh, yeah?" Gabe scoffed as he picked up his pen and added another sentence to his letter. "What's that bible-pusher going to do for my welfare?"

"Your spiritual welfare," Jake explained, his smile unfazed. "You know, it's just as important as your physical."

With a snort, Gabriel signed off the letter and put down the pen. "I don't need to be ministered to," he insisted. "And certainly not by one of your hypocritical 'men of God'." He'd been a skeptic all his life, but knowing about the kind of man his biological father was, had deepened his conviction that religion was a waste of time at best and a cover for jerks at worst.

"Not all Christians are perfect," Jake replied. He had no way of knowing exactly what Gabe was talking about, but it didn't matter to him. There were rotten apples. Everywhere. That was people, and it was life. But there was also a lot of good in people. Maybe a little good in everyone, even the most seemingly depraved in society.

He had to believe that, otherwise he wouldn't be able to do his job with the care and compassion he held. For Jake, all of the men behind these bars were God's sons, too. They'd made mistakes, maybe been led down dark paths, perhaps they'd succumbed to temptations the devil placed in their way. No matter what, though, they were his still his brothers. And they could be saved. Even a man like Gabriel, whose violent temper had caused him to batter a man's brains in.

"You're telling me," Gabriel muttered.

"There are lots of good ones, though."

Folding his letter, Gabriel sighed. They'd had conversations on this theme every day for several weeks. Sometimes they lasted longer than others, usually they were extended whenever he gave Jake the opening to continue it. If he wanted to keep it brief, it was better to keep his mouth shut. He couldn't always manage it, though. And if he were only willing to admit it to himself, he enjoyed debating the issue with him. Just as much as Jake wanted Gabriel to see the light, so Gabe hoped he could shake some of the innocence and naivety out of the young man, who clearly hadn't seen enough of the world to know what it was really like.

"Matt is a good one," Jake added. "I know he's concerned for you. He prays for you."

"Tell him not to bother."

"I pray for you too, Gabe."

Lifting his attention from the letter, he swiveled in his seat. Studying the boyish face in front of him, he rested his elbow on the back of his chair. "You think that'll help?"

"Yes," Jake responded swiftly and certainly.

"You think God cares? And do you think, even if He does, He can do a thing to help me?"

"Yes," Jake said again, his confidence in that simple assertion undented. "It might not always be obvious to us," he continued. "We might feel that He's not listening or that He can't help. But He does and He will. We just need to believe in Him." Releasing the contents of his lungs slowly, he noted the doubt painted clearly in the crinkles above Gabriel's nose. "Matthew could explain it better, if you'd just be willing to talk to him."

Gabe stared at him, one eyebrow raised and the fingers of his right hand rubbing slowly over his brow. He didn't buy it. However, there was something needling him. He wondered if getting to know the prison chaplain would help him to understand his father. Not that he really wanted to understand him for the sake of coming to terms with what happened. But, like it or not, his father was in him. The nature of the man who took advantage of a lonely young woman was also his nature. The genes of the man who looked to everyone who knew him like a devoted husband and clergyman were his genes, too.

That thought made him want to vomit. But it also made him curious.

"Yeah," he murmured. "Yeah, sure. What have I got to lose?"

For a second, Jake thought he must have misheard. And for another second, he assumed Gabe was yanking his chain. As it sank in that he'd heard perfectly, and the man sitting in front of him wasn't joking, he began to smile. "I'll fix it up."

***

Matthew had calm written into his DNA. Gabriel could see that from a mile away. Every movement of his body was measured and controlled. The day they'd first met, he hadn't really paid much attention to that fact, but it was obvious to him now. And he envied it. He wanted calm and peace, he wanted to be able to face life with a sense that it was all under control, rather than spinning away from him into a vortex. That was always what made him lash out; those court ordered anger management classes had taught him that much. A lack of control made him seek control in violence. It was not much use to know that, though, if he couldn't do anything about those feelings of powerlessness. He just wasn't built as some men were, as Matthew was, to take every step in life with an easy stride.

"Hello again, Gabriel," he said. His deep voice filled the room smoothly and easily, but it wasn't loud. "Good to see you again." Smiling, he stopped beside the tiny desk and gently folded his hands in front of him. "How have you been?"

Sitting on the corner of the bed, elbows rested on his knees and fingers laced loosely between his widely parted knees, Gabe titled his face towards the chaplain. He didn't know whether to greet the pleasantries with sarcasm, or answer the stupid question with some sharp retort. In the end, he did neither.

Like everything else in life it seemed, the silence didn't bother Matthew. "Jake mentioned that you might like to talk to me," he said warmly. "What would you like to discuss?"

Tongue moving methodically over the inside of his lower lip, Gabriel pondered the question. What did he want to discuss? What did he want to ask this man? He was hardly the font of all knowledge, but he was one of 'them'. He was like his father.

"Do you believe that God forgives every sin?" he eventually asked.

Matthew didn't weigh his answer for long, and didn't dwell on the motive behind the question. "I believe that God will forgive anyone who truly repents, yes."

That was the big unknown for Gabriel. Had his father repented? He'd obviously never bothered to contact Katherine again. But perhaps, on his deathbed, he'd felt remorse. For what? Five minutes? Was that really all it would take to absolve all the wrongs that had been committed before that?

"So, you just say, 'sorry' and that's that? The slate's wiped clean?"

"No," Matthew insisted calmly. "No, it's never that simple. You have to mean the apology, Gabriel. You have to feel that regret in your heart, and you have to sincerely and honestly seek forgiveness. Preferably from those you've harmed as well as from God."

"I'm not talking about me." Sitting up straighter, Gabriel met the chaplain's calm obsidian eyes directly.

"Oh," Matthew replied, with a slight nod. "Well, it applies universally."

A light huff left Gabriel as he got to his feet. "You think?"

"Yes."

Gabe wondered how it could always be so simple for these people. "How can you be so sure of that?"

Standing firm even as Gabriel moved toward him, Matthew shifted one shoulder in a small shrug. "I believe in the power of God's goodness."

"It's always that clear-cut? No matter how awful the deed, it can be forgiven?"

"There are many things in life that aren't clear-cut, Gabriel. Most things in life, in fact. But any individual, no matter what they've done, can seek God's grace. And if they sincerely and humbly want it, He will offer it gladly."

Shaking his head, Gabe directed his eyes to the ceiling. For the man in front of him, life was black and white. In reality, it wasn't. "Some people don't deserve forgiveness," he muttered.

"It can seem that way," Matthew quietly agreed, his smile fading and the lines of serious thought lining his otherwise smooth brow. "People who've hurt us, or done things that we find too unpleasant for words, can seem beyond forgiveness. I think, what we have to remember, Gabriel, is that we have all done things that other people might not forgive us for. We all seek redemption for our sins, whether they're big or small. We bear the load of guilt. We know what that feels like, how heavy and painful it is to carry. If someone feels guilt, if they truly understand the hurt they've caused to a fellow human being, then they deserve, at the very least, our sympathy."

Gabe swallowed the small amount of saliva on his tongue along with the chaplain's words. "He without sin cast the first stone?" he whispered.

"I believe so," Matthew replied.

He couldn't deny the logic of it. He couldn't deny that there were things he'd done that would be deemed unforgivable by the people he'd hurt. He couldn't deny the anguish that came as a result of his guilt over stupid, drunken things he'd said and done. He'd blocked it. Put his life on a different track. Found solace in Jenny and the children, believing that if his family loved him, he was a better man. That had been his way of seeking forgiveness. And yet-

"Sins are not all equal," he insisted. "Stealing a candy bar from a 7-Eleven isn't the same as rape or murder."

"Of course they're not," the chaplain replied evenly. "And I'm not saying it's easy for us to forgive someone who's wronged us so profoundly. But we shouldn't deny them access to God's grace. And we couldn't even if we wanted to."

"What about men like you?"

"What do you mean?"

"Men like you, who abuse the trust and positions of power your religion puts you in?" A harshness had crept into Gabe's tone, causing his voice to crack slightly.

Matthew paused before responding. "I've never abused the trust people place in me. But- yes, there are a small minority who have, and do, and probably will in the future. We can't prevent that, Gabriel. I wish we could, but human beings are imperfect."

Growing more angry by what he deemed to be an evasive answer, Gabe took another step closer to the man. "What happens to them? Do they still receive God's forgiveness even after they've used His name to do terrible things?"

The chaplain inhaled slowly and moved his head in a sympathetic shake. He wondered what had prompted this line of questioning, but he didn't ask. "I'm sorry, Gabriel, I don't know. If those people have a conscience and come to feel remorse for their crimes, I imagine it must be in large quantities. If that's the case, perhaps the Lord will forgive. I don't believe He ever shuts any of us out if we want Him in our lives. He is a god of love and mercy, Gabriel. Even to those who've hurt his children, and hurt Him. That's not always an easy position to take. But it makes Him all the greater."

The tension in his shoulders lessening, Gabriel took a pace backward. His calves met the edge of the bed and he slowly sat again. As he did, he realized he'd been the one to view the issue simply. He'd deemed it in terms of 'right' and 'wrong' and the 'wrong' of his biological father, and even his biological mother, was unforgivable to him. But Matthew had confused everything. And he was no longer sure whether the righteous anger he was holding onto was justified. He couldn't quite bring himself to let it go either, though.

Noticing the paling of Gabriel's cheeks, Matthew shuffled back a quiet pace. "Would you like me to leave you alone for while?"

Gabe nodded while his eyes remained steadfast on the floor.

"Perhaps we can talk some more? Tomorrow maybe?"

To Matthew's surprise, and Gabriel's own, he nodded again in response.

Chapter Fifteen

Gabriel loosely folded his hands on the table in front of him. When Katherine stretched forward and placed her fingers over his, he didn't pull them away. It was the first time, she was sure, that the gesture had felt natural to both of them. In the previous months, their slight touches had been stilted. At first, he pulled away. Then, as if he were experimenting with the sensation it created, he'd force his hands to stay. Finally, on that day, it was second nature. To both of them, it was comforting. It brought a lump to his throat. And it turned her vision blurry.

"How are you?" she said, her voice low and soft. She always started the same way, not knowing what else to ask. And it was the only question that really mattered to her.

Nine months after she first sat across from him, Gabe had lost the tight hold he'd had on his anger. She was still there. She cared. And he'd come to appreciate that in ways he couldn't have imagined when he first discovered who she was. In fact, he'd become a different person to the one he was when he first discovered who she was.

Part of that change was from her, he knew that. She'd been patient even when he'd been moody, angry and impossible to talk to. She'd gained his trust by sharing so much of her life and her past. The other part of that change he wouldn't bring himself to admit, at least not out loud. Katherine had heard him talk about Matthew, though. And she'd been able to guess the kind of influence the young chaplain must have had on her son. She was glad, too. She wanted him to accept God, not just because it was good for him and for his soul. But because she wanted him to be able to cleanse himself of the truth about his father. One bad apple shouldn't destroy a faith – she was only too aware that her own life would have been much worse if she'd allowed it to.

"I'm..." he began, his eyes settling on their joined hands. He smiled, but it was so subtle Katherine couldn't be sure it was there and was ready to doubt herself. "I'm okay," he murmured, the smile growing stronger and unmistakable.

"Good," she whispered, her lips mirroring the motion of his. "I'm glad to hear that."

Gabriel had reached a place of acceptance. Matthew had told him to 'bear all things, believe all things, hope all things, endure all things'. At first, he'd been dismissive of the passage. Slowly, though, it began to make sense. Perhaps because the only option available to him was to bear, believe, hope and endure.

"I..." Slowly, he swallowed and lifted his eyes to ones he felt sure looked a little like his. They were not the right color, of course. He figured no one in the world would agree that they bore a resemblance to his own. But there was something in them he felt a connection with.

"What is it?" she asked, head tilting as she studied the curious expression on his face as he looked at her.

"I realized something," Gabe continued, his mouth straightening. "I deserve to be here."

Silent, Katherine stared, waiting for him to say more. But for several long seconds, he didn't and all she could do was hold her breath. This was important, and not because it would give that poor man's family and loved ones closure, but because it was important for Gabriel himself. Once he finally admitted what he'd done, he could truly begin to seek forgiveness. And perhaps, one day, he would be able to forgive himself. It would be a tough road; she knew that through experience. But he was about to make the first step.

"I've done some terrible things," he eventually added. "In every part of my life, I've screwed up. I've disappointed everyone."

"I'm sure that's not true," she quietly insisted.

"I took so much for granted. My wife and my children. Every day with them was a gift, and I spent most of my time looking at it as a burden. What kind of father was I?"

"Gabriel," she soothed. "We all take things, even precious things, for granted. We all assume the most important people will be there and we forget that life is fragile. That's human nature. You don't deserve to have them taken away for that."

"It's not just that, though." Sighing, Gabe shuffled his feet, trying to get comfortable and knowing he never would be. "I did bad things. I drank too much, and I had a temper, and I got into fights. I hurt people, Katherine." Holding her gaze, he waited to see the flash of disappointment, the change that would mean she could never look at him the same again. But it didn't come.

Calmly, she brushed her thumbs across his coarse knuckles. "You regret those things?"

"Yes," he replied. "Yes, I regret them. I regret the asshole I was. And I regret that when I had the opportunity to turn my life around with Jen and the kids, I didn't treat that like the gift it was."

"That poor man?" she asked, her tone low and lacking in any accusation. She was horrified by what he'd done, but she was sure she shared in the blame. What had happened to Gabriel would always be linked to the choices she'd made. She couldn't despise him for the things he'd done. And, for both of their sakes, she needed to find a way to forgive him. And she would. She could. As long as he wanted forgiveness.

"No. I... I didn't do anything to him. I didn't even know him." Gabe shook his head. "It wasn't me. But I deserve the punishment anyway. I deserve it for the things I did do."

"Gabriel, you can tell me what happened. I won't judge you." To him, she sounded just like Matthew when she spoke like that.

The answer he offered to her was the same he'd offered him dozens of times before, too. "But I didn't do it. I know everyone thinks I did, but I didn't... I've beaten men up before, even men I'd never met and had no reason to fight. I admit that. I even beat a guy so badly I knocked him unconscious. I was an aggressive, angry man. I'm not painting myself as some saint, Katherine. But I didn't kill anyone." His words were smooth and even serene. There was no rage in his voice now, no trace of the underlying violence Katherine sensed, and feared, in him the first time they met.

Still, things didn't make sense. "You might have been drunk..."

"I was," he admitted. "I got drunk that night, so drunk I passed out in my own bed. I didn't go anywhere, and I didn't fight with anyone."

"But," she murmured, confusion lining her brow. "The police were so sure it was you."

"The police were sure because they found my DNA at the man's house. And I have no idea how that happened. It must have been some foul-up at the lab. I never went there. It's impossible."

Eyes falling away from his face, she stared at their hands. Nervously, she chewed on her lower lip.

"You do believe me, don't you?" he said. "No one else does... but... please tell me you believe me." He hadn't appreciated until that very moment just how much he needed that: one person who'd listen. One person who'd believe him, when everyone else had turned their back on him. Just one person to make him feel as though he wasn't spinning out of control and into some rabbit hole into insanity.

She struggled to swallow as she lifted her gaze again. "Yes. I believe you."

Air left Gabriel's lungs in a rush. As he smiled, he flipped his hands over and grasped hers with fierce tenderness. "Thank you," he breathed.

For Katherine, however, this was not the end of their conversation, but the beginning. "You need to appeal, Gabriel."

A soft smile playing at the corners of his mouth, he shook his head. "I don't need to. I've accepted it. Like I said, I'm not paying for the crime I was convicted of, but I am being punished for the things I've done."

"The things you've done don't warrant spending the rest of your life in jail."

He lifted one shoulder. "Maybe not," he murmured. "But we have to bear the challenges God gives us, don't we? I mean, that's what you and Matthew are always talking about. If this is God's will, then I should accept it."

Katherine eased her fingers from him as she glanced at the clock. "It's time," she said. "I'll..." She let the word linger untethered to anything else. She had no intention of raising his hopes for something she could not guarantee. But she wasn't willing to accept the injustice as easily as he was. She also, unlike him, could think of a way his DNA wound up at that crime scene.

***

As she walked through the double doors, her heart tripped faster than usual. She couldn't make up her mind whether that was the result of fear or a small amount of excitement; the same excitement she'd felt as a teenager when she was in this place – when she was near him. In the end, she determined it was probably both. Like one of Pavlov's dogs, she still reacted to the thought of him. Even now, no longer the naïve and impressionable girl, there was still something about the memory of him that sparked feelings in her she wished weren't there.

She wandered through the hall of empty chairs, paused when she reached the cross at the front of the room, and said a quiet prayer. She prayed what she was about to do was not only the right thing, but also something that wouldn't blow up in her face and destroy the tentative relationship she'd built with her son.

Inhaling slowly, she had time to second and third guess herself. And she did. But something compelled her; the voice she recognized as God's. She moved through a door near the corner and down the short hall to the office. It'd been so long since she was last in this place, but each step was still second nature.

Softly, she knocked on the door, remembering a time she didn't need to knock. That door had always been open for her, making her feel as though someone cared about her. Of course, that had been a figment of her imagination. But it was a figment he'd put there, and he'd done so very intentionally. She knew all that now. She realized she'd been manipulated by a man who knew the rules of a game she'd never even heard of. Nevertheless, she was complicit. He might have been dangling temptation in front of her, but she grasped it. And, at the time, she'd felt precious little compunction about doing so.

"Come in." The voice was croaky, a little hoarse even. But there was some quality to it that hadn't altered over the course of three and a half decades.

It didn't affect her, though. Not like it used to. The man behind that door was not the young thirty-something, who'd seemed so handsome and so much cooler than any other adult she'd ever known. Besides, there was something vital at stake. Adolescent fantasies were so low in the order of importance that Katherine couldn't even pretend to be the girl she was.

She pushed open the door, heart still thudding. He lifted his head from his laptop screen and his brow creased.

"Can I help you?" he asked.

"You don't remember me?" It wasn't a question really. She knew the answer. And she didn't blame him. Who would recognize the fifty-five-year-old woman she'd become as the girl she'd been?

Of course, he looked different, too. His thick hair was receding fast and was now almost completely white. Deep wrinkles had formed around his mouth and nose, and there was excess skin hanging from his neck – a sign he'd gained weight at some point and lost it again. None of that mattered, yet Katherine couldn't help but wonder about the life he'd had between that moment and their last meeting.

"I'm sorry, ma'am," he replied, removing his reading glasses and folding them methodically. "You'll have to excuse me, I see a lot of people move in and out of the area. Were you a member of the congregation?" He'd still got it. That slick, friendly patter that put everyone around him at ease.

Katherine was not at ease, though. In fact, she could only think of one other time she'd been as uneasy: the day she told him she was pregnant. "You could say that," she admitted. "But only briefly."

Leaning back, he cradled his chin and rested his elbow on the arm of the chair. "Are you going to make me guess?" he asked, smiling.

"I'll give you a clue," she replied softly. "You took my virginity on this desk."

His smile disappeared in an instant. His Adam's apple flexed as he swallowed, and then, gradually, he squinted at her. "Katherine," he mumbled. "What do you want?"

There were many things she wanted. She wanted to tell him how much he'd hurt her, how he'd made it almost impossible for her to trust any man, how he'd taken her chance of being a mother away from her, how he'd almost destroyed her. None of those things would come from her mouth, though. The cold look in his eyes told her he wouldn't care. In his late sixties, she wasn't sure he posed a physical threat to her anymore. But there were worse things he could do, more powerful ways to intimidate.

"I need to talk to you about our son," she whispered.

"I don't know what you're talking about." Sitting straight, he shook his head.

"His name is Gabriel Summers," she added, ignoring his obvious attempt to shut the conversation down as quickly as possible. "You might have seen him on the news eighteen months ago when he was convicted of murder."

"Whoever this man is, he's not my problem." Getting up, he groaned softly. But his slightly arthritic legs didn't have any trouble rounding the table. When he reached the door, he flung it open and jerked his head to the opening. "And neither are you."

"He didn't do it," she said, standing firm. Too many times he'd tried to hustle her out of his church and out of his life with that flippant gesture. "Gabriel, your son is sitting in a prison cell for something he didn't do."

With a hand wrapped tightly around the door handle, the preacher shook his head. "I don't know what you want me to do about that."

"He looks a lot like you, John." She wasn't sure where that had come from. Perhaps, on some level, she believed that would touch him. That, suddenly, Gabriel would seem more like a flesh and blood human being rather than a name in the newspaper.

Slamming the door shut, he quickly closed the distance between them. Lifting his right hand, he jabbed his forefinger at her. "Don't you ever say something like that again, do you understand? You were just some dirty little slut, who tried to trap me by getting yourself knocked up."

She'd heard vile words like that from him before. She wished she could have said she was numb to it, but she wasn't. They stung. Even though she knew he'd twisted things in his sociopathic head, his vilification wounded just the same as it always had. Maybe it was because she'd loved him, or at least thought she'd been in love with him. And, on some level, that kind of feeling never truly goes away. It diminishes, it might even become obvious that it was insanity. But it's never completely dead and buried. Insults from someone once loved, and even worshipped, will always cut deeply.

"You're a man of God, John," she replied, careful to keep her voice even and level. She didn't want him to know he'd upset her, and she didn't want to exacerbate his anger. "You know that what happened here between us wasn't right. And you know how we dealt with the consequence wasn't right, either. And now Gabriel is paying the price for all that."

"I don't know how many times I can say this to you, Katherine. Neither you nor that bastard are my concern. I have a family of my own, and if you dare try to..."

"I'm not trying to hurt you or your family," she insisted swiftly. "All I'm asking for is your help in making sure our son..."

"Your son," he corrects. "And let me remind you, the reason your son is in the mess he's in is because he had a tramp for a mother."

Biting the skin on the inside of her lower lip, she quashed the urge to tell him his tune had been rather different when he'd wanted her body. For the time being, her focus was Gabriel. "He was wrongly convicted because his DNA was found at the scene of the murder," she explained.

"I don't care."

"Only you and I know how that could have happened," she added, ignoring his apathy. "We have to go to the police, John. We have to tell the truth about what happened, and that Gabriel has a twin. An *identical* twin."

"Have you told him who you are?"

"Yes," she replied unflinchingly.

For a moment, his mouth dropped open and no words emerged. Eventually, he found his voice. "You better not have told him about me."

"I didn't tell him your name," she sighed. "And I told him you'd passed away. But we're going to have to tell him the truth."

The preacher scoffed as he shook his head. "I told you a long time ago, Katherine, those children are your problem. I am not going to give up my life, destroy my family, my career and my reputation in this community, just because you were stupid enough to not take the pill."

"I'll go to the police alone then," she stated.

"No, you won't." Grabbing the front of her sweater, he tugged her close. As he spoke again, flecks of spittle from his lips landed on her face. "Don't you dare. Don't think I won't hesitate to deny it. I'd tell everyone you were some deluded teenager with a crush on someone she saw as a father figure, and you concocted an affair as a fantasy. Don't think I won't tell them I caught you with other men. I'll say you were prostituting yourself out of my home and that's why you had to go."

He'd made very similar threats when she argued that she wanted to keep the babies. That was when she comprehended just what a mistake she'd made in trusting this man. Her reaction to it now was dulled by the years she'd had to contemplate it. The prospect of having her reputation smeared didn't quite pack the punch it used to. However, he was still a well-respected pillar of the community. His word would be believed over hers, and she would be of absolutely no use to Gabriel if her version of events was dismissed.

"Think about what you're saying, John," she pleaded. "He's an innocent man."

"I am not throwing myself under the bus for someone who means nothing to me." With a push, he let go of her sweater. "Breathe a word to anyone," he added. "And I will make sure you and those boys are dragged through the crap. If any police or journalists come knocking on my door…" He left the rest unsaid. It was tacit, and had been said so many times before it'd almost become redundant.

Katherine sucked in a steadying breath, and realized her legs were trembling. The fact was, despite his advancing years, the man still scared her. "I'll pray for you," she murmured, stepping around him.

He grasped her arm. "Don't bother praying for me, Katherine. Worry about yourself."

"I have," she informed him, dragging herself free of his grip. "I've acknowledged my sins and begged forgiveness of Christ and God. Perhaps you should do the same before it's too late." Moving quickly in case he made another grab for her, Katherine scurried through the door and quickly left the church.

Once she was back in her car, she exhaled air, which had been trapped in her lungs for… it felt like years. Thumbs tapping at the steering wheel, she realized her choices were now limited to one. There was only one person she could talk to about the truth. And that final revelation could be too much for him to accept.

Chapter Sixteen

She was certain it was worse than the first time she'd seen him. It was worse than the first confession she'd made to him, and she knew exactly why. Then, he hadn't known her, didn't trust her and if he never wanted to see her again, she'd lost nothing. Now, he'd let his guard down around her. He believed she'd told him the truth. And she had, just not the whole truth.

Now, she had something significant to lose. Her relationship with him had just started to come good. It was better even than she could have hoped for, and better than she let herself imagine in the best of her daydreams over the decades. And she could be about to ruin it all. But she had to. For his sake, Katherine had to confess the very last of her secrets.

"Has something happened?" he asked, noting the tension in her face as she sat in the chair opposite him.

"Uh-" That wasn't an easy question to answer. The quick and truthful response would be 'yes'. But it was all much more complicated than that one syllable could explain. And he would delve if she tried to brush it off. The better thing would be to confront it head on.

"Katherine?" he coaxed gently.

"Sorry, Gabriel," she replied, forcing a smile. "I've been in a world of my own lately. I- No, first, tell me how you're doing." She would deal with it head on. But she didn't see the harm in delaying it for another five minutes. Perhaps she could find a way to ease into the conversation rather than bluntly announcing that he had a brother – a twin brother.

"Are you sure you're okay?" he wondered, realizing as the words left him that it had been a long time since he'd been concerned for anyone else. The fact of it hit him hard. And it made him feel simultaneously good and awful. Awful, because he didn't appreciate how wrapped up in himself he'd become. And good, because it meant he was starting to care about another human being again. He wouldn't have thought that possible just six months earlier.

Her smile became more genuine as she recognized the worry in his dark irises. Although, it also brought a sharp stab at her chest. She'd only just seen it and she might be about to lose that look in his eyes forever.

"How have you been?" she asked, still trying to put off the uncomfortable subject she needed to broach.

"Not bad," he replied evenly. "I've been talking to Matthew every day this month."

"That's good," she said. She hadn't met this chaplain, Matthew, but she liked what she'd heard of him and hoped that one day she might be able to thank him face to face.

"Yeah," Gabe agreed quietly, not quite believing that he was in agreement with her opinion of it being 'good'. "Yeah, he's actually an alright guy." In truth, he was more than an alright guy, but Gabe couldn't bring himself to say that out loud yet. He'd become a friend. And making friends in that place had seemed impossible. Now and again, Gabe still became frustrated with Matthew's overzealous goody two-shoes act, and the fact he had an answer for everything. But those answers weren't always cute or simplistic. Sometimes, they weren't even things Gabe wanted to hear. But Matthew answered all of his questions honestly, and he couldn't help but respect him for that.

"He's been getting me to read the scriptures," he added. "And- uh- Well, some of it's okay, I guess."

Katherine thought he sounded a little like a teenager who'd been coerced into reading something in a lit class and discovered it wasn't as dry as he'd dreaded it being. Smiling to herself, she imagined she was catching the briefest glimpse of what her son might have been like in his adolescence. It was nice to think she hadn't entirely missed out on it. More importantly, though, she sensed he was on the path to finding himself and finding God.

"You've found your faith?" she asked.

"I wouldn't go that far," he muttered. "It's not... I mean, all the suffering in the world doesn't make any sense if the dude up there-" He paused long enough to point his index finger to the ceiling. "-is on our side."

"These are things we can't understand, Gabriel," she replied softly. "Perhaps they'll make sense to us one day. Or perhaps we'll never quite see the grander plan. But there is one. I'm certain of it."

Gabe hummed with no small amount of skepticism. "Matthew says much the same thing." He might have been tempted to think it was the 'party line', but he trusted both of them to say what they thought and not repeat some mindless dogma. Nevertheless, he couldn't bring himself to believe the same thing. He didn't understand. And he couldn't accept the 'we don't know' explanation. He needed more than that. He needed to find a reason.

"Are you thinking about your own situation?" she asked, as his silence began to make her uncomfortable. "Are you trying to find a reason for your own suffering?"

"I told you last visit, I know why I'm where I am. I know what I did wrong. But what about innocent kids who've never hurt anyone? What about my kids? What about Jen? They did nothing wrong and they're suffering, too."

"The punishment of one person affects those around them," she offered, her voice still gently and calm. She'd already made her peace with all the things he was wrestling with. "There's no way around that, Gabriel. God can perform miracles, but he can't make the whole world work in miraculous ways. There are always consequences. And there'll always be people who don't deserve to be hurt, but who are."

"And God's cool with that?"

"No, I don't believe He is," she replied, ignoring the slight sarcasm in his tone. "I think it hurts Him deeply. But just like we can't always help people who are hurting, neither can He."

"But He's God," he said, shaking his head. "He's supposed to be able to do anything, be anywhere and help anyone who needs it. So if he doesn't help, they don't deserve it?"

She pondered his question for a moment. She'd felt that way sometimes. She'd seen people in need and wondered why the Lord had seemingly forsaken them. "I think-" she began. "Things are not as neat as we would like them to be. Nothing is simple or black and white. We often feel a need for them to be, but they're not. And God doesn't work outside the imperfectness that we exist in."

"But He could do something about the imperfection and injustice."

"Maybe He can't," she replied evenly. "Maybe He'd like to. I'm sure He does what He can when He can do it, but He can't fix everything. He's greater than we are, Gabriel. But that doesn't mean He's as all-powerful as we might wish He were. At some point, we have to accept that He's taken a step back and letting us solve our own messes. Most of the time, for our own good."

Gabe stared hard at the gray wall beyond her shoulder. He saw the sense in what she said, but it still didn't explain the suffering of innocents. They hadn't made a mess. And, in those circumstances, God should be able to intervene.

"Gabriel," she said, her focus leaving his face. She acknowledged she couldn't put it off any longer. He deserved to know. And the discussion about suffering had reminded her that she had participated in that suffering – not just Gabriel himself, but his family too. It all, ultimately, dropped at her feet. And God hadn't been able to do anything for those people, because He couldn't help them and punish her at the same time. Their suffering was, therefore, her fault not His.

"There's something I need to tell you," she murmured.

A confused frown lined his brow as he swept hair, which was getting too long, off his forehead. "You're not going to stop visiting, are you?" he replied, his deep voice managing to sound small. "I... You said you believed me..."

"I do believe you," she insisted. Perplexed, she wondered where this worry had come from. After all, she'd visited him initially in the full knowledge that he'd been imprisoned for murder. Why would that suddenly repel her now, even if she didn't believe him? Whatever the reason, it obviously mattered to him.

"I promise," she insisted, trying to ease his anxiety. She was quite aware that the tension between them would soon go far beyond anything she'd seen before, though. So, largely, the attempt was futile. "I believe you. This thing I need to say, it's not about you." That wasn't quite true, because it was about him. "It's me-" she continued. "It's something I should have told you months ago."

The flush of panic began to leave his eyes, but his brow creased deeper. "What do you mean?"

Shallow breaths moved in and out of Katherine's lungs as she counted the seconds. Those could be the last seconds she ever spent with him. They would almost certainly be the last seconds he'd look at her as though he trusted her and cared about her. And she wouldn't blame him for that. She only hoped he'd understand her reasons.

"Katherine?" he urged.

"I... I mislead you about something, Gabriel," she began, figuring that, as with most things in life, it was better to be honest and humble about her mistakes. We all make them, after all. And she prayed he might recognize that within his own situation and take a more charitable view of her faults – she certainly always tried to do the same with others.

"You... You what?"

"I wasn't entirely candid with you..."

"You lied to me?" he snapped, his upper half straightening and stiffening as his shoulders pushed back.

Katherine shook her head quickly. "No, no. I didn't lie..." She knew what she was about to utter was an agile bit of semantics at best. But it was all she had at her disposal. And it was, at least somewhat, honest. "There was something I kept from you, but I never really lied."

Snorting, Gabriel jutted his chin toward the ceiling. "For heaven's sake," he muttered to himself. "What is it?" he demanded, his face darting back to hers. "You're not really my mother?"

"I am your mother," she replied, trying not to give way under the bitterness of his accusation. She had to stay calm. She had to try to keep him calm, because if he was upset now, it'd pale in comparison to how he'd feel in a few seconds. "Everything I told you about myself is the truth," she repeated softly. Of course, what she'd told him about his biological father being dead wasn't true. But she couldn't reveal that. She couldn't run the risk of testing John's threats.

"But..." she added. "I didn't tell you everything."

Gabriel's tongue moved over the hard ridges of his front teeth and then prodded the inside of his cheek. He eyed the woman in front of him with a subtle squint, trying to work out whether he still trusted her. There were doubts now. And perhaps they were made worse by the fact that, for the last eight months, he'd been sensing this was all too good to be true; that he didn't really deserve to have someone visit, write and give a hoot about him. Life had taught Gabriel a few very valuable lessons, and one of them was: when something seems too good to be true, it usually is. The recent dissolution of his marriage had been another slice of proof, if more proof were needed.

Nevertheless, there were also embers of trust that hadn't quite burned out. He wasn't even sure if he wanted them to sit in his heart. The cynical side of him was ready to toss them out, except there was nowhere for them to go. He was stuck with them. And part of him wanted to cling tight to them, because he recognized how badly they were needed. He had to trust someone. And if she was trusting him about the murder, perhaps he would have to trust her without much evidence, too.

"So..." he murmured, only one question resounding in his head. "Why now?"

"I don't understand."

"If you didn't want to tell me before, why the sudden prick of conscience?"

Katherine shifted, adjusting the hem of her long skirt as she tried to decide how frank to be in her answer. "It... Well, I think I might know what happened. I might be able to explain how your DNA ended up in that poor man's house."

"What?" The word came louder than he'd intended, but he had very little control over his volume. The sound of his voice, and the barked question, seemed to echo around them. A few other prisoners and visitors paused in their conversations long enough to glance over. The guards also raised their heads and stared, a couple of them seeming to anticipate trouble. Gabriel noticed the looks and nodded apology to the two men who had the power to escort him back to his cell without ever finding out what Katherine knew.

"You're going to hate me for this," she said, her words coming fast, as though pushed from her by an invisible force before she had a chance to trap them deep within her own soul. "I understand if you do. It was wrong of me... But... It didn't seem like it would do anything other than hurt you... Now, though, I realize that you have to know."

"Know what?"

"You have a twin," she said quietly, so quietly that she wasn't sure if he'd hear her.

He did. And as the shock took hold of him, freezing every muscle in his body, he was sure he would have heard a pin drop too. "But... But..." he babbled, unable to feel his lips or even his tongue. "How? How could I not have known that? Surely... adoption agencies keep twins together?"

"Usually, yes," she replied, nodding. "Your brother... There was a complication during the labor and the doctor had to intervene. But she was inexperienced, and the baby was hurt."

"Hurt?" he said, demanding the whole story from her. He didn't know that it all mattered right now, and he sensed she thought it didn't. But it mattered to him. It mattered greatly.

"The forceps damaged his head, he had to be admitted into the hospital for a few days. So he was taken away from me, and I was left alone with you."

Gabriel shook his head. "You... You..."

"I was scared. I didn't want anyone to find out about your father, because he'd threatened me if anyone ever did. All he cared about was that you and your brother disappeared."

"So... you...?"

Katherine blinked, and she was surprised to find her eyes dry. Perhaps she'd cried so often over this that there were no tears left. Or perhaps, faced with the reality of what she'd done, she felt as numb as Gabriel did. In some ways, it did feel as though it happened to someone else. It could have been a troubling story in a newspaper or the heart-wrenching plot of a chick lit novel. Except, the chick lit novel would have ended happily. And, in real life, few things ever did.

"I left the hospital with you," she said. "While your identical twin was still being treated for the wound on his head." Her face falling forward, she could no longer look at him. "I left you on the doorstep of an orphanage, and your brother... He was taken to be adopted when they gave up hope of finding me."

"Why couldn't they find you?" he demanded.

"I didn't give them my real name," she replied, her eyes still trained downward. "I couldn't... I..." Suddenly lifting her gaze, her pale eyes pleaded with his darker ones. "Gabriel, if you only knew how terrified I was. I hated what I was doing, but I had no choice."

"You had a choice," he bit back. "You had one, and you chose to look after yourself."

"That's not true, I was thinking about what was best for you. Both of you. I couldn't take care of you. And if I'd kept you and your father had discovered I still had you, he... He would have found a way to take you away from me and ruin all our lives in the process."

Tossing himself back in the seat, he lifted his cuffed hands. "News flash, Katherine! My life has been ruined."

"I know, and that's why I came here in the first place. I wanted to explain and apologize for what I've done, and beg your forgiveness. I wanted to make it right. But don't you see, my finding you may have been a blessing, because now we know why you were suspected of that murder. You're not the only person who has your DNA, Gabriel."

Gabe pushed his chair back and slowly got to his feet. He heard footsteps behind him and one of the guards placed a hand on his shoulder.

"I want to go back to my cell," he muttered.

"Gabriel," Katherine blurted. "Please... We can talk more about this... You have to know why I kept it from you. I didn't want to cause you unnecessary pain."

"What you didn't want," he said, leaning forward slightly, "was life made difficult for you. You were selfish. And if you think I want anything to do with you ever again, you're mistaken. God might be able to forgive any sin, Katherine, but I can't."

Turning sharply on his heels, Gabe tried to stride for the exit. The guard's hand on his arm kept his steps slow, though. And, as he walked through the door in the corner of the room, Katherine felt the tears finally prick her eyes.

Chapter Seventeen

Gabriel sat on the edge of his narrow bed, his fists clenching and unclenching in front of him as he waged with the urge to throw a punch at the wall. His knuckles were already deformed from the last time, where the bones had fused together as best they could. But it wasn't his hand he was worried about. It was his control over himself. That control which he'd fought so hard to acquire, and he was reluctant to let go of. Even more so, because he knew his hold on it could be described as tentative at best. He wasn't sure if he could explain exactly why he refused to let it go, why he couldn't just say, "forget it!" and let it all out. There was a time he would have done. And part of him wanted to be that man again, he wanted to erase the previous few months and the man he'd become while he thought someone cared about him.

Staring at the gray wall ahead of him with eyes that wouldn't even blink, he realized he couldn't entirely abandon this new man, simply because he didn't want to. Yet, he felt himself sliding. Backward. Back to the man who couldn't control his temper, who didn't want to speak to anyone, who couldn't think of a single reason to keep breathing.

Pushing himself off the mattress, he paced a few steps until her reached the wall. He lifted his fist to his shoulder, but it stayed there. Teeth gritted, he howled in frustration before letting the balled hand drop to his side. With another grunt, he punched his thigh.

"Crap!" he yelled.

In amongst the sea of incarnadine rage in which he swam, he knew he would drown if he didn't calm down.

Katherine had lied. His entire life had been a lie, because he had family he didn't know about; a brother he hadn't known about.

But, he had also been given a way out of his current situation. She'd finally given him the truth. And that could, very literally, set him free. He knew that. That thought was prominent in the forefront of his mind. And yet, it was constantly battered by the betrayal and the sense that he'd been cheated out of so much. A brother. He had a brother, and not just any brother, but a twin.

What kind of woman could separate her children like that?

Driving his fist into his leg again, he spun and marched the width of the cell. He couldn't square the woman he'd come to know with the woman who would so callously divide her twin babies. Even the young woman who he'd believed had given her baby up for adoption didn't seem so heartless as to leave an injured newborn in the hospital. In his eyes that made her a monster, just as bad as the biological father who hadn't wanted him. And maybe it made her even worse than him.

The knock on the door caused Gabe to whirl around sharply. And he dragged a hand through his scruffy hair as the cell opened. "Go away!" he barked, expecting the visitor to be Jake. But, as the tall, dark-skinned man stepped inside, he shook his head.

"Not now, Matthew," he sighed. "I'm really not in the mood for your God is great crap."

Matthew's stride faltered, but he didn't retreat. Instead, he lingered in the doorway, glancing over his shoulder at the young guard who had unlocked the cell for him. Jake furrowed his brow and shrugged back, just as confused about what had upset Gabriel as the chaplain was.

"Do you mind if I ask what's happened?" Matthew asked. The perpetual calm in his voice was marginally irritating. And Gabriel wondered whether it was ever possible to vex his serene surface. How far would he have to go to rile him? What kind of insult would finally make him crack? Because no one was as genuinely placid as this man seemed to be. Of that he was certain. Everyone had limits. There were buttons that, when pushed in the right order or the right way, could set anyone off.

"Do you ever give it a rest?" Gabe blurted, turning from the chaplain and shuffling toward the bed. He tossed himself down and rubbed both palms over the rough stubble on his cheeks.

Glancing back at Jake, Matthew said, "It's alright," and, with a nod, encouraged the younger man to close the door.

"You sure?" Jake asked, his bright blue eyes moving from Matthew to Gabe and back again. "I can stick around. I'm off duty in a second anyway. So, it's no trouble to stay a little longer."

"Gabriel isn't going to hurt me," Matthew insisted. He was as sure of that as he could be. He didn't exactly know why he was. After all, Gabriel had shown signs of violence. And his past obviously contained a lot of it. Somehow he did know that it wouldn't be turned on him, though. And, even if it were, he was a big guy. Much bigger than Jake. If push ever came to shove, he was confident he could handle himself.

"Sure of that, are you?" Gabriel grunted in reply. Deep down, he knew he wouldn't raise a hand to the chaplain, either. He didn't even want to. It annoyed him that Matthew's confidence in that was so assured, though.

"Give us a few minutes, Jake." Nodding again, Matthew stepped further into the cell. When he reached the small desk that was bolted to the floor and the wall, he perched himself on the edge of it. The metal flexed a little under his tall frame, but it was easily sturdy enough to take his weight.

He paused there silently, his legs stretched out in front of him and feet crossed at the ankles. He was still and completely quiet until the cell door clunked shut and the locks clicked back into place. Then, calmly folding his arms across his abdomen, he let out a soft breath. "So-?" he quietly said. "Do you want to talk about it?"

"Talk about what?"

"Whatever's gotten you so upset." His head was tilted fractionally to one side as he spoke.

Gabriel knew that gesture, it was his sympathetic look. What he wasn't sure of was whether it was done by design or if it was an unaffected motion. Sometimes, he was sure it was unaffected. In that moment, while he was ready to doubt that any goodness existed in any human being, he figured the chaplain knew how to play the people he wanted to 'recruit'.

"Do you think you get extra brownie points for all this crap?" he muttered.

Oblivious to what had been rolling through Gabe's mind, Matthew shook his bewildered face. "I don't know what you mean."

"Do you think God will give you special treatment if you manage to sign up as many of us to the club as possible? Blessings work like commission, or some crap like that?"

Matthew now knew what Gabriel was talking about, but he was no less confused by the train of his thought. "I don't understand," he said. "I know you're still not convinced by God's teachings and maybe you don't even believe in Him yet. But I thought we were making progress. I thought you believed that I wanted to help you."

"Hmm." Gabriel, leaned back and propped his elbow on the bed. "And why do you want to help me?" he mumbled.

With a puff that blew out his cheeks, Matthew looked quizzically back at him. "I don't even know how to answer that question, Gabe. I want to help, because I want to help. I think I can help. And because I think we should all try to help each other."

"No," Gabriel insisted with a firm shake of his head. "It's never as simple as that. People only ever want to help you if there's something in it for them." And in Katherine's case, it had all been about assuaging her own guilt. Did Matthew have guilt he needed to assuage? What was on this pious man's conscience? Gabriel was convinced there had to be something.

Matthew quelled the urge to answer instantly. He wanted Gabe to think about what he'd said, to consider the possibility of a world where no one did anything for their fellow man without an ulterior motive. However, the expression on

Gabriel's face remained unchanged. If he was thinking at all, he was just as determined he was right as when the question came tripping out of his mouth.
"You've never helped anyone just because you could?" Matthew eventually probed. "Never helped anyone, because you wanted to help? And for no other reason?"

Refusing to respond, Gabriel shook his head. "That's convenient to turn it around. I'm asking you. I'm asking why you have a non-stop do-gooder mission. I don't believe anyone feels so dead set on making themselves a saint unless they feel they have to redeem themselves." That's exactly what it had been for Katherine. Every young homeless person she'd helped had been a small step in righting the horrendous wrong she'd committed. It was all an effort to cleanse herself of sin. And Gabriel didn't believe that any chronic do-gooder was any different. They had to be motivated by something, and guilt was one of the most powerful motivators of all.

"If you're asking me whether I've ever done things I regret, the answer is 'yes'." Matthew said simply. "Show me someone who hasn't and I'll show you a liar." With a shrug, he laughed lightly. "And I suppose you're right. I do help people because there's something in it for me. It makes me feel good, Gabe. It fills my heart with warmth to know that I'm making a difference. Because that's what we all want out of life, isn't it? To feel that our time here has had some positive effect on those around us. Some of us find out how to do that more easily than others."

Gabriel took a deep breath, ready to argue, but he was tiring of the conversation. Matthew would always have an answer. He had answers for everything. And, Gabriel had to admit, he had a point in wanting to make a difference. He supposed everyone did want that. For Gabriel, the difference he'd wanted to make was for his kids. And a fat lot of use his efforts were on that score. Even before he'd been convicted of murder, he hadn't been the world's best role model.

"Shoot," he muttered, his head sinking and his hand fisting his hair.

"Gabe," Matthew said, "obviously something's happened. Now, I can't make you talk about it. But, it might help if you do. So- the ball's in your court. No matter what, I'm here for you."

A few short months ago, Gabriel would have told the chaplain to get lost and not come back. A few short months ago, he would have found the whole thing patronizing. And a few short months ago, he hadn't known that there was a way to actually prove his innocence. But, of course, he couldn't do that alone. One person who would have been able to help him was Katherine, but he'd probably put her off the idea of doing anything for him ever again. He wasn't even sure if he wanted her help. And, in truth, his pride would have made it difficult to ask in any case. However, he would need help from someone. Finding his twin would be almost impossible from where he currently sat.

"Do you believe me?" he asked, lifting his head and letting his hands flop down to his thigh.
Matthew blinked before casting his eyes to the floor. When he finally met Gabriel's gaze again, he still wore an expression of perplexity. "Do I believe what?"

"Do you believe that I'm innocent?"

His bottom lip gripped by his teeth, Matthew considered his reply. “It’s not for me to judge one way or the other, Gabe.”

“But do you believe me?”

“I can’t know what happened,” Matthew sighed. “There are only two people who really know. You’re one of them. The other is God. What matters is what He believes, not what I believe.”

Scoffing, Gabriel shook his head. “I’ll take that as a ‘no’, shall I?”

Unfolding his arms, Matthew pushed himself from the desk and crossed the short distance between them. Sitting on the corner of the bed, he made sure to leave Gabriel plenty of space. And he half-expected him to jump up and start prowling the room again. However, Gabe stayed where he sat. Eyeing the chaplain carefully and trying to anticipate the, no doubt clever, answer he’d give.

But Matthew didn’t have one yet. Pausing, he pressed his hands together and rubbed the palms gently. “Gabe, to do my job, I can’t make a decision about any man’s guilt or innocence in here. I have to minister to you all equally. I just- I can’t think in terms of whether I believe anyone or not. All I’m here for is to listen, to offer comfort and guidance.”

“Well, that’s convenient, isn’t it?”

“No, it’s not. It’s hard. I’m asked to become personally connected to the men here, but I am duty-bound to also keep a distance. It’s not convenient and it’s not easy.” His usual low, calm voice remained, but there was a hint of something else.

Bitterness perhaps. A subtle anger at the fact Gabriel didn't understand how the job placed him in a predicament he'd rather not have. It would be much more 'convenient' to tend to a regular parish. But these men deserved the comfort of the Lord. Some of them may even be able to turn their lives around after they've left these walls. It was important work. But it wasn't easy. It was far from easy.

"You don't keep a distance, though," Gabe muttered.

"Not always," Matthew admitted. "I care," he added, "and it's hard to keep your distance when you care." Brushing his hands together again, he placed them on his knees. "Now, I've answered your questions, but you haven't answered any of mine. What's this all about, Gabriel?"

Turning to face the chaplain, Gabriel's eyes settled on the man's face. "I didn't kill anyone," he said, with no flicker of hesitation and an unrelentingly steady gaze.

Matthew exhaled slowly, and held Gabe's focus in return. "And you want to talk to me about that?"

"What's the point if you're not allowed to have an opinion?"

"The point is to discuss what's bothering you," Matthew replied serenely. "My opinions on anything don't really matter, do they?"

With a flick of his head, Gabe conceded the point. Although, he felt it did matter whether he was believed or not. Now he knew somewhere out there was hard evidence of his innocence, it mattered greatly that he had someone on his side. *Really* on his side.

"I need you to believe me," he uttered, in what sounded almost like a plea.

For Matthew, Gabriel's voice had always had a rough edge, an acerbic tinge when he was in a better mood. And it had been laden with bitterness and anger when he was in a bad one. Never had he asked for anything, much less pleaded for it. And that part of him, which found it difficult to maintain a distance, couldn't help but be moved by it.

"I'm listening," he said, hoping that would be sufficient enough reply without actually having to say he believed something he wasn't yet sure he did. After all, the evidence against Gabriel had been damning. And the way he'd behaved since he'd been in prison was suggestive of someone with the kind of violent temper that could indeed lead to murder.

Gabriel was smart enough to see the subtle verbal dancing that meant Matthew refused to commit himself to anything. But it was the best he'd got. Maybe it was all he'd ever get.

"I found out something today, something that could prove I didn't kill anyone and that I was never at that house," he said.

"Okay," Matthew said slowly, nodding. "If that's true, perhaps you need to discuss this with a lawyer or someone who could mount an appeal."

"I can't afford to hire a lawyer," Gabe quickly replied. "So I need help. I need your help."

Carefully moistening his soft lips, Matthew continued to meet Gabe's eyes. "If there's something in my power, I'll do what I can," he said. "But I can't make any promises, Gabriel."

"Can't or won't?"

"Why don't you just tell me what it is you need from me?" Matthew suggested.

"I need you to track down my twin brother."

For a split second, Matthew wondered if he'd heard correctly. Then, he wondered if Gabriel was joking. Eventually, he shook his head in confusion.

"I was adopted- And I was separated from my twin just a few days after we were born." When Matthew still sat mute, Gabe continued. "Don't you see? Identical twins have the same DNA. So, he must have been the one in that man's house. He might know who really did kill Renaudin. But, even if he doesn't, as long as he admits to being in that house, I'm clear. Right?"

To Matthew, this all seemed more than a little far-fetched. He let the news digest for a few moments before peering at the floor in front of his feet. "You never had any idea that you had a twin?" he asked in no more than a whisper.

"No- My birth mother's only just told me. She realized how the DNA might have wound up at that house, and so she told me the truth. She told me about how me and my brother came to be adopted."

Finally understanding what had got Gabriel so upset, Matthew nodded. He hadn't met this woman, but Jake and

Gabriel had both mentioned her. And she seemed to be having a wonderful influence on the man. He realized how betrayed Gabriel must have felt. He also realized that, despite the fact the situation could easily be slipped into a soap opera, it wasn't as implausible as it might otherwise have sounded.

If there really was an identical twin, Gabriel could be innocent. And, there was certainly no harm in trying to find this man - if indeed he existed.

"Alright," he said, twisting his face back toward Gabe. "Alright. I'll- Well, I'll do what I can. But, I've got to tell you, I'm no expert in tracing people. I will do everything I can for you, though, Gabriel." Inhaling, he tossed his eyes to the ceiling and sought help from the Almighty. "I'll just need to find someone who'll be able to help," he said.

Chapter Eighteen

Shutting his car door with his hip, Matthew clicked the remote lock and rounded the hood. He waited for an elderly couple to pass before trotting up onto the sidewalk, and he smiled at a small boy of about four years old before sweeping through the double doors that took him inside the precinct.

The hectic buzz of a variety of ringtones filtered the air and the movement of busy feet rushed from desk to desk or from desk to coffee machine. At least a dozen voices resounded around the high-ceilinged space and several conversations were being held at once, meaning Matthew only caught odd words and half-sentences.

"No, the perp was wearing a red hoodie."

"Jaywalking."

"I believe so, yes."

"We'll obviously need to speak to your son at some point."

All the noise confusing him, he tried to block it out. Heading to the large, long desk at the far end of the room, he passed a line of plastic chairs with steel arm rests. Two people sitting in those seats were cuffed to them. He wished he could say that was an unusual sight to him. He cast his gaze to both men and offered them a polite nod. Neither of the tattooed bikers bothered to acknowledge him though.

Brushing it off, he kept walking. He couldn't help but think, as he passed a row of silver file cabinets on his right that they were moot in this day and age. In fact, he'd guess there wasn't anything in them. A throwback from the last century, they'd just remained because they were literally part of the furniture.

The young officer at the desk could have been fresh out of school. With a few pimples on his pale skin, he was sweating in the August heat despite the fan that was trained right on his face. Tugging at his collar, he let out a heat-weary exhalation before giving Matthew his gray-eyed attention.

"Can I help you, sir?"

Laying his hands on the desk, Matthew shuffled closer. "Yes, I'd like to see a detective by the name of Meredith Maloney."

With one hand, the possibly teenaged officer tapped at his keyboard. "You have an appointment with her?"

"Um- no," Matthew replied. His decision to come had been spur of the moment. He hadn't even considered calling beforehand to ask if she could make time to see him. Actually, he felt that was probably a subconscious effort to make sure he couldn't receive a 'no'. Because, the truth was, if she did turn him down, he wouldn't know where else to turn. After all, a private investigator would cost money. Money neither he nor Gabriel had.

"I'm not even sure if she's in at the moment," the officer said, still looking at his computer and languidly clicking one finger at the keys. "She might be out on a case. If you want to leave your name though, I can get her to call you." Turning his focus to the man in front of him again, the officer offered an apologetic smile.

"Do you think you could be kind enough to call her?" Matthew asked, reaching into his back pocket. "It's- uh- Well, it's to do with a case she worked on." As he spoke, he pulled the prison ID card from his chinos and laid it on the desk. "I'd appreciate it if you could help me out," he added, nudging the card forward. Matthew wasn't a man who usually tried to skirt around the rules. But this was an exceptional circumstance, and he was willing to bend one a little now and again if it meant achieving a greater good.

The gray eyes of the desk officer slid downwards as a bead of sweat zigzagged from his temple. He swiped the perspiration away before lifting his face again. "We're on the same side, huh?" he asked, smiling. "Well, I suppose I could do you a favor this one time." Holding up his index finger, he reached for the phone and dialed only enough numbers for an extension. His forefinger stayed up, asking Matthew to wait, as he listened to the ringing on the other end of the line.

The seconds ticked by and the officer chewed the inside of his cheek. Finally, kissing his teeth, he gave up and put the phone down. "She's not answering," he muttered. "But, to be honest, she can be like that sometimes. Uh- you're welcome to stop by her office yourself, and maybe wait for her if she's not there." With a shake of his head and a shrug, he added. "I have no idea how long she'll be, but if you're not bothered-"

"I've got some spare time," Matthew replied with his trademark warmth.

"Alrighty," the officer said, getting to his feet. "Go through those doors. I'll buzz you in." Gesturing to the ones in the corner, he lifted his arm and the sweat soaking his shirt became obvious. "Take a left, follow the hall down to the elevators. You want the third floor, and hers is the fourth door on the right."

Confident he could remember that, Matthew nodded. "Thanks for your help."

Turning, he moved to the doors, not bothering to offer another friendly gesture to the two recently-arrested gentleman this time. He knew there were times when one had to accept it was unwelcome. And, on the few occasions, in years past, when he'd been as eager as young Jake to spread kindness wherever he went, he discovered it could be met with anger and unpleasantness. The lesson had been well learned. His offer was always there, his door was always open. But he knew when to leave well enough alone. And he knew, without doubt, the best results came when someone came to him of his or her own volition.

Humming a quiet tune, he strolled along the corridor and stepped onto the elevator. He found himself crammed into it with four uniformed officers, who were clearly excitable rookies enthusing about their lesson on the firing range.

Unlike the ground floor of the precinct, the third story was carpeted. A beige well-worn carpet, which he followed until he reached the door he was searching for. And once he had found it, he paused.

Matthew rubbed his fingertips across the nape of his neck and flicked his eyes up and down the corridor. A couple of cops in uniform passed him. A detective in jeans bumped into his shoulder as he paid more attention to his tablet computer than he did to where he was going.

"Sorry," the man muttered, only briefly looking up.

"No problem," Matthew replied, stepping closer to the door so he wasn't blocking so much of the path. He stared at the nameplate, but continued to hesitate. Meredith Maloney. He had no idea whether this was a waste of time, no idea whether she'd listen or want to help. After all, she was one of the arresting officers. She had testified during Gabriel's trial. She'd believed beyond reasonable doubt that Gabe was guilty. Would she be willing to have her mind changed?

Gabriel had thought not. From everything he'd said about her, she was a dogged- Well, Gabriel had used a word Matthew wouldn't. And he'd suggested Matthew go to anyone *but* her. Nevertheless, something told him that it was worth talking to Maloney. And he always listened to those 'somethings', because he was sure they were guidance from a higher force. So, why was he now experiencing a moment of doubt?

Before he had a chance to lift his hand and knock, the door flew open and the slender woman halted her hasty stride only just before she walked right into him.

"Oh," she said, slightly breathless. "Sorry, I was just-" Making a move to weave around him, she didn't bother to finish what she'd been saying.

"Meredith Maloney?" he asked, not budging out of her way.

"That's my name," she replied. "Don't wear it out or I'll make you buy me a new one." With a sardonic smile, she tried to edge around him again. But the tall, broad-shouldered man wouldn't move. "Can I do something for you?" she eventually asked, lifting her eyes to his.

"Uh- yes," he hedged with a quirk of his head. "Maybe."

She cocked her face at him, trying to remember whether she'd ever seen him before. She couldn't recall him, but she saw a lot of people and her memory wasn't always the best. Although, as she took in his handsome features and strong physique, she figured he was the kind of man she might well remember. As her thoughts drifted to dirtier places, she smiled.

"Well-" she murmured, kicking the door open wider and stepping back a pace. "What is it I can do you for?" Reminding herself to remain professional, but still flashing him a saucy smile, she swung her arm towards the office.

Matthew cleared his throat, and blinked at the woman's grin. He wasn't fresh off the farm, he knew flirting when he saw it. And he wasn't unfamiliar with it. But, he wasn't expecting it here... and not from her. Although, he had to admit, she wasn't unattractive.

"Umm..." He lingered another second before finally stepping across the threshold, which felt a little like a fly stepping into the spider's parlor. And he was aware of the irony of that. He was a big guy, he spent his life ministering to hardened criminals and didn't bat an eye around them. But this woman disquieted him somehow.

She weaved around the desk and sat in her chair. Nodding to the vacant one opposite, she made herself comfortable. "Why don't we start with your name?" she suggested.

Her office was neat, except for the mess on her desktop. There were some manila files in there somewhere, but mostly it was cluttered with a dismembered newspaper, a couple of empty Starbucks cups, and a takeout carton from a Chinese restaurant. Her laptop sat on top of the pile, and was open and on. She'd clearly been working, and he wondered how she managed to in all that chaos.

The rest of the small room was well kept, though. A few pictures hung on the walls, mostly landscape photography, but one was of a family of four. The mother bore a sharp resemblance to the detective with the messy work surface, and Matthew guessed she was a sister. Interestingly, there were no other family photographs, which led him to believe she didn't have one of her own. Although, he could imagine her job might make that more difficult than the average.

He moved forward and lowered himself into the vacant chair. Placing his hands on his thighs, he smiled bashfully. "My name's Matthew Keyes."

Maloney let the name float around her mind for a few seconds before she decided she'd never heard it before. "And what is it you need from me, Mr. Keyes?"

He inhaled, wondering if what he was about to do counted as a betrayal given Gabriel was so dead set against her being the one he asked for help. Perhaps it was. But he couldn't very well walk away anymore.

"I'm the chaplain at the Metropolitan Correctional Center."

Her smile lost its mischievousness and she sat straighter. "Man of the cloth, eh?" Bright eyes widening, she tried to dismiss all naughty thoughts of him. Yet, she found some of them lingered... and became all the more dirty for knowing he was more saint than sinner.

"Not sure I'd put it quite like that," he admitted with a tilt of his head. "But... Yes, I suppose so."

"Well, uh... Okay. So, what do I call you...Reverend?"

"Just Matthew is fine," he replied, offering her one of the smiles that always came easily to him. Now he'd noticed the slight discomfort that had stopped her flirting in its tracks, he wasn't feeling quite so anxious. At least, not about her lustful glances. The bigger issue was still looming. And he remained uncertain of how to handle it for the best.

"Okay, Matthew, what is it that you think I can help you with?" Leaning back, she tried not to let her gaze slide down to his crotch. It took more effort than she'd have imagined it would.

Taking a quick breath, he shuffled far enough forward so he could rest a hand on the very edge of her desk. The only part of it that was bare. "Do you remember a man named Gabriel Summers?"

Thoughts of the chaplain's crotch vanishing, Maloney straightened. "Guy who pounded a man's head in with a tire iron. Yeah, that's not the kind of case you don't forget."

"And you recall Gabriel maintained his innocence throughout?"

It was her turn to take a breath and sigh. "I know what he said. I also know about his history, and I know how he behaved when we arrested and how we questioned him. We're talking about a particularly violent man. A man who was placed at the scene with conclusive DNA evidence."

"But he said he'd never been there," Matthew added.

"Yeah, I remember." She shook her head and released a puff of bewildered laughter. "How he thought he was going to get away with it, I don't know. It's not as though he even had an explanation for how his DNA was found in the house. He just insisted there had to have been a mistake at the lab. But let me reassure you, Matthew, there was no error at the lab. I had that sample checked three times." Scooping her loose hair off her shoulders, she held it back in a loose pony tail at her neck.

Intrigued, Matthew regarded her carefully. "You did?"

"Yes."

"Why?"

She flicked one shoulder in a lazy shrug as she spoke again. "It seemed so strange that he'd stick to the story that he'd never been there when he knew we had the evidence right in front of us. To start with, I just had him pegged as a complete lunatic. But, it became clear he was lucid enough." Tracing an idle pattern on one of the sheets of newspaper on her desk, she added. "I just wanted to make sure we had everything totally on the up and up." Her shoulder repeated the gesture. "And we did."

Her words, and her thorough approach gave Matthew hope. He felt certain she'd listen to him and he was almost sure she'd take him seriously, too.

"So...?" she offered, waiting for the other shoe to drop.

"Gabriel still says he never saw that unfortunate man, Renaudin. And he still maintains that he never set foot in that house."

"I can quite imagine he does," she said with a subtle laugh. "But the evidence speaks for itself, my friend."

"Well..." Pausing, he shuffled forward in his chair. "There may be another explanation for how the DNA got there."

Maloney didn't want to laugh, but she couldn't help the chuckle that erupted as she looked at the chaplain. "Man of God turned man of investigation, huh?" she asked. "You don't look very much like Father Dowling, but go ahead!"

He offered her a self-deprecating and slightly lopsided smile as he nodded. "I haven't been investigating anything. It's not really my- area of expertise. That's why I'm here. I need your help with that part of it."

Lifting her feet, she crossed her ankles on the edge of the desk. "Well, you've certainly got my attention Mr. Keyes."

"Matthew," he reminded her.

"Okay, you've got my attention, *Matthew*."

He drew breath, knowing what he was about to say might sound hokey. "Gabriel recently told me that he has an identical twin."

Maloney made a grand effort to keep a straight face, but her lips betrayed her. "I'm sorry?"

"He has a twin."

"Forgive me for asking what may seem like a stupid question," she said, trying not to sound condescending, although she thought the chaplain was a sap for being suckered in by this hare-brained explanation. "Why wouldn't he have mentioned that beforehand? Why wouldn't he have mentioned it at the trial, or better still the first time we told him we had his DNA?"

"I admit, it seems strange," he conceded, no longer as bashful as when he thought she was checking him out. When you took all of the facts into account, it wasn't as dumb as she was making it sound. He wasn't embarrassed about suggesting it or about letting her know he believed it. So he met her eyes squarely as he continued. "Gabriel was adopted, and he's only just found out he has a brother."

Running her tongue along her top teeth, Maloney stared at his earnest face. There was a small part of her that admired him for being so firmly invested in his efforts to help someone he perceived to be in need of it. She could admire that quality in anyone. She'd never let her colleagues know that, of course, but she wasn't as tough as she liked to appear. However, she still saw a very naïve man in front of her, who was too full of the milk of human kindness to know when he was being fed a story.

"Matthew, I appreciate what you're trying to do here, but-"

"I know," he interrupted. "But Gabriel's birth mother recently made contact with him, and she told him the truth. You can speak to her if you want."

She listened, but continued without addressing his words directly. "I think Gabriel might have sent you on a wild goose chase."

"No." With a subtle shake of his head, he held her gaze. "I understand why it seems-"

As he paused in search of his next word, 'manure' resounded loud and clear in Maloney's head. She didn't offer it aloud, even though it practically screamed to be released from her mouth.

"Fanciful," he eventually landed on. "But I would not be wasting your time if I didn't think there was some truth to this."

Slowly inhaling, she dragged her feet off the desk and sat forward again. "Alright," she murmured. "For the sake of argument, I'll play along with this. We'll agree that there is a twin out there. This twin, who no-one knew about, just happened to be at Renaudin's the night he was killed? The word fanciful is stretching it, don't you think?"

"You don't have to buy it all," Matthew replied softly. "All you have to do is agree to look into it. If there is a twin brother- Well, it changes things, doesn't it?"

Her eyes sank to the laptop and she tried to calculate the odds against the story being true. However, this guy had a point. Proving it wrong, and putting the whole thing to bed once and for all, would just be a simple case of establishing whether the twin was a figment of Gabriel's imagination. If she could do that, then the chaplain on the other side of her desk would at least have learned a lesson: don't trust the weird and wonderful tales of his criminal flock.

"Okay," she sighed, looking at his face again as she shot to her feet. "Okay, why not? Let's find out whether this brother exists." Striding to the file cabinet in the corner of her office, she opened the second drawer down.

Curious, Matthew watched her. "Huh, I thought you'd keep all your files on computer nowadays."

"I like to keep my hard copies, too," she replied, distracted as she searched for the collection of papers she wanted. "Ah, here we are," she said, yanking them out. "There won't be much to help us in here," she admitted before slamming the drawer shut. Looking at him, rather than at what she was doing, she jammed her finger and snatched it free with a yelled, "Damn it!" Shaking her hand, she squinted at the chaplain. "Uh- sorry- I-"

"That's alright," he said, chuckling. "I hear a lot worse at work."

"Oh, yeah," she conceded, walking back to the desk and putting her file down. "I suppose you do." Throwing herself back into her chair, she continued to mutter about her sore hand. "As I was saying," she added, "there won't be much in here. I'll need the name of the mother and any other information you have."

"But you'll help?" he asked, smiling broadly.

"Yeah." Finding his grin both attractive and infectious, she couldn't help but smile back. "Yeah, I'll help." She didn't bother to remind him that he might not get the answer he wanted.

Perhaps that's because she didn't want to be the bitch. Mostly, though, she realized it was because she didn't want to see that grin of his fade.

Chapter Nineteen

Maloney lounged back in her couch. Pulling her laptop off the coffee table, she rested it across her thighs. With a sigh, she reached to her left and the open pizza box that sat next to her. One hand tapping on the keys, she stared at the screen while guiding a large and stringy slice of margarita to her mouth.

Her takeout dinner growing tepid, she chewed it distractedly as her pale eyes scanned the information in front of her.

The TV in the corner of the room was still on, but she hadn't been watching it for over two hours. Providing nothing in terms of entertainment, all it was doing was filling the room with a fluttering glow and the occasional bout of canned laughter from the old sitcom being shown. And she was almost completely oblivious to both.

It hadn't taken long for Matthew to tug her into his cause. She tried to tell herself that was purely professional and detective instinct, rather than an attraction to the man. For the most part, it was true. She was interested from the perspective of a police officer. On the other hand, though, she was interested from the perspective of a woman. Of course, it didn't do any harm that the handsome chaplain was also charming and had a sincere warmth to him that was magnetic. He was a man of goodness. And that was a rare thing to find.

She knew it was a passing fancy, though. He wasn't the kind of man who would ever be interested in a woman like her. The thought of them together was laughable. But the thought of them together in bed wasn't quite so funny to her. She wondered if the man of abundant goodness had a little bad in him.

But whatever the reasons, an interest in him and an interest in his cause had settled in her and taken root. Within minutes of searching, Maloney discovered that a baby had been left at St. Anthony's Maternity Unit. Although no longer identifying as Catholic, Maloney remembered what had been drummed into her as a child. And found irony in the fact Katherine and her boys had been at a hospital named after the patron saint of lost souls. He obviously couldn't find them. But then, he wouldn't. It was all bull as far as she was concerned, which is why she turned her back on the religion at seventeen years old.

From there, her search had told her that a young Katherine Roser had been picked up by a beat cop while she wandered the streets looking disorientated and distressed just two days later. She never told anyone what was wrong, at least, if she did, nothing got written in the brief report. But it seemed obvious to Maloney what had caused the girl's anxiety.

What had started out looking like a flight of fantasy by an insane and desperate criminal was beginning to look more credible. Maloney wasn't going to let herself be dragged into believing this amounted to Gabriel's innocence, though. All she'd established for certain was that a woman had twins and left the hospital with only one, abandoning the other. That may or may not prove that Gabriel had a brother, because that woman might not have been Katherine Roser and, similarly, there was no way to prove that the baby she left with was Gabriel Summers.

And even if it were proven that Gabriel had an identical twin brother, that didn't mean that twin had ever set foot in Renaudin's home. Summers could easily have found out about the situation surrounding his birth and adoption and simply jumped on it as a way to throw doubt on his conviction.

Maloney still had serious misgivings over the amount of doubt this whole thing offered, especially as it turned out the injured baby, who Katherine left behind, was adopted by a family who shortly afterward moved to New York. But her curiosity was certainly piqued.

Mason Heiland had been officially adopted at just three weeks old. The Heilands were considered to be a perfect couple, both in their mid-thirties at the time, they'd been able to have children of their own and were apparently ecstatic to take Mason. During the routine visits, a social worker had glowing praise for the way Mason was being welcomed into his new family. Everything, it seemed, was perfect. Then, Peter Heiland, was offered a job in New York, and the three of them shipped across to the east coast. From there, the Chicago records she had access to ceased.

But with no other relatives in The Windy City, the Heilands would have little cause to visit and Maloney couldn't think of any obvious reason that Mason would find his way back, as he was only two years old when his family left.

In other words, if he had been back in Chicago; if he had met Renaudin and been in the man's house and left a sample of his DNA behind, it was a massive coincidence. The problem was Maloney didn't really believe in coincidences, not the kinds with such long odds against them.

Her front doorbell ringing, she tossed a half-nibbled pizza crust back into the box and heaved herself up from the soft cushions. Putting the laptop on the coffee table, she strolled across the short distance to the door and pulled it open.

"Hey," he said. His usually pristine appearance was notably absent, the knot of his tie loose and askew and his jacket creased.

"What happened to you?" she wondered aloud.

Planting his hand on the doorjamb, he leaned his weight in that direction. "Tough day," he replied. "On top of a tough week... And I... Just..." He blinked and Maloney was sure she saw a glassy film over his dark brown eyes. "I'm sorry," he added, sniffing and straightening before clearing his throat. "I don't know what I'm doing here. It's late and you're probably..."

"Whoa," she replied, grabbing his arm as he took a step back. Firmly, Maloney tugged him toward her even though he tried to yank himself free of her grasp. Unwilling to let go or be shrugged off, Maloney persisted.

"What's wrong?" she asked.

"It's nothing," he insisted, taking another step back as she moved closer. Every time he tried to put space between them, she closed it. "I..." One hand bundled into a fist at his side, he struck the side of his thigh with it. "I'm sorry. Okay, I shouldn't..." Faltering, his voice cracked and his squeezed his eyes tight shut against the tears that had been coating them and were threatening to spill over.

Meredith Maloney didn't think. She didn't pause to consider the fact she was letting him see a side of her that she'd never shown him before. Perhaps that was because he was showing her a side of him that she'd never seen before. Letting go of his sleeve, she shuffled forward and wrapped her arms around him. He stiffened for a second, and she thought he was going to shove her away. However, gradually his limbs softened in her embrace. Slowly, his head sank to her shoulder. And then, after several minutes, his own arms wound their way around her body.

One of her hands moved soothingly up and down his spine. The other found its way to his neck and stroked the nape.

"It's alright, Cox," she murmured. "It's alright." She didn't know what else to say. She didn't even know whether what had got him so worked up was a professional or personal thing, let alone whether it was or could ever be alright. But then, that wasn't really what she was talking about. She was telling him it was alright for him to breakdown. It was alright for him to show a moment of weakness, which she didn't perceive as weakness anyway. It was alright if he didn't want to talk. It was alright if this big, strong man, who always had his act together, just needed someone to hold him. It was alright.

"It... It all went really wrong," he said, his voice hoarse and the words muffled as his breath came heavy against her neck.

"You don't have to..." she replied.

"The guy had a gun and I... It happened so fast... But it was... my fault." As his words came disjointedly, she could only guess at the meaning behind them, but a picture was beginning to build.

"It wasn't your fault." Maloney had no way of knowing whether that was true or not, but she couldn't imagine any scenario where something bad would have been his fault. He was a decent guy. Jensen Cox was a little arrogant, maybe even a jerk at times, he was a snob and a stickler for the rules, and a pain in her behind whenever they'd had to work together. But he was a decent man. He had decency in his DNA. She guessed he was sort of like that chaplain in many ways. There was no way he'd done something awful.

"I hesitated," he said, lifting his face from the comfort of her shoulder and looking her in the eyes. "A split-second. But that's all it took. That's all it took for that officer to get shot. And now she's lying in a hospital and I'm... I..."

Maloney refused to let him go completely, her hands still at his back and the nape of his neck, she continued to offer her comfort. "It wasn't your fault," she repeated. She didn't know if he was hearing her or really listening, but it was all she could say. It was all that mattered.

"You don't... It..."

"Come on," she urged, her hands clutching him tighter as she stepped back and coaxed him with her. "Come inside."

Reticent, Cox stood, his hands still at her waist. He realized he didn't want to leave. Didn't want to be alone. And yet, he couldn't quite accept her comfort, either. He was undeserving of it. And she was Maloney. She didn't do touchy-feely. He didn't either, of course, under normal circumstances. But seeing an almost maternal side to her made him... Well, it came really close to making him like her. Before, she'd had his respect. He didn't dislike her, but he couldn't call their relationship much of a friendship. Now, though, he saw a person of compassion and sensitivity, someone he could imagine himself more than liking.

"Maybe I should go," he murmured.

"Come on," she replied, noting that, despite his words, he still hadn't let go of her. "We can talk."

"I..." Shaking his head, he finally did unwind his arms from around her torso. "I'm not sure I wanna talk about it."

"We don't have to talk about that," she quickly insisted. "We'll talk about something else." She met his eyes and saw the reluctance in them. "You came here for a reason, didn't you?"

Mouth opening, Cox wavered, his lips moving while no speech emerged. Eventually, with a soft sigh, he admitted, "I don't know why I came here... I..." That was the truth. He hadn't been thinking. He hadn't known where to go or what to do. And somehow, he'd just wound up on her doorstep. He hadn't known what he was going to say when she opened her apartment to him. He hadn't known what he expected or even wanted from her. He'd just found himself there.

Letting her hands slide from his back, she stroked her way down his arms, his wrists and then gripped his hands. "Just come and sit for a while," she suggested. "We don't even have to talk at all if you don't want to." As her lips rose in a sympathetic smile, she gave his hands a quick squeeze.

Against his dejected emotions and against his better judgement, the right side of Cox's mouth drifted up in a half-smile and he let himself be pulled across the threshold. Grateful to her, and amazed that she hid so much compassion away, he didn't bother to mention the mess of the tiny apartment. He didn't grumble about the stack of papers on her coffee table or the unwatched TV, or the box of pizza she had to toss on the floor to make space for him to sit.

Instead, as he lowered himself onto the couch, he said, "Thank you."

"That's what partners are for," she sighed as she tossed herself down beside him.

As he leaned his head on the back of the cushions and directed his face to the ceiling, he replied, "We're not partners."

"Not right now," she agreed. "But we were- So, on some level, we always will be. Right?" That made sense to her. That was how it should work. Part of her wanted to tell him she'd missed being his partner, and missed him. But that was getting too sappy than she could bear, even given the situation.

Blinking, he kept his eyes toward the ceiling. "Yeah. Yeah, I guess so." The words, 'I missed you, Maloney' were on the tip of his tongue. But he didn't say them. He tried to remind himself that she was infuriating. Several things about her drove him nuts, her disorganized approach to everything high on that list. Yet, he had missed her. He'd missed her sense of humor and he'd missed her intelligence. He'd missed... Lots of things about her now that he came to think of it.

"Whatever happened," she quietly uttered, her own eyes drifting upwards. "It wasn't your fault."

"You... You can't know that."

"I do," she replied. "I do know it, because I know you."

Slowly, he twisted his face toward hers. The light from the television was flickering across her features, making it difficult to focus on them properly, but he could see her well enough to find the candor in her bright eyes.

"I've missed you, Maloney," he said, his voice quiet. Yet, in the dimness of that room and even above the noise from the ancient episode of Friends, it sounded deafening to his ears. He wasn't going to take it back, though. He couldn't, even if he tried. It was too late. She'd heard.

"Get out of town," she muttered, smiling as she flicked the back of her hand at his chest. Secretly, though, she wished she'd had the guts to say, 'likewise'.

For a while, neither of them said anything. Then, as the credits rolled on the television, Maloney reached for the remote and switched it off.

"You working?" Cox mumbled, nodding to her open laptop and the screen that had just gone to sleep.

"Uh... Yeah," she sighed. Glad to have a subject that might change the mood, and heartened by the fact he felt up to talking, she continued. "It's the damnedest thing. You remember the Renaudin case? And all that crap Summers kicked up about himself never being anywhere near the house and his DNA couldn't possibly have been recovered from the scene?" They were all rhetorical questions. She knew he remembered it just as well as she did. Probably better, because, as he once informed her, he had an eidetic memory.

He began to nod, but she was already continuing.

"Well, there may be some new evidence. I mean... I'll be the first to admit, it's sketchy right now, but it's worth looking into."

"What made you dig back into that?"

Smiling slightly, she shook her head. "You're not going to believe this, but the chaplain at the prison came to see me. And suggested I look into something."

"Look into what?"

Her lips grew crooked she made a doubtful noise and her face tilted. "I can't tell you yet, it sounds too crazy to me. So I know how you're going to react to it, Captain Sensible."

He chuckled under his breath, it was more than he could have imagined himself capable of in that moment. "I... I suppose I better go," he sighed.

"You can stay... if you want," she offered with a shrug. Later, she wouldn't be able to say where that offer came from, what exactly she was suggesting, and whether she wanted him to take her up on it or not.

***

The following morning, Maloney pulled her Ford Fusion to the curb just as Matthew was closing his front door. She tooted the horn to get his attention, and he glanced over his shoulder at her.

"Good morning!" she hollered, the passenger window whirring down as she leaned across the seat. "You going to service or something?"

"Uh... No," he replied, smiling a little nervously as he stepped toward the car and bent forward so he could look at her while they talked. "I was just heading into work to do some paperwork."

"You people have paperwork?"

His smile relaxing, he nodded. "Yep."

"Can you skip it and get in?" she asked with a flick of head that was inviting him to do just that.

"Well, do you mind if I ask why?"

"Got a little lead we can follow," she said, beaming at him. "I don't know where this twin brother is now, but I know where he was. We can ask around, maybe find out whether it's possible that, by some freak of serendipitous twist of fortune, he wound up back in Chicago."

"We?" he echoed. "You need me for that?"

She jerked her head again as her smile widened. "I don't know yet. There might be things you know that can help.

But two heads are always better than one, right? And I can't get any of my colleagues to help me with this... So, I guess, it's you and me."

Matthew straightened and slid his hands into his pockets as he glanced up and down the road, considering Meredith Maloney's suggestion. He was grateful she was helping and he was pleased she was taking it all so seriously. But, could he start getting involved in the investigation? Should he?

Pulling his hands from his pants, he tossed them up before popping the car door open and slipping in. "I really don't know how much help I can be, though," he warned her as he pulled on the seatbelt.

"I don't know that yet, either," she replied. "I guess we'll find out."

"Hmm," he said, wincing as she pulled out in front of a Jeep Cherokee. "So... uh... Where are we going?" he asked, hoping it wasn't too far.

"New York."

"Wh... What?"

"New York," she repeated, tossing him a sidelong glance. "Why? You've got something pressing in that paperwork?" Somehow she doubted it. And she still couldn't imagine what a chaplain would have to fill out paperwork about.

"Well... I... No, but... If we're going to drive, it'll take all day."

She chuckled quietly, as she barely checked her rearview and then changed lanes. "We're heading to the airport. I can have you back for prayers this afternoon… Or whatever it is you do with a gang of convicted criminals."

Not sure whether to take her little jibe seriously or not, Matthew leaned back, but found his fingers clinging to the seat for dear life. "It's… Prayer helps," he eventually said. "Prayer can help all kinds of people. And, don't forget, you catch them and lock them up for a reason."

"I catch them, so the rest of us are safe."

"Most of them won't spend their entire lives behind those bars," he reasoned. "You want to still be safe when they come out, then they have to be rehabilitated. And the only way to do that, Ms Maloney, is to treat them like human beings."

"It's Detective Maloney," she reminded him, although the way he'd said her name wasn't in the least bit condescending. "But you can call me Meredith."

His hands not loosening as the car came to an abrupt stop at a set of lights, Matthew turned his face to her. "We have to find a way to make them believe they have a life out of those walls that can be better than the life they went in with. Otherwise, they go right back where they started or maybe worse. And you just have to catch them all over again."

"And you think God is the way to reform all sinners, huh?" she asked with a small smile.

"Not all sinners, no," he replied calmly. "But I think many can be. And I don't think anybody is reformed by being treated as though they're never going to be fit for normal society again."

Maloney silently nodded. She had to admit he had a point there. She wouldn't consider herself a bleeding heart, but she did know the prison system simply didn't work. Repeat offenses were rife. Jails weren't a deterrent and they weren't reforming many of the men and women who were sent to them. Perhaps there was something to be said for the influence of men like Matthew, and the influence of the spirituality he brought with him.

"Sorry if I seemed a little rude," she eventually said. "I didn't mean…"

"That's okay."

"I guess I'm a bit edgy, because I didn't get a lot of sleep."

Knuckles turning white as the woman beside him put a heavy foot on the gas, he worried even more for his life knowing this reckless driver was also sleep-deprived. "Sorry to hear that," he said. "It's a hazard of the job, I suppose. It must be stressful."

"Ah, well, yeah. But this wasn't really… Well, it was I suppose. Hey, you're a man, if a guy…" She stopped herself quickly with a self-effacing laugh. "No, that's stupid," she muttered. She couldn't ask him about what had happened the night before. She didn't really know if she could talk to anyone, much less him.

"You can discuss it if you'd like to," he offered. "We've got a two-hour journey ahead of us."

"No," she replied, smiling. "No, it's fine. I shouldn't have brought it up."

"Well…" he said, forcing his left hand from its vise-like grip of the passenger seat to rest a reassuring hand on her knee. "If you change your mind…."

"Thanks." She was certain she wouldn't, though. It didn't matter if the night kept plaguing her like it was right now, she wouldn't resort to asking him about it. It was private. It was personal. It was possibly embarrassing. And it didn't have to make sense. Men didn't make sense. She'd learned that the hard way over the years.

"It's fine," she added. "Nothing important." Both of those statements were lies.

Chapter Twenty

Matthew paused at the steps of the townhouse, while his companion trotted up the stoop, taking a couple of steps at a time. The street was a quiet little piece of suburbia lined with trees. It wasn't exactly upmarket, but the people living here were obviously comfortably wealthy. Gabriel's twin, Mason, had grown up in a nice, upper-middle class neighbourhood. He was probably a professional. And Maloney had mentioned, during the cab ride from the airport, that he seemed to have struck lucky with the family who adopted him. So why would he turn into the kind of guy with a grudge against a man he'd never met? Or the kind of man who could take a life?

Matthew was quick to remind himself, though, that just because Mason might have been in the dead man's house didn't mean he was responsible for the killing.

As she reached the door and knocked like a cop before she managed to school the habit, Maloney glanced over her shoulder at the chaplain still on the sidewalk. "Second thoughts?" she asked.

"No," he responded, lifting his eyes to her and silently acknowledging he didn't really know where his thoughts had been taking him. They were largely purposeless, he supposed. "Just... strange to think of these two boys growing up and not knowing anything about each other."

"Yeah." She nodded and parted her lips to say something else, but the door swung open and stopped her intake of breath. Turning to the sixty-something woman with dark gray hair and pale blue eyes, Detective Maloney smiled.

"Hi," she said. "I'm sorry to disturb you. I'm looking for Mr. and Mrs. Heiland."

The slightly plump older woman clung to the door and squinted. "Do I know you?"

"No, ma'am," Maloney replied, reaching into her inside jacket pocket for her badge. "I'm Meredith Maloney, I'm with the Chicago PD."

"Chicago?" Mrs. Heiland's squint strengthened, and she shook a tanned face that looked like she may have recently returned from vacation. "What... What do you want?"

"It's nothing to worry about, ma'am," Maloney assured her quickly. "I just need to ask you a couple of questions about your son, Mason."

Mrs. Heiland wasn't reassured. Her gaze moved over the detective with even more suspicion. "Nothing to worry about, you say. But, you came all this way?"

Maloney's smile was warm and genuine. She had no desire to panic the woman, not only because that wouldn't get her the answers she wanted, but also because there was no need for anyone to panic. Chances were, this would all turn out okay. Mason had probably never been back to Chicago in his adult life, and Gabriel's claims could easily be put to bed.

"It's really no big deal," she insisted. "I'm investigating a case back home. It's nothing whatsoever to do with your family, Mrs. Heiland. But there's a loose end, and, I'm sorry to tell you, I'm one of those cops that hates a loose end."

Mrs. Heiland nibbled the inside of her cheek and continued to look unconvinced. "All this way... just for a loose end?"

Maloney shrugged before sliding her hands into her pockets. "I really hate them," she replied, chuckling.

The older woman's exacting blue eyes moved over Maloney's shoulder and landed on the man lingering at the bottom of her stoop. Matthew offered her a genial smile, but she frowned at him in response.

"It's okay," Maloney said, "he's with me."

That did nothing to ease the lines in Mrs. Heiland's forehead. The longer the woman talked, the more nervous she was getting. What did she want? What had Mason been up to? Had he gone back to Chicago? And if he had been back there, what for?

Maloney considered telling the five-five woman in front of her that Matthew was just a chaplain rather than another cop, but she could tell by the look on her face that it'd prompt more questions and concern. However, she didn't want her to think she'd got two police officers on her doorstep. Well, she was the one on the doorstep. Matthew was close to it.

"He's just a friend," she explained instead. "I'm not here on official business, I just... Well, like I said, just my own curiosity."

Mrs. Heiland shifted her head in a quasi-nod, and released her tight hold of the door. "Okay," she sighed. "What do you want to know?"

"Do you happen to know if Mason has been in Chicago recently?"

Matthew looked on and considered stepping closer, he had, after all, been introduced. Although, the woman had made it fairly clear she wasn't exactly in the mood to welcome guests.

"I haven't seen Mason in several years," she muttered. "I don't know what he's doing or where he is, so..." As her voice crept up with each word, she sensed herself nearing an edge. And stopped. She wasn't going to break down over him again. She definitely wasn't going to break down in front of two perfect strangers. Willing her stiff upper lip in place, she exhaled and stood a little taller. "I'm afraid I couldn't begin to tell you where he is."

"I see," Maloney replied. She'd noticed every tiny flicker of emotion the woman in front of her had tried to hide. She noticed, and she said nothing. She had no desire to embarrass her or probe into things that were clearly painful. The fact the subject of her son was painful was interesting, though. And part of her desperately wanted to know why.

"Well... Could you possibly tell us where he was when you last were in touch with him?"

Pausing for a moment, Mrs. Heiland tried to decide how much she was willing to say, and balance that with how much would satisfy the persistent detective. "I... The last time I saw him was just after his wife left him."

"And when was that?"

"Almost a year ago."

"Where is she now? Do you know?"

"No. We didn't keep in touch." Her words becoming more clipped, and it was no surprise when she grabbed hold of the door and started to push it shut. "Now, if you'll excuse me."

"Mrs. Heiland," Maloney said. "I'm not here to cause any trouble to you, I promise. I just like to..."

"And I like to be left alone," the woman blurted, shoving the door closed with a bang that rattled the lintel.

With a sigh, Maloney stuffed her hands a little deeper into her pockets. For a moment, she just stared at the closed door, wondering how she'd lost control of the conversation so quickly. Then, turning on her heel, she wandered down the steps much more slowly than she'd galloped up them. With a chin near her chest, she studied the ground as she came to a stop beside Matthew.

"Well, that went well," she grumbled.

"So... What now?" he asked, watching her as she thoughtfully studied the sidewalk between her feet.

Her face darting back up, she replied, "We need to find this ex-wife."

"How?"

One hand darting to the back pocket of her jeans, Maloney reached for her phone. "I might know someone who can help us."

***

Fingers tapping restless on his thigh, Gabriel watched the closed door. He wasn't sure if he was trying to will it to open. He might have just been willing the time he'd spent staring at it to pass. Whichever, it wasn't working.

How long? That was the question that kept circling his head. How long? They now knew there was another way his DNA could have wound up at that house, so why was he still sitting in a jail cell? How long was it going to take before he was free? He'd dared to let himself imagine what it would be like. He'd dreamed of it. He'd tasted it. That was his mistake. Because now he'd let hope into his life, the existence he was living wasn't enough. The time things were taking to change was driving him insane.

Finally, with the familiar knock, the locks began to twist. Gabe jumped off the bed and strode the two paces to the opening door.

"Well?" he said.

Jake offered him a smile and a, "good morning to you, too." Chuckling he stepped aside and made room for Matthew.

"Well?" Gabe repeated.

Matthew held up his empty palm. The other hand held loosely to a bible, which rested near his hip. "I'll explain. I'll explain."

"Explain what? I should be out of here by now, shouldn't I? We know there's someone else out there with my

DNA. So that's not conclusive proof of anything anymore, right?" He didn't stop long enough for the chaplain to answer, but it was rhetorical anyway. "So, why am I still rotting away here?"

With a quiet sigh, Matthew made his way to Gabe's tiny desk and lowered himself until his backside was rested on the back of the chair. "It's going to take some time. These things don't work quickly. And, before we can do anything, we need to find your brother."

"And?"

"And I spent the day in New York with Detective Maloney yesterday." When the news was met with an unwieldy roll of Gabe's eyebrows, Matthew chuckled. "She's not that bad. And, keep in mind, she's the one who's helping. She believes Mason might be your brother and she's determined to find him."

Scuffing his feet along the shiny floor, Gabriel moved back to his bed, but felt too fidgety to sit. "So why hasn't she found him yet?"

"She's working on it," he said gently. "We've found out that he was married, and that his wife left him because he was violently jealous. Now, we can't trace her because she's been moved and given a new name to protect her from him... The good news is Mason should have been kept tabs on because of his aggressive history."

"Aggressive history... You mean... He could have...?"

"We just don't know, Gabe," Matthew replied, careful not to let him jump to any conclusions, although he'd connected the dots during the flight home, too. He was pretty sure Maloney had as well, but she wouldn't say as much out loud. He could tell that she had something weighing on her mind during that short plane journey. Some of it obviously wasn't to do with the case.

"Anyway," he added, "the bad news is that he's slipped off the radar in New York."

"What? How the heck did that happen?"

"Resources are stretched, budgets are tight." Matthew shrugged. "You know how the system works, Gabe. It's imperfect, and when he stopped showing up for his counselling sessions, nobody tried very hard to trace him. So..."

"He could be in Chicago," Gabe supplied. "He could have been here this whole time. He could have been in Renaudin's house... and he could have killed him."

Matthew's chest expanded slowly, as he took and then released a deep breath. It was a possibility. He couldn't deny that. But... "Mason Heiland's been living in New York almost his whole life, Renaudin's never lived in NYC, so the chances of them knowing each other are slim. And what would Mason's motive have been? Murders committed by someone who's a complete stranger to the victim are uncommon." As Maloney had reminded him twice during their flight home.

His shuffling feet coming to an abrupt stop, Gabriel spun sharply toward Matthew. "I didn't know Renaudin, either. I had no motive. But everyone's ready to believe it was me!"

"Okay," Matthew quickly said, lifting his open palm and the book he held in his other. "Okay. I'm on your side, remember? And, I think, with a little help, this could all work out."

"Help from Maloney?" he scoffed. "Yeah, I'm sure she's really eager to get to the truth."

"She is helping," Matthew replied. "And I'm certain she does want the truth just as much as we do. She's a little brash, but she's in the job because she believes in justice. She's told me she will get to the bottom of all this, and I believe her." Pausing, he smiled softly. "But she wasn't who I was talking about when I mentioned help."

Some of the tension left Gabe's jaw, but he still stared hard at the man in front of him. "Do you really think He wants to help me?" There was a thick layer of bravado to a question that he wanted to sound rhetorical. Yet, Matthew heard something beneath it. Something scared and almost pleading. As though he were a small boy, desperate for someone to help him, but too ashamed to admit it.

Silently, the tall man pushed himself off the desk chair and took a step closer. His free hand reached for Gabriel's shoulder and gripped it lightly.

"Have you been reading the scriptures?" he asked, his deep voice barely more than a whisper.

It wasn't altogether willingly that Gabe's eyes moved toward the bed and the leather-bound bible that Matthew had gifted him months ago. At first, he resisted it. He'd read bits and pieces. But it had mostly stayed on his desk or on the floor beneath his tiny cot. Gradually, though, he'd become more interested. Eventually, he'd found some comfort and distraction in reading it at night. It helped him sleep. And then, he'd begun to deem it worthy of more of his time and attention. The answer was, yes, he'd been reading the bible. He'd read more of it than at any other time in his life, and he'd found himself wanting to read it. Unlike when he was coerced into doing so as a child, he saw deeper meanings in the stories. He appreciated the messages, and the sacrifices, and the lessons within it.

It hadn't helped him to find his way to Jesus, as Matthew had hoped though. The more he read, the less worthy of grace he felt. And the idea that God and His son, Jesus Christ, might help him seemed too much to hope for.

"He won't help me," Gabe murmured, his gaze slowly returning to the dark brown eyes of the chaplain. "Will he? I don't deserve it." His focus reminded on Matthew, but he began to frown as the man in front of him adopted a small half smile.

Squeezing Gabriel's shoulder, Matthew urged him toward the bed and encouraged him to sit. Slowly, he lowered himself onto the stretch of mattress next to him. In silence, he placed his bible between both hands and closed his eyes. His lips moved almost imperceptibility. His breath was soft and quiet, words he whispered under it were impossible to hear.

Eventually, he opened his eyes and offered the man next to him an even broader smile. "Gabe," he began. "Do you feel ready to welcome Christ into your heart and your life?"

His fingers grasping each other, Gabe rested his elbows on his thighs and hunched forwards. Fixated on the wringing of his own hands, he didn't know where else to look. "I... I don't know. I haven't exactly lived a virtuous life. I mean... I never killed anyone, but I did awful things. I... I'm nothing like Him."

"Can I ask you something?"

Gabe snorted softly as he thought of all the things Matthew had been asking him since they'd met. All of their conversations had been questions. To ask permission now seemed like shutting the barn door after the horse had bolted.

"Go ahead," he murmured with a shrug.

"Do you recognize yourself as flawed?"

His fingers clenching, Gabriel tossed his eyes to the ceiling and laughed bitterly at himself. "Flawed? Yeah. Yeah, I'd say flawed doesn't begin to cover it. I've been a jerk to my wife, a lousy father... A thug and a bully, and..."

"You're not perfect, Gabe."

"No," Gabriel replied. Dejected, he twisted his face to the man next to him. "I'm far from perfect. So, why would Christ want to help me, huh?"

"Because none of us are perfect," Matthew replied smoothly. "We're all flawed. We've all done things we regret. Things that have hurt others and things that were weak. No person to ever walk the face of this planet has been perfect. Except one..."

Holding the chaplain's gaze, Gabriel began to nod. "Jesus of Nazareth."

"He was perfect." Matthew smiled softly as he mirrored Gabe's nod. "He was the one perfect being to ever exist, and he died for us. All of us."

Unable to share in the chaplain's smile, Gabriel shook his head. "Why? Why would He die for someone like me? Someone like... the people here who've done horrific things?"

"So that we could all have a chance at redemption," Matthew explained. "So we could all have the chance to spend eternity with God."

"What if we don't deserve it?" Gabriel muttered.

"He believed we all do deserve it. That's why he was perfect."

Gabriel tried to swallow, but couldn't. He tried to open his mouth, but it wouldn't. As he blinked, he felt the moisture welling in his lower lids and tried to remember the last time he'd cried. Not when any of his kids were born. Not when his grandparents died. Not since he was a child himself. Sniffing back the weakness he didn't want to show, he violently shook his head.

"I don't deserve it."

"It doesn't matter whether you think you do or not," Matthew responded warmly. He could see the glassy sheen on Gabriel's brown eyes and, unlike the man they belonged to, he didn't see those tears as a sign of weakness. They were a sign of something positive. They were a sign that, whether Gabe wanted it to or not, something had touched his heart and begun to move him closer to God.

Reaching across the space, Matthew clapped Gabriel on the back. "You've read, Gabe. You know Jesus doesn't care what you've done. He doesn't even care whether you recognize the wrongs you've committed. He wants you to have a path to God. And, thanks to him, you do."

"But... I..." Faltering, he struggled to comprehend the sacrifice that had been made for him; the suffering that Christ had endured so that he might have a shot at heaven; an eternity in the grace of God. A state of grace he'd done little if anything to deserve.

"Whether you ask for forgiveness or not, Jesus forgives you," Matthew said, rubbing his hand along Gabriel's shoulders and feeling them tremble. "It's part of what it means to be Christian, Gabe," he added. "To forgive even if the person who has sinned feels no remorse."

His breath coming in slight shudders, Gabriel wasn't sure whether he wanted the chaplain's comfort or not. Part of him did. But there was still the old part, the Gabriel who was determined to prove that he was tough and didn't need comfort from anyone.

Pushing himself forward, he found he didn't have the strength to get to his feet. Instead, he fell to his knees. Hitting the cold tiles of the cell floor, he took a deep breath that shivered all the way into his lungs. And then, gradually, silent tears began to slip down his cheeks.

"I... I don't..."

Matthew got off the mattress and knelt beside the man he'd come to care about more than was strictly professional. It was a hazard of the job, of course. But, somehow, Gabriel was different.

"Let it out," Matthew urged. "And let Christ in."

"I want to... I..."

"Then, just let Him," Matthew replied with a smile. "It's as simple as that, Gabe. Christ is waiting. Open your heart to him. Open your heart to hope, and not just for an eternity with God, but for a better life in the here and now. There is always hope. Even in our darkest moments, there's hope. Sometimes that's all we have. It's a precious thing, Gabriel. Whatever you do, don't let go."

Tears slipped down his face, but Gabriel began to smile. "I want that. I want to hope... And I want a better life."

"Open your heart to it, Gabe." Matthew's smile warmed and his hand rubbed the space between Gabriel's shoulder blades.

"I've..." Pausing to sniff, the tears continued to roll, but he forged ahead with a voice that cracked. "I don't like the man I was... I... I want to make up for it... I... I need to apologise to my wife and I want to make things up to my kids."

"You can do all of those things."

"From here?" Gabe muttered, with a doleful shake of his head.

"Keep hoping," Matthew replied. "Hope that you'll get to make it up to them in person. But, trying to make it up to them from here wouldn't be a bad start, huh?"

The skin of his face sticky with salty tear drops, Gabe brushed the back of his hand across his chin and then his cheeks. "Yeah," he whispered. "Yeah, I need to write to them."

Remaining on his knees, Matthew's hand stayed on Gabriel's back. "Let's say a prayer together first." Lips lifted in a broad grin, he tipped his face to the ground and waited as the man next to him did the same.

Chapter Twenty One

Rubbing her sore eyes, Maloney slumped back into her creaking desk chair and sighed. When the still silence of her office was disturbed by a knock on the open doorframe, she muttered a, "yep."

"Still here?" Cox asked, strolling across the threshold. "Thought you wrapped up that suicide four hours ago?" With a slight smile, he made his way towards her desk, and sat himself on the corner of it with a familiarity that came easily to him. They hadn't talked since that night at her apartment. He'd wanted to talk to her, but she seemed to be avoiding him. Politely. But, it was nevertheless avoidance. He knew her well enough to know that. What he couldn't decide was the why. Did she regret it? Did she look at him differently? Was it something she wanted to now forget?

If she was entirely honest with himself, he didn't know quite what had happened between them, either. He didn't know whether it had changed things. No, that wasn't true. He did know. And it had. For one thing, it changed the way he saw her.

"Hmm," she replied, the heel of her hand rolling circles over her closed left eyelid. "I did, but I can't shake this Summers thing."

Smiling at her, he realized he found that relentless streak in her attractive. He always had, he'd just failed to really acknowledge it before. On this occasion, though, the relentless streak was fruitless, he was convinced of that.

"The Summers thing is over," he said, with a subtle shake of his head. "You know we got the right man."

"Maybe not," she mumbled, still looking at the computer screen. "What if we got it wrong? What if we jumped to an admittedly plausible conclusion, and ignored the things that didn't add up?"

Leaning back, Cox rested his hand on the far edge of the desk. His weight tilting to the left slightly, his head mirrored the action as he peered at his... What was she now? He didn't even know that. More than a colleague. A friend? More than a friend?

Maloney recognized the look he gave her as he studied her. "It's not crazy, Cox," she insisted.

"I didn't say it was," he tossed back with the hint of a laugh. "I just think you're wasting your time."

Picking up a pen that rested on the edge of her laptop keyboard, Maloney shook her head. "Everything's always black and white to you, isn't it?" she asked, shaking the pen at him. "It's all neat. You can just ignore the unexplained stuff, can't you?"

"What's unexplained?" he retorted. "The guy's DNA was in the house. And he's got a history of violence. It doesn't get much more open-and-shut than that, Maloney. And you thought so, too." As she continued to waggle the pen at him, he snatched it from her. "Stop that."

She tried to take the pen back, but he lifted it out of her grasp. Slouching back in the chair, she folded her arms. As he began to smile at her, her lips lifted too.

"Can we talk?" he said, turning serious.

"I think you'll find we are," she replied with her grin growing crooked.

"You know what I mean. Can we talk about what happened the other night?"

She had known what he meant, but she was hoping to skirt it again. "Look, Jensen..." she sighed.

"Do you realize that's the first time you've called me that?"

"What?"

"You've always just called me Cox," he said, squinting at her as he tried to figure out where the use of his first name had come from.

"I... I..." Frowning, Maloney sought an explanation, but couldn't find one. She hadn't even realized she'd said his name, and couldn't begin to explain why. "That's not the point," she blurted, giving up the search for reason. "I don't think that..."

"You don't have to do this, Meri," he interrupted.

"Do what?" she replied, trying to ignore the cuteness he'd given her name for the very first time.

"Pretend to be tough, pretend that it didn't mean something." The cold hard truth was he simply wasn't sure whether it had meant something to her. At least, not until she'd said his name. Then, he'd seen the slight blush that filled her cheeks and the confusion on her brow. It was as though she wasn't even sure of what she was feeling. It was as though she was experiencing something new, which she didn't quite know how to define or how to deal with.

"It was... Well, you needed comfort and I... I'm not saying it was a bad idea," she fumbled, keeping her eyes just away from his, because they were making her more nervous. "But it wasn't... I mean, let's not pretend that you and I could..." Lifting her right hand, she rolled it in a vague motion, unwilling or unable to finish the sentence in her head.

Cox understood her well enough, though. Sombre and focused, he had no similar problems meeting her face squarely. "Why couldn't we?"

"Because it's... You and me?!"

"That makes a guy feel special," he muttered good-naturedly. "Yeah, you and me. I don't think it's so crazy. And I don't think you do, either. I think what's spooked you is that... Is that 'you and me' was good." Leaning forward, he brushed a strand of hair away from her face. "It was better than good," he whispered.

It had been good. At least, for her it had been good. She didn't know whether he'd have said the same - until that moment. Mouth suddenly dry, she ran her tongue across her lips. Her heart had started pounding loudly as soon as he'd put his face closer to hers, and all she could think about was his kiss. She'd thought about it several times since that night. She'd even found herself dreaming about it. She told herself it was foolish, and chastised the almost adolescent nature of her fixation. He was just a guy, after all. A guy she'd known for a long time. And she wasn't some sappy teenager with a crush on the quarterback.

"Meri," he added, managing to make her name sound like a gentle caress.

Forcing herself to swallow, Maloney slowly leaned back, removing herself from temptation and a confusion so profound, she didn't know which way was up. Clearing her throat, she turned to the computer screen.

"The thing is, Summers seems to have a twin."

Beside her, Cox's fingers lingered where her face had been. For a second, he struggled to adjust to the sudden change in atmosphere. Gradually, as his hand lowered to his leg, he muttered, "What?"

"Gabriel Summers has a twin brother, we think. Identical. So... Technically speaking, there is another way that sample of DNA could have found its way into Renaudin's house."

"You're really not going to- Wait a minute," he added, his concern in the conversation they needed to have waning slightly as he considered what she'd said. "If he has a twin, why didn't he...?"

"Say anything?" she offered before he had a chance to. "I've been through all this with Matthew. They were adopted separately at a few days old. It's only just come to light."

"Convenient," Cox mumbled. "And who's Matthew?"

Maloney gave a flippant shrug as she replied, "Prison chaplain." And when she received raised eyebrows in reply, she added, "It's a long story, and it's not important. What is important is this twin, Mason, has also got a propensity for violence."

"That doesn't mean..."

"I know it doesn't, but it casts some doubt, doesn't it? It means we could have been wrong. And I can't leave it alone until I know for sure."

For a second, Cox was still and deathly silent. Only his eyes moving, he searched her face and then glanced at her computer screen. "You could be on a fool's errand," he said, meeting her eyes again. "You have any idea how far-fetched this all sounds?"

"Yes, and yes," she replied with a huff. "Why do you think I wasn't tripping over myself to tell you about it?" Reaching for her pen, which rested loosely in the hand that hung at his side, she grasped it back.

"But so far, it checks out," she added, tapping the end of the pen on the corner of her computer screen. "I believe there is a brother. I know he was in New York, and none of his family seem to know where he is now. He has an ex-wife who's had to hide from him... And I have to find him."

"How are you going to do that?" he wondered.

"Find the wife," she replied. It was the only thing she could think of. It was the only real lead she had. She'd checked Mason Heiland's place of work, he'd quit two years ago; just before the murder. And he hadn't been seen since. He had no friends that could be tracked. The abused wife, who probably never wanted to hear her ex-husband's name again, was the only person who might be able to help. And even that was a long shot.

Cox rubbed the pad of his thumb across his lower lip. "Are you serious about this?"

"Yeah," she responded calmly. "Very."

His mouth quirking thoughtfully, he glanced at the floor. To him, it seemed ridiculous. The chances of anyone else being responsible for Renaudin's brutal death were negligible as far as he was concerned. She was wasting her time. Yet, her determination was admirable. He knew he'd never be able to stifle it, but, more importantly, he didn't want to. It was part of what made her 'her'. And he was beginning to realize just how much he liked 'her'.

"I might be able to help," he eventually said.

Lifting her face and her eyebrows, she stopped her restless tapping. "What do you mean?"

"I know someone who might be able to find out who this ex-wife is and where we could find her."

"You're going to help me?" Maloney replied sceptically.

"Yeah," he muttered.

"But you think it's a fool's errand?"

"Yeah," he repeated. "But if it'll make you realize that you're being given the run-around, I'll do it."

She snorted and shook her head. "Thanks," she grumbled.

"Then, maybe, once we have put this whole thing to rest once and for all..." he said, as he reached into his inside jacket pocket for his phone. "We can talk about us."

"Bribery?" she quipped.

"No," he responded coolly. "Just clearing your head of distractions." With a soft smile, he lifted the phone to his ear.

She watched him as he grinned at her. Something about being under that gaze felt very comfortable. Yet, at the same time, it managed to make her very uncomfortable. He saw her; saw something in her that no one else seemed to notice. That was mildly frightening. It was also exhilarating, and it was... nice. Because although she would deny it with every breath in her body, part of her wanted someone to really know her.

"Okay," she replied quietly. She wasn't sure if he even heard, because as she parted her lips, he was already busy saying 'hello' to whoever was on the other end of the phone.

***

Gabriel Summers sat at his desk. A letter lay on the small space between his elbows. His fingers loosely laced together, he closed his eyes as his head drifted down and rested on his clasped hands. He prayed that the letter expressed what he wanted to say. He prayed that Jennifer would read it, and recognize the sincerity in it. He prayed that, somehow, they could repair some of the damage done to their marriage.

He wanted to reach out to his children, too. But they were still too young to really understand, even if he could get letters to them. And there was a larger problem, he didn't even know where to find them. Jen had moved away, and he at least knew she'd wanted to be closer to her family. But she hadn't bothered to give him her new address. That left him with few options. In fact, the only one he could think of was sending the mail to his mother-in-law's address. His ex-mother-in-law. He needed to keep reminding himself that he and Jennifer were no longer married.

He hated that. At the time, when she'd asked for a divorce, he was too filled with bitterness, anger and a hatred for the whole world to really appreciate what a blow it was to him. His marriage was over. The woman he'd promised to love for the rest of his life had left him. And he couldn't blame her. She deserved better, but that didn't make the reality easier to accept.

She and the kids had meant everything to him. He'd just been too stupid and myopic to see it. And now he'd lost them, he didn't know what that meant for him. Who was he? What was he? If he wasn't a husband and father, what else really mattered?

Faith.

Faith was all that mattered. It was all that could matter, and it was the thing he had to cling to in order to sustain him. He would do everything in his power to seek the forgiveness of the woman he loved. He'd get out of that jail cell and prove to her that they could be a family again. In the meantime, he would be the better man he felt she deserved, whether she ever wanted him back or not. That was what mattered. He needed to be the best person he could be; not just for her or for his children, but because he needed to make amends for the man he'd been.

With Jesus' strength to lean on, he would turn things around. He couldn't say for sure how it would end, or whether he'd even taste freedom again. But, no matter what happened to him, he would strive to be a person he was proud to be, rather than the man he was ashamed had been him.

A knock disturbed his silent prayer and he lifted his face to the familiar sight of Jake wandering into his cell. He smiled a little bashfully as he lowered his hands. He knew Matthew must have told him about the 'breakthrough', but it was still the first time Jake had found him in quiet reverence. He shouldn't have been embarrassed by it, but he was acutely aware of the marked change from the man who currently sat before the young guard and the man that young guard had first encountered.

"Hi," Jake said, feeling no such discomfort as he grinned. "It's your yard time."

"Oh..." Glancing to the window, Gabe realized he'd lost track of the time. "Thanks."

"How are you doing?"

Folding the sheet of paper neatly, he ran his palm over the smooth sheet before pushing himself to his feet. "Yeah... I'm okay." Pausing, he rubbed his hands over the back of his jumpsuit pants. "Listen, I'm... I'm really sorry for the way I've sometimes spoken to you. I didn't..."

Jake shrugged. "It's no problem."

"It is," Gabe insisted. "I shouldn't have been such a jerk to you, especially when you were only trying to help me. I... I am truly sorry."

Graciously, Jake tipped his head a fraction. "Apology accepted," he said, his smile growing warmer. "And, you know? I'm still here for you if you need me."

Gabriel opened his mouth to tell him that there was nothing more he needed, but stalled. There was something. The question was: could he ask for it? Should he ask for it? "Uh..." He hesitated another few seconds, wondering if he could get Jake in trouble for what he was about to ask. "I don't suppose there's any way you could help me find an address for someone...?"

Casually, Jake glanced behind him at the still open cell door. No one was moving in either direction along the corridor outside. "Mind if I ask why?" he said, resisting his impulse to immediately agree. He was almost certain Gabriel wouldn't do anything bad with the information he was after. But, he had to be a little cautious.

"I've written my wife..." Eyes dropping, he shook his head. "My ex-wife," he amended. "But I've no idea where she is now. Back in her home town maybe, but..." When he noticed Jake was looking at him with a curious expression, it crossed his mind that the guard was thinking about the things the 'old Gabriel' might do with his wife's address. "I need to tell her how sorry I am," he said quietly, gesturing to the letter he'd so tenderly folded and left on the desk. "I need her to know that I'm... I'm more sorry than she could ever know. For everything. And I..."

"Say no more," Jake replied, nodding. "I understand. And I can't guarantee anything, but I'll do what I can to find out where she is now."

Allowing himself a smile and a flash of hope, Gabriel took a step towards Jake. Lifting his hand, he patted the younger man on the shoulder. "Thank you."

"That's what I'm here for," Jake said. "That's what we're all here for, Gabe. To help each other out."

Gabriel let those words marinate for a moment before he found himself smiling. Jake was right. That is what we're here for. And he was determined to start helping out those around him.

He would also reach out to Katherine again. After all, forgiveness was the cornerstone of Christ's existence. And Gabriel now knew, only too well, what it felt like to desperately need to be forgiven. And if he were honest with himself, he had no right to be angry toward his birth mother.

She had been young, and she had been a position no teenage girl should be in. He thought for a moment about his own daughter. What if one day Amy found herself in that kind of trouble? He wouldn't want her to feel as Katherine had; alone and unable to take care of her babies. Someone should have been there for her. He would be there for his girl if anything like that happened to her.

"I..." Gabriel said, his brow furrowing as he took a step back and turned toward his desk. "I actually have another letter I need to write."

"It can wait," Jake urged with an encouraging jerk of his head. "Get some exercise and some fresh air."

Slowly turning to him, Gabriel paused.

"Come on," Jake continued. "It can't be that urgent."

It was urgent. But it didn't matter whether he wrote it now or in an hour's time, she wouldn't get it any faster. "Okay," Gabe replied, deciding that he'd spend his yard time figuring out exactly what he wanted to say to the woman who gave him life. And then had given him a fresh chance at it.

Chapter Twenty Two

A clock gently ticking and the evening sun streaming through the window, Katherine read the letter with tears in her eyes. But, for the first time in a long time, they were a happy overflowing of emotion rather than the desperate sadness that had gripped her since she last saw Gabriel. Sniffing, she watched some of the blue ink blur as a teardrop landed in the middle of the page. With the pad of her thumb, she tried to wipe it away, but she just succeeded in smearing the whole word. Pushing the paper away to make sure she wouldn't ruin it entirely, she slipped off her reading glasses and rubbed both eyes.

In reality, it wouldn't matter if she did ruin the letter entirely. She knew it by heart. Even if she never had the chance to read it again, even if she was suddenly struck blind, she'd be able to recall every word until her dying day.

Dear Katherine,

I don't know how to begin this letter. There's so much I want to say, but words don't seem enough. I suppose the best place to start is to apologize, although I don't know if it'll mean much now. Please believe that I am truly sorry for the way I spoke to you the last time you visited. I could make excuses for myself, and tell you how frightening it is in here and that I try not to show it, but sometimes I'm terrified. I could say that the truth wouldn't sink in, and it made me lash out. I could tell you that imagining the life I could have had; growing up with a brother, made me go a little nuts. None of that matters. There is no excuse. I should have tried to be more understanding of the situation you were in. I should have tried to imagine what it must have been like to make a decision like that.

And if I had done either of those things, I might have spoken with more kindness and forgiveness than I did. I wish I would have. I would now, that's for sure. I wish I could take it back, but I know I can't. And so, all I can do is offer you what I'm now looking for: forgiveness.

I don't blame you for anything that happened. It wasn't your fault, and I know you would have done it all differently if there was any way you could have done it differently. I forgive you. And I'm grateful to you for bringing me the truth. Not just because it may have given me a way out of this place, but also because it's given me the chance to see things differently. I've opened my heart to so much in the last few days: hope, love, happiness, but mostly Christ. I'm stronger for that, and that's down to you.

If you can find it in your heart to forgive me too, I'd love to hear from you again. I'd love to see you again, so I can say sorry properly. I'd appreciate that chance.

You're in my thoughts and prayers.

Your son, Gabriel.

He had never referred to himself as 'her son', not even during those months they had been forging their tentative, but promising, early relationship. That, even more than his apology, made her heart swell until she thought it might burst at the seams. He had come around. She wasn't sure if she really deserved the olive branch he was extending, but she was grateful for it beyond words.

And now, she could even let herself have a little of that hope he'd written of. She allowed herself to hope that, when he was released from prison, they might have the kind of close-knit relationship she'd always dreamed of having if she ever got the chance to meet her children. She might even get the opportunity to know her grandchildren. She could be part of the family she'd so badly missed over all those years spent alone.

She could be fairly sure, now Gabe had welcomed Christ into his heart, he would also welcome the chance for them all to be one loving family, too. It might not be as picture perfect as The Waltons, and there was plenty of atoning for both she and he to do. But family was too important to squander. Love was too important to waste on petty point scoring. And forgiveness should be given easily and with patient kindness. If they could all remember that, somehow they'd overcome the rest.

Katherine found herself wondering whether Gabel had been in touch with his wife. She remembered how sure he'd been that she wouldn't reply. If he'd written a letter like the one he'd written to her, though, the ex-Mrs. Summers would have to be pretty hard-hearted not to be moved. Nevertheless, she pondered writing her, too. Perhaps woman to woman, she could make her appreciate that Gabriel wasn't to blame and that he was a truly changed man. Of course, he might be irritated with her for interfering. And maybe it was best to let them work it out alone. She made a mental note to at least ask him, though. There might be something, but only with his blessing, that she could do for them.

And, soon enough, he would be free anyway. She was confident of that. She'd spoken to that young detective a week ago, and although she'd begun the conversation sceptically, she'd quickly started to find Katherine's story plausible. And after a little digging, to confirm her version of events at the hospital, it was clear the Maloney woman believed her. What was even clearer was that she was determined to get to the truth, freeing Gabriel in the process if that's where the truth led her. Yes, Katherine was glad it was that determined young woman who was working on helping her son. She'd do everything in her power to find Gabriel's twin.

That thought brought a smile to Katherine's face. Partly because it meant the man she'd gotten to know in that terrible prison wasn't guilty. But it also meant she might have the chance to meet her other son. Of course, that didn't come without a hint of trepidation. What if he had done that awful thing? Would she be able to forgive him? Would she be able to forgive herself?

A hefty knock at the door startled her and wrenched her from her thoughts. The landlord always knocked like that – as though it was his door, so he had every right to break it down if the whim took him.

The tips of her fingers lingered at the bottom edge of her letter as she got to her feet. And they didn't leave it completely until the stretch of her arms wasn't long enough to keep touching it. Sighing, she turned from the small kitchen table and wove her way to the front door. As she wrapped her fingers around the handle, the knock sounded again.

"I'm coming, Mr. Merritt!" she called, drawing the security chain off and edging the door open. "I paid the rent two days ago…" Her gabbled speech came to a halt when she realised the man at the threshold was not her sixty-year-old landlord.

Her mouth dropping open, she stared at a face she recognized well. Except it wasn't quite the same face. This man's brow was heavier. There was something darker in his eyes. And there was a cut under his eye that indicated a recent fight. And if there was any other doubt about who he might be, it was all swept clear away when her eyes found the old silvery scar which ran from his temple down his face until it was level with his earlobe. Unlike the mark under his eye, she knew exactly how that scar had been caused. It'd happened when he was being born.

"You're... You're..." she said, not quite having the breath to speak, but somehow managing to whisper the words.

"Your son," he replied, with a quirk of his lips that couldn't be described as a smile. "Hi, Mom." Stepping forward, he grasped the door from out of her weak hand and slammed it shut with a bang that rattled the jamb.

"I don't... How did you...?" Instinctively, she shifted back. The look in his eyes reminded her too much of his father. And unlike the ageing preacher, he was physically threatening. His shoulders were broader than Gabriel's, and the close buzz cut of his dark hair gave him an even more dangerous air.

"Find you?" Mason Heiland asked, glancing around the tiny apartment while his lips curled. "Well... It's the strangest thing." Strolling forward, he slipped his hands into the back pockets of his light blue jeans. His casual stance blended with the tone of his voice. But there was something underlying both that suggested he was anything but relaxed. Katherine saw it in the tension in his jaw, the slight raise of his shoulders and the tapping of his thumbs against the denim on his backside.

"I was watching the TV," he continued. "And I saw this guy who looked just like me. He could have been my double. My twin." Twisting his upper body to face her, he offered her a flash of white teeth with another of his quasi smiles. "And this guy had been convicted of murder. And so, I thought to myself… who is he? How come he looks so much like me?"

Katherine held his eyes, knowing if she didn't it would be a sign of fear. She felt it alright, but she wasn't going to let it show. She knew from experience that it's best to never let it show. Forcing the excess saliva on her tongue down a very dry throat, she straightened her spine in a show of strength. She wasn't sure how successful it was or how used he was to seeing people he talked to be intimidated. She guessed it was very familiar.

"It's taken you all this time to find me?" she wondered quietly.

"No." He shook his head and turned to face her. "No, it didn't. But it did take me this long to figure out whether or not I wanted to see you."

"I'm sorry," she instantly replied. It was heartfelt, but unlike the apology she'd offered Gabriel, it wasn't laced with tears. Her wariness of the man in front of her wouldn't allow them to glaze her eyes. "I would never have left you if I had any other choice."

"Choice?" He snorted as he lifted one hand and ran it over the back of his head. "What choice do you think I had?"

"I… I…" As her tall son took a step towards her and seemed to tower over her, she took a hurried pace back. "I wanted what was best for you. I wanted to give you a better chance at life… You…" Pausing, she took another tack. "Do you have children of your own?"

Running his tongue between amused lips, he looked her over with almost the same disdain as his father had done more than thirty years earlier. She wondered how he managed to replicate an expression he'd never seen.

"Don't try to talk your way out of this!" he spat. "I'm not here to have some teary reunion. All I wanted was to meet the woman who ruined my life."

"But I..." Katherine glanced at his feet and took another step back, eager to get away from the oppressive heat of his breath. She didn't understand. She could have sworn Maloney said her abandoned son had been adopted by a good family and grown up in a decent area of New York. She'd refused to give her his name, or the exact place he lived, and she understood the reasons for that. But the detective had been so sure that she'd traced the right man. And if that were true, how could the man bearing down on her believe that his life would have been better with a single mother who would have struggled to keep him fed and clothed?

"You took him with you," Mason said, the words clipped and taut. "You took him, and you left me."

"I wouldn't have left you... And I didn't get to keep Gabriel... I had to give him away, too. It wasn't a choice between the two of you."

Rocking his weight back on his heels, he nodded slowly. "Yeah, yeah, he was adopted, too. But I bet he had a better life than me, didn't he? He didn't grow up with this for a start." As he spoke, he lifted his left hand to the aged scar on the side of his face.

Katherine didn't know how to respond. There was no way to reason with the bitterness in him. Bitterness that had no grounding. Gabriel didn't have a scar, that much was true. But he hadn't had a better life. Both young men had struggled with the fact they were adopted; struggled to find their identity and, it seemed clear to Katherine, both let their frustration loose by means of a temper they inherited from their biological father.

"I'm sorry," she eventually breathed. It was the only thing she could say. Knowing it wouldn't be enough to appease him, it was the only thing at her disposal. "I am truly sorry for everything you've been through. Not a day has gone by I haven't thought about you, and that I haven't prayed that you're safe and well and happy. That was all I ever wanted for you."

Mason didn't believe it for a moment. And he didn't even want to. It would simply get in the way of his only goal. Revenge. Revenge for all of the crap in his life; for the fact he'd never been able to forge a proper relationship with anyone, because deep down he knew he hadn't been wanted.

"I think the only person you were thinking about was yourself," he muttered. "And maybe him... Maybe the golden boy, right?"

"I never even saw him until a few months ago," she insisted, although she realized the cold hard facts of the matter were immaterial to him. He had his own version of events, and he wasn't about to be swayed from them.

Nevertheless, she persisted. "I visited him in prison, and I told him the truth. He didn't find it easy, either. But... But he's forgiven me. And I hope, in time, maybe..."

"I will never forgive you," Mason snapped. "I don't want to forgive you, or play happy families with you."

"Okay," she whispered, her hands beginning to tremble at her sides. Balling her fingers into fists, she hoped their quivering didn't show. "You don't have to. You don't have to do anything you don't want to."

"I only came here for one thing," he said, stepping closer.

She took another shuffled pace back, but met the wall and realized she was trapped. Eyes shifting to her left and right, she tried to find a way out, but there was no obvious escape.

"I want you to tell me who my father is and where I can find him."

Fluttering pale eyes finding her son's angry features again, she blinked. "He... He was older than me. He was married, it wasn't... It wasn't simple, and that's why..."

"I want to know who he is," Mason repeated.

"It doesn't matter," she muttered, not sure whether she was protecting the man who's caused her so much pain, protecting herself, or protecting the son in prison who still believed the adulterous preacher was dead. Maybe she wanted to protect the other son in front of her, too. As much as he terrified her in that moment, she didn't want him to be hurt. She didn't want any more violence to come from the hands of her flesh and blood. And she didn't want both of her twins to wind up in jail. The tension in his face suggested he could easily do the latter two.

A scoff of laughter, shook his body slightly as he placed his hands on her upper arms and pressed her to the wall. "Of course it doesn't matter to you, because it was just a grubby little fling and once you'd stopped shoving your legs in the air and realized you were knocked up, you had to put it all out of your life and forget it."

"I never forgot any of it," she blurted, certain it was wholly unwise to contradict and bait him. It wasn't intentional, though. She just couldn't let his accusation lie. "I've lived with the guilt of what I did every day of my life. I never put it to one side. I never forgot him. And I never forgot either of you."

"Well, I'm glad you haven't forgotten," Mason said, his face drawing closer to her as his fingers squeezed her arms tightly enough to leave bruises. "Because I want to know where he is. And you're going to tell me."

"Why?" she whimpered, remaining still beneath the force of his hands, even though part of her wanted to push him away. It would only make it worse if she tried. "Why do you want him? You blame me... So... Whatever it is you want to do, you can do to me."

He tilted his head back to study her, as though she was a strange and undiscovered creature. "You're in love with him? Is that why you're trying to protect him?"

"No," she whispered. "I don't love anything about him anymore. But I do love you. I want to protect you... And if you go to him..."

"What? What do you think he's going to do to me?" he asked in amusement. "He can't do anything to me. And you know the really sick thing? Nobody can. Nobody can, because I'm already dead inside. I've lost everything. And I never really had anything to start with. It was all taken away from me when I was only a couple of days old... because of you."

Without willing them to and without even being aware of them moving, Katherine's hands gently rose to his face. She brushed his chin with her fingertips, before pressing her warm palm to his cheek. "I'm sorry if this is what I've done to you," she said quietly. "I'm so sorry."

Seeming to snap to his senses and realize what she was doing, he grasped hold of her hands and wrenched them from his skin. "I don't care how sorry you are. You're no mother of mine. You're just some tramp."

Katherine winced as he pushed her arms over her head and pinned them there in one of his large hands. She squirmed in panic as she watched him reach to his left and the knife block that sat on the kitchen counter. With a swish of a cleanly sharpened blade, he pulled one of the tools free. For a moment, he glanced at the six-inch knife.

"I'm going to try once more," he said, in a conversational tone so at odds with what he was doing and what he held in his hand. "And maybe you want to think long and hard for a moment about whether this married man who used you like a slut is worth all this..." Turning the blade toward her, he brought it close to her eye.

She closed both reflexively, and the sharp point was soon chilling her eyelid. The pressure was as light as a butterfly's wings, but it held infinitely more violence. "I... I..." she babbled. "Please, I don't..."

"Where is he?" Mason demanded. "Tell me where he is."

"Please... It's..."

"Tell me where he is!"

As he pushed harder with the blade, Katherine felt the sharp prick of pierced skin and shrieked. "No! Stop!"

Recognizing the desperate surrender in her pleas, he pulled back, leaving a small spot of blood on her quickly fluttering eyelid.

"I'll tell you..." she panted. "I'll tell you where he is."

Chapter Twenty Three

The man groaned as he lifted himself from the chair. His lower back had stiffened from two hours of sitting hunched over his desk. Sometimes, he wondered why he even bothered to spend so long on his sermons. The people who came to his church rarely listened, they were simply making sure they got the 'good mark' next to their names for showing up in the house of God. That would make a difference when they were in front of the gates… At least, that's what they believed. He wasn't so sure. In fact, he wondered if anything made a difference. Maybe they were all going to hell. We are all sinners, after all.

That's what he told himself.

When the guilt of his own actions began to creep into the edges of his conscience, he reminded himself that every single human being on the planet was full of sin. His were no worse than any other's. In fact, they were much less than many other's. He hadn't killed anyone. He hadn't harmed anyone. He hadn't forced that girl to have sex with him. She'd wanted it. She would be just as guilty in the eyes of The Lord. Worse even. She was worse, because she was the one who'd brought temptation to him. Like Eve, she had led him into sin.

And once she'd coaxed him down that road, it was impossible to stop. It was her fault then and it was her fault that it had continued. There had been others after Katherine. He'd been more careful with them, though. He'd never risked pregnancy again. And, if he were honest with himself, with all of the rest - maybe a dozen over the course of thirty-odd years - he'd been searching for the same thrill he'd experienced that first time. The first time he'd been unfaithful to his wife. The time he'd taken that girl's innocence. It was a rush like he'd never known before or since. A drug-like high. And no matter how many times he went looking for a second hit, it couldn't quite match the strength and exhilaration of the first.

Still, he kept looking. And in the search for it, he sullied himself and everything he was supposed to represent. He knew that. He knew what he'd done. But he was not responsible for that. For any of it. It was her fault. She had done this to him.

He glanced down at the desk, the same desk he'd been looking at for over thirty years. And if he closed his eyes, he could imagine what it was like. He could almost smell her skin, and taste the vague sweetness that clung to her lips. She'd been a siren. No matter how much she might have played the sweet, innocent and wronged girl, she was a siren. And she hadn't just crushed him on the rocks, she'd destroyed everything that made him a good and decent man. If only he'd never met her...

Dropping his chin toward his chest, he released a heavy sigh. Rubbing his fingertips over a lined forehead, he rued the wasted years. If he could go back and do it all differently, would he? If he were honest with himself, he didn't know. He'd been able to keep his marriage intact, although he sensed his wife suspected he'd fallen victim to temptation occasionally. She never said as much outright, and she seemed content to cling to the life they had, even if it wasn't quite all it seemed to be. He wasn't sure whether he admired or despised her for that. Nevertheless, their marriage survived. He was still looked upon favourably in the neighbourhood. He hadn't lost anything. Would he trade that mind-blowing experience just to hang onto a virtue only he knew he didn't have? No. No, he wouldn't. What was life, after all, without a bit of adventure?

And besides, we're all sinners. Every human being to ever walk the face of the planet has been a sinner. What point was there in trying to live some stupid idealistic life that no one is really capable of anyway?

Lifting his face, he shook it as he turned to the door. He grumbled under his breath about the arthritis in his knees and wondered whether he'd still be able to walk unaided by the time he was seventy. Perhaps it was time to start thinking about surgery.

Easing the door open, he made his way along the hallway and rounded a corner which brought him back into the church. The evening service had long since ended, and the congregation had filtered out hours earlier. So as his eyes glanced at a figure sitting at the back of the room, he squinted.

"Hello?" he said.

A pair of broad shoulders lifted, and a face slowly followed. Dark eyes met ones that were so similar to their own that they could have been looking into a mirror. Any doubt he might have had that he'd made a mistake, or that the woman had lied to him, vanished. This was him.

Standing near the lectern he'd preached from, the older man strained to bring the fuzzy stranger into focus. "Can I help you, son?" he asked.

Mason didn't even try to hide the snort that erupted in him. With a laugh that contained no vestige of genuine amusement, he rose to his feet and slipped his hands into the front pockets of his jeans. "Son?" he muttered. "Do you look on all men as your sons?"

Unmoving, the other man rested a hand on his lectern and weighed how to answer. The edge in the younger man's voice meant something, but he couldn't be sure what.

"Yes," he eventually said. "We're all family, aren't we? All children of God." He wasn't sure how much of that he really believed anymore. But the habit to spew out words that meant little to him was so strong that he felt he might not be able to prevent it even if he wanted to. And he didn't want to. He liked the mask of his piety. His faith. It was what stopped people from looking any deeper and suspecting something darker. They all thought he was above them and above sin. He liked that, it protected him. It had allowed him to do things he wouldn't have been able to otherwise get away with, and it continued to protect him from a past he wouldn't want the whole neighbourhood to know about.

Mason ran a hand through his dark hair while he stepped forward. "All family?" he said. "All one big happy family?"

Frowning, the older man stared hard at the figure which was starting to come into better focus. He glimpsed his eyes. He carefully traced the shape of his face and line of his jaw. And as he did, his heart began to pound a little harder against his ribcage. It wasn't like looking in a mirror. It was like looking at a photograph of his younger self. The resemblance was unmistakable.

"I... I..." Not sure how much the other man knew, he was reluctant to speak, but knew he had to say something. "What do you want?"

"Really?" Chuckling, Mason continued to walk forwards. "No, paternal hug? No, 'how have you been, Son?' No attempt to talk your way out of it?"

Straightening, the man refused to be threatened. But Mason wasn't finished.

"Nicholas Harrington," he said almost whimsically, experimenting with the way the sound of the name felt on his tongue. "Well-respected member of this community. Nicholas Harrington, man of God. Nicholas Harrington, my father."

Pushing himself away from the lectern, the older man stepped close and met the other's eyes, but he couldn't manage it without a flicker of hesitation. "If you want something from me, I'm sure something can be arranged. Money?"

"Money?" Mason blurted. "What kind of money does a small town preacher make? Huh? Unless you're cheating your congre..." Stopping himself mid-word, he chuckled again. "Actually, that sounds like you. Are you pocketing the cash from donations, is that it?"

Nicholas would have moved back if he could, but his feet wouldn't let him do anything at all. "I haven't... Um... I don't have a lot of money, but if...? Look, what do you want? Just tell me what it is you want from me?"

"So, you think I have a right to want something from you?" Mason replied, one hand still plunged deep into his pocket while the other stroked his chin. "Well, that's one thing in your favour, I guess."

Silent and stock-still, Nicholas waited for the man in front of him - the son he'd never met until two minutes ago - to reveal his intentions. It didn't take a genius, however, to figure out that they weren't good. The anger in his tight jaw was plain enough to see. All the preacher could hope for would be that he'd be able to placate him, offer him whatever it was he felt was owed and then convince him to leave. The power was all with his abandoned son, though. Nicholas had nothing to bargain with, and his grown-up child had everything. People would have no trouble believing he was the minister's son. Nobody would have to simply take his word for it, and nobody would even bother suggesting a DNA test. It was as plain as the nose on both of their faces.

"Look... We're both practical men," he said, supposing it to be true and hoping, for his sake, that it was. "I'm sure you understand the way the world works."

"Oh, yeah," Mason said. "I know how the world works. I know that you've messed up my life. And over what... huh? What was so important to you that it was worth destroying a life?"

Trying to figure out whether he was fit enough to fight his son off if it came to it, and it was looking increasingly as though it would come to it, Nicholas silently cursed his aging, aching body. "I didn't ruin your life. I just... I did what was best for everyone concerned."

"What would have been best for everyone concerned is if you'd taken responsibility for what you did like a man. Instead, you ditched you problems like they were nothing. I was nothing to you, wasn't I? And now I've spent every moment of my life trying to work out why I meant nothing. What had I done wrong?"

"It wasn't like that. The decision wasn't about you. For God's sake, you hadn't even been born when I told that woman to get rid of you both."

Before Mason knew it was happening and long before Nicholas could anticipate it, the younger man's fist was jerked up toward his shoulder and thrust forward. His knuckles struck his father's jaw, causing the head to snap back. Nicholas staggered, groping behind him for the lectern to support him. His fingers missed what they searched for and he slumped to the ground, landing hard on his butt.

"People are dispensable to you, aren't they?" Mason said, leaning forward and grasping hold of his shirt front. "Your own sons were dispensable to you!"

"Wh... What would you have had me do?" Nicholas breathlessly gasped. Hands covering his son's, he tried to pry his grip off his shirt, but couldn't get a solid hold of him. "Things... Things were complicated. I had a wife. I had a..."

"You." Mason spat. "That's all you cared about. You." Suddenly relaxing his grasp, he pushed the older man's upper body away from him in disgust. With a step back he added, "In all these years, did you ever think about me? Did you ever wonder where I was, what I looked like, what I was doing? Did you think about me at all? Or was the relief of it all being over and out of your way so great that I never entered your head?"

Nicholas hesitated before replying, trying to remember whether he had ever thought of either of the boys - heck, he hadn't even known they were boys until Katherine sauntered back into his life insisting that they had to go to the authorities with the truth, because one of the twins was in jail for something he didn't do. The honest answer was no, he hadn't thought about them at all. Not once. But, surely, this guy understood that? He knew that life was dog-eat-dog. He knew that sometimes self-preservation had to be the most important thing in a man's life. He clearly wasn't the touchy-feely sort.

Nevertheless, Nicholas didn't have the guts to speak the truth. And he didn't have the guts to lie, either. Instead, he swerved his way around the subject entirely. "What kind of life do you think you would have had with a teenage mother and a disgraced minister for a father? It wasn't simple."

"It was simple to you," Mason said. "You didn't want me, so I didn't exist. Even though you made me. Do you know what it feels like to grow up knowing you weren't wanted by your own parents? Do you have any idea...? Knowing you were a mistake as far as they're concerned. A bastard mistake. And I've lived with the consequences of that everyday." Sinking to his haunches, he rested his elbows on his thighs. "And what about you? What have you had to live with?" Answering his own question, Mason shrugged. "Nothing. You've just been carrying on as before. Making the saps that sit in this church believe that you're some conduit to the Almighty, when you're more rotten than all of them combined. Have you acted as though you care about them? And do they believe you?"

Nicholas shook his dazed head. "I... I was just... It was a moment of weakness. Okay. I was drawn to the woman, and I... I didn't deserve to be punished for the rest of my life for that."

"And raising me would have been a punishment?"

"That's not what I meant," Nicholas replied hastily. "I just meant that... I would have lost everything. For a crazy fling, I would have lost everything. Don't you understand?"

"No," Mason replied, his head shifting slowly from left to right and back again. "I don't understand. And maybe you wouldn't understand why a cheap fling was worth all this if you knew what you'd done. If you knew what you'd turned me into."

"I... I didn't do anything to you."

Mason lips rose in a twisted half-smile. "Yes, you did. You might not realize it, but everything I am is down to you. I didn't know your name, I didn't know what you looked like, but I knew that you casting me aside like I didn't exist was what turned me into this."

Nicholas didn't want to ask what 'this' was. And he sensed he wouldn't need to. Mason was confessing and punishing in equal measure, and he was far from done.

"I spent my life being angry at the world. Because that's what happens when the person who's supposed to love you rejects you. You spend every day feeling like the world has rejected you. And you want to hurt it, because it's hurt you."

Trying to lift himself, Nicholas planted his hands on the floor either side of his hips and heaved. He didn't get far, though. Mason's fist was soon twisting his shirt and pushing him back down.

"Are you listening to me?" he demanded.

"Yes." Nodding, Nicholas tried to look as though he was interested while he was in reality more focused on looking for an escape. Part of him knew, however, that there wasn't one.

"You can't hurt the world, Harrington," Mason continued. "All you can do is hurt the people in it. So that's what I did. I hurt people. Some of them deserved it. Some of them didn't, and I didn't really care which was which. I beat people up. I slapped my wife around, until she proved me right about not being wanted by the world, and left me. And I was so angry with her for that, you know? So damn angry I could have killed her."

Nervously swallowing, Nicholas lifted a hand to his son's chest and pushed. It didn't do him any good, though. Mason remained impassive.

"If you've hurt this woman, you must..."

"Must what?" Mason snapped. "What, Harrington? You tell me. You think you're better than me? You think you haven't hurt women. The woman you impregnated? Your wife? What about the others? Because I'll bet there are others."

"I never..." Nicholas stopped himself, letting the words taper off as he realized the attempt to tell his son that physical violence was different would be in vain. "I understand why you're angry," he said instead. "But..."

"You don't understand," Mason insisted. "If you did, you would never have cast me aside."

"None of us are perfect."

"You're right about that." A subtle smile, Mason nodded, but the tight hold he held of his father's shirt remained. "So maybe people deserve what they get, huh? Maybe the people I've hurt deserved it? Do you believe that, Harrington?"

"I... I..."

"I killed a man," Mason announced. It was as casual as someone else might have mentioned that they bumped into an old friend at the market. "That man my brother was arrested for murdering," he added. "It was me. I killed him. Do you think he deserved it?" Smile growing wider, he added, "More importantly, do you think you deserve what's about to happen to you?"

"Look," Nicholas mumbled, squirming in a bid to cut loose of his son's hand. "I didn't mean for any of this to happen. And I'm not responsible for your actions as an adult. We all have to face what we've done, and..."

"And you're about to face what you did," Mason interrupted, his fist rising again and slamming hard into Nicholas' face. Lip splitting open on impact, blood splattered over Mason's fist and dripped down the minister's chin. Not hesitating, Mason struck him again. And again. And again. The crunch of bone filled the high-ceilinged space as a fist was driven into the minister's nose. Another crack could be heard when the punch found his cheekbone.

Nicholas lifted his arms, trying to shield himself from the torrent of blows that continued to come. He was quickly losing strength to defend himself. And Mason, with a panting, cursing, endless supply of energy kept driving his fist into his father's face without pause and without conscience.

"You low life!" he shouted. "You're just scum of the Earth!"

The blood and adrenaline pounding in his ears meant he didn't even hear the bang of the door opening and scuffing of rapid footsteps. He didn't hear the shout of, "Mason Heiland, get your hands in the air!"

He didn't hear or see or smell anything but his father's quiet groans, the blood that flowed from several cuts all over his face, and the strong metallic scent that came with it. He wasn't even aware anyone else was in the room until a pair of solid arms grabbed him around the waist and at the chest, and hauled him backward. Then there were other arms. Soon, he found himself pinned to the floor.

Cuffs were being slapped on his wrists as someone said, "Mason Heiland, you're under arrest. You do not have to say anything..." The rest of the words tapered off as he wrenched his head up to look at the older man, who was lying motionless a few feet away.

As other officers gathered around the minister, he was blocked from view. Mason's impassive eyes lifted to the ceiling and all he could do was wonder whether he'd done enough to finish the job.

Chapter Twenty Four

Maloney strolled into Cox's small office with a subtle smile playing at the corners of her mouth. She'd been humming a soft tune as she wandered the corridor. But now she waited quietly, hovering at the corner of his desk, until he finally lifted his eyes to hers.

"We've got him for the assault on his mother, and for the attempted murder of his father." As she spoke, she slipped her hands into the pockets of her charcoal, pin-striped pants and shifted her weight onto one hip.

Resting his elbow on the desk beside his keyboard, Cox placed his chin on his fist as he looked at her. And for a second, that's all he did. He just looked at her. He loved seeing her like this – all fired up over work. Happy that she'd done a good job, and content that justice had been done. As though she'd set the world to rights. He had no doubt she would try too.

"Nice work," he said. "Doesn't mean he's guilty of the murder, though." When that didn't wipe the grin from her face, he continued. "It doesn't mean Gabriel's innocent, either." The fact was, he was beginning to have severe doubts about Summers' guilt, too. But he wouldn't admit it. That wasn't how their relationship worked. He had to be the cynical one. Besides, what he'd said was true: Gabriel Summers could well be guilty.

Maloney's smile still remained. "Maybe not," she agreed, with a quick shrug of one shoulder. "It's more than enough to cast reasonable doubt, though. Don't you think?" It wasn't a question.

But he answered it anyway with a smile of his own. "It casts doubt, I'll give you that."

"That's all I was ever aiming to do. What happens now is down to a court of law. My job was to make sure I had all the facts. And until yesterday, we didn't."

Under different circumstances, he might have tried to argue with her. Just for the sake of arguing with her. But he didn't want to. Besides, she was right. Still leaning on his chin, his let his eyes move over her satisfied, victorious features.

"Thank you," she said, the upturn of her lips altering in a way that Cox couldn't quite define, but the change was very obvious to him nonetheless.

"For?" he asked, knowing the answer, but wanting to hear the words from her lips.

"For your help," she replied, only too aware that the conversation they were having could just as easily have been left unsaid. After all, so much of their relationship had been unsaid. So much of their relationship didn't *need* to be said. And it had morphed without her even realizing it. Had he known? She couldn't help but wonder. Although, if she were forced to put money on it, she'd have said he didn't. She guessed it was as surprising to him as it was to her. The difference between them was he seemed to be handling that surprise much better than she was.

Lifting his face from his knuckles, he leaned back in his chair. "Do you plan on showing this gratitude somehow? You know... a quid pro quo?"

"What exactly are you suggesting?" she replied, aiming for indigence. What actually came from her mouth sounded a lot like flirting. Girlish flirting. And part of her was annoyed with herself for letting it out. There was no way to take it back, though.

"Well," he said, letting out a noisy breath of contemplation. "I believe we mentioned getting together to have a proper discussion about us. An uninterrupted, no avoidance kind of discussion."

Now that her cool façade had slipped, Maloney didn't see the point in trying to cling to it. It would only look undignified. And although she wasn't averse to looking undignified, she didn't relish the thought of doing so in front of him – not anymore. "Well..." she began, shifting her weight to the other side and sticking her other hip toward him. "I'm not sure we actually agreed to that as such, did we?"

"Yes, you did, Ms. Maloney," he insisted, getting out of his chair and taking the small step to reach her.

She lifted her chin to look at his taller frame. She wondered if it might be a good idea to move back. The closeness of him was affecting her in a way that it never had before. Her instinct was to move away from it. To stay on the 'safe' side. On the flipside, she was, as ever, reluctant to ever show any vestige of fear. She was loath to call it fear anyway. It was just... discomfort. And what exactly she was discomforted by, she wouldn't be able to say.

"I believe the agreement was extracted in questionable circumstances, though, Mr. Cox," she replied.

"Not at all."

"Really?" she said. "You don't think using a case to bribe me was morally questionable?"

"I helped you find Heiland's ex," he reminded her, taking another small shuffled step until his torso was brushing her breasts. "She was the connection, right? She'd had a relationship with Renaudin. And that's why Mason went after him. Right?"

She glanced down at the way his body pressed against hers, and couldn't decide whether to admit to herself she liked it or not. "That's all true," she replied, her voice softer. The mood between them had grown almost intimate, and the tone of her voice dropped to a whisper as she added, "But justice is your job. You shouldn't be gaining from it."

"Then I shouldn't admit how I feel about you," he replied, both hands lifting until they cupped her face. Caressing her cheeks with his thumbs, he held her eyes solidly. "Because, I met you in the pursuit of justice. So... I should pretend to feel nothing for you in order to uphold some moral ideal? Is that what you're saying?"

Maloney didn't know what she was saying, and she didn't know what to say as he continued to tenderly stroke her face. It didn't seem plausible that any of it was happening at all. "Jensen," she murmured.

"Yes, Meredith?"

"Do you really think...I mean... Isn't this crazy?"

"You tell me," he replied, leaning forward and pressing his lips to hers.

She saw the kiss coming, and half thought she should stop him. But she didn't. She didn't even try. She let her eyes slide closed, and then whimpered softly as his mouth melded with her own. It was a bad idea. She knew that. But somewhere, deep down, she realized that the 'bad idea' ship had already sailed. Maybe it was too late to put a stop to it any of it now. Or, if she were honest, she didn't want to put a stop to it. She wanted to pull him closer and beg him to never ever stop. She wanted to be with him. Always. Because, it was only when she was with him that life made any sense. She wasn't sure when that had happened, but she was even more sure of it as his tongue slipped between her parted lips than she'd ever been sure of anything.

Breath moving raggedly in and out of his lungs, he pulled back. But he didn't let go of her as he said. "Is that crazy?"

Struggling to find breath enough to speak, she shook her head before whispering. "No."

"So...?" he asked, the prelude of a smile forming. "We can talk about us?"

"Yeah." Maloney didn't know if she was doing the right thing, or even the smart thing. Something told her, if she were putting his best interests first, she should put a stop to this now. After all, she'd only screw it up. That's what she did, it was her MO. She screwed things up, every chance she got. "But..." she added quietly. "Are you sure this is what you want?"

"I've known what I want for a while now," he replied, his eyes never leaving hers. "I just need to know what you want."

Sliding her hands between their bodies, Maloney grabbed her ex-partner's lapels and pulled him nearer. "I think you know what I want," she said before ending the conversation with her lips pressed against his.

***

Matthew watched as Gabriel wandered the width of his cell. He'd been back and forth so many times, the chaplain's neck was starting to ache. It reminded him of trying to watch a tennis match. He didn't try to stop him, though. He viewed this burst of energy as a good thing. It was certainly better than the languid, depression he'd seen in him many times before.

"So how long?" Gabriel said, his voice harsh and ricocheting off the cell walls.

"Hmm?" Matthew replied, resigning his neck of the task of following the restless man. His eyes continued to track him, but he felt sure they'd also tire of the job soon. "How long what?"

"How long before I'm out of here?" Stopping next to the wall, he breathed hard through his nose. "They've got him now. They know there's someone else with my DNA. That provides enough doubt to overturn the conviction. I should be out of here already!"

With a rub of his hands across his cream chinos, Matthew got to his feet. "Sometimes, these things take time. The wheels of justice don't move quickly."

"They moved quickly enough to put me in here," Gabriel tossed back, although part of him knew it wasn't quite true. It had taken over a year for him to wind up in jail. But he'd been incarcerated all that time, so it amounted to the same thing as far as he was concerned. He didn't expect Matthew to understand that. How could anybody understand having a chunk of your life ripped away from you?

And it wasn't just a chunk. Because the repercussions of his conviction would last forever. Overturned or not, there would continue to be consequences. The loss of his wife and family being top of that list. Jenny still hadn't replied to his letters. He couldn't even be sure if she was getting them. Jake seemed convinced he'd got the right address, though. But... Perhaps Gabriel wanted to cling to the notion that the address might be wrong, because he would also be able to hold onto the idea that maybe his wife wasn't ignoring his attempts to contact her. That possibility hadn't completely passed him by. But, it wasn't one he was willing to engage too much time with.

Strolling easily across the small space, Matthew placed his hand on Gabriel's shoulder. "What happened to you was unjust. There's no question about that. And you deserve to be freed as soon as possible. But you have to be patient."

"How much more patient do I need to be?" Gabriel blurted, his face twisted toward the man who'd become more than just a chaplain. He was a friend. Perhaps the best he'd ever had. And the fact of that seemed insane. After all, he'd almost hated the guy on sight. He didn't want anything to do with him or his religion.

Now, though, in quiet moments, Gabriel knew that Matthew and his religion – a religion that was now *his* too –

had saved him. There was no way he could have survived without it. And he had to frequently remind himself that if it weren't for Matthew, and Jake, and his biological mother, and the common drive they all shared to live as close to Jesus' example as possible, he would have spent the rest of his days in a jail cell. The truth would have stayed buried.

"I'm sorry," he muttered, dipping his face and taking a slow, steady breath. "I don't mean to yell at you, I know you don't deserve it. I… I can't thank you enough for helping me. You know, I might not always seem very grateful, but…"

"Say no more," Matthew insisted with a soft chuckle. "I was only doing what I could do. It's the same as anyone would have done in my situation."

"That's not true," Gabriel replied. "And you know that, don't you? You know the world is full of selfishness and greed, and people who won't do anything for anyone unless there's something in it for them."

Matthew closed his eyes, and was silent and still for several moments. "It's an imperfect world. And we are an imperfect species. But there are good people around, Gabriel. They're there. If you look for them, you'll find them. I promise you that."

"Because you think there's good in everyone?" he wondered, a cock of his head making it clear the question was genuine rather than sarcasm.

Dark eyes once again meeting Gabriel's face, Matthew squeezed his shoulder. "Most people have the capacity for good in them. Just as most of us have the capacity for bad. What dictates who and what we become is which of those sides of ourselves we nurture. And it's a choice we have to make constantly, Gabe. It's a battle that's never won, until we pass over to the other side. When we're with God, then we can relax. Until that moment, we have to keep striving to nurture the good in ourselves."

Stretching his arm forward, Gabriel laid his hand on the wall. His palm moved gently over painted bricks he'd thrown his fist at several times before. Letting Matthew's words marinate, he considered how he'd nurtured the unpleasant side of himself, and the effect it had had on those around him. "What are you telling me?" he quietly asked, his eyes studiously following the nondescript patterns his fingers made on the wall.

"I'm not telling you anything."

"You know what I mean," Gabe replied, smiling. With a quirk of his head over his shoulder, he found the chaplain's eyes again. "What's the lesson in all of this?"

"I'm not sure that we ever really know all of the lessons that He has for us," Matthew replied ruefully. "But I suppose what I'm getting at is, you get to choose in this moment who and what you want to be. You choose which side of yourself you want to nurture."

"It's not that simple."

"Why?"

"Because... I... It's not like I just lost my cell phone or had my car stolen. It's not a material thing that I can just shrug off. We're talking about my whole life." Brown eyes glassy as he blinked, Gabriel pushed away from the wall and turned his back on it. "I've lost so much. Things that can never be replaced. And you're asking me to let that go. To not be bitter and angry about it."

Matthew shook his head. "I'm not telling you how to feel about what's happened to you. You can feel any way you want to. But I can tell you this much: being bitter and angry won't help anything. It won't bring any of that time back, and it won't bring all the other things you think you've lost back. And the only thing it will do is hurt you."

Leaning back until his shoulders met the cold wall that seeped through his shirt, Gabriel sighed. "You don't understand. You can't understand. How can I just let something like that go?"

"I'm not saying it's simple," Matthew replied. "It's not. But those negative emotions eat away at the host. And they do nothing for the person that it's actually directed at."

"I know that I'm supposed to forgive, but how can I begin to forgive this? My brother must have realized I was being wrongly convicted. And if he saw me on the news or in the papers, he knew long before I did that we were twins. And he did nothing. He was happy to let me take the fall for something he did."

Matthew peered at the floor in front of his feet. "You forgive for your sake as much as anyone else's. You know that, right?"

Gabriel did know that. It was something they'd discussed before on numerous occasions. And he saw the logic. In theory, he knew it was a sound principle. In practice, it was different. How could one ever forgive someone who had ruined a person's entire life?

"You can let this eat away at you," Matthew continued. "Or you can begin to heal and let it go."

"How?" As Gabriel spoke his voice was hoarse.

"Well..." Pausing, the chaplain tried to decide how best to phrase the next words from his mouth. He no longer needed to be as cautious around Gabriel. The man in front of him knew that his intentions were good, and he understood much of what he said. But his next sentence could send Gabe back to depression and disillusionment. "The only way we can ever look at difficult and painful things in our lives is to try to see the things we've gained and learned from them."

Gabriel opened his mouth, but his intake of breath to form words was quickly cut off.

"I know," Matthew said. "It's not easy. And it feels as though you've lost more than you've gained. Perhaps you have, but perhaps you haven't. We won't know that for years and maybe even decades to come. But you have gained things from this experience, Gabe."

Rolling his shoulders, the prisoner fought the urge to fire back a retort. He was calmer than he had been. He was more considered. Whenever he felt the desire to fall into old habits, he remembered Christ, His sacrifices and the immense love He'd shown to all people of the world.

"You've become a better person through this, Gabe," Matthew softly added.

With a slow, but convinced nod of his head, Gabriel began to smile. "I have learned a lot from this. I have become a better man. And I want to be a better husband and father. But... It's just... Will I ever get a chance to be those things? How much longer do I have to stay locked up here?"

"I don't know how much longer. And I don't know whether you'll get to prove yourself as a husband, but as a father I'm sure you will. Even if your wife decides to keep your children from you now, one day they'll be adults. And they'll be able to get to know you on their terms. They'll appreciate the man you are, Gabe. They'll know the you that stands in front of me. And you'll make them proud."

A tear Gabriel made no attempt to stop skated down his cheek. With a sad smile, he glanced to the ceiling. "You think all this was worth it to become a better father?"

"It's up to you decide whether what you've been through was worth it to become who you are now," Matthew replied. "It's up to God to determine why these things happen, and it's also up to Him to give us the strength to endure them," he added with a half-smile. "None of this has been fair or easy. Life rarely is fair or easy, and some get a rougher deal than others. All we can do is learn from everything that comes our way. Help whoever we can. Love as much and as often as we can. And make sure that everything we do shows the best of who we are." With that, Matthew's smile grew larger and he shrugged. "It's up to you what the best of you is, and whether you want to let it show."

Lifting his hand, Gabriel swiped at the salty, sticky tear track that had left a zig zag down his face. "Yeah," he whispered. "You're right." He knew exactly what the best of him was now, in a way that he had never truly understood before. And if that was the only thing he'd gained out of being to hell and back, it was worth it. He would make sure it was. Because he wasn't prepared to have been through it all for nothing.

Chapter Twenty Five

Matthew realized he wasn't breathing and filled his lungs hurriedly. He couldn't have said why he was so nervous. After all, he was used to this kind of situation. He'd met and spoken with many violent criminals. There was nothing new in what he was about to do. Although even as he told himself all that, he knew exactly what made this different. He'd broken the golden rule. He'd become far too attached to this whole issue. Too attached to Gabriel. And too attached to the outcome.

Over the months, he'd tried to urge himself to take a few steps back. But he'd already known it was too late. As he stood outside that door, the ship had sailed so far that he couldn't even see its wake anymore. Lifting his hands from his pockets, he glanced down at both palms before exhaling slowly.

"What's the matter?"

Matthew lifted his head toward the voice and graced her with a slightly bashful smile. "Nothin'" he replied with a brisk shake of his head.

"Big fella like you scared of a coward like him?" she added, as she sidled up beside him and nudged his ribcage with her elbow.

Slipping restless hands back into his pockets, he met Detective Maloney's amused green eyes. "You're in a good mood," he noted, hoping the change of subject would turn the focus away from his nervousness.

The plan worked and Meredith's cheeks flushed a pale pink as she withdrew her elbow from his side. "Well... Sure, why wouldn't I be? I mean, we made the arrest. We've got the right guy this time, and an injustice is about to be set straight. Right? I've got a lot of reasons to be in a good mood."

"Things haven't been set right yet," Matthew pointed out, his lips narrow as he thought of the solemn man he'd left in a prison cell just a few hours earlier. "Gabriel's still waiting to see justice."

Nodding, she glanced over her shoulder at squeaking hinges that announced a uniformed officer entering the small room. "I know it sucks," she muttered, her eyes flitting between the cop and the chaplain. "If I had my way..." she began before pursing her lips. "Things are moving, though. It won't be long now." The apologetic tilt of her face implied she wasn't as content with the explanation as her words suggested. But she had nothing else to offer.

Matthew couldn't argue with her. After all, he'd been trying to get Gabriel to see things that way. Patience. That was all that was needed now. And if the Lord felt there needed to be some transition time, then He knew what he was doing. Nevertheless, Matthew wasn't entirely content with the explanation, either. Gabe had been through more than enough, and what he desperately needed now was to be with his family again - to try to rebuild his fractured, semi-destroyed life. There was little doubt in his mind that he would be able to rebuild it. Maybe he'd have to do it without his wife. And maybe he'd even have to do it without his kids. But, Matthew knew that Gabe was so much stronger now than he had been. And he was far from alone. Jesus was with him.

"With a bit of luck," Maloney added, unaware of Matthew's thoughts. "We can speed the process along."

"And you need my help for that?"

"Well, 'need' is a strong word," she joked, sliding back into a light-hearted tone as she turned to face him fully again. She didn't like to admit to needing anyone. Never had, even at four years' old. Things were beginning to change, though. She was realizing that, whether she acknowledged it or not, she did need things from other people. The first step to admitting that aloud was to treat it with humor.

"I'm getting no place fast with this guy," she admitted, her smile still twisting her mouth. "I thought maybe you could...You know, make him... see the light or whatever it is you do."

Matthew blinked at her and wondered if she was still joking. "That's not exactly..."

"I know, I know," she interrupted. "But, you're good at talking to people. You can be very persuasive. I know that from experience," she added with a subtle laugh.

Matthew found his own mouth shifting in a grin as he recalled their first meeting. "It was easier with you, you cared."

"Maybe there's something this guy cares about," she replied, gesturing to the door with her head.

"Maybe," Matthew agreed. "Or maybe he's a true psychopath who cares about nothing."

"Hmm." Humming, Maloney nodded. "I think even psychopaths care about some things," she said as the door slowly squeaked open again. Standing beside it, she waited for Matthew to move first.

He cleared his throat and ran a hand through his thick black hair before stepping across the threshold and beyond the reinforced steel doorway. His feet echoed on bare concrete around an almost bare room, as he stepped closer to a small table and the man who sat in front of it. A man who looked exactly like the one he'd become friends with over many months previously. A man who looked at him with cold eyes, much colder than any glare Gabriel had ever squared at him.

"Who are you?" the man muttered, his voice a tone lower than Gabriel's, but his accent almost identical.

Eyebrow arching, Matthew looked behind him at the woman who was following him into the room. The question was clear: why hadn't she told Mason what this meeting was about? The answer, though, was also obvious: he wouldn't have agreed to it if he'd known.

"Ah," the prisoner added, his dark eyes moving over Maloney as she leaned against the back wall and crossed her feet at the ankles. "Good to see you again, Detective," he added with a leering grin. "Missed me, did ya?"

"Desperately," she replied flatly, the word doused in sarcasm.

Leaning back in his chair, Mason pulled his cuffed hands back from the table and grasped his crotch. "I'll bet you did, baby. Think about me often, don't you?"

Maloney quelled the gagging reflex and tossed her eyes toward Matthew. In turn, the chaplain puffed out his cheeks, noting how different the twins were. Although, that fact was hardly a complete revelation given the crimes the man in front of him had committed.

"What? You're banging the black dude?" Mason wondered, his hand leaving his body and resting once more on the edge of the table.

Refusing to rise to the childish baiting, Maloney tapped a finger against her thigh as she looked over at Matthew. The chaplain wasn't abashed or even surprised by the behaviour or the language, but he was beginning to realize the task ahead of him might be even harder than he'd anticipated. No one was unreachable, though, of that he was certain. He would just need a little more help from Christ. And there was no doubt He would give it.

"Mason," Matthew began, his voice seeming darker in the confined but cavernous space. "I work at the prison; the one your brother's been in for over two years."

"So?"

"So nothing," the chaplain responded evenly. "I'm just introducing myself. My name's Matthew. I was hoping you'd let me talk with you for a while."

"Free country, right?" With a hefty shrug of one shoulder, Mason sniffed. "But if you're going to harp on the same tune as the stuck-up tramp over there, you can forget it. I'm not going to admit to anything. You wanna pin something on me, prove it!"

His tongue tracing his lower lip, Matthew tossed a quick glance at Maloney. Unaffected by the insult - she'd heard much worse, and some of it from her own family - she rolled her eyes and waited for the conversation to continue.

"You don't have to talk about what happened to us or anyone else," Matthew admitted, his attention moving back to the angry man before him. "But it might help you if you do."

"I'm spending the rest of my stinking life in jail, pal. It makes no difference to me."

Silent, Matthew calmly stepped forward and lowered himself into the vacant seat opposite Mason. "That's true," he conceded. "But it will make a difference to your well being. Don't you want to unburden yourself?"

Squinting, Mason eyed Matthew's face as his lip curled in contempt. "You're one of those Jesus freaks? Man, you really are wasting your time. What were you thinking sweet cheeks?" he added, tossing the question to the woman who still lounged on the wall at the rear of the room. "You think a bible-basher is going to work a miracle here?"

Still, she refused to answer. Confident that Matthew could handle himself, she watched passively and waited.

"No miracles," the chaplain said. "That's the Lord's field, not mine. But I can help you if you want my help."

"I don't need no-one's help."

"What about the people who need yours?" Matthew countered easily.

Laughing, Mason shook his head. "Nobody needs my help."

"What about your brother?"

"I don't have a brother," he muttered. "Just some guy who shares my DNA."

"He's been punished for the things you did," Matthew persisted. "He's still being punished, and you can end that suffering for him. You can do the right thing now, Mason. You can help someone. Maybe that'll feel good."

"Maybe you should go suck some choir boy's penis."

Calmly, Matthew twisted his upper body. His eyes met Maloney's and he saw the loss of spark in hers. She'd given up hope that this would get anywhere. He, on the other hand, had not.

"You know, he reminded me a lot of you when we first met," Matthew conversationally uttered. "You two aren't as different as you might think. And if you'd had the chance to get to know each other..."

"But we didn't," Mason snapped. "We didn't. Okay? So he got the perfect life and I got the crap. He got the unblemished face. He got the wife and the children."

As he listened, Matthew noted that Mason had found out much more about his twin brother than he probably wanted to admit to. He was more interested than he probably wanted to admit, too.

"What did life ever hand me, huh?" Mason demanded.

"I don't know," Matthew replied sympathetically. "But we could talk about that if you want to."

"I don't want to." Closing his eyes, Mason grasped his lower lip roughly between his teeth. The puncture marks left behind almost prompted a steady flow of blood, but not quite. "You know what I want?" he said, his tone shifting as he opened his eyes and stared hard at the man sitting across the table. "I want to meet the miserable jerk who had everything that should have been mine."

"I'm not sure..." Matthew began, but he didn't get the opportunity to say more. Maloney's voice cut across him.

"What will you give us in return?"

"What?" Mason scoffed.

"I can set up the meeting, Heiland," she said, pushing herself away from the wall and crossing her arms beneath her bosom. "But you know you can't get something for nothing in this world. So... the question is how badly do you want to meet your brother? What are you prepared to do?" She knew she was needling him in a way that could easily blow up in her face. He was not the kind of man who responded well to being pushed into a corner, even a metaphorical one, and he especially didn't like to be pushed by a woman. She was either too invested or too cocky to stop. She sensed it was a combination of the two.

"Screw you, Maloney." Tossing himself back in his seat, Mason shook his head.

Meredith had one last move to make, and she knew she had to make it fast to ensure it didn't seem like a bluff. "Fine," she sighed, spinning on the ball of her foot and taking hurried steps to the door. "Like you said, you're going to prison either way. I don't care whether you ever get to be in the same room as your twin or not."

"Wait," Mason hollered.

Maloney allowed herself a surreptitious smile, which she wiped clean away before she turned to face him again. "Yeah?" she said sweetly, trying not to let the phony air show.

"You're not screwing with me? You can set this thing up?"

"Plead guilty, and I'll set it up," she replied matter-of-factly.

***

The old Gabriel would have wanted no part in this. But things were different now. He was different. And there was a side of him that wanted to know his brother. Maybe there was a side that even felt sorry for him. They were brothers, after all. They shared a bond, whether they wanted to admit and, even whether they liked it, or not.

He approached the table calmly. He studied the smirk on his double's face. He eyed the scar, evidence of Katherine's account of their births. Mostly though, he was drawn in by eyes that looked so much like his own, yet not like his own. They were full with resent, anger, bitterness and a violent rage he wanted to hurl at the world. Gabriel recognized those things as clear as day. And he knew why that was the case- because those things had once been in his own eyes. He didn't know whether he'd ever looked quite as darkly at anyone as Mason was now looking at him, but he worried that he might have done. That unpleasantness had existed in him, and he was determined to never let it back into his life.

"Well, well, well," Mason muttered as Gabe settled into the seat and met his brother's eyes without a flinch. "If it isn't the angel Gabriel."

"I'm far from an angel," the much calmer of the two men replied. "I'm not so different from you. I've done things I regret, too. It's not..."

"What makes you think I regret anything?"

Set off balance by the question, Gabriel shook his head. "You- You-" He knew the kind of violence he'd thrown at their father and threatened their mother with. To some extent, he even understood it. But that man's death had to have been an accident. "You meant to kill him?" Gabriel eventually managed to ask, already knowing the answer.

"That jerk screwed my wife," Mason replied casually. "He deserved everything he got."

Gabriel had already learned the basics of the case from Maloney, via Matthew. He knew that Mason's battered ex-wife had had a brief relationship with Alec Renaudin. What he hadn't bargained on was that Mason had tracked the man down with the premeditated intent to kill.

"He- but he-" It was on the tip of Gabriel's tongue to point out that neither Renaudin or the former Mrs. Hieland had done anything wrong, but the fact seemed so obvious the words just wouldn't come.

"You know the funny thing? I bumped into him almost by chance," Mason continued, with cold eyes focused dead ahead. "When I asked him if he knew Claire, he started bragging about how great she was in the sack. Well, I wasn't going to stand there and take that. So- I didn't. I didn't take it. And he'll never speak that way about her again." His chin lifting, he actually seemed proud of what he'd done.

Gabriel watched as a smile twisted his mirror image's mouth. Wondering if that strength of evil lay in him too, he found himself suddenly grateful for everything that had happened to him. Grateful for the turn of events that had steered him away from the path he was on to a different one. A better one. One that, despite all the suffering that had come with it, had led him to happiness.

"You don't have to live the rest of your life this way," Gabriel said, hoping he was right and it wasn't too late for his brother. "There's something more, you just have to open yourself to it."

"There's nothing more. There's nothing for me, because the life I could have had was stolen from me. I could have been you!" he yelled. "If this had happened to you rather than me," he added, pointing to the scar on his head. "I would have had your perfect little life."

Knowing those thoughts intimately, Gabriel had long since banished them from his heart and mind. They did no good. They were just forces of destruction. He wondered if Mason could even conceive of letting them go. They seemed to have become such a part of him it was difficult to know where they stopped and the man behind them began. Jealousy was like a good friend to Mason, always with him even when the rest of the world had abandoned him. In reality it was no kind of friend, though.

"I don't know what you've been through," he began, trying not to earn yet more of his brother's hatred. "And I'm sorry that you were dealt a crappy hand. But my life hasn't been the bed of roses you think it has- I think we might have quite a lot in common. I mean-" Not knowing how much to say, he stopped and focused on the most recent wrong that had been handed him. "The last few years have been hell, you know?"

Mason snickered. "You expect me to apologize for that?"

Quietly, Gabriel considered the question. What had he expected from this? He didn't know. But he did know that it didn't matter whether Mason offered an apology or not.

"I forgive you," he said, his voice strong and clear and his eyes set firmly on his twin's.

Mason was equally convinced in his reply. "I don't want your forgiveness. I don't want anybody's."

Incongruous as it was, a smile drifted across Gabriel's face. He suddenly appreciated something he hadn't before: there was power in forgiveness. There was strength to be gained in letting go of the anger and hurt. It was a gift he offered, but it was also one he received. It unburdened him just as much as it would unburden Mason if only he'd accept the light into his life.

"I forgive you anyway," he said, his smile growing warmer. "That's what we do as Christians."

"Our father called himself a Christian," Mason replied, anger forcing the words out. "You think he was some great man just because that's what everyone saw?"

"People call themselves lots of things." As Gabriel spoke, he realized how much like Matthew he was beginning to sound. He didn't mind, though. "It's not what we call ourselves that matters. It's what we do. By his deeds shall ye know him."

Amused, Mason released the contents of his lungs. "And your deeds?"

"My deeds haven't always been something I'm proud of," Gabriel confessed, with no hesitation or shame. "But I've become better and I will be better. It's never too late. You can change things."

"No, I can't." Straight-faced and with a furrowed brow, Mason shook his head. "And even if I could, I wouldn't want to."

It wasn't just the sight of Mason that was like looking in a mirror. Gabriel knew he and his twin were alike in a number of ways. And he didn't like what he saw reflected back at him.

"Well-" he sighed, getting to his feet. "Maybe some day you'll change your mind." He certainly had every intention of trying to urge him to.

"So, that's it? You're just going to go back to your life?"

“No.” There was not one to go back to. The old one was gone. And, truthfully, he was glad. “I’m going to try to make a new one.” With a brief smile, Gabriel turned to the door and left his other self behind.

Chapter Twenty Six

Detective Maloney settled into the seat, leaned back and took a deep breath. A hand at her thigh, giving a gentle squeeze of comfort, reminded her that she wasn't alone. She turned to look at him and offered a shy smile.

He cocked his head at the expression on her face that seemed so alien on her features. There was nothing shy about Meredith Maloney. Except, he was beginning to understand, there was. She just didn't let everyone see it. There were two of her. The Meredith Maloney, hard-bitten cop that she let the rest of the world see. And then there was Meredith Maloney who was more affected by her work than even she wanted to acknowledge, the compassionate, sensitive, vulnerable Meredith. That version of her was a secret she kept locked away in the safest recesses of her heart. She didn't let just anyone in, but she'd let him. And looking back, he realized that she always had let him see flashes of it. She'd allowed him that privilege. And so, he smiled warmly at her in reply.

Meredith's own grin softened as she felt his warm eyes study her. She had no idea what was going on in his head, but she knew she loved it when he looked at her like that. As if he saw something special and wonderful, something he loved. She was still wary about making their relationship public knowledge, though. She didn't want the rest of the department to look at her differently, or think she readily leapt into bed with her colleagues – there had been one or two when she was younger, but she'd soon learned it was a horrible idea.

This was different, though. It was never just a fling. And it definitely wasn't one now. She'd even begun to imagine the two of them getting married, maybe having a family, and growing old together. That was the kind of relationship that couldn't be kept secret. For now, though, she was happy to share knowing smiles with him; to have something only they knew about. It was romantic and sexy.

"What are you thinking?" Cox asked, as he noticed her smile morphing from nervous to giddy.

"About you," she replied, leaning closer so she could whisper. "About me. About us."

"I like the way you think," he murmured, giving her leg another squeeze before letting go. He didn't want to draw attention to them, although he wondered how much they were really fooling anyone with their sappy smiles and moony eyes. "Hey," he added, stretching an arm across the back of her chair. "Good for you."

"For?"

"This," he said, nodding his head at the courtroom in front of them. It was small, and filling gradually. The pine prosecution and defense desks were already littered with papers and files while the DA spoke to the Summers' counsel. Not that either of them were really necessary, it was all just window dressing really.

Behind the two detectives, one row of the gallery was occupied with faces Jensen Cox recognized, reporters he often saw covering cases he'd worked on. He wondered briefly what angles they'd all take when covering this. It had already been all over the front pages. Some papers had reported it as a catastrophic error by the police and justice system, others had a more lenient approach; painting a situation that was highly unusual and a miscarriage of justice that was, in many ways, unavoidable. Rationally and calmly he took the latter view, but in quiet moments late at night, he had to ask himself whether he'd really done all he could to avoid this. He hadn't done as much as Meredith, that was for sure.

"Well," she sighed. "It doesn't put it all right, but it's a start."

"I'm proud of you."

"Thank you." Turning her upper body toward his, she tweaked with the knot of his tie before running her hand down the length of it. "I'm..." Whatever she'd been about to say would have to wait.

As a door at the front of the room opened, the room fell hush and a voice yelled, "All rise."

Meredith and Jensen stood, and her eyes shifted to the front bench where a pale Gabriel Summers looked uncomfortable in his skin as he got to his feet.

The suit he wore, the same one he'd worn at his trial, was too big. He'd gained some muscle over the previous months, but lost his beer gut, which meant the pants felt loose and the jacket was baggy. It felt wrong, and it made him seem like a small boy, wearing clothes that were bought intentionally too large so he'd 'grow into them'. He reminded himself he wasn't a boy. He reminded himself he wasn't a victim, either. Pushing his shoulders back, he brought himself to his full height and breathed a deep, slow lungful of air-conditioned oxygen.

This wasn't like the first time. It was nothing like the first time. He knew what the outcome of this would be, there was no need to be nervous. He would be celebrating by lunchtime. He'd be free. Yet, there was still a dryness to his tongue and a tension in his throat that made him feel like he might be on the verge of vomiting. He couldn't account for it. He tried to swallow it, force it down and shake it off. But it sat there, a terrible dull weight in the pit of his stomach.

"It's alright, Gabe," the man beside him said. "Like I said, this is all just formality."

As the judge sat at her bench, adjusting her black robe before picking up her reading glasses, she glanced at the room before her and offered a nod to the bailiff.

"You may be seated," he called.

Shuffling of feet, brushing of clothes and clearing of throats broke the tense hush that had descended into the room. But it was brief, lasting only a second or two. And then, the silence was back.

Settling back into her chair three rows in front of Maloney and Cox, Katherine tried to still her jittery hand by pressing it against her thigh. She didn't know why she was nervous. And she'd valiantly hid it earlier when she'd been allowed to see Gabe. She did know, though, that it wasn't today she was worrying about. It was all of the days to come, how her son would cope in a life without his wife and young family.

To her right, Matthew reached across and placed his hand over hers. "It's going to be fine," he whispered. "He's a free man now."

"Is he, though? Really?" Katherine wondered if Gabriel could ever be free of his past – any fearer than she was of hers, or Mason was of his. Gabe may have innocence well and truly on his side, but perhaps the time passed had caused damage that could never be repaired. Some scars simply never heal.

"As free as any of us can be," Matthew replied contemplatively.

Katherine would have asked what he meant, but the judge's voice quickly stopped her attempt to speak.

"Can you confirm for the court that you are Gabriel Summers?" the austere woman said as her eyes fell on the man in an ill-fitting suit.

The answer was simple, Gabe knew it instinctively. On any other occasion the word would slip from him effortless. It was easy as words go, one of the first he'd learned and one he must have used a million times over the course of his lifetime. But it wouldn't come. It stuck in his dry throat, and as he opened his mouth only a slight coughing sound emerged. The world seemed blurred at the edges, but a glass of water was thrust in front of him and he grasped it gratefully. Taking a noisy couple of gulps, he wiped the back of his hand across his lips.

"Yes," he eventually said, the word cracking, but clear enough to be heard at the back of the room.

Maloney flicked her face toward Cox and noted the sombre lines on his brow. "He's been through a lot," she quietly uttered as she rubbed her palm across his upper back. "But he's going to be okay. And it wasn't your fault."

"Maybe," Cox mumbled, glancing at her before adding, "Shouldn't have taken this long, though. And if it wasn't for you..."

"We both did what we could with the information and evidence we had at the time, Jensen." They'd had this conversation before, it had taken various forms; sometimes she was the one beating herself up over it. But the results were always the same, they'd come to agree that there was no way for them to have supposed the truth, and second guessing themselves forever more was the surest way to end their careers. They had to move on. And, for the most part, they both had. But there were moments when the regrets were sharpened.

At the head of the room, the judge twisted in her swiveling leather chair. "As you know, Mr. Summers," she said, "this is not a trial, you're here to be acquitted of the crime you were found guilty of. Do you understand?"

"Yes," Gabe replied.

"New evidence has come to light, which cast doubt over your part in the murder of Mr. Renaudin. And a subsequent confession has put you in the clear." The judge continued to talk, the words almost conversational, as though she wasn't talking about a death and another life destroyed. "Is there anything you'd like to say at this point Mr. Summers?"

Gabriel had imagined that moment for weeks, he'd concocted long speeches railing against a system that had failed him. As he stood there in the fluorescent light from the court room's ceiling, he couldn't summon any of the anger he'd felt when he'd written them in his head.

"I... um..." he began, dredging his mind and his heart for all of the bitterness he'd spent so long nursing. It wasn't there, and he didn't even miss it. "I just want to say that I've forgiven all the wrongs done against me," he said. "I don't hold any grudges and I don't hold any one in this room to blame for what happened." As he came to an end, he smiled and some of the tension left his shoulders.

Behind him and unseen to his eyes, Matthew and Katherine shared a small grin. Katherine's fingers stopped fidgeting and she flipped her hand over to take Matthew's warmly. It was going to be alright, she was sure of it. Her son was going to be alright.

Meredith and Jensen glanced at each other, too. Jensen's eyebrows crept up, Meredith simply offered him a shrug. She couldn't explain the change in him, but she'd already seen it the day Gabriel visited Mason in custody. She was a cop, she could put two and two together, and realized Matthew must have had a hand in the transformation, but it was still difficult to square the man in court today with the man they'd arrested and questioned.

While the judge went through the obligatory legalese, Meredith told Jensen about Matthew's seemingly magical influence. "There's just something about him," she offered unable to offer a clearer explanation. "I guess he must have got through to Summers somehow."

"Yeah," Jensen agreed, his eyes still wide. "I'd say so."

"Who knows? Might even mean he's able to patch things up with his wife," she suggested. In reality, she wasn't sure whether there was a lot of hope on that front, but there was certainly more chance than there had been.

"So," the judge said, raising her voice as she came to the end of her spiel. "You are free to go, Mr. Summers."

There was a light ripple of applause spattered about the room, Gabriel didn't make any overt celebration, though. He smiled softly, almost as though he were worried the whole thing was a dream he might wake up from. The hand that clasped his and shook it firmly suggested otherwise. And when he finally tossed his face over his shoulder and saw the tears slipping down his mother's face, he was convinced. It was no dream. It was real, and for the first time in years, his life was his own again.

As that thought settled like a fallen leaf, creating tiny ripples in a pond, the disbelief gave way to happiness. He felt the swell of tears in his own eyes before he was led from the room.

Chapter Twenty Seven

The apartment was quiet. Almost deathly quiet. The only sound was the constant swish, swish of the cars five stories down. His relationship with that noise was uncomfortable; he found it somewhat soothing, but it simultaneously grated on his nerves. He couldn't decide whether it was better or worse than silence. Silence was familiar and safe and a friend. But it was lonely. And, so much more lonely now that the small house warming party had dispersed.

It hadn't been anything fancy. Very few people had wanted to come. Even fewer had actually turned up. Most of his old friends and colleagues wanted to avoid any resurgence of the media frenzy that had descended when he was first arrested. His wife had refused any contact, even after he'd been cleared. And there were those old acquaintances who still clung on tight to their doubts about his guilt.

So the party itself had consisted of just Matthew, Jake, Katherine and a couple of Jake's friends. They'd eaten pizza and watched the game, it'd been almost as though the whole nightmare hadn't happened. But not quite, the memory of it lingered like a thick fog and tainted everything, even the taste of the pepperoni. Gabe was sure he still smelled like prison, too, and no amount of scrubbing would rid him of that stench. He was still grateful for every single one of the people around him, none of whom would even be in his life if it weren't for what happened. However, he felt the sharp pain of those who weren't there – the ones who'd been cruelly ripped away from him by what happened.

Alone and almost quiet now, Gabe felt that loss all the more keenly. Seated on the couch he glanced around the sparsely decorated room. He'd only gotten a few items of furniture from Goodwill. One of those was the couch he was sitting on, which was a little threadbare in places and so covered with a throw. The other items were a scuffed armchair in the corner and a slightly chipped coffee table. It wasn't much, but he was thankful for it. The TV, a present from Matthew, was still on, but Gabe had long since stopped watching it. The glaring light from it illuminated the room with fluttering greens and blues, while his eyes remained focused on the window.

In many ways the apartment reminded him of his very first place, the little studio he'd rented at twenty years' old. It was small, but serviceable. And yet, it didn't seem small to Gabe, it seemed much bigger than that old studio apartment and infinitely bigger than the place he'd just been calling 'home'. Funny, he thought. He remembered feeling panicked and claustrophobic when he was first in that jail cell. Over time, without realizing it, he'd become accustomed to it. And now, being in a space even slightly larger made him feel agoraphobic. He'd been warned by a psychologist laid on by the prison that that might be his reaction. Nothing could have truly prepared him for the sensation of leaden fear that settled in his abdomen as he stepped out into open air and freedom once more, though. Not only was it a shock to him, but he felt too foolish to tell anyone about it. He should be ecstatic, he'd finally be able to return to his life, he could come and go as he pleased – he had every reason in the world to be deliriously happy, and none to be the nervous wreck that sat on his tatty hand-me-down couch.

Exhaling heavily, he shot up. Both hands rose to his head and swept through his dark hair, which had recently seen the rare treat of a good quality barber. It felt too short to Gabe, though. Too short and too neat. That hair belonged to a man who was employed... and, of course, that was the whole point of the haircut, to turn him into someone who was once again employable.

There was a whole fresh source of anxiety, Gabel couldn't begin to imagine what it would be like to interact with people in the outside world again. His mother had insisted it was easy, no different from talking to her. It was different, though. It was very different, because his employer and co-workers might not hesitate to ask questions about the missing years of his life, the heavily-publicized case and his psychopathic twin. And how would he answer those questions?

Letting his fingers shift to the back of his head, he stroked the nape of his neck as he deliberately slowed and deepened his breaths. "Calm down," he told himself softly. "Just calm down." It was a simple and well-used mantra, but it rarely worked.

His other hand falling to his side, he wriggled the fingers before clenching a fist. Still massaging his nape he turned one way and then the other, not sure whether he wanted to move much less which direction he wanted to move in. Eventually, he glanced back at the couch, and that no longer seemed inviting. Sinking to his haunches, he swayed a little before planting his backside on the floor. The floor was good. The floor was safe. Nowhere to fall. Crossing his legs in front of him, in a way he hadn't done since he was a kid, he closed his eyes and laced his fingers in his lap.

"Lord, I think I need you now more than ever," he began softly, the words no clearer than a faint mumble. "I'm thankful for all I have, and the life returned to me, but I don't know where to go or what to do. I'm frightened, and I need your strength and guidance to get through this. I know you're already giving it, but I... I feel so lost and alone right now. I'm not sure what your plan is for me, but I don't want to screw it up. I don't want to squander the precious gifts you've offered me. So, please. Please help me to stay on the right path. And please take care of Jenny and the kids. Thank you for your constant love. I'll strive to deserve it with every breath. Amen."

By the time he'd finished, breathing it had become easier and the tightness in his chest lessened, but he couldn't prevent his eyes from moving back to the window and the bright lighted sign of the liquor store across the street. Forcing his eyelids closed, he tried to calm the palpitations that tremored in his chest. He knew sleep was going to come hard.

***

Over the next few weeks, sleep went from hard to elusive. The insomnia as bad as his first months in prison, he yearned even more for a good stiff drink to numb him into insensibility. Sweat soaked his mattress as he lay staring at the ceiling, hoping for the occasional gentle breeze to cool the perspiration on his brow.

He'd been looking for work, with the help of someone appointed by the court. But, Daisy (at least, he thought that's what her name was), was more interested in her cell phone than she was in actually helping him. Katherine had suggested he go to her workplace for a couple of afternoons, and he promised he would, but had been successfully putting it off ever since. He was still so scared. Of everything, all the stuff he'd simply taken for granted before all this began. Now, he took nothing for granted.

The buzz of the door was unexpected on a Monday morning, he had no appointments and very few people paid unplanned visits these days. Picking himself up from the carpet and that one spot on the floor that seemed secure, Gabe shuffled with only socks covering his feet. When he reached the door, he pressed the gray button on the intercom.

"Hello?" he said.

"Gabe, it's only me," came the reply of a man Gabriel knew well. "Sorry to pop by uninvited, but wondered if you're free for a chat."

There weren't many people Gabe was glad to see these days, and as he felt himself slipping closer to temptation, he wasn't sure he really wanted him around, either. But, he also knew he had to hang on to the friends he had as though his life depended on it. Because, in truth, it did.

"Sure, Matt," he eventually said, his thumb pressing the pad that unlocked the street door downstairs. "Come right up." Before he'd finished talking, he craned his head over his shoulder to check the state of his living room. He didn't really know why, it wasn't as though it ever looked like a frat house, he was old enough to know how to clean up after himself. And there wasn't anything incriminating, like an empty six-pack or half-drunk bottle of Budweiser, for Matthew to spot. Gabe had just managed to remain clear of the urge to drink again. Only just. And he wondered how much longer he could do it. He needed sleep, he needed to feel the warmth that surrounded him when he had a drink; like being hugged. And that was a sensation he wouldn't readily admit to missing. He needed the oblivion that getting well would bring, then the world might look less threatening.

Tugging the security chain off the door, he eased it open wide enough to spot Matthew walking up the narrow hallway. The chaplain broke into one of those warm smiles that was his trademark. Gabe tried to offer him one as easy in return, but couldn't manage. His was strained and he knew it didn't reach his mouth, much less his eyes.

"Hey," Matthew said, lifting a hand in greeting. He stepped across the threshold with a nod of thanks, and Gabe was reminded again how strange it felt to be in control of who came in and out of his home. "How are you doing?" the chaplain added.

"Fine," Gabe replied before closing the door with a casual kick of his toe. "Fine."

"You know, it's alright not to be fine." Smile growing softer, Matthew idly looked around the room. "It's a huge change, and we all need help and time to adjust to change."

Gabe dipped his face as he slid his hands into his pockets. "Yeah, sure, I know all that." Leaning his back against the door he added, "But I'm okay. Really. It's... It's fine." With a shrug he tried to smile again, but the effort was no more successful than the first.

Matthew's lengthy hum left Gabe in no doubt that he'd failed to convince him. So the chaplain's next words came as no surprise to him. "Katherine's concerned. And, honestly, so am I. We missed you in church yesterday."

Gabe had wanted to go, he just couldn't face it. All those eyes on him, people judging or gossiping. He knew most of them were well-meaning, several had even offered to do what they could to help him get back on his feet. In some ways, though, that was worse than the judging and the gossip. As much as he appreciated the kindness in their gestures, he didn't want to be looked on as fragile or treated like a charity case. It was pride plain and simple, he knew that. But he didn't have a great deal of dignity left after the experiences of prison, and he was eager to hang tight to what small amount remained.

"Actually, the whole congregation missed you," Matthew added. "You're becoming part of the family down there."

Wincing at the mention of family, Gabriel stared at the floor. That emptiness inside himself that he was itching to fill with booze could be summed up in that one word. Family.

"I... uh..." he began when the wait for his reply grew awkward. "I've been...busy. I..." It was as feeble a reason as he'd offered anyone for anything. And as he realized that, his words drifted off in surrender.

"Busy, huh?"

"Yeah, busy. I'm looking for work and I'm trying to make this place habitable and I..." Defensiveness left Gabriel over the course of his little speech. Lifting his face and catching sight of the swell of compassion in Matthew's eyes, he tossed his hands up. "I guess I'm just... I'm not coping as well with all this as I thought I was. Not as well as I thought I would be." His confession came slow, but steady, and he never took his gaze from the man who'd been his anchor in the stormiest of seas. "I've been..."

"Why didn't you call me? Or Katherine? Or Jake?" Matthew asked. "You know we're all here for you."

"I guess," Gabe answered, like a child who'd expected a rebuke and was getting only empathy. "I didn't know how to start. It seems so stupid to admit that… I'm scared."

"Scared of what?"

"Scared of everything," Gabe replied, his voice a whisper. "Scared all the time." Lower lids burdened with tears he tried to wipe them away while clearing those same unshed tears from his throat. "It's ridiculous. I'm a grown man!"

Matthew stepped forward and placed a hand on Gabe's shoulder. Squeezing gently, he sighed. "It's not stupid or ridiculous. And it's not weak either, Gabe. It takes great strength to ask for and accept help."

Swallowing the emotion lodged in his throat, Gabe nodded.

"Imagine you had a friend in your position," Matthew added. "Would you think he was weak for struggling with his new life?"

Gabriel didn't want to admit it, but he knew there was a significant portion of his life when he would have found this hypothetical friend weak. Now, though? Now he'd experienced the soul-destroying system, the fears and the dark thoughts, he couldn't bring himself to judge anyone – even an imaginary someone – for what they might feel on the other side of all that. Repeat offending made sense on some level, because it must have been easy for young men to fall back into the behaviors that had landed them in jail in the first place. And sometimes prison must have seemed like the 'better' option to men, like him, who'd become so ingrained in the system that life outside of the institution was unbearable.

"No," he eventually said, a subtle shake of his head emphasizing the point. "I wouldn't blame them for anything they were feeling."

"Then why are you being harder on yourself? Why do you demand more from yourself than you would from any other man?"

Gabe did the only thing he could do: shrugged. But Matthew's questions were far from finished.

"Why did you stop seeing the therapist?"

He nearly shrugged again, but stopped himself when he realized how childish he was being. "I don't know," he said instead. "It was uncomfortable, and it didn't seem to be working. She wanted me to get in touch with my feelings and stuff, and I just..."

Amused, Matthew smiled as he withdrew his hand and studied the man who had a pinkish blush to his cheeks. "You think it would be a bad thing to be more in touch with your emotions."

"No, I suppose not, but it's not easy and I'm more of a..." Gabe waved his hand in an indefinite circle as he tried to define what it was he saw himself as. "I'm pragmatic, I guess. I see a problem, I wanna fix it. I don't want to talk it to death."

Slowly, Matthew began to nod. "Okay, so what is the problem?"

Before even contemplating his reply, Gabe scraped his lower lip with his teeth. "I've been… I'm struggling not to drink."

Lips pursing in reply, he eyed Gabe quickly before deciding he was telling the truth. The temptation was clearly there, but he didn't look like a man who'd given into it yet. "I'll do everything I can to help," he said. "But that's a symptom, it's not the problem."

"I told you the problem, I'm scared."

Matthew shook his head evenly. "That's a symptom, too. What is it that you need Gabe? What do you lack now that would improve your situation?"

"Where do I begin?" he said with a hollow snicker.

"The most important thing."

Family was on the tip of Gabe's tongue and it almost leapt out when he stalled long enough to consider what it was from his family that he missed most. There were a huge number of things, of course. But mostly…

"I want to feel needed," he mumbled. "I want to feel useful. I want to make a difference to someone."

Matthew's smile returned as he listened, a plan already forming in his mind. He wondered why he hadn't thought of it before. "I think I might be able to help," he said, the force of his grin affecting his words. "But it's going to be a lot of work."

"I'm not frightened of hard work," Gabe replied, finally finding a genuine smile of his own.

Chapter Twenty Eight

The scuff of sneakers on concrete rose up above the raucous laughter. Friendly jibes and the sounds of young, masculine rivalry resonated around the yard as the ball hit the backboard and a swish of net was drowned out by a, "Yes! Suck on that, Halliwell!"

Halliwell, a man of twenty-one, with his blond hair shaved close to his scalp like an army recruit flipped the other man the bird. "You're a prick, Rogers."

Still celebrating his basket, Rogers was unconcerned. Long dark hair in dreads that were pulled back into a ponytail, the twenty-five-year-old Rogers brushed his fingers across his bare mocha shoulders with a chuckle. "Dust it off, my man. Dust it off." He smirked, turning to scoop up the ball that bounced away from him.

The half dozen other men in the game laughed at the good-natured battle for supremacy those two permanently waged.

Gabriel watched from the side-lines, back against the orange bricked wall, one foot lifted behind him and his hands casually dipped into his jeans. He smiled to himself at the men's banter. Chad Halliwell and Tanner Rogers had all but hated each other when they first met. There had been a fistfight over some comment Rogers had made, and the two seemed destined to be enemies. Over time, and with a quiet chat in the ear of each, Gabriel had managed to get them on speaking terms. Now, the insults they traded were light-hearted and he sensed that, deep down, they were becoming friends. He was willing to bet, if push came to shove, both would come to the other's defense.

The game continued and Gabe inhaled a large, cleansing dose of fall air. It had rained that morning, and the scent of damp leaves and grass was mingling with the pepperoni and mozzarella wafting from the pizzeria next-door. He appreciated things like that so much more now. Those seemingly insignificant things one doesn't notice until they've been taken away from one for a sustained length of time.

The basketball clunking on the wall next to him, he shook himself free of his quiet musing. With quick reflexes, he caught the ball on the rebound and tucked it under his arm.

"That's our time for today, guys," he said.

"The winners again!" Rogers cried, tossing both arms around the shoulders of two of his teammates. "Man, you're going to have to raise your game if you want to beat us, Halliwell."

With a shake of his head, Halliwell turned away. But a rueful smile crossed his lips as he wandered across the court.

"See you Saturday!" Gabe hollered after him.

He raised an arm to acknowledge he'd heard, but said nothing. The other men followed, chatting about their plans for Friday night, girls they were seeing, the football later that day, or the college assignments they still hadn't done. Only one lingered behind.

Gabriel glanced at Rogers as he bounced the ball at his feet with one hand, keeping the other loosely tucked into his pocket. He could have asked, 'what's up?', but he waited, knowing the young man in front of him would speak in his own time.

"So... uh..." Sure enough, Rogers started. Running his palms together slowly, he looked to the concrete at his feet, then the ground where the ball repetitively bounced and finally lifted his hazel eyes toward Gabe's face. "Well... I... I mean, I wanted to thank you."

Gabriel only gave the man half his attention, carefully making sure that his full scrutiny didn't force Rogers back into silence. He continued to bounce the ball, glancing down at it occasionally as he caught it. "No problem," he replied with a shrug.

"I just... I wanted you to know I appreciate everything," the younger man added. "Things were pretty rough before and... Well, it's better now."

"Like I said," Gabe said. "No problem." Lifting his face, he smiled at the nervously fidgeting man in front of him and saw a little of himself there. He would have been the same as a twenty-something; except he'd had no one there to help him as a twenty-something. Someone to make him feel like he was worth something, and he could do great things if only he didn't stand in his own way. Life would have been a lot different if he had, but then he might not be in a position to do it for others now. God works in mysterious ways. He grinned again, more to himself than Rogers.

"I... uh... I've got this buddy." Hands pressing together, Rogers glanced over his shoulder. "He's kind of got into some trouble."

"Kind of trouble?" Gabe echoed curiously, with a small smile.

"He had a brush with the cops this weekend. A knife or something." It was difficult to be sure whether he was being circumspect because he didn't know all the details, or if he simply didn't want to reveal them all. Gabe didn't ask. It didn't matter, he knew enough.

"I was thinking," Rogers added. "Maybe I could bring him here...you know, if that's okay with you. You are always saying that we should bring people if we think they need it. And well...he's a good guy really, I don't think he'd cause any trouble. He just...needs someone who's there for him."

Gabe nodded as the younger man talked, giving him his full attention now that he realized it wouldn't prevent Rogers flow – he was too invested in the request by that point. "If he's interested," Gabriel said, "by all means bring him down. I'll have a talk with him and see if there's anything we can do to help."

Breaking into a relieved grin, Rogers stopped stroking his hands. "Thanks, man," he breathed. "He's just got caught up with the wrong people, you know?"

Gabe did know. It was a problem all too common in the men he saw around him. So many of them lacked a sense of connection with their families or their communities, and so they searched for it elsewhere. And they found it, usually, in the worst places. Gangs. Groups of petty criminals. Drug addicts, who swore they'd found the best escape from the troubles of the world. And it all amounted to the same thing. A big pile of trouble for the poor souls who just wanted to feel like they weren't alone in the world.

"I'll do what I can for him," Gabe said, catching the ball underhanded in his palm and holding it there.

"Thanks," Rogers added, flexing onto his toes before adding. "See you, Gabe." With his usual light gait, he followed the route his friends had taken.

As he rounded the corner of the pizza place, Gabe continued to watch him. And just as Rogers disappeared, another familiar face turned in the opposite direction.

Dressed in a pair of pale jeans and a long-sleeved T-shirt that was pushed up to his elbows, Matthew waved and hollered a, "Hey there!" across the space between them. Reaching the edge of the basketball court, he paused.

Gabe lifted his hand and tossed the ball toward his friend. It bounced somewhere between them and Matthew reached out with both hands to catch it as it neared his chest. He smiled as he flipped the orange ball up onto the tip of his finger and spun it.

"How's it going?" he asked.

"Good," Gabe replied. "Really good."

Losing its momentum, the ball wavered and Matthew took it back in both hands. "The group seems to be getting a bit of buzz," he said, his eyes moving to the hoop several feet away. He lifted both hands and hurled the ball in that direction. It bounced on the rim twice before falling back to earth.

"Missed," Gabe chuckled.

Matthew shrugged and turned his focus back to the conversation. "A couple of cop friends of mine were telling me what a difference they think you're making."

Feeling his cheeks warm a little, Gabriel shifted one shoulder. "I'm just doing what I can."

"These guys needed someone to look up to, someone they respected and who really understood what they were going through. You're doing a lot to turn their lives around."

Gabriel hoped that was what he was doing. It was what they had both hoped for when Matthew had first suggested setting up a place where young men who'd had a scrape with the law could go, talk, find support and that sense of belonging they'd been searching for. He sensed he'd certainly helped a few find the right path again, he felt good about what he was doing. And he couldn't remember the last time that was true. In fact, he was almost positive he'd never felt as good about what he was doing. Perhaps that was because, in the past, he hadn't been doing anything truly meaningful with his life.

He'd thought he had been. He'd been focused on earning money, providing for his family. Money was important, he wasn't naïve enough to think it wasn't. But it wasn't the most important thing. The pursuit of it was not the most valuable use of his time. People were more important, yet he'd been too blinded by the things that had been drummed into him from a young age to see it.

Now, he saw everything with crystal clear vision. He knew that we are put on this earth to help others, to make a difference to those around us. To live as Jesus lived and died, with love in our hearts and a boundless desire to help our fellow man.

"They're good kids," Gabe sighed, tipping his head in the direction the young men that had wandered. "It's a pleasure to be able to give them a sense of direction. I think Jiro might apply to college next year."

Jiro had only been coming to the group for a month, before that he'd been dabbling in hard drugs and had been arrested twice. He was close to the point of no return; barreling toward a life that would have brought him and those around him nothing but pain and heartache. Matthew had brought him along to one of the hang out nights and, as with most of the first timers, he'd stood near the corner not saying much to anyone. Gabe was sure he wouldn't come the following week. But he did. He still didn't talk, though. Not until his third night with the group; then he'd opened up to Gabriel and told him he was unhappy, but didn't know how to change.

That was the first step. And Gabe knew how much of a step it was, too. Once Jiro had admitted that much, it was only a matter of time before he let help come to him. Gabe didn't need to do much, except listen and empathize – just as Matthew had done for him many months before. He hadn't even needed to make many suggestions, because the young guy would eventually get there himself. He wasn't stupid, he knew what he needed to do to make a change and give himself the opportunity of a better life. He just needed someone to believe in him enough to support him through it.

"He's getting clean, and he's going to finish off his high school diploma," Gabe continued, smiling as he realized just how pleased he was for the young man. "I offered to help him scope for scholarships. He's a bright kid, I think he's got a solid chance if he sticks with it."

Matthew nodded. “I’m glad for him. I’m glad for you, too. You’re a great mentor, Gabe.”

“Well,” Gabriel replied, with an abashed flick of his head. “I don’t know about that, but I do enjoy helping these kids. I’ve got a sense of purpose again. It feels...”

“Good?”

“Better than good,” Gabe said, chuckling. “It feels great.”

“I’m glad.” Cocking his head back in the direction he’d come, Matthew added, “You want to grab a bite to eat. I wanted to talk to you about expanding the work you’re doing.”

“More kids?”

“Not necessarily,” Matthew replied. “But I’m thinking we could start a program to help men who’ve spent a lot of their life behind bars. Especially those who are later exonerated. I mean, you know better than anyone how tough that can be to adjust to. And... Well, I figured you’d be able to offer a unique kind of support to them.”

Gabe found his head shifting in agreement without really willing it to. He was already excited by the idea. He didn’t know how many people had had to go through the trauma he’d endured, but there had to be others like him. And helping them would be just as beneficial to him as it would be to them.

“Sure,” he eventually said. “Let’s talk about it.” Taking a step forward, he put his arm around Matthew’s shoulder as the pair moved to the sidewalk and headed in the direction of the swelling scent of pizza.

***

The first time he came, he could barely make it through the door without finding it hard to breathe. He'd never had a panic attack in his life, but he imagined that must have been what one felt like. He had to force himself to inhale slowly to the count of five. He had to focus on each step, remembering with every one that what he was doing was important. Matthew had ensured him it would get easier in time.

And as the weeks went by, it did. Crossing that threshold, walking through those corridors and into that room, got easier. The conversations remained difficult for a lot longer, though.

Mason hadn't wanted to talk at all for the first visit. He'd stayed stubbornly silent, studying Gabriel as if he were trying to assess and then judge him. If he reached any conclusions, he kept even those to himself. He couldn't have made it plainer that he wanted nothing to do with his twin and he couldn't have cared less if Gabe ever visited again.

Nevertheless, Gabe had persisted. Partly, because he knew how isolating prison life was. But mostly, because his mother had persisted with him and, if she hadn't have done, things would have been so much more unbearable for him. He didn't know whether he could make things less unpleasant for Mason or not, but he was determined to try. And because Mason never refused the visits, he assumed deep down he must have been glad to see someone. Someone cared. Gabriel had certainly been glad of that when he was on the other side of the small table. He might not have shown his gratitude well – or at all. But he'd been thankful that his mother had cared enough to keep showing up, at least one person in the world had been concerned about whether he was okay.

Letting go of his personal bitterness toward his twin brother had been easier than letting go of his anger over what Mason had done to their mother, though. Gabe prayed every day for a month for a little more forbearance and understanding. He tried to remember that he had also been angry with Katherine, not angry enough to threaten or harm her physically. But he *had* harmed her. Maybe his refusal to see her again had hurt her even more. That weighed heavily on him, even though he'd apologize and she'd accepted.

He hoped that, perhaps, Mason's wrongs would weigh heavily on him, too. If not immediately, at some stage over the course of the rest of his life. He hoped for it, because he knew if Mason ever did feel the weight of his sins, he might be compelled to search for help in carrying that burden. Gabriel knew, of course, no mortal could help in that regard, but Christ could. And would.

"How are you?" Gabe asked, settling into the seat opposite his brother. By that point, after nearly four months' worth of visits, he was no longer unnerved by sitting across from a mirror image of himself. Maybe it was because there was something in Mason's eyes that reminded him they were vastly different people. Their shared DNA wasn't the extent of the commonalities, but they were far from identical in every way.

Mason sucked his teeth before peering down at his cuffed hands. "Fine."

Gabe would have asked if Mason had been talking to Matthew, but he already knew the answer. Matthew had tried, and failed to get through.

"Why do you keep coming here?" Mason muttered, gaze still focused on his wrists. His voice was lower, but it wasn't just the tone that was different. There was a quality Gabriel hadn't heard before, and he wasn't sure how to describe the difference.

"I'm not sure what you mean."

"You've got your perfect life. Why do you keep coming here?" His gaze suddenly darting up to meet Gabriel's, there was a glassiness to his eyes. "You just want to gloat, is that it? The brother who had everything and still has everything?"

Gabriel shook his head in bewilderment, he'd been sure they'd already put that conversation to rest. He didn't perceive himself as having had a 'better life' than Mason. It certainly hadn't been perfect.

"I'm not here to gloat," he said. "I'm here to offer what help I can. I'm here to let you know that you're not alone."

With a scoff that caused a splutter from his smoker's lungs, Mason shook his head. "We're all alone, Gabriel. We come into this world alone, we leave it alone and we're alone every second of every day in between. You might want to fool yourself into thinking you're not. But you are."

Gently Gabriel smiled. "I'm never alone, Mason. And neither are you. Christ is with you, looking after you and loving you." Leaning forward, he placed his wrists on the edge of the table. "And there are people right here who are with you, too.

You can push them away, you can try to convince yourself that you're on an island. But that's not possible. No man is. We're bound together by our common humanity. And when you hurt anyone else, you're hurting yourself, too."

Mason chuckled as he stared at his brother. "Sounds like hippy bull to me."

"Maybe so," Gabe relented. "But I believe it's true. I believe that nobody is ever alone. And I believe that we can do so much more to help each other than we realize."

"You can't do anything to help me. I'm going to spend the next forty years in this place, and when I get out... there won't be a whole lot left to live for, right? When the system gives you life, that's what they take even if they don't take all of your years or sentence you to death."

"Not if you want to make a change," Gabe insisted. "Not if you're willing to see that there's more to your life than you've acknowledged so far. And not if you accept the love of Jesus Christ."

For the first time since they'd met, Mason didn't have a quick answer. He wasn't ready with a smart remark that would belittle everything Gabriel held dear.

"I'm here, because you are my brother. Literally and spiritually," he continued, "so it's my job to care about you, to care for you and love you. And I'll do those things whether you're glad of it or not. Just like I've forgiven you even when you don't want my forgiveness."

Still silent, Mason shifted and the chain between his wrists rattled.

"We're never going to be close," Gabriel admitted quietly. "There's too much between us for that. We're never going to have the kind of relationship I'd have wanted for us, because we didn't grow up together. We don't share all the things that brothers should. But we can have a relationship, Mason. I can support you now. I can be here. And that's what I want to be."

Feet scuffing, Mason fixed his eyes on the surface of the table. "I think you're wasting your time. But suit yourself."

Gabe disagreed. He wasn't wasting his time. And if he wasn't sure of it before, he was certain of it then.

Chapter Twenty Nine

Gabe wandered toward the window with his cell phone pressed to his ear. "Yeah," he said, resting himself on the large window sill and turning his upper body to look down at the street below. "I think it's pretty obvious it's a miscarriage of justice, we just need someone willing to go out to bat." He listened to the voice on the other end as he continued to watch the steady stream of foot traffic on the opposite side of the street.

"That's great," he eventually said, smiling. "Thanks for your help. Yeah, I'll be in touch again as soon as I've had the chance to talk to him about an appeal." He nodded gently to himself as he ended the call and lowered the phone. For a moment, he looked at the screen – the lawyer's number still visible. Then, with a soft, "Yes!" he slipped the cell into his pocket.

He'd been trying to find someone willing to take on the case of a twenty-five-year-old named Phil for more than two weeks. It was a clear-cut case of police coercing a confession, but with no money to pay a good defense attorney and learning difficulties that made it impossible for the young man in question to source legal help on his own, he'd been left to rot by the system. Gabe had found out about his case, purely by chance, when he was visiting another prisoner who was about to be released. He'd felt for the guy, and had seen it as his duty to help. Finally, he'd got somewhere.

Letting his head drop back onto the glass, he peered up at the ceiling and allowed himself a broad smile. He was certain Phil's appeal would be successful, and the poor guy who'd spent two years in jail for something he didn't do, would once again be able to have a life.

Of course, it wouldn't be an easy life. Phil had the deck stacked against him. But Gabe was already formulating other plans to help him. One of the younger guys from the group worked for a mechanic and Phil was great with his hands, it wouldn't be too difficult to get him a job there. He was also thinking about offering him his couch for a while until he managed to find a place of his own. Or there was Matthew, who knew of several halfway houses that might have a room for him.

Gabe felt good about his future. He felt sure that, with a bit of help, Phil could get things back on track. And his own life wasn't far off, either. With a renewed sense of purpose, life was good. Sometimes, it surprised him that he could say that. Life was good.

It wasn't perfect, there were still things he wished for, like contact with his kids and with his wife. But, he knew his existence had meaning. He knew he was contributing to the world and the lives of those who needed help. And that all felt so much better than he could ever have imagined it would feel.

Mouthing a "thank you" to the heavens, he closed his eyes and said a silent prayer.

A knock at the door disturbing the silence, Gabe pushed himself off the sill and strolled across the living room. His apartment was beginning to look like a home now; it was filled with proper, comfortable furniture, it was clean. It was a space fit to come back to and pleasant to spend time in. His chosen path had meant money was short, he knew he'd never be able to get a mortgage and a big house again on the income he was making. But that didn't matter. All he needed was a comfortable, safe and warm place to rest his head. Many of the people he saw, and tried to help, didn't have that luxury. It wasn't something he ever took for granted.

Reaching the door, he unlocked it and edged it quietly open. He parted his lips ready to say, "hello" but the word never made it out of his mouth. Instead, his gaze widened as he looked at the woman standing at his threshold.

In many ways, she looked just the same – the same as the day he'd met her. But she was different from the last time he saw her, too. He was sure she looked thinner. Her blonde hair was longer, there were some lines on her brow that hadn't been there before. She was paler, too. As she wrung her hands in front of her, she was silently observing him in a similar fashion.

Like him, she saw a man she both knew and didn't. He looked so much healthier than when she last saw him. His weight loss had trimmed him down, made him look as athletic as he was in his early twenties. There was color in his cheeks. And there was a brightness in his eyes she wasn't sure she'd ever seen. Maybe she had. Maybe it was there when the kids were born. But it had been a long, long time since it'd been there.

"Jen," he eventually said. A swell of confused feelings swirled in his abdomen. He couldn't remember the number of times he'd imagined her standing there. He'd dreamed about her standing there. He'd wanted to see her standing there. And yet, now she was, he had no idea what to say, what to do or how he should feel about it.

"Hello, Gabe," she whispered, her fingers still squeezing her hands as though she didn't know what to do with them. "I... uh..." She blinked, the beginnings of tears obvious in her glistening eyes. "I..." Hesitating again, she took her eyes from him and glanced down the hall she'd just walked. "Maybe I shouldn't be here," she admitted quietly.

Gabriel leaned against the doorjamb for support, not sure whether she was about to bolt and whether he should try to stop her if she did. Perhaps she was right. Perhaps too much time had passed. Too many things had been left unspoken. Things were too different and too difficult now.

"We should talk," he found himself saying. "If you want to, that is." Even if things were too different and too difficult, there were things that should be said.

"Yes," she replied, nodding. "I'd like that." She tried to offer him a smile, but it trembled and a tear crept from the corner of one of her bright blue eyes.

Gabe couldn't find it in himself to comfort her. Instead, he stepped back, pushed the door wider and made room for her to walk in.

"Thank you," she muttered with the politeness of a stranger. Yet, they were the opposite of strangers. They'd been as close as two people can be. As intimate as two people can be. They'd been one person and, with the children forever connecting them, they still were.

Not sure how to handle the stilted awkwardness between them, Gabe said nothing as he pushed the door closed and watched her. She walked slowly, as though she was nervous about each step. She briefly looked around, headed to the couch as if she might sit, but then changed her mind. Still wandering restlessly, she sniffed back more tears and clenched her hands by her sides.

"Is there something you need from me, Jen?" Gabe asked, as his brain reeled with the possible things that might have brought her to his door. Was something wrong with one of the kids? Was she in trouble financially? Did she want to tell him that their children were about to get a new dad? He figured the last one unlikely, why would she bother to tell him she was getting remarried? It was none of his business anymore, after all.

Jennifer didn't know how to respond to that question, but it did stop her aimlessly moving feet. It also turned her attention toward the man who used to be her whole universe. Did she need something from him? Yes, she did. But she wasn't sure if he would give it. Or if he *could* give it. She wasn't convinced she deserved it.

"I... I came to..." Her breath coming ragged, it made it hard to speak, but she forged on. "I came here, because I wanted to apologize."

"Apologize?" he echoed as his hands sank into his pockets. Head tilting to one side, he studied her carefully. "What do you want to apologize for?" he said. "Not believing me? Deserting me when I needed you more than I've ever needed anyone in my whole life? Taking my children away from me? For..." His voice raising, he realized he was losing control and stopped himself. Biting down on his lower lip, he breathed deeply and let his focus drift to the floor. When he lifted his attention to her again, he shook his head. "A lot has happened, Jen. And I can't pretend I'm not hurt."

Her breath heaving at her chest, she nodded. "I know. I know I hurt you, Gabe. But... Try to see it from my point of view. Everyone thought you were guilty. The evidence was..." It was her turn to halt her flow. "It's not an excuse," she admitted softly. "You're my husband and I should have believed you. But... you didn't make it easy to, Gabe."

"I *was* your husband," he corrected her. He didn't bother to argue with the second of her assertions, though. He knew he had been a jerk when he was arrested. He'd been aggressive, he'd allowed his temper to resort to violence. He hadn't acted like a man capable of assaulting and murdering someone. Deep down, he knew much of that was born of not being believed, even by the people who knew him best. But he realized the way he'd acted was indicative of that something in him that was unpleasant and dark, and had drawn him to violent acts as a younger man. That something that existed in a lot of the guys he was now trying to help. Those men could be hard to love, hard to empathize with and hard to help. They weren't unreachable, though. Far from it.

"You really thought I was capable of killing someone?" he asked softly, not entirely sure where the question came from, but needing the answer. "The man you shared a bed with, the man who fathered your children? You thought I could do something like that?"

"I didn't want to believe it, Gabe." Her eyes filling with tears, her words cracked as she continued. "I didn't want to believe the man I loved could do something so awful. It wasn't easy for me to accept that it was possible. But I do know about the things you did. Terrible things that don't seem like the man I know...and I began to think, maybe you're not the man I think I know. Maybe, the whole time we were married, you were someone else."

Gabe shook his head, "I was always myself with you, Jen. Always. You saw the uglier side of me as well as the good stuff. You saw it all, and you saw me at my worst." Exhaling heavily, he added, "I admit it was bad, but I could never have beaten someone to death."

"I was so desperate to think that," she whispered, staring at his feet with eyes that wouldn't blink. "But the DNA."

"DNA isn't infallible."

"I know that now," she mumbled. "But how was anyone to know back then? I... I had no idea you had a twin."

With a wry smile, Gabe said, "Neither did I."

Jennifer coaxed her gaze to his face and cocked her head. There was something different about him. More different than those physical changes she'd first noticed. He exuded a calm, he was almost serene. Now he had more reason than he'd ever had before to hold a grudge against the world, and for the first time he didn't have one. Despite everything he'd been through, he was relaxed. She couldn't imagine where that newfound tranquillity had come from, but it gave her hope.

"Have you met him?" she asked.

Gabel nodded. "I visit him once a month." With a shrug, he added, "We're not close, but I think it does us both good to talk."

"And you've met your mother?" The hint of a smile nudged her lips, but it was tinged with sadness.

"Yes."

"That's good."

Filling his lungs, Gabe wriggled the fingers in his pockets. "Jen, did you want to say something?"

She shifted her head timidly. "I wanted to say I'm sorry," she repeated. "Really, truly sorry for the way things turned out. I wanted to make sure you're okay."

"If you were concerned for me you could have replied to my letters," he said, regretting the sarcasm in his tone. It was an all too humanly instinctive, but he wished he'd been able to quell it. He knew it was pointless to rake over all that stuff. It was done. But the red-blooded, fallible man in him needed to know why the woman he loved had been so heartless.

Her brow sank closer to her bright eyes. "What letters?"

"The ones I started sending you from prison."

"I... I haven't heard from you since the divorce," she replied.

Gabe squinted at her, but it didn't take long to decide she was telling the truth. For one thing, Jen had never been much of a liar. For another, he could see the guiltless expression of surprise in her eyes. This really was news to her. Slowly nodding, he figured he knew what had happened.

"Your mom obviously didn't want you to get them."

She chewed her lower lip, as her eyes flashed with something more than surprise: anger. "Gabriel, I never wanted to turn my back on you. But I was scared for the kids, and everyone kept telling me I had to put them first and I..." Her words breaking, she tried to stem the flood of tears, but they still came. "I feel so awful when I think of you going through all that alone."

"I wasn't alone," he replied, smiling. He was never alone. For much of his life he hadn't realized it, but Christ was always with him. A constant source of support and guidance, if only he'd known how to turn to him.

Through her tears, Jen started to smile too. "I've missed you so much."

"Why did it take you so long to come?" he wondered aloud. There was no bitterness or accusation in the question, just genuine curiosity.

She carefully met his eyes before answering. "I felt guilty. And I was so frightened that you wouldn't want to see me. Who could have blamed you for slamming the door in my face?"

"There was a time when I might have done that," he replied thoughtfully. "But forgiveness is the gift I give and receive these days."

Confused, Jennifer shook her head. "You forgive me?"

His response was automatic and simple. "Yes." Taking his hands from his pockets, he closed the small space between them. Standing directly in front of her, with her body in reach of him for the first time in what felt like centuries, he kept his hands loosely clenched at his sides.

"We've put each other through hell," he added. "I don't see the sense in hurting each other anymore, do you?"

Jen shook her head as a quivering smile brightened her features. "I know I let you down when you needed me most, Gabe. I know I hurt you and punished you for something you didn't do when you were already being punished. I'm not naïve enough to think we can forget all that, I realize things can never be as they were between us... but I miss you, and the children need you, especially Nate." Pausing, she searched her ex-husband's eyes for a sign of his reaction. It was impossible to read. "He's getting to that age where he really needs his dad around and..."

"What are you saying, Jen?" he said, his calm still making it hard for her to tell what was on his mind.

"I'm saying, the kids need you in their lives. And..."

"And?"

"I need you in mine," she breathed, her gaze darting nervously over his features for the first hint he was going to reject her. "I'm not saying I deserve a second chance, Gabe..."

Lifting his hand to her face, Gabriel silenced his ex-wife with a gentle finger pressed to her lips. "I think," he began, "everyone deserves a second chance. I think *we* deserve a second chance." Grinning, he pulled his forefinger from her mouth. "And you're right, things can't be as they were before." Looking intently into her eyes, he dipped his face close to hers. "They'll be better, Jen. I promise," he added, before grazing his lips softly against hers and reminding himself that she always tasted sweet. Like strawberries.

Chapter Thirty

Fourteen months later...

Gabe whistled as he jogged along the hall. He paused long enough to inhale the scent of gingerbread coming from the kitchen before flinging the door open. He took a breath only to have the biting wind steal it.

"Woo," he gasped, wrapping his arms around his torso and slapping his sides.

He spotted Nate beside the car, groaning under the wait of a shovel full of snow. The boy seemed to have grown up frighteningly fast. He had grown up fast, he was a little man now rather than a boy. It pained Gabe to think of all he'd missed, but he was eternally grateful for the second chance he'd been given.

"Nathan!" he called once he could find enough air to speak at all.

The image of his father, Nate's dark head and dark eyes lifted as he tossed the heap of snow aside. "Yeah, Dad?"

"Come on in, kiddo." Gabe knew his eldest son hated that nickname, but he couldn't help himself. He was determined to enjoy what was left of Nathan's childhood while he could. "Your mom and Amy have nearly finished the gingerbread house."

Any grumbling Nate might have been tempted to do about 'kiddo' died away on his chilly, chapped lips at the mention of gingerbread. The grin that spread across his face was so like the one he used to wear as a toddler that Gabe couldn't help but chuckle. He might have grown up, but some things never change.

"Can I have part of the roof?" Nate asked.

Gabe let his lower lip jut out in thought as he surveyed the front drive and the work his son had done to clear it. "Looks pretty good," he eventually concluded. "I figure all that elbow grease deserves a chunk of roof."

"Yes!" Tossing one hand in the air, Nate dashed as fast as he could, kicking up a shower of snow behind him. When he got to the small front porch, he propped the shovel against the wall and hauled off his boots. Mom's rule. The roof would be out of the question if he flouted it and traipsed muddy snow all through the house.

"C'mon," Gabe urged with a cock of his head and a shiver that moved all the way through his body.

With just thick winter socks covering his feet, Nate ran across the threshold, peeling his coat off as he went. "Dad," he said, tossing his hefty insulated coat on its peg. "Can you help me with my math later?"

"Sure," Gabriel replied, shutting the door before wrapping an arm around his boy's shoulders. With the cold firmly left on the other side, the pair walked down the toasty hallway to the kitchen.

Gabe found his daughter and his wife waiting by the oven. Both wore aprons and had flour smears on their faces. Amy even had white flour in her sandy blonde hair; he figured she'd eventually have dark hair like him and the boys. For the time being, though, she was clinging to that angelic blonde –

except for the flour that made her look as though she might be prematurely graying.

Laughing, Gabe crossed the cream tiles and rubbed his fingers through Amy's bangs. "How's it going, sweetpea?"

"Great," she said, twisting her face so she could beam up at her father. "You're going to like it, Dad."

"I'm sure I will," he replied, smiling. As he tried to sweep the last of the flour from her hair and failed, he turned to Jen. "Where's Jamie?"

"He's in the living room." With a slight tilt of her head, she gestured to the room next-door. "Glued to The Grinch, I think."

With a chuckle, Gabe nodded. "I'll get him," he said, taking a step back. Nate was settling himself eagerly at the table as Gabe passed. "Don't start without me," he warned his son, good-naturedly pointing a finger at him. The mischievous smile Nate offered in reply suggested there could be no guarantees on that score.

Not surprised by that fact, Gabe chuckled as he strolled through to the living room. He found his youngest son sitting cross-legged in front of the TV, leaning so close to it that his nose almost touched the brightly colored screen.

"Hey, Jamie, what have I told you? You're going to get square eyes if you sit that close."

The little boy craned his head an awkward angle over his shoulder and flashed his Dad a grin that was missing a front tooth. "Square eyes would be cool," he said.

Gabe gently shook his head. “They wouldn’t be cool. Besides, the rest of the family’s in the kitchen finishing the gingerbread house. Don’t you want to come?”

Jamie’s toothless smile fell and his brow creased. Glancing at the TV, then back at his father, he tried to weigh what was obviously a difficult decision. Eventually, leaping up from the carpet, he turned the television off and scampered through to the kitchen, yelling, “I want to help with the frosting!”

Gabe stooped to pick up the remote that had been abandoned on the rug. Placing it on the coffee table, he listened to the sounds coming from the kitchen. The excited squabbling between his two boys. The proud, “Look at this, Mommy!” of his daughter and the quiet, contented laughter of his wife.

He’d been missing all of those things for much longer than the time he’d spent in prison. He’d missed it while he’s been right there with them. He should have been enjoying it back then, but he hadn’t. And, in some ways, that loss was tougher to bear. Still, as their happy voices continued to pour in from the other room, he turned to look at the Christmas tree. The decorations glinted with the white lights that were carefully wrapped around it. And those lights blurred a little as Gabe realized his eyes were growing damp. With a smile and a sniff, he pulled himself together and made a move for the kitchen.

He didn’t get far enough to grab a taste of the fresh gingerbread, though. The ting of the doorbell took him back in that direction with another cheerful tune on his whistling lips.

As he eased the door open and let the winter chill hit his cheeks once more, he broke into a broad smile.

"Hey there," Matthew said, holding a gift-wrapped box in one hand and a wreath in the other. "Merry Christmas Eve," he added, offering the wreath to Gabe with a grin.

"Thanks." Taking the pine cone and poinsettia decorated wreath, he turned and looped it over the brass door knocker. Stepping back, he admired the ornament. "Thanks," he repeated. "It looks great." He'd been meaning to buy a wreath, but he'd been busy with a young offender he was trying to mentor.

"You're welcome."

Stepping backwards into the hall, Gabe ushered Matthew in from the cold. "We've got fresh gingerbread happening in the kitchen," he told him as he took his coat from him and hung it on the rack.

"Hmm. Smells great." Matthew paused long enough for Gabe to join him, and the pair wandered to the kitchen side by side.

"Look who's here," Gabe announced brightly.

The three children looked up from their gingerbread construction and waved. "Hi, Uncle Matthew," Amy said. "Are you going to stay for dinner?"

"That's kind of you," Matthew replied, strolling toward the table and eyeing the house-raising that was underway. "But I can't stay long. Just wanted to wish you all a Merry Christmas."

"Hello, Matt," Jen said, drying her hands on a dish towel. "Nice of you to drop by."

"Oh, and this is a little something for under your tree," the chaplain added, holding up the gift he was still carrying.

Gabe thanked him before taking the box toward the living room. Matthew followed, propping his shoulder against the doorjamb.

"Things seem good here," he noted quietly.

"Things are good." Gabe smiled proudly as he placed the present with the others. "It's been quite the journey," he added, sighing as he stood upright again. "But I couldn't be happier with where it's brought me."

Matthew smiled warmly. "Well, you know, I'm really happy for you."

"Thanks." Gabe nodded as his gaze drifted to the carpet momentarily and he wondered what he was thanking Matthew for. Whatever it was, it didn't seem enough to simply say the word. "I... uh..." he muttered, slowly lifting his eyes. "I don't think I would have survived without you."

Matthew drew in a quiet breath. "It was always my pleasure to help in any way I could."

"Yeah," Gabe whispered, his head shifting in agreement. He now knew exactly what Matthew meant by that and how he felt. He'd been able to help people, and knew the deep sense of fulfillment and purpose that came with it. Helping someone in need wasn't just a gift you gave to that person. It was a gift they gave to you, too. A feeling like no other. It was something Gabe now cherished as though his life depended on it.

"Well," Matthew sighed. "I ought to get going. I'm driving up to my parents tonight. I just wanted to stop by and see how you all are."

"We're doing great."

Matthew twisted his upper body back to the kitchen and said a cheery goodbye to the rest of the family, before Gabe walked him to the door.

"By the way," Matthew added. "That young guy you've recently started talking to popped into the halfway house the other day. We couldn't offer him anywhere that night, but I made some calls and got him a bed someplace else."

"That's great."

"Well, I think it might be the first step in getting away from the situation he's in."

The 'situation' was an abusive step-father and alcoholic mother, which made for an unsettled and violent living environment. He was one of those kids who quite understandably fell in with the wrong crowd in his search for a 'new family'. His gang of friends substituted the love he wasn't getting. Gabe was hopeful that with a different group of people around him, offering real support and love, his life might start to look a whole lot brighter.

"Thanks for helping him," Gabe said, patting his friend on the shoulder as he handed him his coat.

Matthew slipped an arm in the sleeve as he shook his head. "You were the one who made him see there were other possibilities out there for him."

Sliding one hand into his pocket, Gabe opened the door. It had started to snow again; thick, fluffy drops that were creating a blanket over the asphalt poor Nate had just cleared.

"You be careful out there."

"No problem," Matthew replied, stepping out into the drops of white. "Forecast was that it wouldn't get too bad." He waved as he made his way down the driveway, leaving large footprints in his wake. "See you in a couple of days!"

"Sure thing," Gabe replied. He waited until Matt was once again in his car and the engine had started before closing the door.

Releasing a sigh, he was reminded of the smell in the kitchen and made quick strides to return to it. Amy and Jamie were messily decorating their house with frosting while Nate chewed on some of the excess that had been cast off. Jenny took off her apron and slumped down onto a stool by the island.

"Long day?" Gabe asked, wrapping an arm around her shoulders and dropping a kiss on her temple.

"You could say that," she replied, smiling as she turned her eyes up to him. "Wouldn't change it though, would you?"

"No way." Squeezing her a little closer, he kissed her head again.

"Dad," Nate called around a mouthful of gingerbread. "Can we open a present tonight?"

"That depends," Gabe replied, "on whether you're all going to head off to bed early so Santa can make his rounds."

With his back to the two younger children, Nate rolled his eyes. He was too old to believe in that kind of thing, but played along for his sister and brother.

"And only one," Jen chipped in. "You want to save something for tomorrow, right?"

"I guess," Nate muttered before shoving another piece of gingerbread into his mouth.

"Hey," Gabe said, "before anyone else has any of that, I want us to have a few moments." Unwinding his arm from his wife's shoulders, he walked to the kitchen table and sat at the head of it. Jen and Nate both followed.

Amy and Jamie looked up from what they were doing, with white frosting around their mouths. The innocent grins they tried to bestow on their dad were fooling no one.

"Let's pray," he said.

Everyone around the table dipped their heads. Amy slapped her sticky hands together and brought them close to her face.

"Lord, we thank you," Gabe began, "for everything you've given us. We are blessed with a house, with food and warmth. Mostly, though, we're blessed to have each other.

Everyone around this table is precious and valuable to our family. And we are grateful for that above all else. Today, especially, we thank you for the love you show us. We thank you for your patience and your wisdom, and we hope to fill our lives with the same unconditional love you give. Amen."

"Amen," Amy and Jamie echoed.

"Amen," Jen quietly uttered as she slipped a hand beneath the table and stroked her husband's knee. "That was beautiful."

Gabe graced her with one of those smiles he reserved only for her. He knew it. He felt the difference; a mixture of love and satisfaction in having earned her pride. No one else had ever made him feel that way.

"I love you," he whispered before turning his focus back to his frosting-covered kids. "Right, everyone upstairs and wash up for lunch," he said.

"But Dad, the gingerbread..." Nate began to grumble.

"Can wait until after lunch," Gabe finished for him with a grin. "Now, go on."

Straying close to adolescence even though he was still a few years off of it, Nate muttered as he got out of his seat. Amy and Jamie were rather more excitable as they jumped down from the table and raced each other for the stairs.

Closing weary eyes, Gabe leaned back and tipped his face to the ceiling as his young brood's running footsteps echoed from above. There was a time that noise would have driven him crazy. Now, he embraced it. They would only be young for a short while. And once they were gone, the house would seem horribly quiet. He appreciated that in a way he couldn't possibly have appreciated before.

"Gabe, honey," Jen said, stirring him from his thoughts.

"Hmm?" Opening his eyes, he turned them to her.

A strange half smile pulled her lips as she nibbled on the lower one. "I... um..." she began, stopping and shaking her head. "I know we talked about this years ago, and we decided that we didn't want to have any more children. But..."

"You've changed your mind?" Gabe, asked tilting his head. The possibility dashed through his brain and he pondered what it would be like. A whole fresh batch of sleepless nights. Diapers. Another college fund. There was a lot to consider, and he couldn't help but wonder if Jen had really thought it all through.

"Well..." she murmured, but got no further.

Gabe figured she might have been aware, as she got further into her thirties, time was running out and the choice might be taken out of her hands. He didn't quite know how to voice that, so he reached out and covered her hand with his.

"Listen, sweetheart," he sighed. "If you want to talk about it, we can. I'm open to discussing it. I want you to be happy. But we've also got to consider what's best for the rest of the family. So... We can talk about it. And maybe in the New Year..."

"No, Gabe," she interrupted, shaking her head. "It's not... It's not that I'm feeling broody and want to convince you to try with me... It's... Well, it's happening."

Gabriel's dark eyebrows shrinking together with the force of his frown, he shook his head. "I'm not following."

"Honey, I'm pregnant."

His frown dissipated quickly, and a moment of shock lifted his brows. However, that was replaced almost instantly with a smile. A smile that grew wider as he took in his wife and his gaze eventually settled on her belly. "You are?" he whispered.

"You're not mad?"

Laughing, Gabe shook his head. "Why would I be mad?"

"Because it wasn't planned. We both thought we were done with three, right? I mean... Money's not..."

"We'll find a way to make it work as far as money's concerned," he insisted smoothly. "If we'd had a chance to plan it, I might have had reservations. But the decision's been taken from us," he added, chuckling. "This little one wants to come into the world." As he spoke, he leaned forward and stroked his hand over her lower abdomen. "This is a gift, Jen," he murmured, his eyelids heavying with tears. "The best Christmas gift I've ever gotten." His focus lifting to her face, he found her close to tears, too.

"I love you, Gabe," she breathed, sweeping the bangs out of her eyes before she covered his hand with her own. "I love you."

"You're the world to me," he replied, his face drawing closer to hers. "You and the kids are everything that's important in my life. And there's plenty of room in my heart for another soul. I will spend the rest of my life treasuring each moment I get to spend with you all."

Her wobbly smile gave way as silent tears skated across her cheeks. Happier than he'd ever felt, Gabriel kissed his wife's lips. "Thank you," he whispered, speaking both to her and God. He was beyond grateful for all the riches he'd been given, and the perspective he'd been granted to enjoy them.

THE END